What will People Say?

What will People Say?

Rehana Rossouw

JACANA

First published by Jacana Media (Pty) Ltd
First, second and third impression 2015
Fourth and fifth impression 2016

10 Orange Street
Sunnyside
Auckland Park 2092
South Africa
+2711 628 3200
www.jacana.co.za

ISBN 978-1-4314-2024-7

Cover design by publicide
Set in Stempel Garamond 10.5/15pt
Printed and bound by ABC Press, Cape Town
Job no. 002756

Also available as an e-book
d-PDF ISBN 978-1-4314-2166-4
ePUB ISBN 978-1-4314-2167-1
mobi file ISBN 978-1-4314-2168-8

See a complete list of Jacana titles at www.jacana.co.za

Chapter One

The South-Easter lifted the smell of pig manure spread across farms in Philippi, crossed Lansdowne Road and dumped it like a wet poep over Hanover Park. Piles of rubbish swept down the streets, announcing the arrival of the wind. Shopping bags jiggered and jived to the beat of the gusts until they hit the wire chain-link fences guarding rows of houses, where they were plastered into hedges of plastic.

The wind screamed through the tunnels separating the rows of three-storey blocks of flats striding across the township. Washing whipped on lines strung high across the courtyards, tied to the metal rails of the stairs flanking the flats. Neighbours' clothing twisted together – a shirt slipped into a jacket, a pink bra clung to bleached-white Jockey underpants. The dark smell of the pig manure, ploughed into the sandy fields flanking Hanover Park, soaked into the garments.

The fine dune sand that blanketed the Cape Flats poured down from the wind, crept under doors and stole through cracks in the concrete. Thousands of Port Jackson trees, imported from Australia to anchor the sand dunes, threw up sneezes of yellow pollen into the wind to seed its march across the flatlands wedged between Table Mountain and the Hottentots Holland range.

In a flat on the third floor of Magnolia Court, the South-Easter's whine harmonised with bickering voices in the lounge. Nicky Fourie leaned over the Formica-topped table in the kitchen and struggled to focus on her geography homework, wincing in the glare of the neon light reflecting off her textbook page. She was learning about the Sirocco and Santa Ana winds. One carried hot red dust from the Sahara across the Mediterranean and the other a hungry fire across California.

There were winds that could drive a person befok. When the South-

1

Easter blew, Nicky could easily murder someone and probably get away with it. The flat's thin walls gave little shelter from the wind screaming for her attention. Her eyes were red and dry as grated nutmeg; her sinuses exploded in protest against the pollen-filled air.

Nicky reached for the toilet roll next to her pencil case, rolled off a piece and blasted out a river of snot. Her right arm went lame and black spots bounced across her eyeballs. Fingers of pain shot off her eyebrows and clawed deep into her skull.

The smell of cabbage bredie drifting in a thick, green cloud above her head made her naar. The green-checked Terylene curtains in the kitchen window flapped a sour kak smell into her face. She didn't have the krag to get up and close the window. She was scared to move her head; the pain slowed down to a throb if she kept it still.

Eventually Nicky was forced to move; the kitchen sink was directly in her line of sight, her head couldn't take it. Mummy had wiped the sink bright after she washed the dishes; its silver shine sliced deep into the tunnels of pain in her head.

No one was going to notice she was in trouble. Mummy and Dedda went bedonnered when the wind came up. They had started on each other at the supper table. They were in the lounge now, where they had been gaaning aan for almost an hour. Their voices were shrill but Nicky couldn't make out what they were saying through the thumping in her head, keeping time with the howling wind.

Vomit dripped into her mouth. She swallowed it down and instantly made herself naar. It was no use trying to stop the hurl; she could feel its burn squeezing back up her throat. She pushed her chair away from the table and got to her feet. She took a left off the short passage connecting the flat's five rooms and paused in the lounge doorway. Mummy and Dedda were too involved with each other to notice her arrival.

Mummy's hands were planted on her lips as she leaned over Dedda and questioned him. "What are you: a man or a mouse?"

Nicky's head turned to Dedda to catch his reply. He was on the couch, his hands folded on top of the *Cape Times* on his lap. He answered slowly, like he was dealing with a fool. "I must be a man if I don't give in to everything a woman wants. Don't you think so?"

"If you were a man Neville, a proper man, you would do the right

2

thing by your family. Why is it so hard for you to do the right thing?"

"And who decides what is the right thing? Only you? I don't think so Magda. I've had enough of your ways."

Nicky couldn't take any more of their skelling. "Stop it you two. Just stop it! You making me sick!"

She held her hand tight across her mouth as she rushed across the passage to the bathroom, making it to the toilet as the vomit poured out of her mouth. It hit the bowl with such force that some splashed up into her face. Her body hukked as another long, sour sausage forced its way up her protesting throat and streamed out of her mouth.

She felt Dedda's hand rubbing her back as she crouched over the toilet. He was muttering under his breath. "That woman's making me sick, she's making everybody sick." His voice went soft. "You okay, my bokkie?"

The last of the cabbage bredie came out of Nicky's cramping gut. She squatted back on her ankles, hot tears rolling down her cheeks.

Neville crouched down next to her, cupping his palm on her forehead. "Sjoe! You boiling up. Come, you need to relax a while. Is gunna be okay, my bokkie. Dedda's here. Dedda's gunna make it better."

Nicky let her dedda pull her onto his lap after he sat himself down on the bath mat. She relaxed as he held her against his chest and rocked her slowly, humming the liedjie he had crooned as long as she could remember. Her snukking slowed, turned into hiccoughs and died down. The marching band in her head was still thumping its painful rhythm but she didn't feel so naar.

She looked up and managed a small smile for Dedda. A crack of light from the lounge across the way streaked over his face in the dim bathroom. There was no mistaking whose child she was; Mummy said she and Dedda were cut from the same cloth. His plump, dark face topped with a mop of curls was identical to hers.

The dimple in Dedda's right cheek, in exactly the same place as hers, smiled at her. "Come, let me clean you up, it will make you feel better."

Nicky got to her feet and sat on the edge of the bath. Dedda flushed the toilet. The sour bredie smell that had crept up the bowl disappeared in a rush of water. She winced when Dedda ran the spluttering hot tap and bright blue light sparked from the gas geyser bracketed above the bath.

Dedda brought her yellow facecloth, soaped and warmed under the tap. Nicky sat limply as he ran it over her hot cheeks and stroked away the dangly earring of vomit hanging from her lip. She came to her feet when he pulled her up and leaned against him until she found her balance.

She took the toothbrush Dedda passed to her and gratefully scrubbed the sour acid off her teeth and her tongue. She held onto the washbasin after she rinsed her mouth. Her head was a spinning, glittering disco ball.

Neville put his arm around Nicky's shoulders and brought her out of the bathroom. "You must get straight into bed, bokkie. The best thing to do is to sleep. That's the only way to sort out a migraine. That and a Grandpa powder."

As they left the bathroom, the lounge light sliced into her eyes like a welder's torch. Nicky lowered her head. She didn't see Mummy as she passed the lounge door, but she heard her voice: "Sleep well, sweetheart."

Neville led Nicky into the bedroom she shared with her sister Suzette. He left the light off and guided her inside. There was just enough space between the two wardrobes and the bunkbed for them to walk side by side.

Nicky dropped onto the bottom bunk like a sack of potatoes. She took the pink nightie Dedda found under her pillow on the top bunk and handed to her.

Neville put a hand to Nicky's forehead. "Put on your nightie, then you get into bed. I'll go fetch the Grandpa."

A question pushed its way into Nicky's throbbing head as she climbed the ladder to the top bunk and slid under her sheet and blanket. Why were Mummy and Dedda fighting? They didn't fight a lot, but when they did it could be bitter. Mummy always wanted everything her way, although Dedda could be quietly stubborn. They were usually careful not to get too loud when they rolled with each other. Mummy always worried that the neighbours would hear.

The walls between Magnolia Court's flats were egg-box thin. Most Friday nights, Mr Oliphant next door came home with a shopping bag clinking with brandy bottles. He'd sip quietly for a while, later his voice would come growling through the walls. Lying in her bed some Friday nights, Nicky heard flesh hitting flesh next door and the screams that followed. She didn't know where to look when she saw Mrs Oliphant the next day.

She had never seen Dedda lift a hand to Mummy. Maybe he was scared she would moer him. Nicky was sure Mummy could give any man the hiding of his life. She was heavy, but it wasn't fat she carried – she was solid as a rock. Dedda's head just about reached Mummy's shoulders.

Neville came back into the bedroom with a headache powder and a big glass of water. He stood next to Nicky's bed and watched while she swallowed it down.

Nicky drained the water down her steelwool throat. As she handed Dedda the empty glass she remembered her question. "Dedda, why were you and Mummy skelling like that?"

Neville shuffled his feet before he answered. "It wasn't such a big thing. It was about the church again. She wants me to get more involved, go to services and help on committees."

Dedda was the best man Nicky knew. She had never in her life come across a man who did more for his family. Mummy said all the time that he was one of few men in Hanover Park who worked for their families. But he never went to church with his family. He never really said why, except 'it's your mother's church'. It was no use asking him, he wasn't going to be saved any time soon. Besides, her head was too sore for any more cross-questioning.

She remembered her books on the kitchen table and sat up. "I didn't finish my homework. I better go do it now."

Neville put a hand across her thighs to stop her from leaving the bed. "It's Friday, Nicky, there's no school tomorrow. You don't have to do anything more tonight except sleep. Just relax, close your eyes."

Nicky lay down and turned her back on Dedda, her cheek resting on her hand. Her eyes closed as Dedda hummed and stroked her back. She tried to ignore the thumping wind outside, the cause of her pain. She pretended it was the sound of waves hitting a beach, and after a while she fooled herself into believing it.

Chapter Two

Neville kept watch over Nicky until she fell asleep. She didn't get migraines often; they came mostly in the spring and summer, when they hit her hard. The doctor could do nothing. All he kept saying was that she was allergic and she would grow out of it. Maybe it would stop shortly, she was turning sixteen next week. He felt sorry for the girlie; there was little he could do to help. He closed the bedroom door gently and headed back to the lounge.

Magda was onto him the second he walked in. "How is Nicky? Is she sleeping? Ag shame, man. You know she only gets like this when the wind blows. Can you smell how foul it is tonight?"

"Ja, I can smell it. Nicky's sleeping. That's the best thing for her."

Neville spotted Magda taking a deep breath. No ways was he picking up where she left off. He had enough of her damned church for one night. As if it wasn't enough that they took ten per cent of your pay packet, they also wanted all your free time.

He lifted a hand like a traffic cop and halted her in her tracks. "Magda, leave it for now. You heard how Nicky said we making her sick. She's sleeping, I don't want to make noise. Leave this church business for another time. I'm gunna fetch Anthony. It's getting late. The boy should have been home already."

Neville left the flat and walked down the stairs to the concrete landing on the second floor of Magnolia Court. He leaned over the metal rail and scanned the courtyard. Washing writhed on the lines below like couples at a disco. His nose twisted; the kak smell on the wind would soak into the clothes and make housewives cross. He could see no sign of Anthony.

As turned to go down the stairs he bumped into his neighbour Moira coming up, a plastic laundry basket tucked into her hip. A lacy red bra sat on top of the pile like a cherry on an ice cream cone. Neville eyed the shapely woman blocking his way; appreciating the way her petticoat showed under her pink-checked housecoat. He smiled. "Good evening, Moira. Do you need a hand?"

Moira lifted a pinkie to her racing car-red lips. "I might, I might. But not with my washing, I need it to do something else for me."

Neville's dimple sunk deep in his cheek. He enjoyed Moira's jas style. She'd been making a move on him since she came to live next door eight years ago. Just a friendly move, nothing serious. She was never desperate for a man. He'd greeted a lot of men on the landing he shared with Moira. He had to come out a few times to calm men down when they were leaving for the last time. Moira had five children with five different fathers, according to Magda. You'd never say it when you looked at her. Everything was still in the right place, and exactly Sophia Loren's size.

Neville's eyes went back to his neighbour's face. "I can't help you tonight, Moira. I'm gunna fetch Anthony. Have you seen him?"

"No I haven't. But you must look sharp. I saw Ougat and his boys walking by earlier on when I went to fetch my washing. Those boys are gemors. I don't like to see them here. Go fetch your boy and bring him home."

Moira brushed up against Neville as she pushed past him up the steps. Charlie's Angel eau de cologne rose up from her cleavage and into his nostrils. The wind hadn't sent her hair home; her Lady Di cut was still in place.

At the bottom of the stairs Neville stopped to turn up his collar. The sandblasted wind had stung his neck earlier, when he walked home from the taxi rank. He looked up at the block of flats across the way. Television images flickered blue through the Terylene curtains in every lounge window he could see, except for one. Maybe their television was repossessed. Or broken, and they were waiting for payday to claim it from the repair shop.

He couldn't stand the way Magnolia Court ... in fact all the blocks in Hanover Park were neglected by the City Council. The yellow pastel paint had long ago stopped trying to hide the grey concrete underneath.

Some of the wooden guards on the stairs were broken; children could fall through onto the concrete courtyard below. No one did anything to stop people from parking their cars on bricks in the courtyard. They became a playground after their engines, windscreens, doors and seats disappeared.

Neville couldn't understand why they called the blocks of flats 'courts'. The only queens around were members of the moffie netball leagues who played on the courts across the road. The players stuffed sanitary towels in their panties to hide their man's parts and make smooth panty lines. They were always flicking up their short skirts, whether they had the ball or not. The moffies drew big crowds to their games.

Neville reached the edge of the courtyard and spotted boys seated inside one of the crocks. He leaned in through a window of the rusting Cortina, pretending not to notice the cigarette quickly being cupped in a palm. "Evening. Any of you boys seen Anthony?"

One of the smokers responded immediately, pointing a finger down the road. "Yes uncle, he's at the park. We seen him there."

"You boys must go home now. It's getting late."

"Yes uncle," the four choroused.

Neville checked his watch. It was still light out at eight o'clock on a February evening, although the sun had gone behind the mountain a time ago. In the distance Table Mountain was a slab of black stone carved into a sky slowly darkening from blue to purple.

He made his way down Lemon Road. On the wall of the next block down, Orchid Court, he saw something that made him stop in his tracks. An American flag had been painted on the wall flanking the pavement. The wall was stained dark from the fires the young men guarding the flag kept going through night. The strong smell of piss on the walls was proof that they never left their posts. There were three young men on duty tonight, squatting with their backs against the flag, their backsides hovering above the grey sand.

Although he walked past Orchid Court every weekday on his way to the taxi rank, Neville saw for the first time that someone had attacked the flag with a thick paintbrush and black paint. The letters JFK were evenly spaced across the stars and the stripes. It meant nothing to him,

8

but he was sure it meant something to the Americans, who had marked Orchid Court as their turf.

Neville stared at the wall and hoped there wouldn't be trouble. Children often got hit in the gangsters' crossfire. Their grieving parents always said the same thing afterwards: 'He was just going to the shop. He was just going to buy bread.' It was time to keep a close eye on his children, 'specially Anthony who was getting to that difficult age. Thirteen-year-old boys never listened; they always thought they knew better than everyone.

He reached the park; shards of broken glass scattered across the grey sandy field glittered in the last of the sunlight. Grass tried and failed to grow in patches of litter at the edges. The park had a set of swings, a metal climbing frame and a roundabout. It wasn't much, but it kept the children off the streets.

He spotted Anthony playing soccer on the field with five other boys. Four of them were still in their school uniforms. Their school bags were the goalposts; they probably hadn't been home since they left for school that morning. Anthony had been home for supper; he had left to play outside seconds after he cleaned his plate.

He was about to call his boy over when he heard a mighty crash. Neville's head swivelled towards a group of young men circling the roundabout. A concrete kerbstone lay on top of the shattered wooden floor of one of its sections. One of the youngsters had another slab lifted above his head, his T-shirt riding up his skinny torso as his arms strained to hold the weight.

"Hey, you!" Neville shouted. "What you think you doing?"

The boy holding the slab turned towards him, gave him a dark look, faced the roundabout and smashed the slab through its floor.

Neville ran towards him. "Hey, stop it! Stop right now! Are you out of your mind?"

The skinny boy split off from the group as Neville came close. "What the fok is got to do with you what we doing, timer? Does this fokken place belong to you, huh? Fok off."

Neville tried not to show his panic as the six young men drew close and made a semicircle around him. He lifted his hands, palms facing front, and spoke in a slow, even voice. "This park belongs to all of us.

9

We get little enough from the council for our children. The least we can do is look after what we got."

"Fok the council. Give your laaities to me, Ougat will show them a good time. You got any girls?" The young man grabbed his crotch and cackled. His friends laughed in tune.

So this was Ougat. Neville had heard a lot about him, from the neighbours. He had been released from Pollsmoor Prison a few months back; he had finally made the big time after two spells in the Ottery School for Juvenile Offenders. Neville heard that Ougat had caught the eye of a gang general in prison. Some said he was the general's wife. There was also a story going around that he had stabbed a prisoner who tried to make him a wife in the showers; and the general was impressed with the way he took a life.

Neville was surprised at how small Ougat was, and how young. He must be older than eighteen if he served time in Pollsmoor, although with his baby face he could pass for fifteen. The boy was short; his closely shaven head barely touched Neville's shoulder. But dynamite came in small packages and the youngster looked ready to explode. His eyes were bulging in his head like the small, ugly dog in the Hendricks's flat downstairs.

Neville wasn't taking any chances with the kortgat gangster; he tried to make the peace. "Look, I don't want any trouble. All I'm saying is think about the children who use this park. What must they do now?"

Ougat leaned forward and pushed his face into Neville's. The two gold teeth flanking the gap in his mouth where his four front teeth were missing gleamed in the last of the twilight. "I can take care of the laaities, moenie worry nie. This here is Ougat's turf and he got a lot to offer, you know mos?"

Neville couldn't make out what Ougat was saying. The other young men were nodding their heads in agreement and one reached out and shared a complicated hand-slap with Ougat that looked like congratulations for wise words. He tried again to stop the boys from wrecking the park. "Just think of the children. Some of us are trying to raise our children decent, and it's hard enough in a place like this."

Ougat's eyes swelled in his face. "You saying Ougat is not decent?

Is that what you fokken saying, you naaier? You can't come here and talk such kak to me. Nooit, my man."

The semicircle of young men took a few steps forward. Neville started to sweat. What had he started here? How did it get out of hand so quickly? He couldn't see a weapon in Ougat's hand but he was sure there was one nearby.

"Dedda? What's going on Dedda?"

Anthony and his friends had abandoned their soccer game and came to stand next to him. Neville drew his boy close and put an arm around his shoulder, smiling and hoping he was hiding how poepscared he was.

"Is okay, Anthony. I was just leaving. Isn't that so?" Neville looked up at Ougat hopefully.

The gangster ignored him while he checked Anthony out. "What we have here? What's your name, laaitie?"

Neville pulled his son into his body and answered for him. "His name is Anthony. I came to fetch him; it's getting dark. Come Anthony, let's go." The boy hadn't picked up how bang he was; Anthony was being difficult, as usual. He wasn't interested in anything he had to say.

"Ag Dedda, just a few more minutes, okay? The score is two-all and one of the teams must win before we can finish."

Neville took a few steps back, pulling Anthony with him. He didn't have the pluck to look in Ougat's direction; he was hoping he wouldn't notice they were moving. He had to find a way to get the boy to listen to him. He spoke quiet but firm. "Come now Anthony, it's late. Say goodnight to your friends. They must also go home now. It's getting dark. Mummy is worried about you."

For once, the boy listened. Neville kept his arm around Anthony's shoulder, turned him round and walked out of the park. Maybe they could get away without any trouble. Anthony and his friends were much younger than Ougat and his ouens, who outnumbered them anyway. There was a good chance they could get away from the baby-faced shower killer.

Ougat's voice was loud at their backs, shrill like a woman's. "Listen to your dedda, Anthony. You be a good boy." His voice changed back to normal. "Tomorrow we can have a game. Your ouens against the JFK. You ouens are good, I been checking you. What you say; you on?"

Neville turned and jumped in before Anthony could answer. There
was no way he was going let his son do anything with Ougat, 'specially
now that he learned he was from the JFKs, who looked set on moving
in on the Americans' turf. "Leave my boy alone, please. He got his
friends, you got yours. Okay?"

Ougat stepped forward, his ouens at his back. "What's your saak,
timer? Why you looking for trouble with Ougat? I'm just being friendly
here. You got a problem? You think I'm not decent enough for your
boy, is that what you thinking?"

Neville raised one hand and kept a tight grip on Anthony's shoulder
with the other. "Leave the boy alone, please. He's only thirteen, he got
friends his own age."

Ougat's gold teeth flashed. "Thirteen's old enough. You know what
I was doing when I was thirteen? I was a man, ask all the kinners who
were around at the time." His ouens laughed as he grabbed his crotch.

Neville nodded and pretended he was impressed. He had to get away;
the gangsters were showing too much interest in Anthony. The boy was
smiling at Ougat like a fool. "I'm sure you were a man. Anthony here's
just a boy. He's not yet ready for anything like that."

"Dedda!" Anthony's pale cheeks filled with red circles.

Neville had enough of Ougat's nonsense. It was getting dark and he
was tired. It was Friday night after a long week. Magda had worn him
out earlier with her nagging about the church. All he wanted was to
get home and finish the paper. There was nothing Ougat could do to
stop him from leaving. He turned and led his boy and his friends away.

Ougat had one last thing to say to Neville's back. "This isn't over,
timer. Don't think I forget you showed disrespec' to me. Ek sal jou
fokken wys. I will show you who is decent around here, you fokken
naaier."

Neville ignored Ougat and walked away fast. He told Anthony's
friends to collect their school bags and sent them home before setting
off for Magnolia Court with his boy. His mind worked overtime as
they walked in the blasting, stinking wind. He hoped Ougat wasn't
planning on starting a turf war with the Americans. There had been
several gang wars since they moved to Hanover Park in 1974, but it had
been a while since there was one this side. The gangsters ducked with

their guns behind the crocks in the courtyards and bled to death there, in front of the children and everyone.

He caught up with Anthony as they reached the flag with the JFK markings on Orchid Court. The boy was cross; he had walked fast ahead of him after they left the park, kicking every piece of rubbish that he passed on the pavement. Neville grabbed his son's arm and forced him to stand still. Anthony looked him in the eye; the boy was almost as tall as he was. He should be – he ate the whole day long. It was a good thing he liked peanut butter and jam sandwiches, else he would eat them out of house and home.

Neville gripped Anthony's arm tight. He had to make sure the boy got what he had to say. He didn't like the look of Ougat and it seemed he got on the wrong side of him. He shook Anthony's arm. "Listen here. You listen when I talk. I want you home every day by the time it gets dark, you hear me? And I want to know at all times where you are."

Anthony's bottom lip drooped towards his chin. "But Dedda, there's no school tomorrow. We were playing best out of five and it was two all. I was coming home just now."

"Don't argue with me, Anthony! You keep away from Ougat, you hear?"

"Why Dedda? What was he saying? Why he saying you disrespected him? Are you bang, is that why you want me to keep away?"

Neville sighed. Sometimes Anthony did see and hear what was happening around him, always at the wrong times. "Just listen to me, okay? I'm not bang, but Ougat is bad news. He's been in prison. There's no need for you to associate with him. You got your own friends."

"But why's he going on like that with you? Why's he saying he will show you? What did you do to him? Aren't you bang he's gunna come after you?"

"I'm not bang. There's no need to be scared. Did you see Ougat's eyes? They looked just like Mrs Hendricks's ugly dog downstairs. What's it called again? A chow-wow-wow?"

Anthony laughed. "It's more like a chow-ugly than a chow-wow."

Neville chuckled and riffled his fingers through the boy's soft brown hair, trying to lighten the mood and to get Anthony on his side so he would mind him. "Did you hear what I was saying to you, about keeping away from Ougat?"

Anthony kicked an empty cooldrink can at his feet and muttered. "Yes Dedda."

"Yes, what?"

"Yes, I will stay away from him."

Neville dropped Anthony's arm. "Let's go home. Mummy is worried."

He lowered his head to keep the stinging sand out of his eyeballs as he walked home with his son and the Friday night stragglers heading from the taxi rank and the bus terminus.

After he tucked Anthony into his bed on the couch in the lounge, Neville switched off the TV and followed Magda into their bedroom. He changed into his pyjamas quickly and climbed into bed clutching the morning paper. The fight with Magda had interfered with his routine. He brought the *Cape Times* home every evening. One of the partners at the law firm where he worked as a messenger gave him his copy every day after he was finished with it.

Magda had calmed down and watched a TV show with them after he came back with Anthony. She hadn't said another word about the church. But she was distracting him from the newspaper again. She was putting on her nightie.

Neville knew full well that Magda didn't like him to watch when she got undressed or dressed. Her church got her all confused about being naked, like it was something to feel ashamed about. She didn't want to go to the bathroom to get changed, so she banned him from looking in her direction when she took off or put on her clothes. He shook the newspaper so she would think he was reading.

He watched skelmpies as Magda took off her dress. She stood in her petticoat while she hung the blue Viyella garment in the wardrobe. Next, she pulled her petticoat's straps down her arms and lowered the beige nylon to her waist. She took off her bra and quickly pulled her nightie over her head. Neville spotted her breasts, reflected in the dressing table mirror. They were fuller than when he first encountered them, after she fed his three children, and he smaaked them more than ever.

He focused on the paper when Magda took a seat on the upholstered stool in front of the dressing table and began rubbing Pond's cold cream into her pale cheeks. He heard the crackle of electricity as she brushed out the brown hair that hung to halfway down her back. She kept it tied in a ponytail most of the time. It was a pity, Neville thought; she looked like a hot mama when her hair was down.

He looked up when she got into bed next to him, holding the Good News Bible. Magda was on a mission to finish it. She started months ago, got stuck in the Old Testament. She frowned her way down a page, her tongue creeping out of her mouth as she tried to remember who begat who.

Neville concentrated on the newspaper. It was filled with the kind of news he never saw on television – of protests in townships across the country and the detentions and shootings that always followed. When would it come to Hanover Park?

The news made him worry about Suzette; she was somewhere out on the streets. He lowered the paper and turned to Magda, careful with his words. He hadn't told her about Ougat. There was no reason to worry her; nothing happened that she needed to know. "What time did Suzette say she was coming home? It's getting late."

Magda bookmarked her page and closed the Bible. "She should be back soon, she said half past nine and it's almost ten o'clock. They got a lot of work to do, to get ready for the church fete."

Neville held his tongue. There was the church thing again. Magda took his children to the Church of Eternal Redemption, Nicky and Suzette were members of its youth group. Anthony was being baptised later in the year; Madga would expect him to do more for the church afterwards. After what he saw and heard in the park earlier, Neville promised himself he would never complain about his children being in the church – there was so much worse things they could be involved in.

He reached over and took the Bible from Magda. "You go sleep. I want to finish the paper. I will wait up for Suzette."

His arm brushed against Magda's breasts as he placed the Bible on her bedside table. He paused and looked around while he enjoyed the heat of her breast against his arm. The bedroom was cluttered with furniture. The imbuia suite they bought on hire purchase five years ago looked good in the showroom, but it was far too big and too dark for their small room. The wardrobe covered half the window, keeping the bedroom in permanent twilight.

Soon after Magda fell asleep, Neville heard the door to the flat closing carefully. He got out of bed and caught Suzette as she was about to enter the bedroom she shared with Nicky. "How was your meeting?" he whispered.

"It was okay. Only a few people came. They always stay away when there's work to do. The church fete is going to take up a lot of time."

Neville looked up at his oldest daughter; she was two inches taller than him. The puppy fat she had carried tightened at the edges when she grew up. When did she get so beautiful and why hadn't he noticed? Of all his children, Suzette favoured her mother the most, although her skin was lighter than Magda's and Anthony's. Her light-brown hair hung in a fat plait down her back. All she got from him was his small, sharp nose. Neville was so taken up with her beauty he forgot why he had come out into the passage.

Suzette opened her bedroom door. "Night, Dedda."

Neville remembered what he wanted to say. "Don't make noise when you go in. Your sister's got a migraine. She was vomiting earlier."

"I'll be quiet. Night, Dedda."

"Night, my bokkie."

Suzette had been almost four years old and still struggling to say Daddy when Nicky started talking. They were too cute to correct so Neville became all his childrens' Dedda.

He waited while Suzette closed the bedroom door gently. If he hadn't been so distracted by her looks he would have said something about the smell of cigarette smoke rising off her breath and her clothing. What could he say? She was in her last year of school, on her way to becoming a woman. He joined his sleeping wife. He could relax; his family was safe at home.

Chapter Three

Anthony kicked every stone, bottle and tin can in his path as he walked home from school. His shoes were worn down to grey at the toes. He had rubbed in extra black polish that morning. He didn't want Mummy to see what he had done to them; when she bought the shoes two months ago, she warned him that this pair had to last a full year.

It had been another kak day at Forest Glen Primary. Anthony was glad it was his last year there; he couldn't wait to get away from the place. He would be one of the youngest at high school, but that was orrite – he was used to being the baby. It wasn't so bad; most times when he was in trouble Mummy said he was too young to know better.

Rushdie in his class brought a porno magazine to school. He stole it from his father's secret stash and charged twenty cents for a look. Anthony was the last to get a turn. He didn't have twenty cents, he wasted all of first break begging friends to lend him money. He got the magazine minutes before the end of second break. The cover had come loose from its staples and someone's lunch left a smear of fat on the big breasts of the centrespread model.

He sat with the magazine on his lap, ignoring the sharp mixture of Jeyes Fluid and piss in the stainless-steel urinals lining one wall of the boys' toilet. He was so deep in his study of a dark patch of hair between a model's thighs that he didn't notice the door of the stall had opened and someone was watching him.

"What do we have here? Educational material, perhaps?"

The sarcastic voice gave Anthony such a skrik that he dropped the magazine onto the floor. His stiff piepie shrivelled in his grey shorts.

He watched as Mr Pieterse stooped to pick the magazine up and

17

paged through it slowly. The skinny teacher looked like a snake in his shiny silver suit. Fok! Why did he have to be the one that was caught? Other boys had done exactly what he was doing. It wasn't fair!

Mr Pieterse had the same look on his face as the boy Anthony grabbed the magazine from when it was finally his turn. He licked his lips as he turned the page from side to side. He spotted Anthony's stare and grabbed his arm roughly, pulling him off the toilet. "Let's go to the office and see what Mr September has to say about this."

Anthony dragged his shoes on the floor as Mr Pieterse led him to the principal's office. He had been there last week, when his class teacher took him in for not doing his Afrikaans homework. He had to listen to Mr September's long lecture about 'utilising your potential to the maximum' and 'adhering to the high standards of this school'. Anthony was scolded again for not being more like Nicky who had been a star pupil at Forest Glen Primary three years ago, passing standard five with five As.

The principal wasn't in his office. Mr Pieterse told him to wait in the corridor outside and went to the staff room. Anthony leaned against the wall with his hands behind his back, cradling his backside. He was probably in for it.

The bell rang and pupils began strolling towards their classrooms. A few of them stopped to stare or giggle at Anthony, including Rushdie, the porno-loving bastard. He had the nerve to stare hard. Anthony stared silently back at him.

Mr September came slowly down the corridor, followed by Mr Pieterse. "Well, well, if it isn't young Mr Fourie again. Please come into my office."

Anthony stood in front of Mr September's desk and watched while he forced his fat gat into his chair. He grunted three times, like a vark sinking happily into a mixture of mud and shit.

He stared at the glass ornament on Mr September's untidy desk, the kind that threw up white snow when you shook it. This one had a miniature bridge inside. People who had been overseas, like Mr September and his Aunty Violet, kept it on show for the rest of their lives. There was a red pencil bag in a shape of a London bus next to the ornament.

Mr Pieterse dropped the magazine onto the desk. "I found him in the toilet with this, sir." He opened the magazine onto the centrespread.

Mr September stared at the picture. He closed the magazine and pushed it away from him. He criss-crossed his fat slapchip fingers and stared across the desk at Anthony. "I am disgusted by this filth. You brought such filth into my school, this place where decent people send their children. You have decent parents. We go to the same church, for God's sake! What do you think your parents will say if they find out that you brought such filth into my school?"

Anthony stared at the glass ornament. There was a tiny flag on top of the bridge. It was red, white and blue. On the base of the ornament were the words 'Tower of London'. He hated ornaments. They were good for nothing except collecting dust. Every Saturday morning he had to dust the cabinet in the lounge that was filled with ornaments and school photos. There was a small trophy that had to be dusted every week. Nicky won silver at the primary school Eistedffod for a phoney poem about daffodils.

Mr September's shouting made him jump and pay attention. "Look at me! What will your parents say if they find out?"

Anthony looked up into Mr September's sweating face. "They will be disgusted, sir."

"That's right! And they would be right to be disgusted."

Mr Pieterse chimed in. "Sir, I'm also disgusted."

Anthony was glad when Mr September thanked Mr Pieterse for bringing the matter to his attention and sent him on his way. Mr Pieterse was a piemp.

Mr September waited until they were alone before he spoke again. "I couldn't bring myself to tell your parents about this, and I'm sure you don't want to disappoint them either. Am I right?"

"Yes, sir."

"Then bend over."

Bending over the desk, Anthony rested his head on his folded arms. The worst part was waiting for Mr September to start. He took his time as he fought his way out of his chair and dragged his vetgat around his desk. Anthony heard him wheezing as he bent down to slide open the cupboard next to his desk. What cane was he choosing? The thin ones stung but the thick ones left a lasting pain.

Then came the part Anthony hated second most. The whistling noise before the cane landed on his bum. It didn't land; Mr September was taking a practice swing. A heavy hand came down in the middle of his back. There was a pause.

"I think I'll give you six of the best. That will teach you not to bring filth into my school."

Six! Anthony was sure he would get only four. He'd never got six before. This was gunna be fokken sore.

Mr September took a long time between strokes. The first one landed at the bottom of Anthony's bum, where his thigh connected. Then a pause, with heavy panting coming from behind, before the whistling started up again. Mr September was a master caner. He never landed a stroke on top of another. He could spread the pain evenly.

After the third burst of pain, Anthony couldn't believe the caning was only halfway. He sunk his teeth into his arm to keep his mouth too busy to cry. His bum felt like Mr September had pushed a hot chilli inside.

There was a small break in the caning while Mr September moved across to take care of the other cheek on Anthony's bum. The cheeks on his face were dry. The fat vark would be looking for tears afterwards. Think eye of the tiger. Will to survive.

Mr September wasn't finished after the caning. He forced Anthony to look at him while he gave another kak boring lecture about decency and disappointed parents before sending him back to his class.

Mrs Smith stopped talking in midsentence when Anthony opened the door to his classroom and thirty-nine pairs of eyes stared at him as he made his way to his desk. He sat down carefully, but still an 'eina' squeaked out as his bum connected with the hard wooden seat. The class laughed and didn't stop until Mrs Smith told them to keep quiet. Anthony hated them all. Naaiers!

Rushdie cornered him immediately after the bell rang at the end of the day. A few other boys who had enjoyed the magazine also gathered round.

"What happened?" Rushdie asked, a thick frown joining his eyebrows.

Anthony stared hard at him. "What you think happened? I got six of the best."

"Six! That's kak, man."

"Tell me about it."

"Where's the magazine?"

Anthony pushed hard into Rushdie's chest, forcing him to take a step back. "Where the fok you think it is? It's on Mr September's desk. I bet you he spent the whole afternoon enjoying it, the bastard."

Rushdie held his palms up. "I need it back, man. My father's gunna moer me when he finds out it's missing."

"What you want me to do? Go ask Mr September for it? Why don't you go tell him it's yours and you want it back?"

"Did you tell him its mine?"

"Whose gat is sore? Yours or mine? What you think I said?"

"Just checking, no need to get so aggro. I'm also in the kak man, not just you."

The boys wanted to see how bad the caning was. Anthony led them to the toilet and dropped his pants. There were a few whistles when his bum came into view. He craned his head over his shoulder and saw the swollen red stripes, burning as much as it had during the caning.

Brian whistled through his teeth. He was also a regular visitor to Mr September's office. "You got to give it to him. Mr September is a master. My gat took four days to come right the last time he moered me."

Anthony pulled up his pants. "Show's over, you guys have seen enough."

Anthony's school shoes were badly damaged when he got home. The municipal workers had been on strike for three weeks. Rubbish filled the pavements and spilled into the gutters. There was plenty of ammo. He pretended that everything he kicked on the way home from school was Mr September's vark-ugly face.

He dropped his school haversack on the lounge floor on his way to the TV. Nicky heard when he switched it on and came into the lounge. "Howsit?"

"Orrite." Anthony kept his eyes glued to the TV. He practically lived on the couch. It was his bed; the family could watch TV only as long as he was awake. His sisters didn't want him in their room. He had a wardrobe in their bedroom; they forced him to knock and wait for permission every time he came to fetch something.

There was kak on the TV, the Afrikaans children's programme *Liewe Heksie*. Anthony hated it but he stared at the screen, waiting for Nicky to leave him alone. He had a lot on his mind. It wasn't fair that he got into trouble when so many boys did exactly the same thing he did. He was feeling sorry for himself, the moer in with Mr September and his bum was fokken sore.

Nicky didn't get the message. "You want a fried-egg sandwich? I just started making one for myself."

"Okay. Gimme six slices."

Nicky came back a few minutes later with the sandwiches and two cups of tea on a TV tray. Anthony watched without moving as she nearly tripped over his haversack.

He was still hungry after he gobbled down his sandwiches. He checked out Nicky, sitting next to him on the couch, reading a book while she had her bread and tea. Her second and last sandwich was in her hand; if it had been on her plate he would have gryped it. He turned back to the TV, pretending he was watching the tarty show.

Nicky interrupted his thoughts again. "How was your day?"

"Kak. I got moered. Six of Mr September's best."

"What did you do?"

"I got caught reading a porno magazine in the boys' toilet."

"I don't understand why you boys are so into porno. Why is it? The Bible warns against lust; is bad for you."

Nicky was driving Anthony out of his mind. The last thing he needed today was another lecture. "Leave me alone, okay? I got enough kak on my plate already. I don't need any from you. You sound just like Mummy. You better not tell her, or Dedda, what happened to me today, you piemp."

"But I really don't understand why boys want to look at naked women's bodies. Girls won't stare at pictures of naked men, even if there was magazines like that."

Anthony got to his feet, wincing as his bum left the mock leather couch. "We all can't be like you, Miss Perfect Nicolette Fourie who got five As in standard five. Some of us are interested in other stuff. Leave me the fok alone." He slammed out of the flat. There was no peace inside.

Chapter Four

Friday night, party night. Suzette had been planning this one for a while. She told Mummy she was helping her friend Charlene make crafts to sell at the church fete. She said they were going to work late into the night because few people had volunteered to help. The lie worked; she could sleep out. Mummy agreed that it wasn't safe to walk home when she was done.

The whole year Mummy had been on her case. She wasn't allowed to go anywhere or do anything. All her friends went to bioscope and nightclubs at the weekends. She was eighteen already, but still going to matinee shows with her sister and brother. Mummy said it was for her own good. Her childhood was ending and it was time to learn to be a woman. The lessons started with Mummy teaching her to iron shirts. It was bladdy unfair. Why did she have to iron Nicky's and Anthony's stuff? They had hands, didn't they?

Suzette was already a woman and making the most of it. Mummy wanted to teach her to be a wife but she wasn't ready to be one, definitely not. There was a lot she wanted to do before she got tied down to a man. Like party all night.

She hadn't lied about everything. She was sleeping at Charlene's house – after she went with her friend to a party in Heathfield. Charlene promised that her cousin's twenty-first was going to be a befokte jol. There would be good music, lots of food, booze and young men.

Suzette left the flat wearing a frilly pastel-blue dress that would have looked good on a six-year-old. Mummy bought all her clothes at the factory where she worked; they didn't make jeans there. She planned to change into Charlene's clothes before they left for the party – something lekker tight-fitting that showed she was hot to trot.

∽

Charlene's cousin's house was pumping when they arrived. Suzette could hear the music from the bottom of the road lined on both sides with cars. The smell of smoke drifted in the warm summer air. She poked Charlene in the ribs as they entered the house. "This is a kwaai place, you didn't tell me you had such sturvie people in your family."

Charlene smiled. "They not rich, my uncle is a school principal and my aunty is a teacher."

"Ja, but this is a double storey. Yoh, look! They even got a swimming pool. Tell me, they got any sons?"

"There's Keith, although I dunno about him. He never keeps a girlfriend for long."

"Just watch me, okay?"

"Okay."

The birthday girl, Sharon, loved her present from Charlene. She let loose a small scream, hopped up and down and gryped her cousin hard after she tore open the wrapping. "Personalised towels, I love it!"

Suzette also expected to get sheets, towels, tablecloths and kitchenware as birthday presents when she turned twenty-one. Mummy bought a kist for her on her eighteenth birthday; it was used as a coffee table in the lounge. So far the only trousseau Mummy had put in the kist was Tupperware she bought at parties hosted by women in her prayer circle. She always bought the cheapest things in the catalogue; all Suzette had to take to her new home when she married was a water bottle and about ten ice trays.

Suzette and Charlene followed Sharon through the house into a large, built-in kitchen filled with women. Sharon introduced Suzette to her mother Lynette, her aunts, cousins and friends. A woman leaned over the sink, washing meat. At a counter to her left, two women marinated chops and chicken; to the right, rolls were being cut and buttered. A table in the middle of the kitchen was surrounded by women making salads.

Sharon crossed the kitchen to the stove where pots filled with potatoes were bubbling on all four plates. "I got two more pairs of hands here. You got more knives, Mummy? They can peel. Sorry to rope you in like this, girls, but we running late. Why my sister had to choose today of all days to have an emergency Caesarian, I don't know. We were at the hospital the whole day."

Charlene squeezed into a gap at the kitchen table. "No problem cousin. What must we do?"

Suzette wondered what people would say if she went to sit on the barstool in the corner and watched. She took the knife on offer and started scraping a carrot, slowly. She hadn't come here to work; she came to party.

She was stuck in the kitchen while Lynette entertained the crowd of workers with the dramatic story of her grandson's birth. Lynette looked far from ready for her daughter's party – her hair was up in rollers and a pink housecoat covered her generous curves. She chopped a mountain of onions while she spoke. Fat tears rolled down the cheeks of the woman standing to her left.

"Who would have thought Rhoda would struggle like that?" Lynette asked and continued her story without waiting for an answer from the women hanging onto her lips. "I always thought her hips were made for babies. And that husband of hers, Miles, he's so foolish! He insisted he wanted to be there when they cut the baby out. He fainted at the first sight of blood. The doctor had to leave what he was doing to pick him up from the floor."

The kitchen filled up with laughter. Lynette waited for it to stop before she went on. "The doctor just started, so he didn't have to worry about dropping the baby when he jumped to pick up his daddy. Rhoda said she was more worried about Miles than she was about herself. And she was the one that was all cut open like a snoek."

The laughing women worked fast. Suzette helped them carry the food out into the yard when it was ready. A green canvas covered a paved area outside the kitchen, fairy lights strung along its edges. Two trestle tables were set up in a corner. One was covered with platters of snacks – chips, dips, chicken wings, cold meats and savoury biscuits slathered with egg mayonnaise and tuna mayonnaise. The other trestle buckled under the weight of alcohol, soft drinks and glasses.

The smell of charred meat drifted across the yard from a built-in braai next to the pool. Suzette saw a group of men tending to the meat, every one of them hanging onto a drink. She crossed the lawn carefully in Charlene's borrowed high heels and joined them.

A young man wearing a denim shirt and jeans stepped forward to introduce himself. "Hello there. I'm Keith, the birthday girl's brother."

Keith introduced Suzette to the rest of the men. She paid no mind to any of their names; she only had eyes for one. Charlene's cousin was a George Michael look-alike, only darker. With brown hair, not blonde – styled like the Wham singer's, standing high off his forehead.

Suzette hadn't managed to hold onto a boyfriend. A few guys had come and gone since she found out that they were good for something; but none of them hung around for long. They wanted to get it on all the time and it was hard to provide with Mummy and Dedda keeping watch.

She made the mistake last year of bringing a boy home. She really smaaked Sedick and she thought Mummy and Dedda would like him. He was respectable; he hadn't gone under her clothes once since they started seeing each other after school. He came to ask if he could take her to the bioscope. Dedda chased him out and Mummy went on and on for months about it; Suzette was either a loose woman or she was about to convert and change her name to Sumaya. True love waits, Mummy said, and it was definitely waiting until she found a nice boy who belonged to their church.

Keith was older than most of the boys she'd been with but she could see by the way he was checking her out that she could get him if she wanted. She took up position next to him, pretending not to mind the thick clouds of smoke rising from the sausage on the braai, soaking its fatty smell into her skin and her borrowed clothes. She could handle him easy; he had all the usual lines.

"So what's a girl like you doing here all on your lonesome ownsome? Your boyfriend gone to get you a drink?"

"No, I came with your cousin Charlene."

"You got a boyfriend, right?"

Suzette shook her head. "No boyfriend, still looking for Mr Right."

"Right, I see."

She tucked her hand on her hip and pushed her breasts out towards Keith. She had practised the move in the mirror in Mummy's wardrobe; it always worked on the boys. "What you see?"

Keith stared for a while before he whistled through his teeth. Got him!

She made herself useful while the men braaied the mountain of meat, carrying chops, chicken and sausage to the kitchen when it was done and bringing the next batch of raw meat to the fire. She made sure Keith's glass, and hers, was never empty.

The DJ set up on the patio turned up the volume and got the party pumping. Men pulled women onto the dance floor. Kool and the Gang, Stevie Wonder, Whitney Houston, Michael Jackson and Earth, Wind and Fire kept them there.

The music stopped for the speeches. A plump man with a comb-over too thin to cover his bleskop pulled Sharon up against him, took the microphone from the deejay and told the crowd that twenty-one years ago he was in a bar with friends, getting drunk. He found out at midnight that his daughter had been born three hours earlier. He had to wait for the laughing to end before he could continue.

"That's how it was in those days. We didn't stand next to our wives while the doctors cut them open. We stood in the waiting room, smoking one cigarette after another."

"Or sat down in a bar, drinking one beer after another," Lynette shouted at her husband, drawing even more laughter.

"Nevertheless, I wasn't there when my daughter was born. I'm not proud of that, but it's the truth. I'm sorry, my baby, I'll always be there for you from now on."

The birthday girl gave her father a big hug.

Suzette was already bored, but there was more to come. Sharon's parents presented their daughter with a carved wooden key symbolising her freedom into adulthood. The birthday girl gave a speech, most of it thanking her parents and everyone who helped make her party a success. An uncle proposed a champagne toast and led the singing of Happy Birthday and She's a Jolly Good Fella. Candles were lit and blown out. A photographer took snaps for Sharon's twenty-first birthday album.

Platters of braaied meat came out from the kitchen, and the fifty-odd guests tucked in. The food disappeared in minutes.

Suzette shared a lounger next to the pool with Keith while they ate.

They had been talking nonstop since they met at the fire. She liked what she was hearing. Keith was a definite candidate for a boyfriend. He was an apprentice boilermaker, working at the Simon's Town docks. He was twenty-two and still living with his parents, but he owned a car.

The music started up again, calling people back onto the dance floor under the canvas. The DJ played Suzette's favourite Peaches and Herb song, Reunited. Keith claimed her, chasing off every man who tried to cut in. She pressed her breasts against his chest as his hand stroked up and down her back. By the end of the third slow number they were French kissing in a corner and she could feel his hard-on pushing against her stomach.

Keith whispered in her ear as the song ended, "Come with me."

Suzette let him pull her off the dance floor. They were about to go into the house when she stopped in her tracks. "Wait a minute, there's something I must do."

She made her way through the dancers towards Charlene, whose hol was covered in the firm grip of her dance partner. She tapped her friend on the shoulder. "I'm going with Keith. Watch me."

Charlene lifted up her head from her partner's shoulder and nodded.

Suzette went back to Keith and followed him through the house to his Ford Escort parked in the driveway. He opened the back door, pushed her onto the seat and lowered his heavy hips onto hers. His mouth drukked hard onto her lips, his thick tongue pushed into her throat. His hands gryped her breasts, hard. She was just about to push him off when he sat up.

Keith's voice was hoarse. "Wait, let me close the door."

Suzette took her chance, pulled her legs free and struggled to sit up straight. "No, you wait. Give me a minute, not so fast."

Keith gave her a look before he slammed the car door. Suzette was shocked at how his face changed. George Michael was gone and something vrek ugly had replaced him.

Keith growled like a pitbull ready to attack. "Why did you then come here with me? What did you think I wanted? What are you? A cockteaser?"

Suzette pulled away as Keith reached for her, but there was nowhere to go. She strained against the car door; the window winder digging into her scalp as Keith pulled her down, trying to pin her underneath him on the seat.

She could hear people shouting out goodbye as they walked down the path to the front gate, metres from the car. She was about to say something when a heavy hand came down on her mouth. She started to worry.

There was a tap on the car window. Charlene's voice. "Suzette, you okay in there? Suzette, you orrite?"

She slid out from under Keith as soon as he started lifting his heavy body off her. "I'm orrite. Wait there, Charlene, I'm coming." She opened the car door.

"Cockteaser," Keith hissed.

Doing her best to pretend nothing had happened, Suzette walked around the car, linked her arm with her friend's and strolled back into the house, swaying her hips. "Sjoe, that was close. Thanks for watching, Charlene. You came just at the right time. A minute later and I dunno what would have happened. I can see why your cousin can't keep a girlfriend. There's something very wrong with him."

Mummy was in the kitchen doing the ironing when she came home the next morning. The table was piled high with neat rows and the plastic laundry basket was almost empty. This was a kwaai surprise. Suzette's hangover wasn't too bad, but it left her in no mood for housework.

Magda smiled when Suzette dropped into a kitchen chair. "I thought I should give you a hand today. You working so hard on the fete. Shame, were you up late?"

Suzette didn't have to lie. "We went to sleep around three o'clock."

Magda sighed. "I really don't know why it's so hard to get people to do the Lord's work. It's been seven years already and the church is still not finished. This year, thank God, all the work is on the inside. If everyone paid their tithes there would be no need to make the fete such a big thing. I make sure your dedda contributes, even though he's too lazy to get up for Sunday services. Promise me that when you start working, you'll give your fair share."

Suzette had to lie. She had big plans for her pay, and first on the list was a pair of tight-fitting faded jeans, like the pair Charlene loaned her for the party. "Yes, Mummy."

"Do the right thing, Suzette. That's all the Lord asks of you."

"Yes, Mummy."

"Ag, I don't know why I'm giving you such a hard time. You a good girl, Suzette. Make us a cup of tea, won't you?"

Suzette took a Grandpa while she waited for the kettle to boil. Looked like she was stuck in the kitchen for a while. She had no smaak for a conversation about the church, but while Mummy did the ironing, the least she could do was listen. Mummy ironed fast; years of working in clothing factories taught her to sweep her arm up and down the garments without leaving a single crease behind.

She sipped her tea and listened with half an ear to a long list of complaints about the lazy church congregation. Was Mummy always like this? She couldn't imagine her on a dance floor. Mummy wasn't bad looking; if she lost around ten kilograms she could look ten years younger. Her skin was still good, she was two years away from forty and there wasn't a line on her pale face. She had nice hair, it was a pity it was always tied back. If she had it styled to frame her face like Purdey she would look bemoer.

Suzette tried to picture her parents on a dance floor, but she couldn't. She saw Mummy leading and Dedda following. She hid her smile in her mug while she took a big slurp of tea.

She went to lie on her bed with Charlene's copy of *You* magazine after Mummy finished the ironing. She chased Keith out of her mind when he crawled in. She wasn't going to let him spoil what was looking like a lekker weekend.

Chapter Five

Nicky got to school half an hour before the bell rang. The sun was up over the Hottentots Holland mountains, the building was warm in its yellow rays. She was lucky to be at Hanover Park High; it was the best-looking school in the area. It was built with red bricks and the walls inside were painted yellow. Only a few windows were broken.

In 1980 Hanover Park High was like all the other schools in the township. The boys punched holes through the thin prefabricated walls. The winter wind cut like dry ice across the students' cheeks when it poured into the classrooms through broken windows. The 1980 school boycott, which spread through the whole of South Africa, started at Hanover Park High. The pupils demanded that their school be maintained, and equal education to white pupils. The school was damaged so badly in the protests that the House of Representatives – the coloured 'parliament' with little power – had to rebuild it. The work finished just before Nicky started high school.

She sat at her desk, frowning over her trigonometry homework. A whisper in her ear made her jump so high that her knees hit the bottom of the desk. She twisted around in her seat and glared at the boy standing behind her. Who else could it be? Kevin had a tarty smile on his face, like he expected her to be happy to see him. "Kevin, are you mal? You nearly gave me a heart attack."

Kevin's smile disappeared. He pushed his shoulders up and shoved his hands into the pockets of his olive-green jacket, pasted with political badges. A black beret sat on top of his curly brown hair. There was a badge on his beret, with a picture of a man with a thick black beard, also wearing a beret. He shrugged. "Sorry man, I was just greeting you. How you doing Nicky, you okay?"

Nicky stared down at her maths book. "I'm orrite."

"What you doing?"

"Checking my homework."

"What is it?"

"Trigonometry."

Nicky wished Kevin would go away. Couldn't he see she wasn't interested? He was in a class above her, in standard nine, but he kept seeking her out. She once made the mistake of talking to him about politics. He agreed with everything she said; since then he kept trying to recruit her for the Congress of South African Students, even after it was banned. She wasn't interested in politics. Okay, she was. Politics was interesting. She just didn't want to get involved. Her schoolwork and the church youth took up too much of her time.

Kevin didn't get the message. His black eyes smiled in his dark face. "So, are you coming to the SRC meeting in second break?"

Nicky turned her mouth down. "Isn't the meeting for standard nine and matric students only? I don't know anyone in standard eight who goes."

"They won't chuck you out. There's no age limit on political consciousness. We planning something big for the tenth anniversary of June 1976 uprising. There's work to be done. Children younger than us are at war in other countries. If our parents won't stand up to the regime, it's our duty to do so."

Nicky never once heard Kevin talk like a normal person. He made speeches. Sometimes he used words she didn't understand, and he didn't even notice. It irritated her. She looked the words up in her dictionary. Dichotomy meant dividing things in half. She had to get him to leave. She had maths first period, and the bell was going to ring any minute. "Okay, Kevin, I'll come to your meeting."

"Good. See you later."

Nicky felt bad when Kevin smiled at her again before he left. She told him she would go to the meeting just to get rid of him. Must she tell him the truth? Too late, he was already gone. She went back to checking her homework, trying to shake him off. She just started when another interruption came. This one was okay; Shirley was her best friend.

Shirley came borrelling down the aisle between the desks, panting as she shoved herself onto the seat next to Nicky. Mummy said she was built like a dressing table. She had a short neck and her breasts grew onto her stomach; there was no gap between them. She gave the best hugs.

Nicky faced her friend. "What's going on with you? Why you in such a state?"

"Yoh, Nicky, I got such kak news. Sorry I didn't meet you on the corner this morning. I was late."

Nicky usually walked with Shirley to school and home again. Her friend lived three roads up from Magnolia Court, in a row of houses on Apple Street.

Nicky frowned. "Is okay, I came early to school. What happened?"

Shirley twisted her legs and her fingers as she spoke. "My mummy came to speak to me this morning before she went to work. She says I must leave school the end of the year. Mummy says standard eight is enough. I can get a job at her factory with a standard eight pass."

Nicky covered her mouth with her hand. Although she knew lots of girls left school at sixteen, this was kak news. Mummy went on all the time about how she started her first job at fifteen. Nicky wouldn't start working until she was twenty-four, when she would be ready for her articles. Dedda took her school reports to work and the partners at the firm said they would give her a bursary to study law if she got into the University of Cape Town. Her teachers told her she could make it. They wanted her to be the first student from Hanover Park to go to UCT.

She gryped Shirley's hands to keep hers steady. She had to help. What could she do? "I dunno what to say to you Shirley, this is really kak news. Haai Jirre, you still a child."

"I know, but my mummy needs my help. Since my daddy died it's been difficult. She got four children to feed. My sister Karen left school in standard eight to work with her. Now it's my turn."

Nicky didn't know what to say to make it better for her friend. There wasn't much you could say about a kak situation like this. She rubbed Shirley's shoulders as they drooped onto her chest. "I promise we will still be friends."

Shirley spoke through tight lips. "Ja, but I'm gunna miss school. I'm gunna miss all the times we spend together."

"We will still see each other, promise."

Nicky gave her friend a hug. The bell rang and the classroom got too noisy to talk. She struggled to concentrate for the rest of the school day. Shirley's desk was in front of hers. She stared at the back of her friend's neck, a dark spot under straightened hair that stood away from her head, wondering what to do to make it better.

Kevin was waiting at the school gate when Nicky and Shirley strolled out arm in arm at the end of the school day. He stepped forward as they came near. "Greetings ladies, can I escort you today?"

Shirley giggled. "Of course you can, right Nicky?"

Nicky didn't want Kevin walking with them. He was only after one thing. She hadn't gone to the SRC meeting at second break; she was too busy sukkeling with Shirley's problem. She still hadn't found a solution. As she expected, it didn't take long – two steps out of the gate and Kevin started on her.

"So Nicky, I was expecting to see you in the meeting this afternoon. There's work to be done. We planning to bring the country to a stand still for the tenth anniversary of the '76 uprising."

Thick, dark irritation filled her face. What must she do to get Kevin to leave her alone? Nicky didn't want him to escort her anywhere. She wanted to be alone with Shirley; she was planning on going home with her. Shirley shouldn't be alone on a kak day like this. "I had other things on my mind, okay?"

"What can be more important than the struggle?"

Nicky stopped and planted her fists in her hips, staring daggers at Kevin. "A lot, you idiot. Shirley, for an example. She's much more important than your blerrie struggle. She got a big problem. Her mother wants her to leave school and go work in the factory with her."

Kevin turned to Shirley, his face squeezed up like a lemon. "You'll be a semi-skilled worker fed to the machine to become another alienated unit of capitalist labour."

Nicky felt like her head was about to burst open like a dropped watermelon, the irritation was so thick. No one could get to her like

Kevin. "Speak English Kevin! This isn't time for a political speech. Shirley needs help. She's not an issue. She's only sixteen and she must go work to feed her brothers. You such a blerrie fool!"

Kevin looked like a foster child on his way back to the orphanage. "Of course I think that's really kak, Nicky! There must be a way out. We must strategise, see what we can come up with."

Shirley smiled at him. "You think you can see a way out of it?"

Kevin gave a couple of firm nods. "Let me think on it for a while. As Lenin would say: What is to be done? That's what we must figure out."

Nicky stared at their backs as Shirley and Kevin walked away without her. That boy had a nerve! Didn't he see he wasn't wanted? She was going to come up with a solution for Shirley's problem. They didn't need him. Why was Shirley hanging onto his words like he was her saviour? She rushed to catch up with them.

The girls' route home took them past the taxi rank at the Hanover Park Town Centre. The rank fed routes into town, Claremont, Wynberg and Mitchells Plain. Gaartjies shouted out destinations and ushered people into revving sixteen-seaters; pushing flesh and parcels inside as they slid the doors shut.

Nicky, Shirley and Kevin wove their way along the pavement between people streaming to the rank and the hawkers lining the sides. Most were selling vegetables, but there were also stalls with tinned goods, bags of bright orange chips and loose cigarettes. A bakkie blocked the pavement, its back piled high with snoek. A plump man covered with a red-stained, yellow plastic apron gutted and beheaded his silver, toothy catch while customers waited. The fish was wrapped in newspaper and exchanged for a five-rand note. Nicky could smell the sea on the bakkie as she walked past.

A toothless, skinny man jumped onto the pavement and blocked their way. He waved a packet of ripe, red tomatoes in their faces. He flashed his gums and offered an invitation. "Squeeze my tomatoes. Feel how firm they are. They lekker like your tette."

Nicky jumped back as the hawker's free hand reached out towards her breast.

Kevin stepped forward and shoved his chest into the hawker's. "Watch it, show some respect."

Nicky pulled him back. "Leave him Kevin, is okay. He does the same thing every day. He don't mean nothing by it."

Another hawker pushed Kevin aside to wave a bag of onions in Nicky's face. He promoted his goods in a singsong voice. "Uiwe, uiwe; juicy uiwe virrie meire."

The girls giggled. Kevin relaxed.

Shirley bought tomatoes and onions. Kevin dug into his grey school pants and found enough coins for a bag of onions.

Nicky walked behind Shirley and Kevin as they left the town centre, listening to their conversation. Shirley was planning a beef stew for supper. Kevin was giving advice.

"The secret to a good stew is making a thick gravy. You must use at least two onions Shirley, maybe even three, 'cause your family's bigger than mine. Braise it well at the start. The onions soak up the flavour from the meat. It melts as you cook and makes a lekker thick gravy."

Shirley shook her head. "I dunno if that will work. It's near the end of the week. My mummy don't have much left, so I got only bones for the stew."

"It will still work, I'm telling you. If you got little meat then it's more important to have a lekker thick gravy. The onions will catch the flavour from the bones."

There was nothing Nicky could add to the conversation. Mummy did most of the cooking. She and Suzette were only roped in on weekends; on weekdays they were expected to do their schoolwork. Mummy gave them the kak jobs like slicing onions and peeling potatoes. Most nights Mummy stood up from the supper table and started preparing the next night's meal. She finished the food off when she got home from work.

Kevin walked with them all the way to Shirley's house. Nicky didn't know where he lived; she hoped it wasn't nearby. He bowed over Shirley's hand like the Count of Monte Cristo and kissed it as he was leaving.

Nicky finally had enough. Shirley had been talking nonstop with Kevin all the way home. She was all worked up about Shirley's problem, but the blerrie fool was giggling with Kevin like she didn't give a damn. Her irritation burst out and poured through her mouth. "Must you be so tarty, Kevin? You must see how you look. Like a blerrie fool."

Kevin wiped his smile off his face and took a step back. "Ladies, I'll see you around."

Shirley turned on Nicky as he walked away stiffly. "Sjoe, how can you be so rude? Can't you see he's just trying to be nice?"

Nicky stood her ground. "Why can't he just leave us alone? Why must he interfere in everything? Every time I look up his face is in mine. Can't he see I'm not interested in joining his struggle?"

Shirley laughed. "He's not in your face because of the struggle. He smaaks you. Everybody can see that. He smaaks you stukkend."

Nicky's chest went cold. "Who's everybody?"

Shirley giggled. "Only everybody who looks in Kevin's face when he talks to you. You so blind Nicky."

Nicky shoved her hand into Shirley's chest, sending her off the pavement. "Don't talk rubbish! Kevin's got a one-track mind. He wants me to join Cosas. He wants me to get involved in the struggle."

Shirley sniffed. "There's none so blind. The whole school knows he smaaks you."

A scene from a black-and-white film started up in Nicky's head. She was sitting on a chair listening to Kevin and nodding to everything he said. She had no mouth; her skin was smooth under her nose all the way down to her chin. She shook the picture out of her mind and went with Shirley to fetch her younger brothers from the neighbour next door. The woman collected the boys at their primary school and watched them until Shirley got home.

Nicky did her homework at the kitchen table while Shirley gave her brothers sandwiches and started preparing the beef stew. She took note of the three onions Shirley put in the pot. Shirley said she was mal to do her homework on a Friday afternoon, but she was grateful when Nicky also did hers.

After a lot of thought, Nicky came up with something to make her friend feel better before she left. She reminded her that the church youth camp was in two weeks – Shirley would get away from her family for four whole days over Easter.

She walked fast to Magnolia Court. The gangsters would soon be coming after the Friday night pay packets. Mummy made her children promise they would be off the streets when it got dark; 'specially on

Friday nights. Two years back, Mummy had walked into a woman crying as a gangster pressed a flick knife against her throat. She could do nothing but watch the woman lose a week's pay and walk her home.

The Fouries had Kentucky Fried Chicken for supper most Friday nights. Mummy was tired by the end of the week and Dedda was flash with his pay packet before she took out the church tithe and the rent money. Nicky sat opposite Suzette at the kitchen table; Dedda and Mummy faced each other. Anthony was on a corner between Dedda and Nicky, his elbow digging into her ribs as he cut through a chicken breast.

Nicky turned to Dedda. If anyone could help Shirley, it was him. He picked up a lot of information at the law firm; he knew all about human rights. "Dedda, Shirley's got a big problem and we dunno what to do."

Neville looked up from his plate. "What is it, my bokkie?'

Nicky told him about the problem; but before he could open his mouth, Mummy jumped right in.

A deep frown carved across Magda's forehead. "I don't know what's wrong with the young people of today. It's like they scared of hard work. I lost two more girls on my line today. The factory was advertising for models and two of my girls got the job. God only knows how I am going to fill my order next week. We'll have to work overtime; I will be in trouble because the girls must be paid extra."

Nicky couldn't work out what this had to do with Shirley. She wasn't scared of work; she was too young to work. Mummy kept gaaning aan about how important it was for her daughters to finish their schooling, why couldn't it be the same for Shirley? It was no use asking, no one could get a word in when Mummy was on a roll.

"After all I did for those girls, this is how they thank me. They go off prancing for the buyers. Some of them even model lingerie. Decent girls don't walk around in their lingerie in front of strange men. But they want to earn big money after working only for a few years."

There was silence at the table. Nicky had nothing to say. This had nothing to do with Shirley, but still, she felt sorry for Mummy. Her feet swelled up like pumpkin fritters when she worked overtime because she had to walk the line to make sure the girls did their work properly. This was the life Shirley was facing; and most of Nicky's classmates who would be swallowed up by the factories. Dedda said people like Mummy – who lived in Hanover Park and worked in the factories nearby – were walking tools.

One day when she was a lawyer earning big bucks, Mummy and Dedda could stop working. She would give them money every month. They worked hard today so their children didn't have to work hard one day, that's what Mummy always said. Nicky understood and she was grateful.

Suzette broke the silence. "How much do they get for modelling?"

Magda started up again. "Far too much, because it's not real work. They might as well stand on a street corner; it's the same thing. I wonder what their mothers have to say about what they doing. Lord knows; you'll never see me stooping so low for money."

Nicky burst out laughing. A piece of chicken went flying out of her mouth onto Anthony's plate.

He picked up the chewed flesh and threw it back at her. "Sies, you disgusting!"

Nicky was hukking with laughter. "I'm sorry, I'm sorry. It's just that I was picturing Mummy as a model, walking up and down a ramp."

There was another silence. Magda started laughing first, then everybody joined in. Nicky gave up. They had all forgotten what she was saying about Shirley. She would try to speak to Dedda about her friend's problem when Mummy wasn't around. It was no use trying to talk to him when she was there.

Chapter Six

Anthony recognised the five men outside his school gate. It was Ougat and his ouens, the young men who had talked to Dedda in the park a few weeks back. They were ragging the girls as they left school, whistling through their teeth and reaching out to touch the pretty ones.

Anthony snatched a look at them. He was deep in conversation with his friend. Delmar had missed *The A-Team* on TV the night before and Anthony was catching him up on how Mr T had blown up a airport hangar and taken out fifteen armed men single-handedly. He heard a shout, but kept walking and talking.

"Hey laaitie, wait up!"

Someone grabbed his arm from behind. Anthony came to a halt, turned and faced Ougat. He frowned. "What you want?"

Ougat flashed his gold teeth. "No need to get aggro. Ougat's just being friendly here. I got a invite for you, to come to my place. Is not far from where you stay."

Anthony pulled his arm free. "Why must I come to your place?"

"I got something for your Daddy, to show there's no hard feelings for the other day."

"What happened between you and my dedda?"

Ougat's smile went wider. "Nothing. That's exactly what I'm vertelling you. There's no hard feelings. We chommies, me and your dedda."

Anthony stood his ground. Delmar was on his shoulder. He was big for his age; he had started shaving already. "Why must I go to your place? You can bring it yourself."

Ougat wouldn't give up. "Just come for a short while. You must mos

41

go past my place on your way home. Is on your route."

Anthony didn't know what to say. He had promised Dedda he would stay away from Ougat. He was gunna be in trouble if he went with him. But Dedda also said there was no reason to be bang of Ougat. He took another look at him. Ougat did look like the chow-wow downstairs; his face was too small for his bulging eyes. He sounded like he wanted peace with Dedda. Anthony said goodbye to Delmar and went with the ouens.

Ougat lived on Peach Street, on a row of maisonettes – double-storey houses in sets of four, two upstairs and two below. A set of concrete stairs led to the top floor. There was a business operating in the front yard of Ougat's ground floor home. Wooden poles creakily held up a canvas roof overhanging the front garden, flapping as the South-Easter struggled to lift it free. The walls were corrugated-zinc sheets nailed together. A bright, black JFK was painted on the sheet at the entrance.

The shebeen's floor had once been the maisonette's front garden. The hundreds of feet that had visited had tramped it down a bit, but the grey Cape Flats sand was hard to settle. The wind brought in the salty taste of False Bay through the gaps in the canvas. A brazier burning orange added warmth and smoke to the establishment.

Anthony had never been in a shebeen. There was one in a backyard at Orchid Court, near his house. He had gone there with friends sent to fetch their fathers. Dedda warned him never to go inside. A man was stabbed to death there.

It took a while for his eyes to adjust. As his eyes focused to the dim light, he saw there were nine men on the shebeen's wooden benches, every one of them holding onto a bottle of Carling Black Label.

A square piece of board and plastic milk crates made a table in one corner. Four men seated around it slammed dominoes down. They held their pieces between the fingers of one hand, leaving the other hand free to lift a bottle.

Brenda Fassie's Weekend Special blared from a hi-fi powered by a long extension cord snaking through the lounge window. It also fed a naked bulb hanging from a nail on one of the wooden poles holding up the roof. Anthony tried to peer into the front room of Ougat's home, but the canvas kept it too dark for him to see inside.

He looked around for Ougat and found him deep in conversation with a beautiful girl. Like Mummy would say, she looked ready to pop any day. She looked ripe to Anthony; juicy and ready to eat.

Ougat waved for Anthony to wait. "Gimme me a minute, laaitie, I got to sort out something here."

Anthony watched as Ougat pulled the pregnant girl down onto a bench in the corner of the shebeen, near the hi-fi. Ougat listened and nodded while she talked, he didn't say anything. When the girl stopped he pulled a stack of notes out of the back pocket of his jeans, peeled off a few and handed them to her. She kissed him on the cheek and left.

Ougat strolled over to Anthony and slapped him on the back. "Kinners, hey? They give you a few minutes of heaven, then you must fokken pay up for the rest of your life. You got a woman?"

Anthony's cheeks got very hot. "I haven't got one at the moment."

Ougat threw his words back at him with a false, high voice. "I haven't got one at the moment. Hey ouens, listen to this laaitie. He speaks like the fokken queen of England. I haven't got one at the moment, he says to me when I ask if he's got a kind."

The shebeen's customers laughed along with Ougat.

Anthony turned to walk out. He didn't want to be there. If Dedda found out, he would be in big kak. There was nothing wrong with speaking proper English, why was that so funny? And he didn't like being called a laaitie, he was as tall as Ougat.

Ougat caught up with him before he got to the door, gryping him round his shoulder. "Hey laaitie, don't take it so hard. Ougat is only making jokes. Can't you take a joke? Eksê, if you got trouble with the kinners, you come to the right place. Mr Lover Man will sort you out one time."

Ougat settled Anthony down on the bench where the pregnant girl had sat earlier. "You see, you got to mos know how to chaff the kinners. Without the vocals you don't get to hear the tune. Then you got to warm them up slowly, 'specially if they kinners who don't give it out so easy. They will all give you a naai, but some like to be persuaded first, see what I mean?"

One of the customers interjected, lifting his bottle in Ougat's direction. "Hey laaitie, you learning from the master. Ougat here

43

specialises in kinners, he once did a ten-year-old and ended up in reform school. Lucky he was only thirteen so they didn't call it rape, just interference."

Ougat glared at the man. "Hou jou bek, Frankie. Just because you made my sister pregnant doesn't make you my fokken brother. Watch what you say to Ougat."

Frankie fell silent and wrapped his arms around his chest. His cheeks sunk into his gums as the smile disappeared off his face.

Ougat turned back to Anthony. "Don't listen to his kak. Ougat here never once had to force a kind. All of them says no, so it's up to you to show them that they can do with some of your loving. You got to start with kisses, even if the kind got a really vrot mouth. Kinners like kisses. You see this? You know what this is?" Ougat opened his mouth wide and pointed to his missing four front teeth.

Anthony shook his head, no.

"A passion gap, that's what it is. For the French kissing. You know mos, French kissing."

Anthony shook his head. His cheeks were getting hot again.

Ougat pushed his tongue in and out of the gap in his teeth. "It's like so. With a passion gap, you can get your tongue right down her throat."

Frankie interjected again. "And a passion gap's a lekker thing to have in prison; makes it easier to get something else down your throat."

Ougat was on his feet in seconds. He crossed the shebeen, screaming at Frankie. "I told you to hou jou bek!"

Beer bottles dropped onto the floor as the domino players dived out of the way. Ougat punched Frankie in the face. He dropped onto Frankie when he fell down onto the sandy floor and moered him, fists shooting up and down. Frankie curled up and covered his face with his hands, not even trying to get a shot in.

After a few minutes Ougat stopped punching, got to his feet and started kicking. Then he grabbed Frankie by the collar of his shirt and dragged him out of the shebeen. He gave him one last kick in the ribs after he dropped him on the pavement.

Anthony lifted his hands and stared at them. There were red half-moons on both palms where his nails had gone in deep while he watched Frankie's beating. He'd seen lots of fights. Been in many of them, behind the boys' toilet after school. He'd won some. He'd never seen anyone fight like this before, except on *The A-Team*. Ougat could be as strong as Mr T. He could drag a man a distance. He had handled Frankie alone without asking anyone for help. Frankie was taller and heavier than Ougat but he didn't stand a chance.

Ougat came back inside the shebeen. His bright black eyes bulged above his high cheekbones as he smiled at Anthony. "What you think laaitie, you like my moves?"

"Yoh! That guy was bigger than you. But you handled him, just like Mr T. Tell me, you like *The A-Team*?"

Anthony never found out why he had been brought to the shebeen. He hung out with Ougat, his ouens and his customers for hours, listening to their stories. A few of the men had been in Pollsmoor. They showed him the exercises they did in the prison yard and how to take a man down.

Ougat had a karate chop to the back of the neck that made a man fall to his knees. He got a customer to help with a demonstration. Then he got four of his ouens to line up for Anthony to practise the move, but he couldn't get one to drop.

After Anthony left the shebeen, he walked down Lemon Street towards Magnolia Court. It was true what Ougat said; he didn't live far away. As he neared the park, he spotted some of his friends and ran to join them. "Hey ouens, wait 'til you see the moves I got!"

Anthony told Elviro to stand in front of him and drop his chin. He went behind him and lifted his hand up, his fingers pressed together tightly like he was saying a prayer. He brought his hand down between Elviro's neck and his shoulder blade. To his surprise, the boy dropped onto his knees in the sand.

His friends were impressed. Those who had older brothers practised hard so they could use Anthony's move to defend themselves. The boys sat on the rails of the broken roundabout after their session to plan who they would take on first.

It was getting dark when Anthony got home. He hadn't been home since he left for school in the morning. Maybe Mummy and Dedda weren't home yet from work. He knew how to make sure Nicky didn't squeal. He was gunna threaten her with his Ougat move.

It was later than he thought. Dedda was the moer in. He started shouting the minute Anthony walked in the door.

"Do you know how worried we are? I was just coming to fetch you! Where were you? Why don't you listen to me?"

Mummy walked into the lounge. Anthony melted his eyes at her, like a baby watching a nipple coming out of a bra. She fell for it and pulled him away from Dedda.

"Ag, don't be so hard on him, Neville. This is the first time he's been this late since you last spoke to him. You won't do it again, will you, Anthony? You won't make us worry again?"

Anthony snuggled into Mummy's soft chest. She was always on his side. He was her baby boy, her one and only. Dedda was always jumping down his throat for the smallest thing.

As he fell asleep on the couch later that night, Anthony remembered the Mr Lover Man conversation. It was nothing like the stories he heard at school from boys who claimed they went all the way with girls. This was true life.

That pregnant girl in the shebeen was very pretty. Her black hair was thick and shiny, and her shirt buttons popped at her breasts. Anthony's hand went into his pyjama pants and found his piel. Before he left the shebeen, Ougat had promised to hook him up with a befokte kind he could naai 'til she couldn't walk straight.

Chapter Seven

Suzette stared out of her classroom window. The field beyond the school buildings was dusty in the wind. There was a tarred area, the size of a netball court. It had no lines and no posts. The boys played soccer there; car tyres marked out their goalposts. All the way to the plastic-lined fence the field was loose soil, with small patches of brown grass.

She dragged her attention back into the classroom. Mr Van Niekerk was drawing on the board, mumbling with his back to the class. She had stopped listening to him months ago. Of what use was biology? How would it help her now that she knew something about the sex life of a spider and a pinecone?

She put her cheeks in her hands and sighed. School was kak boring. She was only here because Mummy and Dedda were so strict about it. It was their plan that she finish school, not hers.

Dedda and Mummy had her life all worked out. They found a college where she could learn typing and shorthand next year. Dedda said the secretaries at his law firm were very clever, and they earned well. The firm had appointed the first coloured secretary this year. He planned on her being the second one. No thank you very much, Suzette wanted to tell him, but she couldn't until she came up with Plan B. Secretaries wore white shirts and grey skirts. And kak beige pantyhose.

Her whole life was kak boring, not just school. She could do nothing without money. Mummy gave her two rand a week pocket money if she helped in the house. Now that she was smoking, drinking and clubbing, it didn't go far. Everyone was going to the Galaxy nightclub on Friday night to celebrate Ebrahim's eighteenth birthday. She didn't have enough to get through the door. Her friends were sick and sat of her holhanging; she never paid them back. How could she, with only two rand a week?

Could she ask Dedda for money? She never did before. What reason would she give for wanting it? She couldn't see how he could help. He handed his pay packet to Mummy every Friday evening. She brought out her pay and they sat at the kitchen table making piles and putting them into envelopes: the church tithe, Dedda's taxi fare, Mummy's fare, food money, rent, burial plans and whatnot.

Nicky had money; she was saving to buy textbooks for university. Nah, it was no use. Suzette had tried her a few times and she always got nowhere. Nicky was a complete waste of her time.

How was she getting into the Galaxy on Friday night? She gave up trying to solve her problem, turned to face the window again and started up her favourite daydream: A boyfriend drives into her life in a Ford Cortina. He takes her to bioscope every Friday night and to Truworths on Saturday mornings where he says 'choose whatever you want baby, I want my girl to look like a model when we step into the Galaxy tonight'.

A befokte idea jumped into her head. Maybe she could be a model! Her friends said she was the best looking of all of them. They were always nagging her to enter beauty contests. The winners never got cash prizes, just sashes and bouquets. What was the use of that?

Mr Van Niekerk's voice faded far in the background as she began to work out whether she had it in her to be a model. It was easy work; all they had to do was stand around and look bemoer while people took photos. She could do that.

How could she go about becoming one? Didn't Mummy say something the other night about her factory hiring girls to model their lines? She got so worked up because the models earned a lot. Did she have the pluck to go for a job at Mummy's factory? She wouldn't survive her first day. What about another factory?

Suzette shot up in her desk. That's what she would do. A small scream of excitement leaked from her mouth.

Mr Van Niekerk stopped teaching and looked straight at her. "Suzette, is there something you don't understand?"

Why was he picking on her? "Yes, sir, everything you said this year."

The class turned to face Mr Van Niekerk and laughed. Suzette smiled. She hadn't lost her touch. Her teacher's face was as red as the beetroot served with a Sunday roast.

Suzette stood naked in front of the full-length mirror at the back of Mummy's wardrobe door. She had bunked school, heading back to the flat after everyone left. Today was the first day of the rest of her life. She was going to find out if she could be a model.

First, she wanted to make sure she had what it took. Her outfits spoiled every look; they were too old fashioned and covered too much of her body. She stood in her underwear and examined herself in the mirror. Not bad! She looked good from every angle.

She skrikked as a door banged shut. It came from next door. Someone was leaving Aunty Moira's flat. She was still alone. She relaxed, crooked her arm into her waist and stared some more. This wasn't a good body; this was a befokte body. Suzette wanted to see it all. She took off her underwear. She had never done this before.

She stared. Her skin was creamy like butter, fairer than Mummy's. None of the magazines she read used photos of coloured models. She didn't want to model skin lighteners and hair straighteners. She could say she got a tan on Clifton beach. Could she pass?

She stepped closer to the mirror to examine her face. There wasn't a mark on her skin, not like some of her friends whose acne left scars and holes in their cheeks. Her breasts were high on her chest. Mummy insisted that she wear a bra every day. She said it was immodest for girls to walk around like ripe figs on a tree. Her stomach was flat and her pubic hair was neat, not that anyone she modelled for would see it.

Suzette had enough pluck to sell herself. She had told her friend Charlene about her plan yesterday. Charlene was convinced it would work and suggested she look in the Yellow Pages for modelling agencies; you were supposed to find everything if your fingers did the walking. She checked it out as soon as she got home from school and found three pages of modelling agencies. What did they do?

She got dressed and went to the lounge. She sat on the couch and

49

lifted the Yellow Pages onto her lap, licking her finger as she searched for the right page. She chose a name she liked and dialled the number.

The woman's voice on the other end of the phone was very larney. "Make You a Star Agency, can I help you?"

Suzette swallowed and spoke as larney as she could. "Yes please. I want to find out about becoming a model."

"Do you have a portfolio?"

"What's that?"

"It's an exemplar of your work."

She got such a skrik she put the phone down. She didn't know what the woman was talking about. She tried the next number in the book. This time, she was ready when the phone was answered and spoke fast.

"Hello. I want to become a model, but I don't have a portfolio. Can you tell me how to organise one?"

Another larney voice. "You have to get to a studio, professional photographers shoot portfolios."

"Will they charge me?"

"Oh yes, it costs around R200 to put one together."

Suzette put the phone down again without saying goodbye. She was getting nowhere. She wanted modelling to solve her money problems, not make bigger ones. She would try one more agency before giving up. She crossed her fingers, kissed them and dialled.

She had only one question. "Can I come see you if I don't have a portfolio?"

"I'm sorry, no."

Suzette leaned back on the couch and cried snot en trane. She had been so sure that all she needed was her good looks to become a model. She didn't want to go to secretarial college so she could get a kak job in a boring office. Mummy would expect her to hand over her pay packet every Friday night. She definitely didn't want that life. She picked up the Yellow Pages again, licked her finger and turned to Clothing Manufacturers. She chose a factory in Athlone.

She was ready when the phone was answered. "Have you got any openings for models?"

"We make men's overalls, we don't need models."

She struck it lucky on her next call. She may have found her ticket out. Planet Fashions in Retreat was interviewing models next Thursday. She wrote down all the details with a shaking hand.

Suzette bunked school again on the day of the interview. She took a taxi to Lansdowne Station. She stole a train to Retreat, changing third-class carriages every time she spotted the gaartjie. She didn't have money for a ticket. Seemed like the preacher raining spit through the carriage as he spread the word of Father God didn't have a ticket either; every time she changed carriages she found him at her shoulder.

Planet Fashions was in a three-storey building near the station. It looked like a prison from the outside; there were a few small windows. The factory was surrounded by a chain-link fence topped with razor wire. A steel gate guarded by a man in a black uniform holding a baton was the only entrance.

The reception area was a dark brown space with green plants in pots in the corners. About six other women had arrived before Suzette, and there were two behind her as she came in. Did they all come for the model interviews? Most of them had kwaai bodies. Suzette stared down at her 34B chest after checking them out.

The girl standing next to her noticed what she was doing, laughed and pressed her elbow into Suzette's ribs. "Don't worry about that, your size of your tette is not so important."

Suzette turned to face the young woman, who was gebou in all the right areas. She needed all the help she could get. "What's important then?"

Melanie knew what was what. She had worked at Planet Fashions until a year ago when she left to have a baby. She told Suzette that Mr Strauss, the owner of the factory, was looking for sexy girls. He wasn't interested in size; he wanted girls who could make the buyers place orders. The factory hired over eight hundred women; he had to make sure they kept their jobs.

Suzette watched Melanie closely. She could see what she meant. Melanie was plump, and the skin on her face creased when she smiled. When she moved all of that disappeared. She kept tucking her blowdried brown flicks behind her ear, and she held her hand open wide on her thigh when she leaned forward to talk.

The noise level went up in the reception area; the women were on the move. Suzette walked behind Melanie as they went through a wide door into a canteen. The windows on the walls she hadn't seen when she entered the factory went from the floor to the ceiling. From the inside, the place didn't look at all like a prison. It was filled with light.

The canteen was lined with trestle tables and wooden benches. Four urns on a table hissed in a corner. A door at the other end led into a dressing room. Steel cages filled with handbags and clothing, secured with Yale locks, lined the brick walls. In the centre were rows of benches divided by metal rails.

Suzette looked around. The women were getting undressed. Some of them were down to their underwear already. They were hanging their clothes on the rail between the benches.

She pinched Melanie's arm as they came to a halt. "Why's everybody taking their clothes off?"

"It's a lingerie factory, domkop. They need to see you in your underwear."

She hadn't expected this. She looked around again. The women were all wearing sexy underwear. There was a lot of lace, French-cut bikinis and a tanga or two that left very little to the imagination. What should she do? If she was going to make a fool of herself it wasn't going to be because she ran out of the room. Suzette took her clothes off, as slowly as possible.

Melanie laughed when she spotted her trying to hide her underwear under her hands. Mummy had bought it – a white cotton bikini and a white cotton, front-fastening bra. Suzette turned away from the laughter and reached for her dress.

Melanie grabbed the dress from her hands. "Wait up girl. Don't get so cross so quickly. There's nothing wrong with what you wearing. They also make this kind of broeks here. If you want to get this job then listen up. It's not what broekies you wear, it's how you wear them. When you go show what you got, think about pomping. You done that, haven't you?"

Suzette pulled her body tight and high. "You think I'm a child?"

"Ja, I think you a child. How old are you?"

She hoped she kept her face straight while she lied. "Twenty."

"Okay, if you say so. When you walk in there, think about someone you want to pomp. If you do that, just watch, you will get this job. You got a lekker body."

Suzette hung back as one by one the girls went into a room leading off the dressing room. She shivered as the room emptied, thinking about her 'look'. Her best pomp was with Aunty Moira's eldest son Mark, who lived next door. He was her first – and still the best she had. But he dropped out of school when his uncle got him a job at the council as a rubbish collector. His hands were never touching her again, no matter how much she smaaked him.

Finally, there was only one girl ahead of her. Suzette licked her lips, thinking about Mark, remembering the first time with him. It was her turn; she walked into the room. Directly ahead was a small wooden platform.

She heard a voice. "Get onto the stage please."

Suzette walked onto the low stage, thought about Mark, and turned to face the room. There was a man in a chair to her left, so short his feet didn't touch the ground. He was leaning forward, straining to see. His lips were thick and red, and his grey hair spiked around his small pink bleskop like people standing around a grave.

He didn't greet her or introduce himself. "Walk up and down the stage."

Suzette walked. She didn't look at the man she thought was Mr Strauss; he would steal the image of Mark out of her head. Her legs stretched wide as she made her way down the stage; she felt nice and loose.

The man told her to stop after she turned around and reached the middle of the stage. She stood like a statue, her hand rested on her hip and her right knee lifted and crooked just like Melanie showed her.

The man looked her up and down. "How old are you?"

"Twenty one in May."

"Have you done this before?"

"No. But I always wanted to be a model."

"What's your name?"

"Suzette Fourie."

"Okay, you can go now. Leave your phone number at reception and we'll get back to you in the next few days."

Suzette had a burning question. If they phoned when Mummy was home that would be the end of it. "Sorry, sir. Will you phone in the morning or in the evening?"

"During working hours, we'll let you know then."

"Yes, sir. Thank you, sir."

On the train back home, she worried about the call from Planet Fashions. How was she going to make sure she answered the phone? It was easy to get Nicky and Anthony to do what she said, but how could she control Mummy and Dedda? Suzette tried to work it out but it was hard to concentrate. Her head was filled with a new daydream: shopping for jeans at Kenilworth Centre with her first week's pay.

Chapter Eight

Nicky's eyes scanned the parking lot at the Church of Eternal Redemption, looking for Shirley. It was half past six on Good Friday morning. The hired bus was leaving at seven o'clock to take them to Koelbaai, a campsite up the coast. It was hard to spot her friend – forty boys and girls were going on the church camp. Many of their parents had come to say goodbye. Pastor Williams, his wife and four deacons were standing at the side of the bus, supervising children as they put their bags inside.

This was Nicky's third camp, and she still didn't understand why it was so important to get new clothes for the long weekend. Some of the girls' bags were so heavy they looked like they were running away from home. Their parents had to start an Easter lay-buy soon after they got the Christmas clothes out of the shops.

She spotted Shirley standing at the entrance to the church. She waved but couldn't join her; she had to go with Dedda, Mummy and Suzette to greet Pastor Williams.

The tamaai pastor's boep hung almost to his knees and his floppy breasts came to just above his belt. He probably went to a special shop to buy his clothes – his pants bulged like a revival tent. Standing next to him was his skinny wife, who looked like a mouse when the thick black hairs growing out of her chin quivered. Pastor Williams saw them coming. He wiped his hand over the thin strands of oily hair covering his bleskop before he held it out to Magda.

"Mrs Fourie! It is always a pleasure to see you and your beautiful family. You are truly blessed."

Magda held onto his hand. "That's what I keep telling them all. We should be grateful for everything He has given us."

"And Mr Fourie has graced us with his presence! Long time no see. You looking good."

Neville stared at Pastor Williams's stomach. "You looking very well."

Nicky left her family when Shirley came to join her. They put their bags into the bus and went to greet their fellow church youth members. Some of the children were jumping up and down with excitement; this was their first holiday ever. The deacons started herding their young flock into the bus. Dedda and Mummy came to say goodbye.

As Nicky made for the bus Suzette pulled on her arm, forcing her to turn. "Keep away from me for the next four days, Nicky. You got your friends, I got mine. I don't want to set eyes on you again 'til we come back."

Nicky stuck her tongue out at her sister as she watched her going up the steps of the bus, wiggling her bum all over the place. She turned to Shirley. "Suzette thinks we so interested in her. I don't want to know what she gets up to; the little I know is bad enough. If Mummy must find out what all Suzette does, I dunno what will happen."

As the bus pulled out of the church grounds in a cloud of white exhaust smoke, there was a hammering on the door. Pastor Williams told the driver to stop, the doors whooshed open and Kevin came on board.

Nicky questioned Shirley as he came up the aisle. "Why's Kevin here? He never comes to church."

Shirley smiled. "I dunno, but I reckon this is gunna be a very interesting weekend."

Nicky got the horries as Kevin spotted her and walked towards her seat with a stupid smile on his face. Just her luck, there was a seat available across the aisle from hers. Marlon sat alone at the window; no one would go near him. He was built and the sweat that ran from his armpits into his fat breasts smelled almost as bad as Tietieland, the township next to the sewage treatment works near the Athlone power station.

Kevin planted himself next to Marlon, stuffed his haversack under his seat and swung his legs into the aisle to face Nicky and Shirley. "Hello ladies, long time no see."

Nicky hissed a hello in his direction, the horries still creeping around on her spine. If what Shirley said was true, everybody at the camp was going to have a lekker skinner session. They would be looking for signs that she was involved with Kevin. She had to keep him at a distance. "What you doing here? I thought you comrades didn't believe in God. Why you coming on a church camp?"

Kevin's smile went wider as he explained. "Well, in order to lead the masses you have to know them. And what better place to get to know people than at camp? We all going to be squeezed into tents together, we have to share one ablution block, it's the perfect opportunity."

"You mal, you know that? Who studies people in ablution blocks?"

Kevin smiled like a fool. Nicky turned her back on him, starting up a conversation with Shirley. The bus turned onto the N2 at the Athlone power station and headed east towards Somerset West. As it passed Crossroads, Nicky leaned across Shirley's short lap to look out of the window. Most of the shacks in the squatter camp were made of zinc sheets, but some were only squares of wooden poles with black plastic sheeting whipping in the wind.

She spotted a yellow bulldozer parked at the edge of the camp. Dedda's firm had taken the Provincial Administration to court to stop the demolition; it was in all the newspapers. Priests were fasting at St George's Cathedral for the squatters. Nicky prayed every night for the lawyers to win; these people had little enough and they were about to lose it all.

Kevin stood up and leaned over her head. He spotted the bulldozer. "Look at that; it's pathetic the way the boers treat our people. Their dogs' kennels are better than some of these houses."

Marlon growled from his seat. "What you mean, Kevin? That's not our people. These people don't belong here, man. Cape Town is for whites and coloureds only. That's the law. These people must go back to the Transkei where they came from."

Nicky turned in her seat as Kevin faced Marlon. She was convinced that Kevin was about to get on his moer. No one lolled with Marlon and came out on top. Maybe Kevin stood a chance; he loved to argue.

Kevin took Marlon on. "How can you say they not our people? Aren't you church-going people supposed to believe God created everyone in His image? How can you think you different ..."

Marlon interrupted, turning up the volume of his Barry White voice. "Are you calling me a kaffir?"

There was a sudden movement in the bus. Necks craned from seats nearby and some children came down the aisle to watch. Marlon's attacks never lasted long, but they were always worth taking note of, as a reminder not to lol with him.

Kevin kept his voice level. For once, he didn't sound like he was making a speech. "Never. You will never hear me using that word. All I'm asking is why you think you better than these people."

Marlon's voice filled the bus that had gone silent with anticipation. "I asked you a question first. Are you calling me a kaffir?"

Nicky could see Marlon wasn't interested in anything Kevin had to say. Was there gunna be a fight? She had seen that look on Kevin's face before; when he kept at her to come to his meetings. He didn't know when to give up.

Pastor Williams pushed his big body down the aisle. "What's going on here? Move aside; let me through. Is it you causing trouble, Kevin? Come sit with me in the front of the bus."

Nicky's breath escaped through lips pressed hard together after Kevin changed seats. She didn't look in his direction as he collected his bag and followed Pastor Williams. He might see she felt bad for him. Although he drove her dilly most of the time, she didn't want him to get hurt. She had been thinking about him a lot since Shirley told her he smaaked her. There was no way she would take him as a boyfriend. He wasn't too bad looking – his hair curled up lekker cute under his beret. His stupid smile was sometimes cute. But they had nothing in common. All Kevin went on about was the struggle. It would never work.

She was too young for a boyfriend, although most of the girls in her class had already broken their virginity. When would she find the time for a boyfriend? Her university studies would be even harder than school. By the time she graduated she would be twenty-four; that was late to start dating. But sixteen was too early. She liked being sweet sixteen, never been kissed.

The bus left the national road at the Strand and sputtered exhaust smoke all along the coastal road, past beautiful beach after beautiful beach with Whites-Only signs. Koelbaai was the only coloured beach on the eastern flank of the False Bay coast. About two kilometres of white sand stretched out in front of the grassed campsite. The beach claimed a couple of lives each summer. A deep trench lay hidden beneath the rolling white foam of the breakers. A swimmer caught in the backwash was almost guaranteed to be washed out to sea.

Nicky wanted to throw herself into the water the minute they arrived at the campsite. The heatwave that had arrived earlier was predicted to last the weekend. There was no chance to jump in the waves. After they pitched the tents and had lunch, Pastor Williams herded his flock onto the grass to listen to his lecture about God's perfect young people. Girls should be modest, he said. Boys should grow into strong men who could take firm control of their households. He read from the Bible. His wife played guitar and led them in songs of thanksgiving and praise.

They sang Nicky's favourite, the one that always got her going at the top of her voice: "A volunteer for Jesus / A soldier true. Others have enlisted / Why not you? Jesus is the captain, / We will never fear, Come and join his army / As a volunteer."

They had just started the chorus for the second time when Mrs Williams's guitar went silent. Nicky was the last person to stop singing.

Pastor Williams was frowning. His eyes picked out Kevin, sitting on the grass in the front row, his olive-green jacket wrapped around his body in the boiling sunshine. "Kevin, what is that you were doing?"

Kevin put an innocent look on his face. "Who me? I was singing the song."

"No you were not. What was that you were singing? Come on, let me hear it."

Kevin got to his feet and turned to face the congregation. He marched in time to the tune. "A volunteer for MK / A soldier true. Others have enlisted / Why not you? Slovo is the captain, / We will never fear, Come and join Umkhonto / As a ..."

Pastor Williams's sharp voice shut him up. "Enough!"

"I was just doing what you said I must do."

"I said enough. I have had enough of your blasphemy. I thought you were interested in joining the youth, that's why I let you come with us this weekend. Seems I was wrong, you had ulterior motives, to spread disbelief among my folk. I won't have it, you hear me? Sit down and keep quiet."

"But I am interested in the youth. Very interested."

"You keep quiet. I have had enough of you. I don't want to hear from you again this weekend."

Nicky held her hand to her mouth to cover her smile at Kevin's cheek. When would he learn to keep his mouth?

After an early supper of braaied chicken, potato salad and rolls, the young people were finally set free. Nicky and Shirley took a walk along the beach and climbed to the road above to watch the sun set behind the Constantiaberg range across False Bay. They seated themselves on the hot stone wall flanking the road and looked out onto dark blue water flecked with the wide orange rays. The girls competed to see who would first spot the evening star after the sun dropped behind the mountains. Nicky let Shirley win, even though she had seen it a full minute earlier.

They were about to return to the camp when Nicky spotted something on the waves. Tubes of neon-white light skittered in the fat rollers headed for the beach.

"Hey Shirley look, there's phosphorescence! Remember? We saw it the first time we came here, three years back. It's befok beautiful."

"What's it made from?"

"I dunno, something to do with wave energy, I think. Or maybe dead plankton floating in the waves."

Shirley giggled. "You not so clever, hey? How you gunna get into university if you dunno stuff like this?"

"Just shut up and look. God made it, okay? That's what Pastor Williams would say."

Shirley whispered after a few minutes of silence. "Yoh, it's the most befokte thing I've ever seen in my life."

The phosphorescence danced on the waves. The show began far offshore where swells formed in the dark water. Light skimmed across the water until the waves broke. As they hit the trench near the beach, the waves threw the light into the air like Guy Fawkes fireworks.

Nicky folded her arms around her calf, rested her chin on her knee and gazed out to sea. Heat released from the tar on the road behind wrapped her like a shawl. Crickets and cicadas screamed into the darkness at their backs.

Nicky felt something stroking the back of her neck. She screamed, jumped up, turned and saw Kevin. Who else could it be? "Kevin, I'm gunna kill you, I swear. Are you out of your mind to give me such a skrik!"

Kevin's smile was crooked. "I was just making a joke. Can't you take a joke?"

Nicky pulled Shirley to her feet. "Let's go, Shirley. Kevin is spoiling a good time – again."

Kevin followed them as they climbed down to the beach, talking nonstop. "I'm sorry, I'm sorry. I didn't realise you would get so the moer in." He jumped in front of Nicky as they reached the beach. "Wait up, Nicky, give a guy a chance. I'm sorry, okay? I said so ten times already."

Nicky stopped. For a change, she could teach him something. "You know, Kevin, for someone who thinks he has the responsibility for everybody's freedom in his hands, you can be blerrie childish sometimes. Shirley and I were having a befokte time, but you can't stand it that we're interested in other things besides your blerrie struggle, can you? You just have to spoil everything all the time. No wonder you don't have any friends, just comrades who have to put up with your arguing at meetings."

For once Kevin had nothing to say. Nicky realised that her words had hurt him. Now it was her turn to apologise. "I'm sorry, okay? It's just that you make me so mal."

Kevin's voice was soft. "It's okay. Now I know you don't take me for a friend."

Shirley stepped between them. "Jirre, must the two of you go on like this? You skelling like a old married couple. It's okay Kevin, we had to go back to the camp anyway. It's already dark."

Kevin turned to Shirley. "I was looking for you, actually. We need to talk. Your father worked at Plascon Paint when he died, didn't he?"

Shirley frowned. "Ja, why you ask?"

"'Cause I went to the advice office at the town centre to ask if they could help find a way to keep you at school. Abigail who works there asked where your father was employed. When I told her she said there was a union at the plant. She phoned their head office and found out they had death benefits for their members. Was your father in the union?"

Shirley thought for a minute. "Ja, I think he was. The man who got him the job was a member so my father also joined."

"Then if your mother didn't already claim it, there's money for her. She must phone the union and arrange to go see them. You don't have to drop out of school."

This was the best news Nicky had heard in a long time. She had been feeling guilty because she hadn't been able to come up with a scheme to help her friend and this sounded like a kwaai solution. Maybe Kevin wasn't an all-talk, no-action fool after all.

Shirley squealed and hugged Kevin. "Really? You not joking? I can sommer kiss you I'm so happy." She pulled Kevin towards her and planted a fat one on his lips.

Nicky's insides dropped down to her broeks as she watched Shirley kiss Kevin. How mal was that? She didn't even like him. It must be because Shirley claimed he smaaked her. For a while, it felt good, even though she didn't smaak him back. Now she had proof that it wasn't true. He had his tarty smile on his face when her friend pulled away.

They walked back to the camp, celebrating Shirley's good news all the way. Their group was gathered around a fire chowing up Port Jackson logs, with Mrs Williams leading them in a singalong.

At ten o'clock the adults told them to get ready for bed. Mr Williams did a headcount and realised two young people were missing, a boy and a girl – one of them was Suzette.

Nicky hadn't seen her sister since supper. She was trying not to look in her direction. Suzette had been wearing a tight sleeveless T-shirt and denim shorts so short her broeks stuck out at the bottom. Where did she get that outfit? Mummy definitely didn't buy it. It was no problem keeping away from her like she wanted; Nicky was embarrassed. The boys crowded around Suzette like flies on braai meat, coming back for more when the hand that swatted them away disappeared.

Part of her wanted to crawl under her blanket and let her sister deal with Pastor Williams. But when Mummy heard bad news about one of her children she made life hell for everyone at home. Nicky slipped away while a search party sorted itself out. Metres from the campsite, she heard footsteps coming up behind her. Did Pastor Williams find her already?

It was Kevin. "I was just gunna cough. I didn't want to give you a skrik again. Are you looking for your sister? Let me come with, I owe you."

Nicky was still feeling bad about her ugly words earlier. Kevin wasn't an idiot all the time. He came up with a strategy to help Shirley. It seemed like a good one. She nodded and set off, moving away from the glowing campfires. The moonlight was bright enough to point out a white sandy path leading to the rock pools at the end of the beach.

Nicky came to a halt. She heard noises in the bushes to the side of the path. She put out a hand to stop Kevin. "Shh. I think there's baboons up ahead."

Kevin listened. "That's not baboons, that's people. Hello, who's there?"

The noises stopped and two heads came up from behind the bushes. Suzette and Edgar. Suzette had taken off her T-shirt and her bra, her jewels were all on display. It was too late for Nicky to check Kevin; he could see what she could see. What must he think? She hoped he didn't think she was also like that.

She screamed at her sister like a fishwife, she was so bedonnered. "Suzette, you in big trouble, you better come back to camp with us. Pastor Williams and other people are looking for you. Jirre Suzette! It's a church camp! Why did you come if you just wanted to get up to your usual nonsense?"

Suzette fastened her bra behind the bushes, pulled on her T-shirt and stepped onto the path. "Hou jou bek, Nicky. You know nothing about what I get up to. It's none of your business. I told you to stay away from me; why won't you fokken listen?"

Nicky fell into a bush when Suzette pushed her aside and made her way down the path, Edgar keeping close on her heels.

Kevin stopped them in their tracks. "Wait, hold up a minute. You in big trouble, you two. What you gunna tell Pastor Williams when you get back?"

Suzette looked blank. Edgar the same. Nicky couldn't think what to say.

Once again, Kevin was the man with the plan. "Tell him you were sitting on the wall next to the road watching the phosphorescence on the waves. Tell him it was so beautiful you forgot the time."

Suzette and Edgar nodded.

A vein swelled fat in Nicky's forehead. Nobody got on her nerves like Kevin. She turned on him after Suzette and Edgar left. "Why did you help them? They were up to nonsense; they should have sorted it out themselves. Why did you have to steal my memories to give it to her? Must you always interfere in my life?"

Kevin's voice was small. "Ja, but what if Pastor Williams found her? She would have spoiled your weekend. What would your parents say if she was caught? I was just trying to help."

"And what are you? The Helpmekaar Society? People always cover up for Suzette. She gets boys to do anything for her and you just like all the rest of them."

Nicky stomped back to the camp, her fists clenched tight. She had been looking forward to this weekend for a whole year; and Kevin had spoiled it. He and Suzette better keep their distance from her; she couldn't hold herself responsible if she got them good.

Chapter Nine

Neville pulled a reflective orange bib over his black T-shirt. His trousers were also black. He didn't need a jacket. There wasn't a breeze to shift the heat rising off the soil in Hanover Park after four days of temperatures thirty-five degrees and higher. He checked his torch to make sure it had battery life.

Businesses and factories were shut for the Easter weekend. The shebeen at Orchid Court had been packed when he passed it on his way home from the rank on Thursday night. Neville checked it out again this morning; it was crowded at eleven o'clock. The men on the benches didn't look too happy. Their hangovers sat heavy on top of the rest of their gripes: the supervisors on their backs, the wives who bitched at home, children who always needed something.

Neville walked into the lounge where Anthony and Magda were watching a film. He had hired a video machine and ten tapes for the long weekend. He wanted Anthony indoors as much as possible until he went back to school. Most of them were action films the boy would watch over and over again, but he had also selected two romantic comedies for Magda.

They were watching *Jewel of the Nile*. Magda turned away from the TV and frowned. "Must you go, Neville? You know my nerves are shot. I'll be up all night worrying about you."

Neville had joined the neighbourhood watch. He was going out on patrol for the first time.

He had been recruited by Herbert Ontong who lived in nearby Lily Court. Neville often saw him at the taxi rank and they sometimes walked home together. They had been crammed next to each other on the back seat of a taxi to town a few weeks back. They were deep in conversation as the Hiace overtook the peak-hour traffic on the N2 in the emergency lane.

Herbert was an executive member of the Hanover Park Civic Association. He had recently lost his seventeen-year-old son to a stabbing. They got Rodney as he walked home from school, on the field across the road from Lily Court. His body was found under a Port Jackson tree with four stab wounds to the chest. Rodney bled to death a few metres from home. Herbert could think of no reason why his son was murdered, and the police hadn't done more than take a statement from him.

Sour acid rolled across Neville's stomach as Herbert spoke. It could so easily have been Anthony, or one of his girls. He would tell the girls to walk home together from school and check if Anthony had a friend who walked the same route home.

Herbert explained how the neighbourhood watch would work. They were using the civic association as a springboard to launch the organisation. Many of its members had already volunteered. They had divided Hanover Park into blocks they would patrol to keep an eye on the gangsters. The watch would alert the police if the young men did anything more than loiter.

Neville joined up before the taxi got into town.

Magda wasn't impressed. "Why must you patrol the streets? Isn't that what the police is for? What you gunna do if someone with a gun comes at you?"

Neville had no intention of changing his mind, but he had to keep Magda calm. "I'm not sure what we gunna do. We not supposed to try to make arrests. Herbert said the watch had a meeting at the Philippi police station. They promised to come if we alert them."

"Neville, I'm bang. I don't want to lose you. I don't think I can cope on my own."

"My bokkie, this is something I got to do. Hanover Park isn't safe. The gangsters are different today. They not the gentlemen thieves we grew up with in District Six. I think the bulldozers didn't only break down houses in the district, they also broke something inside people's hearts."

Magda had to agree. "Ja, there was gangs in District Six but it was safe on the streets. Remember how we used to stroll down to the Parade for milkshakes when we were courting? We used to walk home late at night and never a hand was lifted against us. I feel really bad for Herbert. There isn't a worse thing than losing a child."

Neville capitalised on Magda's sympathy. "If a search party had been organised to look for Rodney, maybe he would have survived. We got to keep an eye on our children if the police won't do it. If the gangsters see eyes watching, maybe they will hold up a little."

"Ja, but why must it be your eyes?"

"There is no police station in Hanover Park. That's one of the demands of the civic association, and I support it. When you call for help they take a long time to come from Philippi. Sometimes they don't have a van available. There's people in Hanover Park who are sick and tired of the situation. You got to admit, it's getting worse. People are getting killed."

Magda nodded. "That's exactly my point! Why must you go out on the streets when it's so dangerous?"

"I need to keep our children safe, Magda. I have to keep a watch on Anthony all the time, you know he doesn't listen. I worry about the girls – and you, my bokkie. You all walk the streets at night for your church activities. Either way, one of us is gunna worry."

Magda ran out of arguments.

Neville kissed Magda and Anthony goodbye and headed to Herbert's flat in Lily Court, where the watch patrol was meeting at seven o'clock. It was getting dark; summer was coming to an end. It was still cooking; the heat wave was holding for the girls' church camp. He was glad they were far from home. There was something he hadn't told Magda. She would have got the horries if she found out that the neighbourhood watch was on the lookout for a full-on gang war. JFKs were being painted over American flags in every direction.

Herbert briefed the volunteers crammed into the lounge of his groundfloor flat. Nine men had come, and one woman who looked strong enough to carry an ox. Everyone wore dark clothing and reflective vests.

Neville listened close while Herbert outlined the situation on their block. A group of young men had been loitering on the corner of Lemon and Peach streets where they kept a brazier going all night. They were suspected of selling Mandrax. There was a shebeen on Peach Street, open day and night. The watch had information that Ougat, who ran it, had been recruited by a general inside prison and sworn to establish the JFKs in Hanover Park. He was marking out turf, and it wouldn't be long before the Americans came to give him a klap. Neville could believe it. He had only met Ougat once in the park, but he reckoned he was befok enough to take on the biggest gang in the township.

Herbert mapped out the route his group would follow. There were six other block watches operating in Hanover Park tonight until the sun came up at five o'clock. They would go out in groups of two, and remain together at all times.

Neville carefully noted the addresses of the watch houses on their block in his pocket-sized notebook. The people who lived there had working telephones and would make them available if they were needed. The Philippi police station knew they were going out on patrol tonight, they had provided the reflective vests. Neville wrote down the phone number of the police station.

He was glad when he was paired with Herbert. The man was serious and deeply motivated by the pain of his son's murder. Herbert had a thick neck and chest like a weightlifter. His afro added inches to his height. Neville was bang. He didn't know what he would do if the war started tonight and he was caught in the middle of it. All they had against the gangs were torches and the police station's phone number.

The streets were crowded with children, organised into teams for cops and robbers, skipping rope games, soccer and netball matches. Small bodies crowded the pavement outside a house where a sprinkler was turned on, dancing wildly in the spray. Herbert and Neville shooshed the younger children inside and gave curfews to the older ones, warning that they would be coming back later to check on them.

The smell of fried snoek drifted onto the streets from hot kitchens. Everyone ate pickled fish on Easter weekend, even the Muslims.

As they passed a group of men leaning over the open bonnet of a car parked under a streetlight, Neville confided his dream to Herbert. "There's this car I got my eye on. A Mazda 323, a blue one. I don't mind second-hand."

Herbert smiled. "I got a brother who's a mechanic. He's fixing a car for me. I found it at the scrapyard. It was hit from behind so the engine's still going strong. I could get him to check out the car for you, make sure you don't get ripped off."

Neville was grateful. "It will take a while before I can get it. I can afford the monthly payments, but my wife keeps giving ten per cent of our wages to the church. She won't hold up while I get a car."

Herbert came to a halt. His voice was stiff. "My church was a great comfort to me after my son died. I tithe. I know that when someone is in need, there will be help available."

Neville zipped his lip. He should have thought before he spoke. He hadn't meant to krap open Herbert's wound.

The pavement was baking hot on Orange Street. Neville's confidence went up a little as his vest began to shine under the streetlights. He slowed as they neared a group of young men leaning against the wall of Oleander Court. A paraffin drum filled with wood stood at the ready but wasn't needed; the day's heat clung to the darkness.

Neville stood back while Herbert approached the men. He told himself he was watching out for Herbert, but he knew he was just being a bangbroek. There were five of them and the only authority he had was a green vest. He forced himself to move closer.

Herbert made eye contact with all the men as he shook their hands. "Evening gents. Nice night, hey?"

The men mumbled greetings and stared at Neville and Herbert with dumb eyes.

Herbert kept up the conversation. "We from the neighbourhood watch. We patrolling here on the weekends. There's been a few incidents recently and we want to make sure it doesn't escalate."

One of the young men responded while the rest stared blank-faced at the unemployed brazier. "What incidents?"

"A young man was stabbed on that field four weeks ago."

Herbert pointed across the road to the scene of his son's murder. Neville turned his head to look. He couldn't see a Port Jackson tree; it must of been cut down after Rodney's body was discovered leaking blood into its roots.

The young man pulled his peak cap down his forehead and responded in a flat voice. "Dunno nothing about a stabbing. We just chommies getting together here."

Herbert wasn't giving up. "We had reports that there's been people selling Mandrax around here. You know anything about that?"

"Wietie. We dunno nothing. We just hanging here, minding our own business."

"Keep an eye out if you see anything. We got our eyes out as well."

Neville could feel the men's eyes drilling into his back as he moved off with Herbert. "They look like they up to no good, don't they? You think they JFK?"

"Dunno. We haven't identified all the members yet. So far we know about Ougat and his lieutenants Majiet, Skelm and Oegies. We still collecting intelligence."

Neville was impressed by the watch. He couldn't remember when last he walked the streets of Hanover Park so late. He was usually in bed around nine o'clock, ten for the latest. He got up half past five on weekday mornings so he could get to his office in town by eight o'clock.

On Peach Street bright light leaked onto the pavement from a ground-floor house with a zinc structure covering the front garden. Neville heard voices shouting above loud music as they drew closer. Herbert pointed out a JFK painted black on the zinc sheet closest to the entrance.

They stood in the doorway and stared into the shebeen. Two women danced in the middle of the sandy floor, their skirts tucked into their broekies, while the men filling the wooden benches cheered and jeered. Neville watched the women's hips swaying in time with the disco music. It had been a while since he had been to a dance; Magda's church didn't allow it. It didn't allow drinking either.

He spotted Ougat dancing towards the women with hips thrust forward and his tongue sliding in and out of his mouth like a lizard in the sun. Ougat pulled a woman towards his groin and bumped up and down her leg in time to the music.

Neville pulled Herbert out of the doorway and questioned him nervously on the pavement. "What you planning? That was Ougat dancing there. Are you gunna take him on? I think we must keep an eye on this place, we don't need to go inside. It looks okay. They just dancing."

"Ja, but did you see how dronk those women were? They asking for trouble. How you know Ougat?"

Neville explained how he had met Ougat in the park a few weeks back. "I can see he's trouble, but I haven't heard him associated with violence yet."

"He will get violent, I'm telling you. The Americans won't stand for his kak. They can't afford to let him move in on their turf. All the gangs are running businesses, with their booze and drugs."

"Ja, but until he gets violent we got nothing on him. Leave him alone for now, we can keep a close watch through the night."

Neville was grateful when Herbert agreed to leave the shebeen. He had no smaak for another confrontation with Ougat.

A few hours later, as they turned onto Peach Street, a woman's scream cut through the night. Another, louder scream, coming from Ougat's shebeen. Neville couldn't keep up with Herbert. He was heavy, but fast on his feet.

When Neville entered the shebeen he saw Herbert kneeling on the ground, bent over a young woman in a yellow sleeveless dress. The drinkers filling the benches watched silently without lifting a hand to help. Blood poured from the woman's nose and one eye was closing under its swelling. She moaned as Herbert pressed a handkerchief to her nose.

Neville noticed movement to the side of the shebeen. Ougat stood near the front window of his house. He took off his white T-shirt and threw it inside. A young man next to him pulled off his sweater and handed it over.

Herbert looked up and growled at the shebeen's customers. "What happened here?"

Ougat pulled down his replacement T-shirt and went to kneel next to Herbert. "She was dancing like mal ding and the next thing we saw she dropped down and hit her head on a bench."

Herbert pointed to the woman's temple. "Nonsense. Someone hit her. Look, there's a bruise here. And there's one here on her chin and it looks like her nose can be broken. Did she fall three times against the bench?"

Ougat shrugged. "Wietie. I only saw her fall once."

Neville found his voice. "Did anyone else see what happened?"

The customers shrugged or took unconcerned sips from their beer bottles. A man lay passed out on the sand in the corner. He was face up under a bench with his legs sticking out into the middle of the floor.

Ougat kicked the unconscious man. "She probably fell over this bra. Fokker can't keep his drink but it don' stop him from trying."

Herbert looked up at Neville as the woman moaned again. "Go three doors to the right from here. They will help you. Call for an ambulance."

Neville ran out of the shebeen to its neighbour down the street. The house was in darkness but lights came on inside soon after he started banging on the door. An old woman pulled the curtain aside at the lounge window. Neville smiled at her. "I'm a member of the neighbourhood watch. I need help. I need to use your phone."

The woman opened the door, clutching a pink towelling gown across her breasts with one hand. "Come in. I heard screaming earlier. What happened?"

"There's a woman who needs an ambulance. They say she fell down in the shebeen. She's bleeding a lot. Please, where's your phone?"

Neville dialled the emergency services, told the operator what happened and gave the address. He didn't know the street number of the shebeen; the old woman supplied it. He listened to her complaints about the shebeen after he hung up, promised the neighbourhood watch would try to get it closed down and headed back to his partner.

While they waited for help to arrive, Neville and Herbert tried to make the injured woman comfortable. She wasn't much older than Suzette. Her short sundress clung tight to her curves. Herbert got Ougat to fetch a blanket from his house, and placed it carefully over the woman lying in the grey sand.

Neville couldn't understand why they couldn't lift her from the ground. "Why don't we take her inside while we wait for the ambulance?"

Herbert explained. "You can't move a patient, in case of a neck injury. I learned that in a first-aid course."

"That sounds useful, maybe we should organise one for the neighbourhood watch."

Herbert nodded. "That's a very good idea. Will you organise it? "

"Definitely."

The shebeen's customers went back to their beer bottles, ignoring the injured woman while they waited for the ambulance. Another man who couldn't hold his drink slid off a bench and landed on his gat without waking up.

Neville kept a nervous watch on Ougat. The gangster had taken up position at the entrance to the shebeen, holding whispered conversations with a stream of young men who arrived and left with complicated handshakes. Neville was convinced Ougat was responsible for the damage to the woman's face. His T-shirt must of been stained with her blood. Try as he might, he couldn't figure out how to confront him.

The ambulance arrived more than an hour later. The paramedics complained while they worked. This was their fifth callout since their shift started at six, and it wasn't midnight yet. They lifted the woman onto a stretcher and carried her out of the shebeen. Ougat and his customers crowded around the ambulance to watch her being lifted inside.

Neville felt very important. It was his first night on patrol and he had already helped someone. She might have been in worse trouble if he hadn't been on the streets keeping an eye on things. After the men filed back into the shebeen, he went inside, walked over to the hi-fi and turned down the music for an announcement.

"Gents, a minute of your time, please. My friend here and me are from the neighbourhood watch. We a new organisation that will be patrolling the streets every weekend night from now on."

Ougat responded. "What for? You got nothing better to do?"

Still pumped with the power of helping a woman in need, Neville didn't spot the gangster's tone. "We keeping an eye out for trouble on the streets. Keeping a watch for people in trouble and people causing trouble."

"Who the fok are you, Superman?" Ougat's customers and ouens laughed with him.

Neville went on, brave like a sheriff in a shootout. "We people from the neighbourhood who's sick and tired of the robberies and the murders and the drugs and the gangsters."

Ougat's eyes were popping in his head. "Why? What the fok they do to you?"

Neville's pluck was starting to fail him. He remembered that it didn't take much to get Ougat worked up. He had tried to keep his warning friendly, it didn't look like it was working. "Nothing, they did nothing to me. They killed my friend here's son a few weeks back."

Ougat's cheeks stretched but he wasn't smiling. "Regtig? What's the name of the gangster what killed his son?"

"I don't know. The police are still investigating."

Neville looked to Herbert for help. His partner was at the entrance, waving at him to come out. He made it halfway across the floor before Ougat gripped his arm.

"Did you hear what Ougat asked? What's the name of the gangster what killed him?"

"I dunno."

"Then how you know it's a gangster?"

"I dunno."

"You people so quick to blame gangsters for everything. You must watch yourself. I know who you are. Raak wys. You can't come in here accusing people."

"I didn't accuse anyone of anything."

Herbert arrived to help. "Let him go, Ougat, we got to get back on patrol."

Ougat turned to Herbert. "Your friend must watch out. He can't just come in here with such kak. Someone can take it the wrong way."

Neville's legs were shaking as he and Herbert left the shebeen. This was his first night on the neighbourhood watch and he had already caught Ougat's attention. At the end of Peach Street he dropped down onto the pavement kerb. His legs were pap tired; he couldn't walk another step.

Herbert sat next to him and placed a warm arm around his shoulder. "It's orrite. It's not so bad. We got out before it got really bad."

"I'm not sure. My mouth ran away from me. You think Ougat marked me?"

"I dunno. But I think we must give you another block to patrol for a few weeks. I also want to rotate, go out with each member of the team so I can be sure everyone knows the beat."

Neville was grateful. "That's a good idea. I don't think I want to see Ougat for a while. This is the second time I been in his sights. I don't think he likes me."

When the sun came up Neville parted ways with Herbert. They had heard gunfire popping in the distance at three o'clock. They called the police from one of the watch houses but they couldn't find out if help had been dispatched. Herbert planned on asking the Philippi police for walkie-talkies so the watch patrols could keep contact with each other.

Neville walked home pumped with pride. There hadn't been another incident on their block after they helped the woman at the Peach Street shebeen.

He still wasn't sure what they could do against gangsters, the cockroaches that crawled out of the walls after the kitchen lights went off. The watch members' torches cast a light on their activities, but it was dim.

Chapter Ten

The wind drove cold rain into his face but Anthony didn't care. He'd rather be outside than at home. Mummy kept finding things for him to do, even though he worked hard the whole morning. He had dusted and polished all the furniture in the flat after Suzette swept the rooms. Nicky cleaned the bathroom 'til it was shining. Nothing they did was good enough for Mummy. She kept fussing because her prayer circle was meeting at the flat.

He escaped after lunch when Mummy called Suzette and Nicky into the kitchen to make a platter of savouries while she iced the cake. Dedda was so involved in a rugby match on TV he hardly looked up when Anthony said he was going next door to Auntie Moira's. No ways he was gunna be in the flat when the church ladies arrived.

It was embarrassing the way Mummy gaaned aan and aan about her children when people came. The way she went on you would think that Suzette was the only child in Hanover Park to make it to matric. She made sure everyone memorised Nicky's reports. She said his hair was so fine and his skin so fair it was no wonder he had been Baby Jesus in the church's nativity play three years in a row and chosen to play Joseph when he got too big for the crib. The visitors pretended like they were happy for Mummy, although he could see in their faces that they didn't like people who took a brag all the time.

He headed for the park. He was friends with Aunty Moira's son Enver, but he didn't smaak like playing with him. Enver was also thirteen, still playing baby games like snakes and ladders. It was difficult to play at Aunty Moira's flat. Enver's younger brothers and sisters were always knocking things over or crying to play with them. Aunty Moira's place was as noisy as his was gunna get when the prayer

76

circle singing started. He was better off outside.

Anthony sat on a swing in the park, waiting for something to happen. No chance of that, no one else was mal enough to be out. The few people on the street kept their heads down as they hurried through the drizzle. He started to shiver. His Drimac jacket kept his top dry but his jeans were getting soaked. He had to get out of the rain soon.

As his eyes landed on the broken roundabout he remembered Ougat's open invitation to his shebeen. Dedda said a woman had been hurt badly there last month but Ougat wouldn't hurt him, they were chommies. The one time he had gone to the shebeen, Ougat treated him like he was one of the ouens. Anthony checked to see if anyone he knew was watching, then he ran all the way to Peach Street.

He headed straight for the glowing brazier in the corner of the shebeen, nodding a greeting to Ougat's ouens. Their gapped-tooth grins showed him he was welcome. The young men all wore peaked caps pulled down over closely shaven heads, two of them hiding more of their faces under dark sunglasses. There was no sign of their leader.

Anthony rubbed his hands together over the flames to warm them up. As they began defrosting, his bum felt cold as a virgin's bed. He turned his bum to face the brazier and smiled as he remembered Ougat's promise to find him a befokte kind.

There had been improvements to the shebeen since he was last there. The rickety domino table was gone and there was a kerem board in the middle of the floor, perched on top of an oil drum. Anthony was good at kerem. The church had a board and a table tennis set they brought out for fundraising games evenings. He didn't scheme he would get a chance to play soon; the board was surrounded. He walked over anyway to find where Ougat was.

Ougat's skeel friend Oegies looked up from his shot when he asked. "Dunno where's Ougat. He had to go somewheres for his Ma. Ask her, she's inside."

Anthony stepped carefully into Ougat's lounge. The shebeen's canvas roof kept the front room dark and there wasn't much light coming in from the back either. The TV was on, blaring above the music drifting in from the shebeen. In its glare Anthony spotted a large woman and a small, skinny boy sitting across from the TV on the couch, staring at the screen. The woman's moon face was as big as Jabba from Star Wars. It was topped with a beige swirlkous made from the panty part of pantyhose.

"Hello Auntie."

The woman didn't look away from the screen as she answered. "Who you?"

"I'm Anthony. I'm a friend of Ougat."

"Who your parents? Do I know them?"

"I dunno Auntie. We live in Magnolia Court. I'm a Fourie."

"I dunno any Fouries."

"Does Auntie know where Ougat is?"

"He went to the shops for me."

Anthony perched his cold bum on the edge of the couch. It was the only place to sit. The TV and a video machine were on a big wall unit across from the couch. The rest of the shelves were stuffed with a set of hair rollers wrapped in a net, several empty beer bottles, baby bottles and plastic bags. There was a chair matching the couch, piled high with clothing.

Ma Ougat was watching the same rugby match as Dedda, Western Province versus Northern Transvaal. The players piled on top of each other in the middle of the field. The ref blew the whistle and the men slowly lifted their huge bodies off one another. The player at the bottom of the pile got to his feet and swayed, blood pouring from a cut in his forehead. Ma Ougat grunted and turned from the screen to find her cigarette packet.

She turned to Anthony after she lit up her smoke. "Ougat will be back soon. I can't get to the shops. I don't get out much. It's my arthritis; makes it hard for me to walk."

Anthony slipped down onto the couch, squeezing the small boy closer to Ma Ougat.

"Shame Auntie, it must be hard."

"You dunno how hard. If it wasn't for Ougat I dunno what we will do. Our Moslem neighbours complain all the time about our business to the rent office. They were here today to poke their noses where it don't belong. We pay our rent on time. They must tell me how I am supposed to support us if I can't work. I tried to get a grant but the welfare said they don't give it for the arthritis, I'm well enough to work."

Anthony was sorry he had sat down; he wasn't interested in the woman's problems. He could hear shouts celebrating the winner at the kerem table; he wanted to go back into the shebeen to challenge for a game.

Ma Ougat trapped him with her complaints. "Ougat's young, but he takes care of all of us. Not one of his three sisters is working. That boy works very hard."

"He's a good man, Auntie."

"My girls all got babies, how they supposed to work, huh? Who's gunna look after the babies?"

One of the babies crawled into the lounge. It was wearing a grey babygro that maybe once was white. Streaks of brown ran down both its legs. A sour smell followed it into the room, cutting through the smoke from Ma Ougat's cigarette. The baby crawled to the couch, pulled itself up and tried to climb onto its grandmother's lap. She shoved it off her swollen legs and it started screaming loudly the instant its head hit the floor. The boy seated on the couch between Anthony and Ma Ougat stood up and rushed out of the room.

Ma Ougat screamed. "Gloria! Come see to your child! His nappy is leaking all over the place here. Gloria!"

A girl came into the room, knuckles rubbing into eyes that refused to open all the way. She looked about sixteen years old and seven months pregnant. "What's wrong Mummy? Can't a person even sleep for a hour?"

Ma Ougat tsked. "Can't you see what's wrong? Can't you smell him? When last did you change this child's nappy?"

The girl stared at her screaming baby. "I dunno Mummy."

"Pick the child up. Be careful how you pick him up, the kak's running down both his legs."

"Ag Mummy, can't you change him? I don't like kak nappies." Gloria stood frozen above her baby, on the floor on his back, kicking his legs in the air.

The toilet smell was getting worse. Anthony stood up, desperate for the peace and quiet of the shebeen.

Ma Ougat pointed a swollen finger in his direction. "You stay right there. See what a lazy bitch of a daughter I got."

79

She turned back to face Gloria, shouting above the screaming baby, the blaring television and the music pumping into the lounge from the shebeen. "If you old enough to make babies, you old enough to change them. That's the rule in this house; you know it, you lazy bitch. You haven't got one baby out of nappies and you already got another one coming. You girls got to learn the hard way. I did."

Gloria shouted back. "Is not my fault! I didn't even want this one!"

"Whose fault is it then? Did I make you pregnant?"

Anthony was sorry he had come inside. He should have waited in the shebeen. When Ougat walked into the lounge it felt like the saviour had arrived to deliver him from evil. Ougat dropped the shopping bags he carried in and took off his wet anorak. "What the fok's going on here? I can hear you people from down the road."

Ougat ignored his mother and sister as they tried to drown out each other's explanations and bent down to pick up the baby, holding him under his armpits with outstretched arms when he realised what the problem was. He forced Gloria to take care of him and dropped down onto the couch next to his mother, rubbing her swollen hands between his.

Ma Ougat pulled away and lit another cigarette, ignoring the one burning in her ashtray on the arm of the couch. She handed it to her son and lit another one.

"Ougat, we got problems. The people from the rent office was here again while you were out. They gave us notice to demolish the structure in front. They say we haven't got permission to add onto the house. I told them we haven't got space inside for all of us, 'specially now that your sisters have all got babies, but they said it didn't look like anyone was living out front. They say we have to demolish it in a week. What we gunna do?"

Ougat soothed his mother. "Don't worry yourself so much. I got contacts at the rent office. I will sort it out come Monday."

Anthony couldn't believe his eyes how gentle Ougat was with his mother. The man with a reputation all over the neighbourhood was talking to his old lady like she was a baby.

Ma Ougat complained through a stream of cigarette smoke. "My nerves are shot. Your sisters are no help. They expect me to do everything. The nurse at the day hospital warned me last week that my blood pressure is getting high. Don't be surprised if I drop down dead one day."

Ougat put an arm around his mother's shoulder. "Don't let it get to you Ma. Relax. I'll sort it out one time on Monday. There's people at the rent office I can weetie to make the complaint go away."

"People who want a slice of our business, I reckon. How we gunna survive if we must bribe everyone? There's a lot of mouths to feed in this house and more on the way. You must speak to your sisters, Ougat. You got to get them to the clinic for the injection. If they wanna be so opetoet we can at least make sure they don't make more babies. We haven't got space in the house for another one."

Anthony left the lounge quietly, too embarrassed to listen to more about Ougat's sisters' sex lives. He was at the kerem table when Ougat came out a few minutes later.

Ougat slammed his fist on the table, sending some of the round disks onto the floor. "Fok those Slamdiens next door. My ma goes befok every time someone from the rent office comes here. Those fokken Slamdiens think just because they keep halaal no one else must mos drink. I'll fokken show them what happens to piemps."

Ougat lit the fat joint one of his ouens passed to him and held the smoke in for a long while before exhaling.

He passed the joint to Anthony after a few drags. "Here laaitie, share a skyf."

Anthony waved his hands in the air. "No thanks."

Ougat shoved the joint in his direction. "Take it laaitie, don't give me more kak."

Anthony held the joint between his thumb and forefinger. The tip was wet with Ougat's spit. The last thing he wanted to do was put it between his lips. But he did, pulling softly and choking when the smoke went down the wrong way.

Ougat cackled and klapped Anthony on his shoulder blade. "That's why I like you laaitie, you always good for a laugh. I missed you. You make a man forget how kak his day is."

Anthony passed the joint back to Ougat. "I don't even smoke cigarettes, how am I supposed to smoke that?"

81

Ougat refused to take it. "No laaitie, try again. You will like it, I swear."

Anthony pulled again, and again he coughed. On the third pull, he managed to keep the smoke inside his lungs, so he took two more puffs on the joint before passing it on.

He knew he had come to the right place when Ougat chased two players off the kerem board in the middle of their game so they could play. Anthony beat him three games in a row. There was something he could do like a man.

When Ougat gave him a beer it was even more difficult to swallow than the dagga smoke. It tasted like soapy water used to wash dirty socks. Ougat didn't insist that he finish the beer, he rolled and passed over another wet joint. Anthony didn't hesitate to put it between his lips, pulling like he had been smoking for years.

He thought of the argument he watched earlier – the part where Ma Ougat said she wasn't responsible for Gloria's pregnancy. It was the funniest thing he ever heard. He started giggling and couldn't stop.

Ougat's gold teeth shined as he smiled. "You lekker gerook, laaitie."

If he told Ougat he was laughing at his mother, he'd probably get on his moer. This thought made Anthony laugh even harder. He was about to piss in his pants but he couldn't stop.

Ougat rubbed his hair. "Laugh lekker my friend. You amongst brothers here."

A man with dreadlocks creeping down his head like cobras stepped into the shebeen, dripping wet. He greeted Ougat with a complicated handshake. "Heita bra, what gives?"

"Is cool in the school. Got some trouble with the slamse next door but it's nothing Ougat can't handle. I'm gunna sort them out one time."

"Irie mon, brothers got to learn to live together. Christian, Muslim, Rasta, we all worship the same God. Brother, how about some spliff? Say maybe a R2 bankie?"

"Sure, stay cool, I can sort you out one time."

Ougat turned to Anthony. "Laaitie, do me a quick favour. There's a house two doors down with a car parked in front. Open the boot and get me the plastic bag inside."

Anthony took the key Ougat held out and headed outside into the rain. A battered red Mazda was walled into the front garden where he was sent. It was going nowhere; it was up on bricks and the gate wasn't wide enough for it to pass through. Inside the boot was a black refuse bag, tied tight. Anthony brought it back to Ougat.

"Shot laaitie." Ougat open it, reached inside and took out a plastic bank bag filled with dagga. He handed it to dreadlocks, took his money and gave the bag back to Anthony to put in the boot.

Anthony played game after game of kerem with Ougat and his ouens. He was introduced to all of them, but only remembered a few names. Lippe Pitbull was a name he wouldn't forget in a hurry, or Oegies with the nasty squint. Skelm kept his dark sunglasses on while he played a mean kerem game; coming close to beating him.

The dagga made Anthony a bemoerde kerem player. When he leaned over the square board, his eyes could focus on nothing else except the round disks and the four corner pockets. Most of his shots ended with the kachung of a disk hitting the back of a pocket before sinking.

As he left to go home hours later, Ougat pulled him aside. "Don't think I forgot what I promised you. Ougat's still checking out for a lekker kind for you."

Anthony thought of Gloria's baby. "No rush my bra, I'm in no hurry."

He could hear the prayer circle's singing as he climbed the stairs to the top of Magnolia Court. Anthony opened the front door. There were about twelve women in the lounge. The older ones sat on the couch and the kitchen chairs. The younger women, including Nicky and Suzette, sat on the floor. There was a Bible on every lap.

Anthony stepped carefully across the women's legs and ducked into his parents' bedroom before Mummy could start bragging about him. He closed the door behind him, to block the false voices singing the Lord's praises. Dedda was on the bed, reading a thick Arthur Hailey novel. Anthony slumped down next to him.

He fidgeted after a few minutes of watching Dedda read. "Can't you bring the TV into the bedroom when the church people come? There's nothing to do. I'm bored. How much longer they gunna stay?"

"I can't. Mummy doesn't want the TV on while she's at prayer, you know that Anthony."

"But why must we all suffer when she's doing something? Other people also live here."

"Anthony, if your mother must hear what you saying! Find something to do. Haven't you got homework? Now's a good time to finish it."

"We didn't get homework yesterday."

"Still, go fetch your books, you can study. The June exams is coming up in three weeks. You got to get used to studying early. Next year you gunna be in high school and that's a lot more work. There's a big difference between standard five and standard six."

Anthony couldn't give a fok. He didn't know when his exams started. He had a timetable in his haversack; he hadn't looked at it once after he wrote it down in class.

"I can't get my books, my school bag is in the lounge."

Neville sighed and put his book down. "So where were you now, before you came in?"

"I told you Dedda, I went to Aunty Moira next door."

"What did you do there?"

"Nothing, just played with Enver."

"So what did you play?"

"Just some games."

"I'm only asking because I'm interested."

"We played snakes and ladders Dedda."

Anthony closed his eyes to show that he wasn't available to answer any more stupid questions. The dagga was wearing off. He understood now why people got gerook. It made a boring life seem interesting for a while.

Chapter Eleven

Nicky wasn't sure if Shirley still wanted her as a best friend. They walked to school together most days, but Shirley was pulling away. She had something new in her life. The struggle, of all things.

Who would have thought that Shirley had it in her to become a comrade? It's not that she was stupid, although some things did take long to sink in. She was getting a one-track mind, just like her new best friend Kevin. They were like converted people who went around asking everybody if they had accepted the Lord into their hearts. Only they said Lenin. Shirley hadn't been seen in church for weeks.

At first, it made sense to Nicky that Shirley was spending so much time with Kevin. He had solved her problem. Her mother had gone to the union and they did have death benefits. The family could keep going for a while. Shirley could go all the way to matric.

It was a big thing Kevin did. Most people wouldn't have cared if Shirley disappeared from school. Hanover Park High had eight standard-six classes and two matric classes. Almost half of the children who had started high school with Nicky were already gone. More would leave at the end of standard eight. With a junior certificate, they could attend college and study to become a teacher, nurse or social worker. Or work in a factory.

Nicky had other friends to keep her company when Shirley had meetings during school breaks, but she missed her best friend. Her other friends also had one-track minds – they were tuned in constantly to their boyfriends. Or they skinnered about boys they smaaked. Nicky had no backseat vrying stories to share. She pretended she was interested while she listened to all their hot and heavy details.

It was a difficult time. The June exams were two weeks away.

Suzette's results would determine whether she could write her matric subjects on the higher or standard grade at the end of the year. Anthony was going to high school next year. Nicky heard Dedda and Mummy's fussing, but they didn't have to keep a check on her – she had a goal and she was working towards it.

Shirley didn't seem to care about the exams. All the way to school she nagged Nicky to come to a meeting after classes, to discuss June 16.

Nicky wanted to go home to study. "Jirre Shirley! Don't you ever give up? I'm not interested, okay? This is no time for meetings. The exams is just around the corner."

"Ag please. Just this once. I hardly see you nowadays. Kevin will also be at the meeting."

It seemed to Nicky that when Kevin helped people, he expected something in return. If she had found a solution for Shirley, she would have asked nothing from her. Good deeds were their own reward, Mummy always said. She tried to bargain. "Tell you what, why don't I come home with you this afternoon? We can study together, like we always do before the exams."

"Nicky! You not listening to me. I'm not sure we gunna be writing exams. There's talk of a boycott because they expect us to write on June 16. It must be a public holiday. We got to commemorate the children who laid down their lives for our liberation a decade ago."

Nicky worked out that Shirley's struggle talk meant the comrades were organising a school boycott, in the middle of the exams nogal. "Are you mal, Shirley? This is a important exam for the matrics. Why you want a boycott?"

"Because we want our demand to be met. We want June 16 to be a public holiday. In America they demanded a Martin Luther King Day and they got it. We can have a Hector Pieterson Day."

"Who's Hector Pieterson?"

"He was the first child killed by the police in Soweto in 1976. He was twelve years old."

"I never heard of him. So why you want to boycott again? What if someone else gets killed?"

"That's a chance we must take. They not gunna give in to our demand if we don't do anything. We must show them we serious. It's been ten years since children laid down their lives in Soweto and our education is still kak."

"Can I come to the meeting and argue against a boycott? What if I come and say we should rather ask the school to change the timetable so we don't write on June 16?"

"All opinions are allowed. That's the way we do it. We not calling for a boycott. We having a meeting to discuss whether we should have a boycott. Come discuss with us."

"Okay, okay. I'll come! You don't give up easy, do you?"

Nicky was determined to argue her point. The comrades were asking for a lot if they wanted students to sacrifice their exams for a Hector Pieterson Day. Most people never heard his name.

The meeting was held in a classroom after school. The wooden desks had been pushed up against the walls to make space for the 80-odd pupils who turned up and sat on the floor. Nicky knew most of them, by face at least. All of them, except Kevin in his olive-green jacket, were wearing the navy-blue tracksuit winter uniform. The room quickly became hot and stuffy despite the cold north wind blowing rain through eight broken windowpanes.

Nicky was bored soon after the proceedings started. The comrades argued about the minutes of the last meeting after it was read out. They had been gaaning aan for 15 minutes, interrupting each other so badly that none of them finished making a point. She was stuck in the corner furthest from the door. She was cross that she hadn't chosen a space near the front, where Shirley sat next to Kevin. She could have stood up and left. Until she had seen it with her own eyes, she would never have believed people could argue more than Kevin. He said the comrades were fighting the boere, but it sounded like they were fighting each other.

She wondered if she had the pluck to stand up and talk in front of so many people. There was more people at the Eisteddfod four years ago and she managed to recite a poem on the stage in front of them and win silver. She took a book out of her haversack to write down her argument. The matrics would be badly affected if they didn't write the

June exams. There were other ways the students could commemorate Hector Pieterson. The SRC could demand that the principal changed the exam timetable so no one wrote on June 16. They could have a Hector Pieterson programme instead; tell everyone who he was.

Nicky's head went up when someone shouted above the skelling. It was Roger, the SRC chairman. There were girls in Nicky's class who smaaked him, who were considering joining the struggle so they could spend time with him. Roger had bright green eyes under blonde hair as thick as Robert Redford's.

Roger held up his hand. "Comrades! Can I have your attention! Let's get on with the agenda. We have a special visitor today. Comrade Mariam, a student at Alexander Sinton, is here to speak to us about the significance of June 16. Comrade, the floor is yours."

Nicky looked up from her writing as a young woman, no taller than a 12-year-old, came to stand in the front of the classroom. Mariam fidgeted with the big black-and-white checked scarf draped over her head, making sure her hair was all tucked in. Her soft voice just about carried to the back of the class.

"Good afternoon comrades, I bring greetings from the students at Alexander Sinton. We have voted for a school boycott, and I have been sent to share our position with you."

The classroom went quiet as Mariam's words sunk in. Athlone's biggest high school had decided to boycott. Nicky lifted her pen, ready to take notes. She had to argue against everything that was said.

Mariam adjusted her scarf again. "The boers are getting desperate. Despite their state of emergency, they have not killed the people's hunger to be free. People from all walks of life are getting involved. Workers are striking, mothers are marching; our consumer boycott is hitting them hard in their pockets."

Mariam's fringe crept onto her forehead, her brown curls soft as a baby's. Her voice and her words were very adult. Nicky was impressed. She forgot to write down what Mariam was saying; she was concentrating too hard on the message.

"Let me share with you how desperate they are. I was detained for 21 days. I was released last week. They tried to break me by all means possible. They told me they knew everything the students were planning for the June 16 commemoration. They said my comrades had betrayed me. But I wouldn't break. So one day they put me in a car and drove me to a beach somewhere on the west coast. It was me and three boers in the car."

The classroom was silent. Nicky was almost too bang to hear what happened next. Dedda said detainees were moered badly. His firm was acting on behalf of a detainee who was suing the government for torture.

Mariam's voice had little emotion. "There was no one else on the beach. They took me onto the sand. One of them said to me I better talk. I told them nothing. A boer kicked me behind my knees and I dropped down. I was pushed from behind and I fell flat onto my face. A boer put his foot on my head and pushed it into the sand. I couldn't lift it up, he was too strong. I fainted after a while and they threw sea water onto my face to revive me. Then they pushed my head back into the sand until I passed out again."

Nicky was shocked. When Dedda spoke about torture she imagined detainees moered by the police, with fists or batons. How did they come up with this method? Mariam was so small. She must have been bang when the policeman stood on her head. In her mind the security police were as dik as rugby players.

Mariam stood straight and her voice grew louder. "I didn't betray my comrades. I had nothing to say to them. After a while they took me back to the Milnerton police station and told me to pack my bags, I was being released." She paused and adjusted her scarf, tucking away a curl that had crept onto her forehead.

"Comrades, they can beat our bodies into submission but they cannot defeat our minds. Freedom is coming. Students started a wave of protest in 1976 and we are going to roll it across the country until freedom day arrives. Amandla!"

The students roared back: "Ngawethu!"

Mariam stood in the front of the classroom, her clenched fist high above her head. Roger came to join her, with the smile that made the girls go jas. He raised one eyebrow as he addressed the classroom. "All those in favour of a boycott?"

Nicky folded her arms as every hand, except hers, rose into the air. In the front row Shirley was holding onto Kevin's shoulder while she lifted her bum in the air so her hand could go higher. Kevin raised a clenched fist.

This wasn't a debate, but it was a vote. Nicky could almost understand why everyone supported Mariam. She spoke like the Pentacostal preacher at the tent revival meeting she went to with Mummy last month. Mariam took everyone with her, just with her words. After such a speech, there was no way she would persuade the students not to boycott.

Nicky walked home with Shirley and Kevin after the meeting, arguing all the way about what happened. Shirley and Kevin were adamant. A vote had been taken and the rest of the school would be asked at assembly the next day whether they supported the SRC's call for a boycott. It was a democratic process, Kevin insisted.

Nicky wasn't sure. Only one position had been put to the vote at the meeting. It was only democratic if people were given a choice.

Kevin agreed. "Ja, I suppose that is the best way to do it. But did you see how many hands went up? I think you were the only person who didn't vote for a boycott."

Nicky shook her head. "The students were swept up on emotion. They didn't listen to both sides of the debate. I was gunna suggest other things they could do instead of a boycott."

Kevin had no time for her suggestions. "You don't understand, Nicky. It's not that we want Hanover Park High to have a commemoration. We want the whole of South Africa to have a public holiday. We want to send our message to the boere, not the principal. That's why we organising for all the schools to boycott."

Nicky wasn't sure if he realised what would happen next. What if the boere didn't like the message? "Don't be mal, Kevin. You want to bring the boere to our school? The things Mariam said sent grille down my spine. Why didn't everyone else get bang? I would just give in, the minute they came to detain me. I would be poepscared, 'specially now that I know what they will do to me."

Kevin laughed. "It happens every time. The more the boere hit back, the more angry people get. I got involved in 1980 after a boy in our street was shot and killed by the police. When people see the boere are not winning even with all the security laws behind them, they get more brave. They run into the bullets like they believe it's going to dissolve like Disprin. The youth are at the frontline of the struggle. When one falls, there's another ten to take his place."

"I think you mal. You gunna get hurt badly. Then don't come say I didn't warn you."

For the first time, Kevin shouted at her. "You don't know what you talking about, Nicky. You hardly go anywhere outside Hanover Park so you blind to the situation in the country. You must catch a wake up. South Africa is burning. Go to Athlone and you will see barricades in the streets. Hanover Park will erupt next, just you watch."

Nicky lifted her chin. "I do know what is happening. I read the newspaper every night and I watch the news on television. My dedda's law firm is representing detainees, and they fighting for the people of Crossroads. They won a interdict last week against the demolition."

Shirley joined the argument. "That's what I don't understand about you, Nicky. You say you want to be a lawyer but you don't seem to care about the law. Lawyers fight for justice, like Nelson Mandela and the people at your dedda's firm. You only interested in the law because your dedda says you must be a lawyer. You must think for yourself for a change."

Shirley's words cut deep. Of course she would know exactly how to hurt her. Shirley knew everything about her.

Kevin chimed in with a softer voice. "Nicky, Shirley's right. You very clever, but you got no direction, no focus. I also don't understand why you say you interested in the law then you do nothing about it. You don't have to wait 'til you graduate to start fighting for justice. If you stood up now people would follow you. There's a lot of people who admire you."

Nicky noticed Kevin didn't say he admired her. "I'm not doing nothing about it! I am focused. That's why I'm going home now, to study. So I can pass. So I can finish high school with good enough marks to go to university. Can you think of another way a person can become a lawyer? If any of you can think of another way, let me know."

She left Shirley and Kevin at the top of Lemon Street and marched home. Kevin was probably going home with Shirley. She could imagine the two of them together, holding hands and talking about overthrowing the regime. She was never gunna talk to the two of them again as long as she lived. They attacked her personally because they knew she was right about the boycott.

She did care about the political situation. She just didn't have time to get involved. She was helping people, through the church. When members of the congregation were sick, they took food to their houses. They cooked Christmas lunch for the old-age home. And she helped Shirley with her problems. It wasn't true that she never went out of Hanover Park. She sometimes went to bioscope in Wynberg, she went shopping in Claremont with Mummy, and she went on the church youth camp to Koelbaai.

Nicky hurried home, scared without Shirley. The comrades were so busy taking on the boere that they couldn't see what was happening under their noses. They were more worried about children in Soweto than the children of Hanover Park. When the war started last week between the Americans and JFKs, she promised Dedda and Mummy that she wouldn't walk home alone. They thought she walked with Suzette, but her sister hardly ever came home straight from school.

Almost every zinc fence and vibracrete wall she passed on her way home was painted with flags, symbols and names. Pang was very popular; his name was everywhere. There were numbers spraypainted onto the walls, 26, 27 and 28. The Americans and the JFKs left their mark on every place a paintbrush could reach.

There was a slogan painted in thick black paint on the vibracrete wall surrounding the soccer field, Don't Vote in Apartheid Elections. The comrades were almost invisible. You didn't find them on every street corner.

The flat was empty when Nicky got home. This was the third day in a row that Anthony was missing in action. His school finished an hour before hers, and she wasted time at that stupid meeting afterwards. He should have been home long ago.

When Suzette came in, Nicky asked if she had seen Anthony. Suzette hadn't noticed that he was coming home late every day, and said she didn't care. Nicky watched, irritated, as her sister arranged her textbooks on the kitchen table before lying down on her bed with a magazine. Suzette always made sure she was at the table when Mummy came in.

Nicky was studying maths in the lounge when her brother strolled in. "Where were you, Anthony? Mummy and Dedda are gunna be home just now. You gunna be in big trouble if they must find out you were out the whole afternoon."

Anthony flung down his school bag and glared at Nicky. "How they gunna know I wasn't here? Are you gunna squeal? Fokken piemp. Mind your own damn business."

Nicky didn't know how to talk sense into Anthony. He was getting ruder by the day. He was getting difficult now his voice was breaking. But she saw how he pretended in front of Mummy that he was still her baby boy. "Your exams are starting soon, Anthony. When you gunna study if you out every day? Mummy told you to stay home 'til after the exams."

Anthony's voice went up and down as he tried to shout. "Maybe I don't need to study. Did you ever think of that? You think you so clever but you can only get high marks if you work hard every day. Some of us don't sukkel with learning like you."

Nicky turned back to her books when Anthony stuck out his tongue. She said nothing when Mummy came home and praised all her children for studying the whole afternoon.

She watched the TV news with Dedda after supper. The first story was about riots in the Vaal Triangle. There were tyres burning on the streets. Soldiers on the back of Casspirs shot teargas and bullets at stone-throwing people. During the break for the adverts she told Dedda about the meeting and the decision to boycott the June exams.

"Jirre, that's bad news Nicky. When does the boycott start?"

"I dunno, Dedda. Kevin said the SRC is calling a special assembly tomorrow to vote on the boycott. The exams are starting Monday, so I suppose that's when."

"It's been a while since there was political action in Hanover Park.

It's been quiet here, considering what's happening everywhere else. Do you think the students will boycott?"

"Maybe, Dedda. From what I saw at the meeting, they not even thinking about what will happen if they do. Other schools are boycotting, so they gunna join in."

Nicky told Dedda about her argument with Kevin and Shirley. "They so unfair. 'Specially Shirley. She thinks if she do something I must follow her. She don't listen to anything I say."

She sniffed away the snot that came up her throat as she spoke. "It's not like I got lots of friends, Dedda, that's why I'm so cross with Shirley. The others girls in my class are only interested in boys. They think I'm phoney 'cause I do my schoolwork. I miss Shirley, Dedda."

Nicky grabbed onto her dedda's hand when he reached for hers. She hukked as she struggled to keep in her tears. Shirley and Kevin had been spiteful this afternoon; they didn't give her a chance to have her say about the boycott.

Neville's voice was soft. "What do you think is the right thing to do?"

"I think it's right to write the exams, Dedda. But I don't like the things Shirley said. It's not like I don't care about what's happening in the country."

"I know you care, bokkie. And you should. It's getting worse. I don't think this can go on much longer. But I think you too young to get involved. At your age there's only one thing you can do to help. You can get an education. That's your contribution. South Africa needs good lawyers. You care about people; that's why you will make a good lawyer. You must stay focused."

Mummy came into the lounge from the kitchen, drying her hands on her apron. "What's going on here? Nicky, why you crying?"

Neville explained that her heart was sore because Shirley didn't want to be her friend anymore. He also told Magda about the boycott plans at Nicky's and Suzette's school.

Nicky's chin dropped onto her chest as Mummy immediately flew into her. "So when is this boycott starting Nicky?"

"I dunno, Mummy. I went to a meeting this afternoon …"

"You went to a meeting? When was this meeting? Where was it?"

"After school, Mummy. It was in one of the classrooms."

"Why did you go? Didn't you promise to come home straight after school to study? I thought I could trust you, Nicolette. You, of all my children. I can't be home all day to check up on you. I expect you to listen when I tell you something."

Neville interrupted. "It's to be expected, Magda. There's an uprising on the streets. It was only a matter of time before it hit the schools."

Nicky felt bad when Mummy turned on Dedda. But there was nothing she could do to stop the steamroller with hands on her hips.

"This is all your fault, Neville. You so busy with the neighbourhood watch you not keeping watch on your own children. It's because you keep going to meetings all the time, Nicky's following your example."

Neville kept his voice even. "I don't go to meetings all the time Magda. I go to one meeting a month and I patrol one night a week. There's people doing much more than that, 'specially now that the Americans have taken on the JFK. I don't do more for the watch because I want to be at home with my family. We already spoke about this."

Magda completely ignored what he said. "And you keep coming home from work with stories about how your lawyers is fighting for people in jail. The police won't put them in jail for no reason. This country is falling apart. People got no respect for the government of the day."

"My bokkie, most people didn't even vote for the government of the day. That's why they in the streets. You got to admit the protestors got a point."

"Huh! Have you seen what they doing? They burning libraries and schools and community halls; the very things they saying they protesting for."

Mummy and Dedda took each other on and didn't even notice when Nicky left the lounge. She didn't want to listen anymore, 'specially not to Mummy. It was unfair that she was in trouble for not coming straight home from school. She was the only child in the house listening to her parents.

Chapter Twelve

Suzette strutted down the stage and swivelled on one leg when she reached the other end. She pushed her hips out and rested her hand on her right hipbone. She held the position while she counted slowly to ten, then she walked to the centre of the stage. She swivelled again and faced front. She could do the catwalk exactly like the contestants in the Miss Universe competition she saw on television. She had been practising. It was hard to do it in high heels, but she liked the way they made her hips sway. Stilettos made it easy to walk sexy.

Mr Strauss from Planet Fashions had finally come through. Three weeks after she had gone to the factory in the hopes of finding a job, the phone rang. Suzette rolled off her bed and rushed to the lounge. "I'll get it! I'll get it!"

Nicky grumbled from her seat on the couch, right next to the phone. "Orrite! I'm not desperate to be your secretary."

It was a man's voice. "Hello, is that Suzette Fourie?"

"Yes, it is."

"It's Mr Strauss here, from Planet Fashions. Remember you auditioned for a spot as a model?"

"Yes, I remember."

"Well, we wouldn't have chosen you ordinarily, I think you're a bit too young. But we've discovered one of the women we hired is pregnant. I have an opening if you're interested."

Suzette had to put her fingers in her mouth to stop her scream from coming out. She managed to get out one sentence. "When do I start?" She concentrated hard on what came next. "Okay, I'll be there at eight tomorrow. Bye."

Nicky had been staring in her face the whole time she was on the phone. Like she was so interesting. As soon as Suzette put the phone down, Nicky started on her.

"Where you going tomorrow, Suzette? Aren't you going to school?"

She stared at her sister. "Why should I? The students voted today for a boycott."

"But the boycott is only starting next Monday."

Suzette couldn't stop her hand when it came down on Nicky's cheek. The girl was getting on her nerves. She had a job as a model. This was the most exciting day of her life, and her fokken idiot sister was trying her best to spoil her mood. It had been a long time since she hit Nicky. She forgot how quickly she tjanked.

She stared at her sister. "I'm not that interesting. I told you before, keep out of my fokken business."

Hanging onto a rail in the crowded compartment of the quarter past seven train to Retreat, Suzette tried to figure out how to keep her job a secret from Mummy and Dedda. She couldn't work out how to tell them she had dropped out of school. They would march her straight back.

The boycott was the best thing that could have happened. She had been sure she would fail maths, maybe also biology, this term. Now that worry was gone. That fokken Nicky better hou her bek. She was the only person who knew something was up – and she was sure to notice when Suzette stopped going to school.

She didn't want to give up on her dream. She was a model. It was okay to start in a factory; everybody had to start somewhere. She needed to earn money for a portfolio. She was planning to present herself at a modelling agency. In the past three weeks she read every interview with a model that she could lay her hands on. She had gone to the library for the first time in years.

At the factory, the receptionist directed her to the dressing room. It wasn't eight o'clock yet; she was the first to arrive. She went to the urns in the corner of the staff canteen to make a cup of tea. It was icy cold in the empty dressing room.

She heard a familiar voice as she was spooning in her sugar. "Look who the cat dragged in! I never thought I'd see you again, girl."

Melanie swayed her wide hips from side to side as she made her way across the canteen.

Suzette smiled at the girl who had helped her at the interview. "Hello, Melanie. Mr Strauss called yesterday. He said one of the girls dropped out because she was pregnant, I must come in today."

"Ja, it's that stupid Crystal. You would think she would learn by now how babies are made, she got two already. It's like that girl never heard of Depo, even though she's been working in factories since she was sixteen."

Suzette knew about Depo Provera. She had been on the injection since she was sixteen. Every six months she went to the family planning clinic in Wynberg. She couldn't go to the Hanover Park clinic, Mummy would find out the very same day. Now it would be even easier; mobile clinics went to all the clothing factories in Cape Town dishing out the injection.

She turned to Melanie, who was making a mug of tea. "So what they want us to do? I never worked as a model before."

"Ag, is gunna be easy. There's no buyers coming in today. Mr Strauss just wants to see how we look in the latest line. We don't model the whole day. Most of time we work as packers, or in the factory shop."

"Is Mr Strauss in charge of the models? I thought he was the owner of the factory."

"Mr Strauss takes a big interest. I think he only makes underwear because of the models. He's harmless. He keeps his eyes open and his zip up. Here he comes."

Suzette and Melanie followed Mr Strauss into the dressing room. Four other girls had arrived while they were making their tea.

The sun poured icy winter light through the dressing-room window but Mr Strauss wiped sweat off his forehead with a handkerchief before he started speaking. "Morning everyone. Are we all here? Ah, the new girl is here. Have you introduced yourself to everyone?"

Suzette gave the girls a small wave.

Mr Strauss waved his hand in her direction. "So … er … tell them your name."

"Suzette Fourie."

Mr Strauss's voice got bossy. "I'll get someone to bring the new line in, then we can start. Suzette, come with me, we need to talk."

Suzette followed her boss through the reception area and up a flight of stairs to his office. She had never seen such an untidy place in her life. All the furniture was covered in paper and pieces of fabric. Some of the paper was turning yellow.

Mr Strauss showed her to the one empty chair before seating himself behind his desk. "Sorry about the mess. I inherited the factory from my father two years ago and found the office like this. I need to get everything archived on microfiche."

Suzette nodded although she didn't understand a word. She got what Mr Strauss had to say next and she liked it. She would earn R80 a week. The best part of the job was that she finished at four o'clock. She could make it home before Mummy and Dedda.

Mr Strauss gave her a R20 advance. It was more than enough for a weekly train ticket and her taxi fare. She needed high-heeled shoes for the job and a gown to keep warm in the dressing room. Charlene could supply them until she was flush.

The day after she got her second pay packet Suzette bought a befokte pair of red stilettos at Cuthberts in Kenilworth Centre. It was the first pair she spotted, but she tried on several other pairs at all the shopping centre's shoe shops. She went back to the first shop and bought the red shoes she liked best, with the ankle strap. They hurt like hell until she got used to them.

Suzette stood on the stage with her leg cocked, wearing a white nightie that just covered her panties. It wasn't so difficult standing half naked in front of strange men and women. None of them looked at her in the wrong way; they were only interested in what she was wearing.

She stood stockstill with four other girls on the stage while the buyers examined the garments and questioned Mr Strauss. She spotted one of them giving her a look. She had noticed him earlier. He was very good-looking. Older than her; in his twenties, maybe twenty-five.

A white man. His eyes travelled all over her body.

Suzette put on her posh Naomi Campbell look when he smiled at her. She could see in his eyes that he liked what he saw. When she walked off the stage she stretched her legs wide so he could get a good look.

She checked with Melanie in the dressing room. "Did you see that man staring at me?"

"Course I saw, he didn't have eyes for anything else. Maybe he'll make a move."

"He's white!"

Melanie laughed. "There's lots of white men that like dark meat. Where do you think coloureds come from?"

Suzette hadn't thought about that. She thought coloureds came from each other. She kept quiet while she worked things out. Naomi Campbell had white boyfriends. Supermodels didn't follow the rules.

When she left the factory at four o'clock he was waiting for her, leaning against a white Golf parked at the gate.

He smiled as she came towards him. "Hi, howzit?"

Suzette didn't know what to say. She wasn't used to talking to whites. "Hello."

He put out his hand. "I'm Neil. After I saw you, I told myself there was no way I was leaving without introducing myself. What's your name?"

Suzette checked him out while she shook his hand. She had never before seen blue eyes with brown hair; she thought it only came with blonde.

The blue eyes smiled. "Can I give you a lift? Which way are you going?"

Suzette hadn't expected this. She couldn't take a man like this to her house. She couldn't take any man there. "It's far, you can just give me a lift to the station."

Neil wouldn't give up. "Where do you live? Maybe I'm going your way, you never know."

A group of women coming out of the factory stopped to stare. Melanie was among them. She lifted the back of her hand and kissed it loudly. Suzette looked away. She didn't want to laugh and sound stupid.

Neil was waiting. Suzette thought up a lie. "I stay in Lansdowne, it's far from here."

"I know where it is. Come, I don't mind taking you. I'm going to town and it's not too far off the highway."

Suzette got into Neil's car. As he closed her door and walked around the car, she caught Melanie's eye through the window. She pointed two of her fingers to her eyes. Melanie gave her a thumbs up.

She stared at Neil skelmpies as he pulled away from the factory. He was even better looking up close. His hair had a curl that grew onto his wide shoulders. The hands on the steering wheel had long fingers. She liked that.

They drove past Parkwood as they headed down St George's Drive. Suzette stared out of the windscreen. There was no park and no wood, only three trees on the sandy field flanking the township. The South-Easter had bent them into crooked fingers pointing north. In the afternoon drizzle, Parkwood's blocks looked the same as Magnolia Court – the grey concrete was dark where the paint had worn off. There was no way she was going to let Neil drop her off at home, what would he think?

Neil kept the conversation going. "So how long have you been a model?"

Suzette still wasn't sure how to talk to him. "Three weeks."

"Really? I've also been in this job for three weeks. Is this your first job?"

"Yes."

"Me too! That's really kiff. Already we've got so much in common."

Suzette relaxed a little. It was true what Neil said; they weren't so different. It was easy to talk to him.

Neil turned and smiled when he stopped at a red robot. "So when did you finish school?"

Suzette skrikked. It wasn't so easy. She had to stop and figure this out. She told everyone at the factory she was twenty. "Two years ago."

"What did you do before?"

What story could she come up with? She knew what. "My parents sent me to secretarial school. It was kak, I hated it."

"Ja, I know what that's like. I tried university for three years.

101

Managed to fail my first year once and my second year before I gave up. So now we've both found ourselves in the fashion business. Are you enjoying it?"

"It's okay. I just started out. I don't mean to work for long at the factory. I'm saving up for a portfolio."

It was so much easier to talk to Neil when she didn't have to lie. But there were some things he didn't need to know. By the time they reached the Lansdowne turnoff from the M5 highway, Suzette had made up her mind that she wanted to see him again. She just couldn't figure out how. He was asking for directions to her house. What could she say? She couldn't take him there!

"Um Neil, I got a problem. My parents will be fok ... very angry if they must see you with me. They very Christian and they strict about what I do. I can't bring you to my house, I'll be in big trouble."

Neil frowned. "I don't understand. What does Christian have to do with you seeing me again? I'm not Jewish or anything."

Suzette went quiet. How could she explain it? She didn't understand at times how Mummy's mind worked. "They don't allow me to go out with men. They very strict about what I must do until I get married."

Still he didn't get it. "But how are you supposed to get married if you don't get to meet men and go out with them and see if you like them?"

"You supposed to meet boys at the church. They don't like you to marry outside the church."

"Ah, I get it. But I want to see you again. What must I do, join your church?"

Suzette couldn't believe that a man like Neil was interested enough in her to join the Church of Eternal Redemption. "I will find a way, I promise. If they must find out, I'll be in big ka ... trouble. You understand?" She was finding it difficult to speak proper English with Neil. He had a beautiful voice. She sounded so coloured when she spoke.

Neil finally understood. "You have to give me your phone number, though, so we can plan to get together again."

"No, you can't phone our house! Give me your number. I promise I will call."

Suzette got Neil to drop her at the corner of Lansdowne Road and Blomvlei Road. The Hanover Park taxis picked up passengers there if they could squeeze them in. She walked like she was going somewhere until Neil drove away, then she hailed a taxi. She checked her purse when she took out her fare; Neil's phone number was safe inside.

Chapter Thirteen

The neighbourhood watch social evening started early for its members. They had a meeting before the festivities began. The watch had recruited forty new members. It was so big it needed a constitution and an executive committee to control its activities.

It had been a long time since Neville had been to a party. He splashed out on a new pair of Wrangler jeans. He thought he looked like a cool cat in them, but no one at home said anything as he left for the Hanover Park Community Centre.

He was looking forward to the evening. He had lived in Hanover Park for twelve years and the watch members were the first vaste friends he had made. You got to know people well when you patrolled with them. The dark streets and the gunshots brought out their deepest fears.

Neville was elected as an additional member of the executive committee at the meeting. He hadn't realised that the watch's members regarded him so highly. Herbert nominated him for the position. He recognised that Neville had organised first-aid training for the watch and that his job at the law firm was very useful. They needed legal assistance – victims of crime and police action had approached them for help.

Herbert was unanimously elected chairman of the neighbourhood watch. The meeting came to an end and the members moved the rows of chairs to the side of the hall to make space for a dance floor. The crowd swelled as their wives, husbands and children arrived for the party. The smaller children raced for the jungle gym and swings of the crèche based at the community centre.

Four big braai stands had been set up in the courtyard, meat sizzling on all their grills. Herbert and Neville found space for two near one of the sawn-off oil drums. The smell of the meat warmed Neville's cold bones. It hadn't rained for three days and there wasn't a cloud in the icy sky. June had been his worst month on patrol; it rained cats and dogs for the first eight days.

Neville declined Herbert's offer of brandy and Coke. He hadn't touched dop since Magda joined her church eight years ago and made him swear on the Bible that he would give it up. He hadn't been a big drinker anyhow; only at social gatherings to put himself in a party mood. Getting elected to the executive committee had lifted his mood as high as it could go.

He turned to Herbert, rubbing his cold hands in the white smoke billowing up from the braai. "It's a pity my wife wouldn't come, this is gunna be a lekker party."

"Ja, why didn't you bring her?"

"Her church don't like parties. And she's in the moer in with the comrades, she wants nothing to do with you guys. Don't take it personal though."

Many members of the neighbourhood watch were comrades. Herbert had asked Neville to join the civic association, but understood when he said he was needed at home. If Magda had come to the party she would have found out that the comrades were just like her. They also wanted their children to be the best that they could be. Neville used to think he was aiming high wanting Nicky to be a lawyer. The comrades thought a law degree was the first step to becoming a president.

Moegamat waved his braai tongs across the fire. "So Neville, what's your wife's beef with the comrades?"

Neville checked to see if Herbert was also listening. He needed advice. "Shame, she had a bad experience. Last week at the taxi rank she saw students searching women's bags as they got off. If they found someone shopped at a white supermarket, they vandalised their food. They were trying to force a woman to eat raw eggs to teach her a lesson. Magda and some other women chased them off. She came home in a foul mood. She's been gaaning aan about the comrades ever since."

Herbert whistled between his teeth. "Sjoe, that's kak. The youth are going to lose the support of the community if they act like that. That's a sure way to alienate people."

"Magda doesn't want to hear anything about the comrades. She's as scared of them as she is of the gangsters. In fact, she wants me to pull out of the watch but I told her I won't."

The men gathered round the fire worried about the youth. If it wasn't the gangs making the streets dangerous, it was the comrades. Or, as Neville heard some of them tell it, the police were the danger as they hunted down the comrades.

Neville argued that the comrades should be brought to order. "It doesn't mean that because they under attack by the police that they got the right to attack old women. This kak must be sorted out. I don't want to worry about Magda, she uses the rank every day."

Moegamat's red fez stuck to his head as he nodded hard. "I'm with you my bra. There's enough kak on the streets, we don't need more from the comrades. Besides, they supposed to conscientise the community, to get people on their side."

Herbert had a way forwards. "The youth must start a campaign to popularise the consumer boycott. They must explain why it is wrong to buy at white shops. We want to hit the government where it hurts the most, in their pockets. It's internal sanctions. It's a good way to build black solidarity."

Moegamat lifted a ring of wors from the grill. "Hey guys, this is a party! Lighten up! Come get it while it's hot."

Neville carried a platter of meat into the hall. There were about one hundred people at the social evening. Their body heat chased some of the chill out of the hall, but the floor tiles were cold under Neville's feet. The ceiling was high and cold stole inside through broken windows. The plate on his lap piled with a lot of meat and a little salad warmed his thighs while he ate.

The DJ cranked up the music after the meal. Saturday Night Fever poured into the community centre. The floor filled up with John Travoltas flinging their hips and arms around wildly while people dancing nearby ducked for cover. The watch members boogied on down with their wives and children. Their patrols took them away from home. They were throwing their families a lekker party to show their appreciation.

Neville watched teenagers grooving in a corner of their own on the dance floor. He felt bad; hadn't thought of inviting his children when

Magda refused point blank to come. Was it too late to fetch them? He checked his watch. It was past nine, Magda would have a fit if he took the girls out so late.

He watched Herbert dancing with his wife Chrysanthea, sending their large bodies across the floor like they were skating on ice. Chrysanthea looked only into Herbert's face as he guided her through the crowd. Neville admired the way women could dance backwards. You had to trust a man to do that.

Herbert came to sit next to him when the song ended, pulling a bottle of brandy out from under his chair and pouring some into a glass. He added Coke, gave the glass to Chrysanthea, filled another one and passed it to Neville. "Have a drink Neville, it will loosen you up. You sitting here like you got observer status."

"No thanks, I'm fine."

Herbert waved the glass in his direction. "You don't drink?"

"My wife's church don't allow it."

"I thought you said you don't believe in her church."

"I don't, but …"

Herbert grabbed Neville's hand and wrapped his fingers around the glass. "Take it."

Neville took a sip. The brandy burned a sweet way down to his stomach. He clicked his tongue against his palate. He had forgotten how lekker this drink was. He leaned back in his chair, swirling and sipping his drink, chatting to Herbert and Chrysanthea. They had met at ballroom classes. They started dancing together when they were fifteen, won junior gold at the championships a year later and were engaged on her eighteenth birthday.

Crysanthea smiled at Herbert. "We haven't danced competitively for almost twenty years now. But we occasionally hit the dance floor."

Neville put his drink between his knees and lifted his arms into a ballroom dancer's position. "You two look good together. I'm not even sure I got any moves left. It's been a long time since I danced."

Herbert stared into his glass. "We used to go dancing on the first weekend of every month. Since the murder we haven't gone out much, this is our first social evening."

Chrysanthea reached over and gave her husband a squeeze. He held onto her tightly for a few minutes before pulling away.

There were still no arrests for Rodney's murder five months back. Neville could see the Ontongs were still feeling very eina. He didn't know what to say. He took another sip of his brandy. It was warming him up lekker inside.

Herbert wiped his eyes. "Ag, to hell with it. We came here to party. Neville, go show my wife a good time on the dance floor."

Neville's glass was empty. He placed it under his chair and reached out his hand to Chrysanthea. "Madam, if you would do me the honour?"

A Luther Vandross number was playing. Neville hoped he wouldn't make a gat of himself on the dancefloor and guide Chrysanthea around like a bumper car. He was sure he could remember how to jazz. He used to be good at it. He led his partner into the middle of floor; guiding her with a hand resting in the small of her back the way Herbert did it. All the moves came back to him and Chrysanthea responded to every one he made. He managed to bend her over his knee when the song ended.

Neville allowed Herbert to persuade him to have two more brandies. What Magda didn't know wouldn't hurt her. He danced again with Chrysanthea, with a few other men's partners and some of their daughters.

When the party ended at midnight he wasn't ready to stop. He hadn't had such a good time for a long while. He had to find a way to persuade Magda and the children to join him at the next social. If Magda came he couldn't drink. That wouldn't be so lekker.

Neville swayed on his feet on the pavement, watching the caretaker lock up. A frown creased up his face. What was Magda going to say when he got home? She was going to be the moer in. He had to find a 'splanation for his good mood.

He sang the lyrics of the DJ's last song in a sad voice. "Baby, do you undershtand me now? / Sometimes I feel a little bad ... mad ... sad / But I'm just a soul whose intenshinsh are good. Oh Lord, please don't let me be mishunderstood."

He ended the chorus with a dramatic twist, bumping into the caretaker and falling to the ground. How did he get there, he wondered, and stayed down while he tried to figure it out.

Herbert lifted him to his feet. "You lekker aan. Don't worry, we'll see you safe home."

Neville sang and danced with an imaginary partner all the way home. Why was the night ending now? Just when he was starting to have a good time. He didn't want to go home to Magda. She didn't know how to get it on.

He complained when they reached Magnolia Court. "Don't take me to Magda. You can't dance when you down on your knees. Can't we go find another place to dance? I can dance with you, Crysanthea. I can't dance with Magda, she thinks you will burn in hell if you have a good time."

He grabbed Chrysanthea's waist and spun her round while he sang in a sad voice. "Oh baby / Don't you know I'm only human, / And I got thoughts like any other man."

Herbert pulled him off his wife. "Come now Neville, it's late. Go home to your family. Go upstairs now."

"She'll never undershtand," Neville muttered as he made his way up the three flights of stairs. He hung off the metal rail on the first-floor landing, peering through the washing lines in the courtyard below. He spotted the Ontongs and shouted at their backs as they walked away. "I got thoughts like any other man!"

He checked on them again as he reached the top. There was still a chance they changed their minds and were coming back to take him dancing. He couldn't spot them.

Light spilled onto the third-floor landing. Moira's front door was wide open. Neville peeped inside. There was no one in the lounge. Instead of heading left to his front door, he knocked on his neighbour's and walked into her flat.

Moira came into the lounge. "Was that you shouting, Neville? You okay?"

"I'm fine, I'm great, I'm bemoer," Neville said, dropping onto the couch. "The night is still young. Have you got shomething for a man to drink?"

Moira frowned. "Neville, you drunk! I never seen you drunk before."

"I'm not drunk, I'm a just a shoul whose intenshins are good. But at home I'm mishundershtood. Pour a man a drink, won't you?"

"The only drink I'm giving you is coffee. Haai Neville, it's good to see you having a nice time. You getting old before your time. Live while you still got the energy, that's what I always say."

Neville found it hard to concentrate. Why was Moira talking so much? Why was she taking so long to bring his drink? A man was getting thirstier by the minute. He frowned. "So where's the dop?"

"Stay here, I'll bring it."

Neville inspected Moira's lounge while he waited. It had been a while since he had been inside her flat. Her display cabinet had the usual school photos of her five children. Their forced smiles showed off how many baby teeth they had lost since their pictures were last taken. Instead of fancy crockery that only came out for guests, there was a collection of miniature liquor bottles in the cabinet. He had definitely come to the right place.

The room looked like a crèche. There were children's things everywhere. Toys on the floor, clothes draped on the chairs and the couch. Neville wondered how they all fit into the two-bedroomed flat, but the children were nowhere to be seen or heard.

Moira came back into the lounge with two mugs. She made space for them on the cluttered coffee table and sat next to Neville on the couch.

"What's this?" he asked, peering into the mug. "I asked for a drink." His happy mood was disappearing. Did Moira also misunderstand him?

"It's coffee. It's all you getting. You got to get home to Magda. It's late. Drink up, then you can go home."

"I don't want to go home!" Neville protested loudly. "I want to go out. I want to drink. I want to dance. Put some music on, I want to dance."

He glared at Moira. Her Lady Di flecked hair dropped down onto a red jersey dress. The V-neck showed off her cleavage to its full advantage. The dress clung in all the right places on a body gebou like a Coca-Cola bottle.

"Lady in red," he crooned. "Come dancing with me."

He reached across the couch and tried to pull Moira to her feet, but something went wrong. He expected her to get up with him; instead he fell down. His nose landed in her nice-and-firm cleavage. Her breasts smelled delicious.

He sniffed deeply. "Charlie. You one of Charlie's Angels."

Moira tried to push him off, but she pressed his hips into hers as she lifted his shoulders. Neville could feel through his new Wrangler jeans that he was getting interested. He smiled and pressed into her hip.

"Neville!" Moira squealed. "What you doing? Get up! Get off me!"

"What's wrong?" he asked innocently as he sat up on the couch. "Don't you want to dance with me? If we was dancing your body would be so close to mine."

"We not dancing Neville. We drinking coffee. Drink up so you can go. What will Magda say if she must find out you drunk and dancing at my flat late on a Saturday evening?"

"What Magda don't know won't hurt her," Neville said, pushing out his bottom lip. Moira was spoiling his evening. He had been lekker happy when he stepped into her place but she made him feel like a doos in minutes.

Moira stood up. "Ja, but what Magda finds out will hurt me. I heard what she says about me; she and all that witches from her church. They think I'm a hoer because my children got different fathers. Don't think I dunno what your wife says about me."

"I hear you. Don't shout. It's loud and clear. I'm going home now." Neville tried to get on his feet, but gave up when Moira pushed him back onto the couch.

"Don't be so foolish. Finish your coffee. There's no reason for you to go right now. You will wake up everybody. I heard you coming up the stairs."

Neville began to feel like a doos. It had been a lekker evening. There was no need to end it on a bad note, no need to spoil Magda's evening. Moira was right. She understood.

Chapter Fourteen

Anthony went to Ougat's shebeen most days after school. As long as he got home before Mummy and Dedda came from work, he was safe. His exams were coming soon; the primary school wasn't out on boycott. Suzette and Nicky were lucky. They didn't have to study. He didn't have to study also; his schoolwork wasn't so hard.

Nicky tried to force him to sit with his books, but he gave her no notice. No one put her in charge of him and he had no time for her scheme to make him as phoney as she was. It was none of her fokken business what he was up to. She better keep her blerrie mouth shut. Suzette hardly looked in his direction. She was only interested in herself.

His friends were kak boring. All they did was watch TV and pretend they were actors from their favourite shows. He used to be Murdoch from *The A-Team*, the clever one. His new friends, Ougat and his ouens, were like real-life actors. Although he still called him laaitie, Ougat was treating him like he was one of the ouens. Anthony was helping to build his business. The shebeen on Peach Street was only one part of Ougat's scheme.

Anthony wasn't stupid. He knew he was hanging out with the Junky Funky Kids. He wasn't a member of the gang; they didn't involve him in their war with the Americans. From what he heard in the shebeen, the Americans fought dirty. He learned to hate them as much as Ougat's ouens did. Marewaan, who was built like Mr T, cried like a baby when he found out they shot and killed his younger brother. The ouens had taken revenge for Marewaan; two Americans stupid enough to come out into the open were vrek.

Ougat said he didn't like the war. He was a businessman and it was bad for business. Customers stayed away from the shebeen for fear of an attack. Anthony hadn't seen a gun or a knife at the shebeen, although he had seen people being moered with fists, and once a man tried his luck with a broken bottleneck. Ougat had sorted him out one time and the man wasn't seen again.

Anthony was delivering parcels all over Hanover Park. Ougat said no one would hassle a decent-looking boy in a school uniform. He took out Anthony's schoolbooks and stashed newspaper-wrapped parcels in his haversack. Anthony was paid well, up to five rand a week depending on whose turf he had to cross. Ougat showed him how to be on the lookout for gang signs as he moved across the township. He warned Anthony not to look direct into the faces of the ouens hanging on the street corners.

He was delivering mostly dagga. Ougat was still selling bankies out of the boot of the car parked at his neighbour's house, and he started a wholesale business after he found a supplier in the Eastern Cape. That's why the Americans attacked him; they were fokken jealous of how big his business was growing. Ougat was also dealing Mandrax, five rand a tablet. More and more customers were asking for pille.

At first Anthony didn't know what to do with the money he earned. For a while, he was the main man at school, buying cooldrinks and slapchips and pies for his friends at the café across the road. When they started asking where the money was coming from, he stopped being Mr Big Stuff.

He spent some on cigarettes and dagga. Ougat wouldn't supply him for free. He put the rest of his cash in a plastic bag and hid it behind Mummy's other pride and joy, the twin-tub washing machine in the bathroom. It took him a while to figure out where to hide his stash. There was no place in the flat that he could call his own.

There was nothing better than a skyf while he was hanging out at the shebeen with Ougat's ouens. He was learning to sabela, to speak prison slang. The dagga loosened the ouens' tongues and the stories they told were bemoer. Anthony could almost see the grey Pollsmoor cells and the cruel warders they described.

It sounded to him like it was kak in prison, dirty and violent, but the ouens spoke like they missed the place. They were a brotherhood inside. That's where they formed the JFKs. They kept the spirit going on the outside. They came together every day – most were at the shebeen from morning 'til night. Anthony had to go to school. His principal, Mr September, was a deacon in Mummy's church. She would find out quickly if he bunked.

The ouens liked nothing better on a winter's day than gathering around the brazier, sharing a skyf and reminiscing about the old days. They all knew one another's stories.

"Remember the day that frans came to sit his gat down next to us in the yard?" Skelm opened the afternoon's tale, passing along a three-blade joint after exhaling a stream of smoke through his wide nostrils. The smoke curled into his peppercorn hair like a bush fire.

"What's a frans?" Anthony asked. He was picking up their weetie, but sometimes it was difficult to keep up.

"He's a moegoe. He belongs to no one. He's on his own," Oegies explained.

"How do you get to belong? Do you pick the gang you wanna join?"

Skelm laughed, his pink gums gleaming between his passion gap. "That's a story for another day. Don't interrupt laaitie, I got a thing going on here. If you interrupt I forget where I am. So this frans drops down and thinks he's one of us."

"Drops like a big drol into a toilet pan," Riedewaan said in a serious tone. The manne got the hysterics.

Oegies continued after they calmed down, rubbing tears from his squint eyes. "This drol lands between us. We can't believe what our eyes is seeing. Anyone can see we in the middle of a serious conversation."

"Ja, that was a big one. Ougat was being released the next day, we had arrangements to make," Riedewaan added. "The man was giving us his contacts on the outside. We all had to remember well. And this frans schemes he can just listen in, like James Bond."

Oegies chimed in. "Maynard had the weights, remember? He was always pumping, thinking no one would figure out what a moffie he was."

The story paused for another round of laughter. Anthony almost pissed himself. Imagine, a moffie at a gang meeting. He was probably eyeing their haircuts.

Skelm stopped laughing first, so he finished the story. "So Maynard gets up, casual as anything, and he drops the weight into the fat frans's lap, on his piel. Fok hom. I hope his piel never naai again. Who the fok do he think he is? What do he take the Junky Funkies for? Fokken poes. We should have gotten Maynard to give him a stywe naai with that weight. Maybe that's what he came looking for in the first place."

Anthony felt his piel shrinking in his school pants. He reached for the bankie in his tracksuit pocket; another joint would make the ouens loosen up a bit. He liked the way they trusted him to hear stories they would never tell franse.

Ougat gave Anthony a heavier task the next day, to take goods to Boeta Ismail's house in Acacia Street. There was a lot to deliver; he had to make a few trips. It was only a fifteen-minute walk from the shebeen, but he had to cross Hanover Park Avenue to get there.

It was getting benoud on the main road through the township. There were barricades every day, burning holes into the tar, and young people throwing stones. Their targets were the lorries that drove down Hanover Park Avenue, transporting goods from the surrounding farms and factories.

Black smoke poured into the grey sky from the barricade of burning tyres in the middle of road. It forced vehicles to climb the pavement to continue their way. When the lorries slowed as they passed the flames, stones rained down. On his first trip to Boeta Ismail's house, Anthony saw boys throwing stones at a bread lorry. The driver accelerated but a stone shattered his windscreen before he got away.

Taking the next load to Boeta Ismail's house, Anthony got the jitters. As he waited to cross Hanover Park Avenue, two police vans trailing a Casspir came screaming towards him. He didn't know which way to turn: to try to reach his destination or race back to the shebeen.

In a split second, he decided to cross the road. He could make it. The vans were still a distance away. He hoped the goods in his haversack wouldn't break if he ran. As he reached the other side of the road, he slipped on the wet kerb and fell. He was too bang to look behind him to see how close the vans were. When the police arrived they might think he was one of the stone throwers and arrest him. How would he explain what was in his bag? Anthony got up and ran with arms pumping, following the comrades sprinting away from the police.

He could hardly talk when he arrived at Boeta Ismail's house. There was nowhere to sit after he took his haversack off his back and sukkeled to catch his breath. The lounge was packed, mostly with electronics like televisions and hi-fi sets. Anthony had been adding to Boeta Ismail's supply, carrying kettles, toasters and linen from Ougat's place in his haversack. Mandrax users didn't always have cash for their purchases so Ougat let them pay with whatever they could lay their hands on.

Boeta Ismail came into the lounge, his huge belly making a tent as it pushed out his white kurta. A white kuffiyeh perched on oily jet-black hair. His face was framed by thin sideburns that grew down his cheeks and met under his chin in a triangular beard. He looked more like an imam than a dealer in stolen electronics. He reached for Anthony's haversack, opened it and removed a Betamax video machine.

"What's wrong boy? Was someone chasing you? Is it the Naughty Boys? They been moving in here lately."

"No Uncle, it's the police," Anthony panted, blowing on his palms that had scraped up gravel when he fell.

"Where? Are they outside?" Boeta Ismail headed for the door.

"No Uncle, they on Hanover Park Avenue. The students are stoning there, and the police came just as I made it across."

"Good, they must keep the police busy. I need to move some stuff today. You okay? You want some sugar water?"

"No Uncle, I'm okay. I just wanna catch my breath. That's the last I'm bringing today. Ougat says I must get the money from you."

Anthony took the envelope from Boeta Ismail and returned to the shebeen. It was safer there than on the streets with the comrades and the police.

Ougat's shebeen had a new addition, a pool table. The floor had been cemented; it was level enough. The table took up most of the floor space. Beer drinkers on benches surrounding the table were forced to duck when players pulled back their cue sticks. Anthony was just as good at pool as he was at kerem. Maybe even better. He got five-ball breaks a couple of times. None of the ouens could beat him. They called him the general of the pool table.

Anthony leaned over the table, a cigarette hanging off his lip, squinting through the smoke as he lined up on the black ball. The ouens who had been crowding around the game moved away, breaking his concentration as they headed towards the entrance of the shebeen.

"What's up?" Oegies dropped his pool cue onto the table and followed the ouens to the door.

"Hey!" Anthony protested. "I'm on the black! Come back and let me win you."

Oegies was tall enough to see over the men's shoulders as they crammed into the doorway leading onto the pavement.

"What's going on?" Anthony asked.

"It's Jackie Lonte," Oegies shouted. "Yoh! Check his BMW. Bemoer set of wheels he got."

The crowd backed away from the shebeen's entrance as Lonte entered. Anthony couldn't see over their heads. All he spotted was the cowboy hat on Lonte's head and the orange scarf wrapped around his neck. Ougat waited for him at the front door to his house. Lonte reached out and pulled Ougat's skinny shoulders into his chest.

Lonte's two men, who had been fastened onto their boss's shoulder as he came into the shebeen, closed Ougat's front door and took up position. They had no necks, their chins dropped straight onto their huge chests. Another bruiser stood guard at the shebeen's entrance, turning away customers and curious neighbours.

Anthony had listened when Dedda spoke about Lonte. Dedda came home from his neighbourhood-watch patrols with stories about gangs and gangsters. Lonte was the leader of the Americans, the biggest gang on the Cape Flats. The Americans had been at war with the JFK for more than a month. Anthony was kak nervous; the enemy had come into Ougat's territory.

He wanted to leave, but Lonte's ouens weren't letting anyone out. There was nothing to do, except wait with Ougat's silent ouens for the meeting to end. He lost his smaak for pool, turning Oegies down when he asked for a revenge game. Anthony didn't want to be the general of the pool table any more. The real thing had arrived.

When Lonte left an hour later, Anthony struggled again to see his face. Ougat's ouens surrounded him, reaching out to shake his hand. When he finally found the pluck to push through the crowd to see Lonte, it was too late. As he reached the pavement he caught a glimpse of the big shot's leg lifting into the back of a bottle-green BMW convertible. A bodyguard slammed the door and got into the driver's seat. Children raced the car down the street as it pulled away silently.

Ougat's manne swarmed around him as they came back inside the shebeen. One after another they threw questions without giving him a chance to explain.

"Hold up!" Ougat lifted his hand into the air. He cleared the shebeen of customers and neighbours, closing the door when only Junky Funky members and Anthony were left inside.

"Jackie came to call a truce. He says we ahead in the war, its nine of us vrek against fourteen of his ouens." Ougat waited 'til his ouens stopped cheering before he went on. "Jackie also came to make a alliance with the JFKs."

"Nooit!" Oegies interrupted. "If we won the war why must we seek alliance with the fokken Americans? What kak is this?"

Ougat frowned. "Jackie recognised that we the winners in the war with the Americans here in Hanover Park. Everyone will know that. They prepared to give over some of their turf to us. What you dom fokkers don't realise is that we not in the killing business. We need people alive, they our fokken customers."

Marewaan, who had killed two Americans in revenge for his brother's death, whispered like he was in a church. "Yoh! Jackie Lonte recognised us! That's befok."

Ougat smiled. "Ja, Lonte says we people he can work with. He got word from the man inside to make this alliance. He got people everywhere. Up the West Coast. All the way to Beaufort West. Maybe even as far as Joburg."

"What business is he in?" Marewaan asked.

"Same as us. Mandrax mostly. He says he can get supplies; he got contacts overseas and everything. They looking for someone to distribute in Hanover Park, so he came to me, the main man."

Ougat took a handshake from each of his ouens before he went on. "We moving up the supply chain, that's what Jackie said. But first he wanted me to swear a truce, so I did."

"Mandrax is fokken expensive," Marewaan said. "How we gunna sell wholesale in Hanover Park?"

Ougat's gold teeth shone as he explained. "Jackie's got it all planned. When he brings in his supplies he's gunna bring the price down. We gots to persuade our rookers to switch from dagga to Mandrax. We gunna offer it at the same price. And we gunna take it to all the other merchants in Hanover Park. Jackie will organise alles."

Oegies frowned. "Why must we help other merchants? They can mos find their own supplies."

Ougat klapped Oegies over the head. "Dom fokker! Didn't you hear what I just said? I said we gunna be suppliers. You get it?"

Oegies nodded, his squint eyes wobbling in his head.

Ougat stared hard at all his ouens, Anthony included, before he went on. "We gunna be organised, you hear me? This is the biggest deal you naaiers have ever been part of. Don't fok it up. For you or for me. You fok it up and you wish you never was born."

The shebeen went quiet. Anthony stared down at the floor. He didn't know what to think. The war was over, that was good. Ougat was getting involved with Lonte; that was the big time. Lonte had a reputation. He wasn't a man to cross. Anthony didn't want Lonte to take note of him; he was only thirteen. He didn't want Lonte thinking he was too close to Ougat. He was so deep in his thoughts, Ougat had to call his name twice before he heard.

"Anthony! I wanna weetie with you. Inside!"

Ougat's house hadn't changed since Anthony first saw it. It was still a dark, dirty cave. The shebeen had been renovated but nothing had been spent on cleaning the house. Anthony breathed through his mouth when he followed Ougat inside.

Ougat chased his mother and two sisters out of the lounge, promising to tell them later what Lonte wanted. It took a while to get his mother out. She kept on about what a sophisticated man Lonte was. "The suit

Jackie was wearing! I'm sure it was Carducci."

Anthony sat down carefully on the greasy brown couch when Ougat took a seat and patted the space next to him. He wondered where Lonte had sat during the meeting. Wearing a suit like that, he probably decided to stand. He hoped Ougat wouldn't keep him long. He had to get to the flat; Mummy would be home soon.

Ougat leaned forward. "Listen up, laaitie. I'm very chuffed with you. You know how to keep your bek and you been working very hard. I'm gunna need you in this new operation, you hear?"

Anthony swallowed hard. What did Ougat want with him? He had Jackie Lonte. If he got more involved with Ougat would that mean he was also involved with Lonte? "Ougat, I dunno. I'm only thirteen; I must be home by a certain time. I must go now; it's getting late. I'll be in trouble."

"Wait up laaitie, won't take long. You got the money from Boeta Ismail? You take all the goods?"

Anthony had forgotten about the envelope in his haversack. It seemed like a while since he raced the police on Hanover Park Avenue. Ougat opened the envelope when Anthony handed it over and took out a ten rand.

"Take it, laaitie," he said, waving the note in Anthony's chest. "You did orrite."

"It was a bit benoud today," Anthony said. "There was police everywhere. The comrades were stoning lorries on Hanover Park Avenue."

"You must be wise," Ougat replied. "You don't wanna be caught up with that kak. Next thing the police catch you with a bag full of Mandrax."

Anthony's nerves jumped like fleas under his skin. He wiped his wet palms on his pants. He licked his dry lips. He didn't want to deliver Mandrax. The Junky Funky Kids were getting too serious for him. He was only thirteen. "Uh Ougat, I got to go. I'll be in big kak if I get home late. I'll come by tomorrow, okay?"

Ougat sighed. "Orrite. But there's something I wanna talk to you about. I think you and me, we got a connection."

"Okay, we can talk tomorrow when I come by."

Anthony walked home poepscared. He didn't want to get involved with Jackie Lonte. Maybe it was time to give up his friendship with the JFKs. What would happen if he got caught with Mandrax? He would go to jail for a long time. How was he gunna explain that to Mummy and Dedda?

Later that night, when he was sure everyone was asleep, Anthony crept skelmpies into the bathroom. He reached behind the twin tub and pulled out his plastic bag. He went back into the lounge and opened his haversack in the dark. He took out five bankies filled with white tablets. Ougat had shoved it into his haversack before he left the shebeen and told him to keep it safe.

Anthony took the ten rand note from his tracksuit pocket. He put the money and the Mandrax in the plastic bag, pulled the TV stand away from the lounge wall and hid the bag behind it. He went back to his bed on the couch and stared at the front door for three hours before he fell asleep, listening out for policemen coming up the stairs.

Chapter Fifteen

The security police came at four o'clock in the morning for Kevin. His mother said they pulled up in six cars. Policemen jumped over the walls and surrounded the house, some of them carrying machine guns. They searched the whole house, turned it upside down, looking for Lord knew what. They wouldn't say where they were taking him when they left.

There wasn't going to be a school boycott, or a June 16 commemoration. All political activity was banned under a new state of emergency and thousands of people were detained the morning before it was declared. Student ringleaders were swept up across the Cape Flats and the rest of South Africa.

Nicky heard the news from Shirley when she arrived at school. The girls hadn't walked together for weeks. They hadn't spoken since the argument about the boycott.

Shirley came rushing up to Nicky as she walked into their class, jumping up and down and shaking her fingers in the air as as she spoke. "Did you hear about Kevin?"

"What about Kevin?" Nicky walked to her desk, opened her haversack and took out her maths book. The boycott was no excuse to fall behind on her schoolwork. Mummy and Dedda sent her and Suzette to school every day. Mummy said she didn't want them roaming the streets dodging stones and teargas; or at home, making boycott babies. Suzette hadn't been at school for three weeks. For all Nicky knew, she was pregnant already.

"Kevin's been detained!" Shirley announced dramatically, forcing her to pay attention. "The police came to his house this morning and took him away. They also took Mariam again, you know, that girl from

Athlone who spoke at our meeting when we decided to boycott."

Nicky dropped hard into her desk. She had warned Kevin this would happen, but the news still came as a shock. "How long they gunna keep him?"

Shirley shook her head slowly. "I dunno. I just heard he was picked up. I also heard they banned all June 16 meetings and boycotts. It looks like we gunna have to write exams now."

"I'm glad I kept studying while the rest of you were marching and singing outside in the rain."

Shirley hung her head. "I didn't study. Now I'm gunna fail and my mother is gunna take me out of school. I know she's gunna. Nicky, I'm too young to work."

Nicky had no sympathy. Her mind was all over the place with Kevin's business. She wondered if the police would hurt him. She wondered if he was scared like she was. She knew what the police did to detainees. "Shirley, I haven't got time for your problems now, I'm too worried about Kevin. Will you come with me after school? I want to go to his house to find out what happened."

"Ja, I'll come. Maybe there's still a chance of a boycott. I'm sure the comrades will be angry because Kevin's detained. Maybe they'll burn down the school."

"Ag, you talk such nonsense." Nicky smiled at her friend. It was good to have Shirley back in her life. She missed her foolishness.

When the girls got to Kevin's home they had to squeeze into a lounge filled with people. Nicky recognised Roger, the SRC chairman. Everyone else was a stranger.

Mrs Van Wyk, a small woman with a big boep in a blue dress, was seated in an armchair in the corner. The bun behind her head was heavy with grey, wiry hair. She looked old enough to be Kevin's grandmother. A handkerchief twisted between her fingers as she cried quietly. A young, skinny woman sat on the arm of the upholstered chair, her arm crooked around Mrs Van Wyk's round shoulders.

"Thank you for coming, thank you," Mrs Van Wyk said after Nicky and Shirley pushed their way through the lounge to greet her. Shirley had met her before; she introduced Nicky.

The old woman's eyes were wet as she raised her face. "So you're Nicky! Kevin talks about you all the time."

Nicky was so embarrassed she didn't know where to look. Shirley was smiling at her like a mal idiot.

"Come sit here by me." Mrs Van Wyk pulled Nicky onto the arm of her chair. "Meet Shamiela, she's been very kind."

Nicky smiled at the woman seated on the other arm. Her long, skinny, denim-wrapped legs were crossed like a dancer's, one over the other. "Nice to meet you."

Shamiela's teeth gleamed white in her sharp-featured, dark face. "Same here. I also heard about you from Kevin."

Nicky was confused. What was Kevin saying about her to all these people? Why was he talking about her? Most of the time she had nothing good to say to him. He could get her worked up like nobody else. But still, she was more his friend than his enemy – she hoped.

Mrs Van Wyk burst into tears, talking through the handkerchief she held against her mouth. "Kevin's so fond of you Nicky. He'll be glad you came. Thank you for coming. I really don't understand why he's been taken from me like this."

Nicky's eyes went big in her head. What was Mrs Van Wyk talking about? She was talking about Kevin like he was dead. She looked around. The people crammed into the lounge were talking in low, serious voices. A woman came in, carrying a plate of scones. It was looking like a funeral.

She turned to Shamiela, searching into her eyes across Mrs Van Wyk's head. "Is Kevin okay? Do you know anything? How long they gunna keep him? Where's he?"

"He's at Victor Verster Prison. My husband Moegamat's also there. From what we heard so far, they took hundreds of people this morning."

"Where's Victor Verster? I never heard of it."

"It's a prison in Franschhoek. Near Paarl."

Nicky had no idea where that was. At least someone knew where Kevin was. That was one less worry. "I'm sorry to hear about your husband. You must also be worried."

Shamiela smiled, rubbing Mrs Van Wyk's back. "This is the third time Moegamat's been detained. He knows how to handle it. You mustn't worry so much, Mrs Van Wyk. They all being held together. There's people inside who will look after Kevin. There's boys much younger than him at Victor Verster. I read in the papers that they cry themselves to sleep at night."

Mrs Van Wyk twisted her handkerchief between her fingers. "Our family never had anyone in jail before. I wouldn't know what to do when I go visit him. How will I get to Victor Verster?"

Shamiela patted the old woman's shoulder. "Don't worry about a thing. The Detainees Parents Support Committee will organise everything. You have to go to police headquarters at Caledon Square to request a visit. Someone will come take you to Victor Verster. Maybe I'll get a visit on the same day and I'll be the one to fetch you."

"You people are so kind, thank you. I don't know how I'm going to get through this. My heart is weak, you know? When the police burst in this morning it took a lot out of me. I didn't think my heart could take it. Kevin is my only child. How will I cope without him?"

Shamiela shook Mrs Van Wyk's shoulder. "Don't worry yourself so much. We got lawyers working on their case. They already looking at this new state of emergency to see if they can challenge it in court. The detainees won't be in for very long, you'll see. We not gunna sit quietly. We gunna work on campaigns to demand their release. We organising a march for sometime next week."

Mrs Van Wyk shivered. Nicky rubbed her back, her hand bumping into Shamiela's as it curved around the old woman's crooked spine.

Mrs Van Wyk's worries piled up. "I can't march, not with my dicky heart. How am I supposed to pay for a lawyer? We survive on Kevin's daddy's pension; it's not a lot. Since my late husband died, life has been difficult. I can't cope without Kevin. My boy does everything for me."

Shamiela reassured Mrs Van Wyk that she wouldn't have to pay a cent for the lawyer; the support committee would cover the costs. She stood up to leave. "Nicky, can I see you outside for a minute?"

Shamiela was skinny but she moved fast, cutting her way across the crowded lounge. Her long black ponytail danced across her hips as she moved. Nicky was impressed with the way she had calmed Mrs

Van Wyk, and with all the arrangements she was making. She joined Shamiela in the tiny front garden, crowded with people who had come outside for a smoke. "You must be so worried about your husband, Shamiela. And still you got time to help Mrs Van Wyk."

Shamiela shrugged. "Don't worry, I'm okay. We used to this kind of harassment. Moegamat knows how to look after himself. It's Mrs Van Wyk I'm worried about. Her health isn't good and she's working herself up to a complete state about Kevin's detention."

"Ja, she's acting like Kevin is dead. I got such a skrik when I came in and she was talking like he was gone forever. When did you say he was coming out?"

"We don't know. The boere declared an indefinite state of emergency. I need your help, Nicky. Kevin speaks highly of you. Do you think you can keep an eye on Mrs Van Wyk? You know, pop in every day and help her with the things Kevin used to do? The woman's got no other family; Kevin is all she has. I can't be around all the time, there's a lot of work to be done now that so many people have been taken."

"Of course, its no problem," Nicky replied quickly. "Shame, I feel for Mrs Van Wyk. She's all alone now."

She was burning to know what Kevin said about her. How could she ask without sounding too interested? The truth was she was interested in him. Was this the right time to ask? She had to find out otherwise it would drive her befok. "Um, Shamiela. You said Kevin talked about me. What did he say?"

Shamiela smiled. "He talks about you all the time. He says he likes arguing with you. You the only person who can make him lose an argument. Sounds to me that he likes to be around you."

Nicky's cheeks went hot despite the cold wind blowing across her face. "I think that's what I like about him also. We fight a lot. But in a nice way."

She said goodbye to Shamiela and went back into the house. She made tea for the constant stream of visitors, most of them activists. The news had spread and they had come to keep Mrs Van Wyk strong. Parents of other detainees came to introduce themselves and offer support.

It was getting dark when Nicky packed away the last of the cakes and food the visitors had brought. There was enough to keep Kevin's mother going for a while, and some to share when visitors came. Mrs

126

Van Wyk thanked her again and again when she left. She cried when Nicky promised she'd be back the next day.

Nicky tried to keep it cool with Mummy in the kitchen after supper but it was no use. Mummy wanted her to have nothing to do with Mrs Van Wyk or the comrades. Nicky was the hell in. She was the only child in the house who was behaving, but she was the only one in trouble all the time. Suzette was missing in action and Anthony got home every day just before Mummy. Why was she the one getting it?

She planned to reason with Mummy but everything came out in a shout. "Mrs Van Wyk isn't well. I'm not involved with the comrades! All I'm doing is going to her house to see if she needs anything. She might need something from the shops."

Magda shouted right back. "What if the police is watching her house? You'll be the next one they throw in jail."

"They won't be watching. She's just a old woman. She can't even walk far, she's sick, dammit."

"Did you just swear at me Nicolette Fourie? Don't you swear at me! You losing respect, that's what is happening! That's what the communists want. They want to destroy family life. What will people say if they must find out my daughter is involved with communists?"

"I'm not involved with communists! You must come to Mrs Van Wyk's house and look at her and tell me she's a communist. You dunno what you saying!"

Magda turned away and shouted in the direction of the lounge, her voice loud above the noise of the TV. "Neville! Come listen to your daughter. Since she got involved with the comrades she lost all respect for her parents."

Nicky stared daggers at her mother. Her fingers were spread wide on the kitchen table as she leaned forward like a lizard and stared across it. Nicky leaned back against the kitchen sink with her arms folded and her eyes opened wide, refusing to blink. It was unfair that she was being treated like she was the naughty child. What she was doing was a good thing.

Neville came into the kitchen. "What's up my bokkies? I can hear you two from the lounge."

Nicky tried to explain but Magda started talking at the same time. Her voice was louder so Dedda turned to her to listen.

"Neville, this child won't listen. She argues when I talk. She's getting involved with the comrades again. Did you see the news? They put thousands of people in jail today. That's where Nicky's heading. You try talking some sense into her."

Neville turned to face Nicky. "What's going on, my bokkie? Why you making your mummy so upset?"

"Dedda, Mummy's not listening to me. You listen to this. Kevin was detained today. His dedda is dead; he lives alone with his mummy. Mrs Van Wyk is sick, Dedda. She can't walk to the shops or anything. I promised her I would stop by tomorrow, to see if she needs anything. Mummy says I must stay away."

Nicky didn't stop to breathe until she reached the end. She was sure Dedda would understand. He always listened. Mummy was always so busy laying down the law that she never bothered to hear what other people said.

She was gatvol of Mummy always thinking that she was up to no good. Suzette drank and smoked and discoed and vryed with boys, but Mummy didn't turn her suspicious eyes on her. Anthony could do nothing wrong in her eyes. Nicky was no squealer, but she knew things that would turn Mummy's attention from her, big time.

She turned to Dedda. "Listen to this good Christian woman. Listen how compassionate she is. There's a sick woman sleeping alone tonight and she can't find sympathy in her heart. The comrades don't live like that, they support each other."

"Who you talking about Nicolette?" Magda leaned over the table. "Who's this 'she' you telling your dedda about? Is she the dog's mother?"

Nicky ignored her and waited on Dedda for the verdict. He was stroking his cheek, thinking it through. Eventually, he made up his mind. "Magda, she isn't getting involved with the comrades, all she's doing is helping Mrs Van Wyk. I think that shows a lot of Christian compassion."

Magda turned on him. "Take her side! I might as well not be here, you all ignore me so. You let the children get away with murder Neville. Soon Nicky will be in jail or dropping out of school because of a boycott. Is that what you want?"

Nicky looked across the table at Mummy, making sure she didn't smile. Mummy was changing colour like a crayfish in a pot of boiling water. It took her a while to find her voice and then it came out roaring.

"Don't you come running to me, Neville, when your daughter is in jail. Don't you come looking to me for help. God knows I try to do my best for my family. But you? You just undermine me. It's dangerous out there, you know it."

Neville's voice went hard. "Why do you always think the worst of the children, Magda? This is a good thing Nicky is doing. She learned it from you."

"They good children because I keep a close eye on them. But not you, Neville. You want them running around in the streets getting up to no good."

Nicky had heard enough. She left the kitchen and joined Suzette and Anthony in the lounge. They both pretended they were watching TV when she walked in.

Suzette couldn't keep her tongue for long. "You in trouble again, Nicky?"

"Mind your own blerrie business." Nicky was tired of Suzette's attacks. She hadn't squealed to Mummy about her, although she came close a few times. Suzette better watch out. When they found out she was bunking school she was gunna be in deep kak.

"Why's Mummy going on about jail?" Anthony asked, his face screwed up like he had swallowed kak. "Are you in trouble with the police, Nicky?"

"Kevin was detained today. I promised to help his mother, now Mummy's scared I'm going to jail also."

Anthony stared nervously at the TV stand. "Is the police coming for you? Are they gunna search our house?"

Nicky wondered where this was coming from. Anthony was never interested in anyone except himself. "No, you idiot. I'm not involved with the comrades. Didn't you hear what I said?"

129

"Just asking," Anthony said, turning back to the television.

Nicky gaved up on her sister and brother and went to her bedroom to study. They paid her no mind when she warned them they were headed for big kak. If she did badly in the exams she wouldn't know who to blame: Mummy for upsetting her so much or the boere for making her worry about Kevin.

Chapter Sixteen

Lying on her bunk bed, one hand resting on her cheek and the other pushing a pillow up between her thighs, Suzette closed her eyes and thought about Neil. About last night. She couldn't hardly believe what happened. She wasn't sure what the fok was going to happen next.

Neil wanted to see her again. Could it be that Suzette Fourie – of Magnolia Court, Hanover Park, nogal – had a white boyfriend? If Neil wanted to see her again did that mean they were involved? How did it work with her other boyfriends? Mark, Aunty Moira's son from next door, thought it was forever after just because they had naaied a couple of times.

She wasn't sure if naai was the right word for what she did with Neil. What was the right word? Making love was the word in Mills & Boon romances, always at the end of the book. Fucking sounded better. That's what people in America said on TV. Both words were better than naai or pomp. She would listen to what Neil called it and use that word from now on.

Suzette couldn't think anymore. Her brain and her bones were lame like jelly and custard. She pushed the pillow higher up between her legs. She was shivering up there. Mummy was expecting her to iron the washing, but she couldn't get off the bed. She needed to rest up a while. She needed time to think about what happened last night.

She had kept Neil's phone number safe in her purse and forced herself to wait three days before she called him. She didn't want to come across too desperate, although she was too bang to wait another day. He might forget who she was.

Melanie, her chommie from work, bet two rand that Neil wouldn't remember her. Melanie stared into Suzette's mouth as she spoke to him on the payphone in the cafeteria at Planet Fashions. Neil said straight away he had been waiting for her call.

He wanted to see her. "I've got friends coming round on Friday night. Are you free? Can you join us?"

Suzette's social life was non-existent. Her school friends were getting on with their lives, she wasn't there to see it happening. She was planning to catch up with them at the Galaxy soon. She had paid back her advance from Mr Strauss and was getting her full wages. She could pay her own way at the nightclub door; buy a drink for one or two people.

"Ja, I can come. I'm not doing nothing on Friday night." Melanie's open-mouthed stare was making Suzette nervous. That sentence didn't sound like it came out right.

Neil understood. "Let me give you my address. I'm right in town, it's easy to find."

Suzette had a few minutes alone with Neil after she sent Melanie to find a piece of paper and a pen. She struggled to think of something to say. She didn't want to sound stupid again.

Luckily, Neil jumped in. "I've been thinking about you a lot. Have you been thinking about me?"

"Ja, yes," Suzette stammered. "That's why I phoned you, 'cause I was thinking about you." That sentence also sounded wrong.

"Then it's a good thing that we're seeing each other soon, isn't it?"

"Yes."

"Come at six o'clock, okay? Can you make it then?"

"Yes."

Suzette took down his address, said goodbye and turned to Melanie. "Not only did he remember me, he wants me to meet his friends. Two rand please." She held out her hand.

Melanie brought her new black Melton jacket to the factory on Friday morning. It would go well with Suzette's new jeans and red stilettos. Melanie also donated a tube of red lipstick; she promised it would send Neil out of his mind.

Suzette lied to Mummy and Dedda. She couldn't exactly tell them she was going out with a white man they hadn't met. She said it was Charlene's eighteenth birthday party; she was sleeping at her house afterwards. It was safer that way. If she came home late she could sleep at Charlene's house. If she didn't come home, Mummy and Dedda would never find out.

She took a train into town. Her third-class carriage had plenty of hard plastic seats available. People were hanging out of the doors of crowded trains heading onto the Cape Flats at the end of the working week. Suzette was glad her carriage was empty. There was nothing to distract her from her thoughts.

Her brain worked overtime all the way to town. She was definitely interested in Neil. How to get him interested in her? What did white people talk about? Maybe they could talk about the factory. They were both in the clothing industry. But what would she say after that?

Suzette followed Neil's directions to the top of Wale Street. Next, she had to walk to the Planetarium. She didn't know what that was, and forgot to ask when Neil was on the phone. Luckily, the man selling peanuts at the bottom of Parliament Avenue could show her exactly where it was.

Neil's flat was opposite the round-roofed Planetarium. His block was painted bright pink with a white stripe at the top. It was nothing like the courts in Hanover Park. Suzette pushed open a wide door, with a wooden frame and frosted glass, to get into the lobby. It was lined with white pots filled with thick ferns that dropped like fans onto the spotlessly clean black-and-white tiled floor. There were only four floors, but the block had a lift, old-fashioned with shining brass and a mirror.

The corridor on Neil's floor overlooked the Gardens. Suzette had been there once. Mummy and Dedda brought them to town two years ago, to see the coons marching on New Year's Eve. They had walked through the Gardens under a full moon afterwards. It had been so bright they could see the goldfish in the ponds.

She straightened her hair and her clothes before she knocked softly on the door at flat 403. Neil opened almost straight away – before she was ready to see him – with a big smile. He took her hand and pulled her inside, apologising because his flat was so small. "It isn't much, just a bachelor."

Suzette didn't know what a bachelor was, she looked around curiously. She had never been inside a white person's home before. Neil's flat was much bigger than her family's. He didn't have as many rooms: just a kitchen, a bathroom and a big, open space on two levels. There was a screen behind one of the black leather couches. Neil's bed was probably behind it; Suzette couldn't see a bedroom. There was a desk with a computer on the top level. Floor-to-ceiling windows at the back were filled with Signal Hill. It was a befokte flat.

Neil guided her to a couch. "My friends are only coming at seven o'clock. I asked you to come early because I want to spend some time alone with you."

Suzette said yes when Neil offered a beer and watched him walk to the kitchen to get it. He was better looking than she remembered. She didn't get a good look at his body the day he drove her home from the factory. His blue-checked shirt was tucked into jeans filled with a nice round, firm hol. She got nervous again. She must think before she talked, she couldn't say words like hol. She had to use proper English; try to sound like a girl from Lansdowne. She had to remember to use sturvie words, like Simon Templar in *The Saint*.

Neil brought two beers and sat next to her. She took a bigger sluk of the icy cold drink than she meant to. She wiped her chin with the back of her hand. It was difficult to act sturvie when she was so nervous. What was Neil saying? She had to concentrate.

"So tell me about Suzette. I'm interested."

Suzette didn't mean to lie but one rushed out of her mouth. "Well, you know I live in Lansdowne, you dropped me there." No ways was she going to tell Neil she was from Hanover Park, 'specially now that she had seen his kwaai place.

"And? Come on, don't be shy. I'll go first. Where do I start? Okay. I dropped out of university in June. Took me three years to get halfway through my second year. Oh yes, I already told you that. My uncle got me a job as a buyer, and that's how I met you."

Neil waited. Suzette took another sip of her beer, careful not to spill down her chin again. She would try to stick to the truth. If Neil didn't find her interesting, that was that. She had high hopes thinking she could make a white man smaak her.

"I live with my parents and my sister and my brother," she said carefully. "My mother's a manager at a factory and my father works at a law firm in town."

She was glad Neil didn't ask the name of her mother's factory, or what Dedda did at the law firm. In Hanover Park, the first thing people wanted to know when they met you was who your parents were. Once they knew that, they made up their minds. They let their sons go out with you, or they kept them at home.

Neil wasn't interested in her parents, only in her. "Tell me about your job. You look good on stage, I must say."

Suzette's cheeks got hot and swollen. Neil had seen her in underwear. He wasn't the first man to see her with her clothes off; she didn't know why she was getting so skaam. On the stage she was a professional. "I'm just starting out there, at Planet Fashions. I'm saving up for a portfolio. A few agencies said they would be interested in looking at it."

"I'm sure you will succeed. You're very beautiful."

The heat came pouring out of Suzette. She couldn't stop it, hard as she tried, it was unstoppable like the lies. She lifted her beer bottle to her cheek to cool it down.

When a knock came at the door, Suzette couldn't believe it was an hour since she came. Neil spoke nonstop. He followed everything that happened in the fashion industry. He showed her magazines so bemoer she couldn't believe it. *Vogue* and *Cosmopolitan* from overseas. Naomi Campbell was also his favourite supermodel.

Neil went to open for his friends and led them inside. Suzette stared with her mouth catching flies as a woman walked into the flat like she was coming off the page of a magazine. She had jet black hair and a pen-straight fringe on a high forehead. Her lipstick was bright red in her spook-white face. Her black dress clung tight to wide hips that swung in tune with her black stiletto steps.

Suzette hardly looked at the man who followed. All she noticed was that he was tall, blonde and dressed casually like Neil, in jeans and a blue-and-white-striped Western Province rugby jersey.

Neil introduced Suzette to his best friend Cameron and his girlfriend Maureen. He went to the kitchen while they shook hands and the couple sat down on the couch opposite Suzette.

"So Suzette, how long have you known Neil?" Maureen raised a thick black eyebrow and leaned forward.

"Not long, since Monday. I met him at work."

"Oh?" The eyebrow went up again. "And where is that?"

"At Planet Fashions in Retreat."

"What do you do there?"

Neil came back, carrying a bottle of wine and two glasses. "You're off-duty tonight, Maureen. Relax a while. You can start your interrogation later."

Suzette was grateful. Maureen was making her bang. Did she think it was wrong for her to socialise with whites? It wasn't against the law, was it? What did Neil mean when he said Maureen could interrogate her? She didn't look like she worked for the police. Her clothes were too kwaai. She couldn't chase after anyone in that outfit.

When Neil said he had to get the meal ready, Suzette offered to help. She didn't want to stay in the lounge with Maureen, who had something clever to add to everything that was said. Cameron had started a conversation about the Chernobyl explosion in Russia. Suzette had seen something about it on the news, but she knew nothing about power stations. Maureen was worried about the Koeberg power station exploding; she had worked out how many people would die an hour after the explosion, how many would die in a month and how many would die years later. Suzette listened but didn't open her mouth once; she was bang they would see who she really was – a stupid matric girl from Hanover Park.

The kitchen was divided from the lounge by a counter, so Neil could talk to his friends while he cooked. He and Cameron got involved in a repeat of a rugby match they had seen on TV, remembering all the major moves from start to finish. Suzette knew nothing about rugby. She could talk a little about soccer; there were a lot of Man United, Liverpool and Arsenal supporters in Hanover Park. Maureen paid them no mind; she picked up a magazine and paged through it.

Neil didn't need much help. He asked her to make a salad, but all she had to put in the bowl was lettuce leaves and small red tomatoes. He didn't use mayonnaise or salad dressing; he gave her black vinegar to pour over it. Neil boiled spaghetti and heated tomato sauce that he poured out of a jar. Suzette wondered how readymade sauce tasted. Mummy made it from scratch, with lots of garlic and grated ripe tomatoes.

Neil grabbed her round the waist and kissed her cheek as she placed the salad next to his huge bowl of spaghetti on the kitchen counter. "You're a star, thanks."

Suzette got hot again. Neil had pressed up against her when he kissed her. She spotted a smile on his face when she stole a look as he called his friends over to dish up.

The food was good. The vinegar on the salad leaves was sweet, not like the white kind everyone in Hanover Park used with spoons of sugar when they made pickled fish and beetroot. Neil only served spaghetti and salad. Suzette thought maybe he cooked the meat earlier, but there wasn't any – even though he had visitors. There wasn't any pudding afterwards. Maybe that was why white people had so much money; they didn't eat it all up like coloureds.

They ate with plates balanced on their laps. Suzette was careful not to sluk the spaghetti loudly up her chin and into her mouth the way she usually did. She copied Maureen, twirling it around her fork before lifting it into her mouth. It was a clever way to eat spaghetti.

Suzette listened while Neil caught up with his friends. It turned out Maureen interrogated people because she was a journalist, at *Fairlady* nogal! Cameron did something with computers; Suzette didn't understand a word he said when he spoke about work.

After they cleared their plates away, Cameron pulled out a bank bag filled with dagga and began rolling joints. Suzette didn't like dagga. She had taken drags from her friends' joints and pipes; all it gave her was a dof headache that hung around in a bad mood for two days afterwards. She preferred alcohol, but she had already downed three beers. She decided to cool it a while; she didn't want to get too loud.

She took a few drags when the joint came her way. Neil and his friends were being nice to her but she was tense from keeping her guard. She needed to relax a while. She could do this. They didn't speak like Simon Templar. They swore a lot, although they said fuck not fok. They said lakker, instead of lekker. Kwaai things were either lakker or kiff.

The dagga was nothing like the majat supplied by Hanover Park dealers. It didn't make her dof at all. It loosened her tongue, the words came bubbling out after she shared a second joint with Neil and his friends. They were clever, but she could understand most of what they said. They didn't mind if all she had to offer was questions.

Suzette learned a lot after Neil told Maureen she was a model. Maureen knew everything about the supermodels, and she was happy to answer questions. She knew which models were sleeping with rock stars and which ones were drug addicts. When Maureen told her how much they earned, Suzette couldn't get her head around it.

Neil and Cameron were having a separate conversation. Suzette tuned in and tried to figure out what they were saying. They were talking about call-up papers. It sounded like they were checking to see if they came yet.

Neil sounded worried. "I haven't been using this address, but I suppose they can track me down at my parents' place."

"That happened to Brian," Cameron said. "His parents gave the defence force a forwarding address, can you fucking believe it?"

"Yes, I can. My father will probably do the same. He's furious that I dropped out of university. I wouldn't put it past him to phone the fuckers and let them know where to find me. Shit! You think he's already called them?"

"Nah, he won't do that. He's a progressive, isn't he?"

"He will. He's pissed off because I didn't want to suspend my registration and go to that fancy clinic he found in Miami." Neil stood up and walked up and down the lounge. "Fuck! Fuckit, fuckit, fuckit! They're probably coming any day now. Maybe I should move."

Cameron held up a hand. "Cool it broer. Don't go para on me. Relax. No one's looking for you. If they do come, there will be plenty of time to make a plan."

Suzette couldn't make out what the men were talking about. "What's a call-up paper?"

There was a silence before everyone started laughing. "Fuck it. It's Friday night," Neil said, plopping down on the couch next to Suzette. "We should be having a good time, not letting those bastards get us down."

"They're talking politics, Suzette," Maureen explained. "They have to decide if they're going to duck here forever, fight a losing battle or leave 'til freedom comes."

"Oh," Suzette frowned. "Politics is boring."

"Too true," Cameron smiled, reaching for the bankie on the coffee table to make another joint. "It is fucking boring. Let's fire up our evening."

The dagga made Suzette talk and laugh. Maureen was very funny. She could imitate almost anyone, had them rolling on the couches with laughter. No one seemed to think Suzette had no right to be there. No one said anything about the fact that she was a bit darker and a lot poorer; they spoke to her like she was one of them.

When Maureen and Cameron left just before midnight, Suzette got nervous again. Should she stay or should she also leave? She wanted to stay. Neil seemed interested. He had put his arm around her when he sat on the couch, but he was very jumpy. He couldn't stay long in one place.

She went to the toilet while Neil said goodbye to his friends. The four beers she drank made litres of piss; she had plenty of time to think. She was jas for Neil, no doubt about that. When he smiled she could see how he looked when he was a small boy. He had nice hands; she wanted them to touch her. Suzette decided that if Neil wanted a naai, she would oblige.

She felt suddenly shy as she left the bathroom. She didn't know how to proceed. It was easier to make conversation with three people than with one. With Maureen gone the flat was quiet.

Neil had turned off the kitchen light, closed the curtains and was coming down the steps of the upper level. "I was just going to put on some music. What would you like?"

"Anything. Anything's alright with me."

"Come, check it out. I've got everything."

Suzette joined Neil at the wall unit flanking the lounge wall. She had never seen one so big. He must have hundreds of books and LPs. She found it hard to focus.

"I like jazz," she said, after pretending to look at a few LPs. She couldn't think with Neil standing so close to her. She could smell him. There was a strong sweat smell but she didn't mind; it showed he had a lot of energy. Men who liked jazz knew how to move their bodies.

"My kind of girl! Let's see what I've got for you."

Suzette admired Neil's hol again as he leaned forward to flip through his LPs. She had never really taken notice of men's holle before, but she couldn't take her eyes off Neil's – it was ripe like a peach. His bum was ripe like a peach, she reminded herself, not his hol.

Neil chose an LP and put it on the turntable. It wasn't like any jazz Suzette heard before; there were no vocals, just instruments making sounds like cats on heat. He raised an eyebrow in her direction. "Good hey?"

She smiled. "Good."

Neil reached behind a book and brought out a small wooden box. "Now we can start a party. I kept my stash for us." He took Suzette's hand and guided her back to the couch. He opened the box and placed a small mirror and a bag of white powder on the coffee table.

"Cocaine," he announced. "My uncle Ronnie paid for a ticket last month to New York Fashion Week. He thought it would get me interested in my new career as a buyer. Thanks to Uncle Ronnie's generosity, I got turned onto the top dealers. The fashion industry knows how to party."

Suzette had seen cocaine on TV, but never the real thing. She watched every move Neil made. He poured some powder onto the mirror, reached for his wallet and took out his ATM card. He sliced the powder into four rows and diced each line. He opened his wallet again and took out a ten-rand note. He rolled it into a tube and pulled the mirror towards him. He put the note into his nostril, positioned it at the edge of a line of cocaine, and sniffed deeply, pushing the tube along the line until it disappeared up his nose. He handed the note to Suzette and moved the mirror closer to her.

"I never done this before." she said nervously.

"It's easy, just do what I did."

"What does it do to you?"

"It makes you feel fantastic. It takes you to the top of the world and keeps you there for a few hours." Neil shifted closer and stared at her. "You don't have to if you don't want to. It will make you feel great, I promise."

Suzette had done a lot of things for the first time since she arrived at Neil's flat. She had survived so far. Alone with him, there was a chance the evening could get better. His eyes were shining as he looked at her.

She copied him and managed to get a line up her nose. It fizzed to the top of her skull like sherbet; then it dropped down. It burned down the back of her throat, worse than when seawater went up her nose. Her face felt thick with snot.

"Fuck, this shit is A-grade," Neil said after he snorted a second line.

Suzette held up a hand when Neil pushed the mirror her way again. She first wanted to check what it did to her. She could try everything once, but that didn't mean she had to like it.

When Neil jumped up again to turn up the volume on the hi-fi, she leaned back on the couch. She could feel the blood moving through her body. She could feel it pumping to the tips of her fingers and her toes and all along her scalp. The light burned into her like she was staring into the floodlights at Athlone stadium. She covered her eyes with her hand and complained.

Neil lit candles, leaving one on the wall unit next to the hi-fi and bringing one to the coffee table. The candle's flame was bright, but Suzette couldn't look away after he placed it in front of her. She could see the heat shivering in the air around the flames. "I feel like I can see better, hear better and feel better," she said, stretching her legs out on the couch. "I can feel my body working. I can feel my lungs going in and out."

"I know, it's the same for me. Come here." Neil sat down and pulled Suzette's head onto his lap, stroking his fingers through her hair. "Just relax. You're going to feel great any minute now."

"I already feel great." Suzette's ears had tuned into the music. She picked up the bass, hidden deep under the wailing cats. It matched the throbbing between her legs. She turned onto her side to stare at the flame dancing on the candle. Neil's fingers crept under her jersey and stroked up and down her back. Her skin lifted up under his fingers.

The music had stopped when Neil took the last of their clothes off. He sat on the couch, staring at her body. "Fuck, you're beautiful."

Suzette propped herself up on her elbows and looked down at herself. She had to agree. Her skin looked lighter than normal on the black leather couch. Neil had left her red stilettos on. They made her legs look more shapely than they really were.

Neil pulled her up. "Come to bed with me. Sex is fucking fantastic on cocaine."

There were no complaints from the guys Suzette had naaied. But with Neil, she was at her best. She couldn't get tired. Neither could he. The only break they took, a short one, was to snort another line of cocaine each. Her tongue was stuck to the top of her mouth. Her hair and her body were wet with sweat. She lifted herself off Neil. "Wait a minute, I need water."

Neil leaned back on the pillows. He was ready for action. "Bring me a beer, won't you? Bring a few."

The clock in the kitchen said it was twenty past four. Suzette definitely liked cocaine. Neil was right. "Sex *is* fucking fantastic on cocaine," she whispered.

She filled a beer mug with water and drained it like a camel at an oasis. She filled it again and went to fetch beers from the fridge. She brought the drinks to the bed and dropped down next to Neil, who had just snorted another line of coke. "Fok!" She crawled down to the bottom of the bed and turned to look at the wide, wet puddle on the sheet. It was icy cold on her bum.

Neil dipped his fingers into the puddle and licked them. "Hmm. You taste delicious. Come here, I know a place where you'll be warm." He pulled her on top of him.

When Suzette woke up again, she was still lying on Neil. Her mouth tasted like a desert and there was sand on fire the back of her nose. She was stretched wide open, all the way up to her womb. Smacking her lips together, she climbed off Neil and the bed without waking him up. The clock in the kitchen said it was ten o'clock.

This was another first. She had never spent the night in bed with a man before. All the boys she had naaied lived with their parents. They couldn't bring girls home unless they married them. She had lost her virginity on the back seat of a car; sometimes she used the front seat. The last time she had a naai was at the church camp in April almost three months back, when Nicky and that comrade friend of hers came to interrupt her in the bushes.

After Suzette got dressed she stood over the bed and took one last look at Neil. His hips were small and his shoulders were wide. His eyelashes curled down almost to his cheekbones and his lips were red and swollen. She went to check on hers in the bathroom mirror. If she walked into the flat with a mouth like that Mummy would know exactly what she had done all night. She had to remember to keep her bottom lip in.

She didn't want to wake Neil; he looked so at peace. But it was time to go. She shook his shoulder. He didn't move, so she shook him some more.

Neil's eyes opened. "Morning beautiful," he smiled, pulling her down to the bed. He saw she was dressed and frowned. "Why have you got your clothes on?" He struggled with the button of her jeans. "Get naked woman, and come here."

"I can't, I got to go home," Suzette pushed his hands away. "I'm sorry, I got to go."

Neil sat up. "Do you want me to take you?"

Suzette didn't want to lie to him again about where she lived. "No, I'm fine on the train. We don't live far from the station." She lied, even though she meant to stop.

"When am I going to see you again? What are you doing tomorrow?"

"I got to … I have to go to church. I can come after lunch."

"Call when you're ready. I'll come fetch you. I'll pick you up where I dropped you the last time."

"Okay, I'll be there."

Suzette kissed Neil one last time. Not too hard or too long, she didn't want Mummy noticing her fat lip.

As usual, Mummy was in a kak mood when she got home. She was angry with Nicky and Dedda but she was taking it out on everyone. Suzette tried to stay out of her way as much as possible but it was difficult in the small flat. Still, the situation wasn't so bad. Mummy was so busy monitoring what Nicky and Dedda were up to that she hardly took notice of her.

"Is this the time to come home?" was the only greeting when she walked in.

"Sorry Mummy, Charlene and I sat up the whole night talking. I only went to sleep at four o'clock." The last thing Suzette wanted was an argument with Mummy. She was feeling good; all she wanted to do was climb into bed.

"You need to help around the house. I can't do everything. Nicky's only interested in helping Mrs Van Wyk. Anthony's gone to the shops with your dedda. I did the washing and I hung it up. You can take it down later and iron it. You girls do little enough around here."

Mummy didn't look like she was overworked. She had her feet up on the couch and was holding the latest *You* magazine.

"I'm just going to lie down 'til the washing gets dry, Mummy, then I'll see to it, promise," Suzette said, heading to her room and closing the door on her mother's complaints.

She pulled the duvet over her head, breathing in the smell of sex on her body. That was the word she was looking for. The word to describe what she and Neil did. She remembered what he had called it. Pushing the pillow between her legs, where she was shivering, she fell asleep.

Chapter Seventeen

Anthony was in big kak at home. So big that he got a hiding with a belt. Dedda had klapped him a few times, but this was the first proper hiding he gave. Anthony had to bend over the bath while Dedda hit him. The bathroom was too small for Dedda to get his aim right, so the belt landed on his bum, his back and his thighs. It wasn't as eina as the canings he got from Mr September at school but, still, he cried. It was more from the skrik he got that Dedda was hitting him like that than from the pain.

He brought his report home on the last day of school before the July holidays, expecting it to be bad. All his teachers had made the exams more difficult than usual. He could only answer two questions on his maths paper; he didn't know what the rest was about. It was the same with the geography paper, although he answered all the questions as best as he could.

Mummy opened his report when he gave it to her. She said nothing while she read it. The lines on her forehead crinkled like corrugated iron as her eyes moved down the page. Then she sat down on the couch and cried. She wouldn't stop and she wouldn't give the report to him to see. She was still holding onto it when Dedda came home.

If Mummy hadn't got the horries like that, Dedda wouldn't have hit him. Dedda was just trying to prove something when Mummy said it was his fault. When Anthony went into the lounge crying after the hiding, Mummy stopped tjanking, pulled him to her and gave him a tight squeeze. Looked like his hiding made her feel better.

When he finally got to look at his report he saw he had failed, one time. He had only passed two of his five subjects, English and history. He never usually studied, just looked at his work the night before. This time around, he hadn't even done that and nothing he heard in class had stayed in his head. His marks had never been as good as Nicky's – they would never be so good – but he had never failed a subject before. None of the Fourie children ever failed a subject or a term; not even Suzette who sometimes just scraped through.

Dedda and Mummy weren't finished with their punishing. He had to stay at home for the whole three-week July holiday and study every day. Mummy wanted Nicky to keep watch over him, but she refused. She was going to Mrs Van Wyk's house every day to cook and clean for her, like a good daughter-in-law. Dedda said it was unfair to expect Nicky to stay at home; that started another fight with Mummy.

Suzette was instructed to make sure he studied, but Anthony had hardly seen her for weeks. She left the flat every morning after Mummy and Dedda and came back all mysterious just before they came home from work.

Anthony was bored out of his mind. He took his schoolbooks out of his haversack and put them on the kitchen table. He sat down and opened his history textbook. He looked at the words on the page but his eyes weren't interested in reading them. He got up and made a cup of tea and four peanut butter and jam sandwiches. He took his lunch to the lounge and switched on the TV. The programme was kak for babies but he watched it anyway.

When he finished the sandwiches he went to stare out of the lounge window. The courtyard below was filled with children playing and women hanging washing, taking advantage of a sunny winter day. If he left the flat to play with his friends and one of them told someone and that someone told Mummy, he would be in more kak. Mummy had told all the neighbours she was on speaking terms with about his bad report and his punishment. She kept reporting back to him what neighbour said she was disappointed and who said he could do better.

There was one place he could go and no one would find out. Anthony hadn't gone near Ougat's shebeen since Jackie Lonte's visit a month back. He was bang. He was sure people went to jail for a long time for dealing Mandrax. If he was arrested he would be in even bigger kak with Mummy and Dedda.

But if he went to the shebeen, no one there would squeal on him. He had only seen one person from Magnolia Court there. Ricardo, from one of the flats across the courtyard, came every day to buy pille. He wasn't gunna tell anyone where he saw Anthony. It had been a long while since he had a game of pool. Oegies had come close to beating him a few times. He was probably ruling everyone else at the table now that the general wasn't there.

Anthony waited 'til after lunch. Mummy called him during her break, to check up on him.

"Hello my boy. Are you studying?" She said the same thing every day.

"Yes, Mummy."

"What you studying?"

"History, Mummy."

"You a good boy, Anthony. You make Mummy proud of you."

"Yes Mummy. Bye."

Anthony changed into someone else when he walked into the shebeen. His shoulders dropped down and his arms hung loose. A boy ran all the way there; a man with a heavy load between his legs walked slowly inside.

Ougat was playing pool with Oegies. He looked up as Anthony walked into the shebeen and flashed his gold teeth. "Hoesit," he said, as though he had last seen him the day before.

"Still hanging," Anthony gripped his crotch.

He gave Ougat a palm-slapping, finger-snapping, shoulder-bumping greeting. Anthony walked around the shebeen, greeting the ouens one by one. The regulars on the wooden benches lifted their bottles in his direction.

Nothing much had changed. There was a new poster of Bob Marley stuck to the zinc wall. His head leaned back, his eyes were closed and long dreads swung in the air around his face. The pool table still dominated in the centre of the cement floor. The benches flanking the walls were filled with customers, at two o'clock on a Thursday afternoon. Must be pension day, Anthony thought. Grannies had to provide for everyone in the house.

He bought a bankie from Riedewaan. He had run out of supplies, it had been weeks since he had a skyf. He sat down with a newspaper and began cleaning the dagga. He pulled the heads off the small branches, crumbled them between his fingers and brushed them up the folded newspaper so the seeds rolled down onto the floor. He rolled a three-blade smoothly, took four skyfs and passed the skyf to Marewaan who was waiting on the bench.

Anthony had a lekker buzz on when he got onto the pool table. He lost the first game but after his second turn he ruled. No one could get him off. His eye was in. Every shot went exactly where he planned it to go.

Ougat kept busy as the shebeen filled up with customers. His sisters helped, bringing cold beers from the freezer in the backyard. Mandrax rookers streamed in and out like skinny clouds of smoke.

It felt good to be among the ouens again. Anthony shifted over when Ougat came to sit on the bench next to him after he took a break from the table to make another skyf. Ougat put an arm around his shoulders. "Everything okay laaitie? I haven't sighted you for a while."

Anthony shrugged. "Don't take it personal. I'm under house arrest."

Ougat pulled back and stared. "Nooit! Did the varke get you? You sentenced already?"

Anthony smiled. "Is my parents; they put me under house arrest."

Ougat frowned. "What's up laaitie? What they find out? You want me to sort them out one time?"

Anthony had to be careful. People Ougat sorted out ended up badly, like his neighbour. Mr Slamdien squealed to the police about the shebeen and before long, he was in deep kak. Someone piemped him; the police raided his house and found Mandrax hidden in the yard, exactly where they were told to look. Mr Slamdien appealed to his neighbours when they came out to watch him being pushed into the police van. He was innocent, he said, someone had planted the drugs. The crowd stared in silence. After the van drove away, neighbours stood a while on the pavement to talk about the skandaal. Some believed Mr Slamdien, most didn't. Anthony thought the drugs were planted, but he said nothing.

He didn't want his parents sorted out by Ougat. "It's orrite. I failed my exams so I'm in kak at home. I can take care of it."

"So what if you failed? I only got standard five and look how good my business is doing." Ougat looked proudly around his crowded shebeen. "School is for moegoes."

"True," Anthony agreed. "My parents also didn't finish high school. I dunno why they say we must finish. Next year I'm gunna be in standard six."

"And still a virgin. I haven't forgotten my promise, laaitie. I'm still gunna fix you up with a lekker kind."

Anthony blushed. "Is okay. I'm in no hurry."

Ougat was generous. He was a businessman but he took time to show interest in a bangbroek laaitie. Anthony wondered why he had been so scared of Ougat after Jackie Lonte's visit. He was welcome at the shebeen any time, to smoke a skyf and play pool. He didn't have to do anything else if he didn't want to.

He was forced to abandon his next pool game. Some of the customers were lekker aan; they were up and dancing and bumping into Anthony's arm or the table. Ougat cranked up the volume and Michael Jackson's Rock with You blasted into the neighbourhood; there had been no more complaints about loud music after Mr Slamdien was arrested.

Anthony rolled another skyf and took it across to Ougat, working behind a table in the corner, slipping LPs onto a befokte new Blaupunkt hi-fi with an amp. He skimmed through the record stack while he waited for the skyf to be passed back. He didn't recognise most of the groups, Ougat seemed to favour music made by people with big Afros and tight pants.

The skyf made Ougat mellow. He came out from behind the table when Jermaine walked into the shebeen and greeted him with a big hug. "Long time brother, long time!"

Jermaine had been a regular at the shebeen until he disappeared a few months back. Anthony thought he was a Junky Funky, but none of the ouens seemed to care much when he stopped showing. Like Anthony, Jermaine was English-speaking and seemed to have gone far at school, but he had no interest in finding regular work. Ougat kept him busy.

"Ja, it's been a while," Jermaine said. "A lot happened since I last saw you. I thought I better come catch you up."

Ougat chased three customers off a bench and sat down with Anthony and Jermaine to hear the news. Anthony passed the skyf to Jermaine, who took three big hits before exhaling a wide stream of white smoke.

Jermaine started his story. "So I'm a father again."

Ougat interrupted. "What's new? You probably made a soccer team already, all on your own. Dunno why the kinners so mal for you."

Anthony could see why the girls chased after Jermaine. His straight hair was almost blonde and he had bright green eyes. He showed off his six-pack under white T-shirts tucked tight into his jeans. Jermaine could probably get a naai with a click of his fingers.

"Ja, I got a few laaities," Jermaine agreed. "But this time is different. I'm married now."

"Married! Nooit!" Ougat leaned back to stare into Jermaine's face. "Are you fokken out of your fokken mind? What you go do that for?"

"My wife's family is religious. They took it badly when she told them she's pregnant. Before I knew it they called the imam and organised the whole thing."

"The whole thing? Are you gesoenat?" Ougat stared down at Jermaine's zip.

Jermaine turned bright red. "No, I was circumcised already when I was small. I didn't have to do that. I got a new name. I'm Junaid now."

Ougat burst out laughing. Anthony snorted so hard snot shot out of his nose. He wiped it on the back of his hand, deposited it on his jeans and rocked the bench with his laughter. Hanover Park's Mr Casanova was trapped in a must-get-married. Was this the end of Jermaine's, sorry Junaid's, jas ways?

The young husband's face was serious. He stared at the Bob Marley poster while he waited for Ougat to stop laughing. "I got a baby daughter," he said when he got a chance to speak again. "She's almost a month old. Her name's Julayga."

"So how many girls is that now?" Ougat asked.

"Three girls."

Anthony felt sorry for Junaid. A few months ago, his big laugh was the first thing you heard as you walked to the shebeen and the last thing you heard when you left. Now he wasn't even smiling.

"Ougat listen, I'm sorry I haven't been around," Junaid said softly. "It's not easy for me. My wife's brother is a Nice Time Kid and I will be in big kak if he must find out I'm here."

Ougat frowned. "So what's the problem with you being here? I got no trouble with the Nice Time Kids. What about us? We tight?"

"Ja, of course. We tight. But I got another problem Ougat. That's why I came to see you. My wife and me are living with my in-laws and it's rough. They got a boy and three girls still at home. I need to find a place to stay. I need help with rent money. Just 'til I find a job."

Ougat smiled and klapped Junaid hard on his back. "My broer! You've come to the right place. Ougat will sort you out one time."

Anthony stared with realisation at Ougat when he reached into his back pocket. There was two meanings to Ougat's sort you out. It could mean he would fok with you one time if you fokked with him. But it could also mean he was there for you when you needed him. Anthony saw how Ougat gave his mother and sisters money every time they asked; and any neighbour who came with a sad story. No wonder they all believed Mr Slamdien was a drug dealer.

Ougat took out a stack of money, peeled off a few notes, kept them, and handed the pile to Junaid. "Here you go, brother. Come see me when you get a job. You got no obligation to me 'til you working. Best of luck, my broer."

Ougat patted Junaid on his back and stood up. The needle had reached the end of the LP, lifted up smoothly and swirled onto its rest.

Anthony went to hang with the ouens. Seemed he hadn't missed much while he was away, they were telling the same old stories. They were kwaai stories though. He missed the shebeen; it was the most interesting place in his kak boring life.

The dagga made him lekker loose. When Ougat played Get Down On It, Anthony got up to dance. A young woman joined him and got him to do the bump. His moves were smooth as he jiggeyed up and down and around her hips. He tripped over her feet and fell onto the floor as the song ended.

Ougat stretched out a hand to lift him to his feet. "Come laaitie. I wanna weetie."

Anthony followed Ougat through his dark lounge and kitchen and into the backyard. It was also cemented and enclosed by zinc sheets, filled with two chest freezers and stacks of Black Label crates. A naked bulb hanging from the roof crackled as it tried to shine some light. No wonder Ougat's place was a spook house. He came to a standstill in front of Ougat, who had seated himself on a chest freezer, and waited for him to talk.

"Listen up laaitie, I'm very chuffed with you," Ougat started. "You know how to keep your bek and you been loyal to me and the boys. You been working hard in the business. We gunna make you one of us."

"One of what?" Anthony couldn't figure out what Ougat meant.

"We plan on making you a full-on Junky Funky."

Anthony got such a big skrik he went deaf. Ougat's lips were moving but he couldn't hear a word. He could only do one thing: think. He couldn't think and listen at the same time. What must he think? His parents, and the police, thought gang members were criminals. Ougat was doing criminal things, selling alcohol and drugs. He was the leader of a war that killed more than twenty people.

"Don't you think I'm too young?" Anthony asked. His brain couldn't think of anything else to say. Anyway, that was what he was thinking.

"Nooit, man. I wasn't much older than you when I became a full on Junky Funky. You ready, I scheme."

Anthony didn't feel ready. He had only come to the shebeen for a couple of games of pool and some company. He didn't expect this to happen. He decided to be honest. "Ougat, I'm bang. I got bang some time back already, when Jackie Lonte came. That's why I stayed away from the shebeen 'til today. I don't wanna get involved in illegal things."

"You already involved. Don't you fokken get what I'm saying?" Ougat's thin voice went higher. His forehead shrunk to half its size. His black eyes bulged as he inhaled and pushed out his chest. He looked like a skinny, short, coloured Hulk. "You piemped to anyone about Jackie and me?"

"No, no, I didn't," Anthony fell over his words. "I will never tell. Who will I tell?"

"You better hou jou bek. You will, 'cause you gunna be a full on Junky Funky. Your dedda is in the neighbourhood watch, right? When Jackie brings my supplies I gunna need storage. Fokken police not gunna search a watch member's place. You got my pille, right?"

Anthony had thought about bringing the Mandrax tablets he had hidden behind the TV stand. He decided to leave them there. Nicky complained about soldiers in Casspirs patrolling the streets and searching young people. He didn't want to be caught with the pille.

"Ja, I still got your pille. But I dunno about Mandrax. You can go to jail for a long time if the police catch you." Anthony was so deep in the kak he was swallowing it. He had to find a way to get out before it got deeper. "I want to think on this. Can I tell you my answer tomorrow?" He needed more time to come up with a reason why he couldn't become a Junky Funky.

Ougat jumped off the freezer and stood chin-to-chin with Anthony. "Don't fok with me laaitie. Djy's myne. You belong to me. Tell me now – are you with the Junky Funkies or against them? Or you think you too kwaai for us?"

Anthony didn't see Ougat's hand until it smacked into his cheekbone. His teeth knocked together. His eyes boiled in redhot tears. There was only one thing to say. "Ja, I'm with the Junky Funkies." Any other answer would set the gang on his gat. Someone would come sort him out.

Ougat grunted. "You be here eight o'clock on Thursday. I got something extra special lined up for you. Tell your dedda you won't come home 'til late."

Tears poured down Anthony's aching cheek, curved around his chin and dripped down his neck. If he opened his mouth he would tjank like a baby. Ougat didn't look like he minded when he nodded his reply. He couldn't stay here a second longer. He had to go home. He rushed to the kitchen door, stopping to nod again when Ougat shouted at his back.

"Don't let me come looking for you, laaitie! You don't want that."

A small boy ran home from the shebeen, crying all the way. Anthony was poepscared. His life was a horror film and he couldn't see a way back to his bioscope seat. He didn't want a knife in his back. He also didn't want to be a full-on gangster. He was too young. Going to the shebeen was the worst idea he ever had. He should have stayed at home with his schoolbooks.

He kept his head down as he sped across the courtyard at Magnolia Court and rushed up the stairs. His face was filled with tears and snot. Anthony threw his keys down when he came into the flat, went to the bathroom and washed his face in cold water. He checked his right cheek in the mirror. It was a bit red; that was better than blue or purple. Mummy was coming home soon. He had to pull his face straight.

He went to sit at the kitchen table with his books. He had to work hard to stop crying again. He bent his head over his history textbook, forcing his mind to concentrate on the war between the Dutch and the British in 1795 for control of the Cape. His cheeks were dry when he heard Mummy's key in the front door.

Chapter Eighteen

Nicky got to know Kevin very well while he was in detention. He was his mother's favourite topic of conversation. She saw Mrs Van Wyk every day – for an hour after school while she wrote exams and more when the July school holidays started. She had known Kevin for two years but she knew nothing about his home life. The more she found out, the more she admired.

Unless Mrs Van Wyk was a liar, and Nicky didn't think she was, Kevin did everything for his mother. He wasn't only her son – he was her shopper, cleaner, cook, gardener, family and best friend. Mrs Van Wyk called him 'my little man' when she wasn't calling him 'my gift from God above'.

Kevin's mother didn't spare any details. She had him when she was forty-four years old; a year after her change of life had started and she had given up on having a child. Her heart was damaged during her three days of labouring to give birth, she hadn't been able to do much since then. After his father died when he was nine years old, Kevin took over the running of the home.

Nicky didn't know how Kevin coped. He did well at school, he always had meetings to attend and his mother needed him to do almost everything for her. She made Nicky tired. When Mrs Van Wyk's neighbour offered to send a plate of food every night, she kissed the woman. That left her with only the cleaning and some shopping. It took long hours to comfort Mrs Van Wyk every time the security police tried to break her dicky heart.

Mrs Van Wyk went four times to the security police headquarters in town to apply for a permit to visit Kevin. Each time they made her wait for hours before they told her they weren't issuing any permits;

155

she had to come back next week. They refused to accept the parcels of clothes and food she put together carefully. They wouldn't take Kevin's schoolbooks. Mrs Van Wyk came home from her trips to Loop Street with palpitations.

The Detainees Parents Support Committee did a lot. There was always someone available to drive her to Loop Street and back. Relatives lucky enough to get visits brought news about Kevin. Three weeks after he was detained, Mrs Van Wyk received a letter from Kevin. Nicky read it until she had it memorised.

"My darling Mummy," his letter started. "I think about you every day. I close my eyes and imagine you are giving me one of your warm hugs. I can feel your arms around me."

Nicky whispered the loving opening words of the letter into her pillow every night. She woke up every morning with her arms wrapped around her waist; she never used to sleep like that. She was doing things she never did before, thinking things she never thought before.

"I know you are worrying about me but you mustn't," Kevin wrote. "We are very comfortable here. Our days are organised. We study or have discussion groups in the mornings and we have games in the afternoons. We have a soccer league, and it turns out I'm a very good goalie. I prefer to play chess but the guys insist I stand in the goal posts. I'm getting very fit."

The lines that got her all worked up came next: "Please tell Nicky that I heard she's been coming to help you and that I will be forever grateful. You can rely on her, Mummy; she is one of the best people I know – after you, of course."

Kevin ended his letter urging his mother to be strong. "I will be home soon. The end is in sight. Apartheid's jails are getting fuller by the day but the streets are still thronging with people demanding freedom. They can't hold us back any longer. One day you and I will live in a free country, and this separation will look like a small sacrifice. Hugs and kisses, Kevin."

The letter was filled with good news, but Mrs Van Wyk cried like her heart was breaking when Nicky took it from her trembling hands, opened it and read it. She needed a lot of comforting afterwards.

Mrs Van Wyk had visitors every day. People from all walks of life came: black and white, rich and poor. A heart surgeon whose son was detained after he spoke at a student rally at UCT gave Mrs Van Wyk a free consultation at his rooms at City Park Hospital. He changed her medication, but she remained convinced that Kevin's detention was going to be the death of her.

The families of the detainees were angry. No reasons other than the state of emergency were given for the indefinite detention. No one was brought to court to prove that they had broken the law. Some of the people caught up in the swoop weren't politically active, but their relatives – and their friends like Nicky – were getting involved as a result.

Mrs Van Wyk received permission to visit Kevin one month and ten days after he was detained. She begged Nicky to go with to Victor Verster, not that she needed any convincing. It was a chance to get near to Kevin, close to one of his hugs.

Shamiela took them; she had a visit with her husband Moegamat on the same day. Nicky admired Shamiela. Nothing got the pint-sized woman down. It didn't faze her when her husband was fired from his job when his boss heard he was detained, she said the struggle would provide. She left her two children with her mother and campaigned night and day for the release of detainees.

Shamiela had persuaded her to join a picket outside the security police headquarters. Mrs Van Wyk said her heart couldn't take it, Nicky could hold up the placard the committee had made, demanding Kevin's release. From the pavement outside she couldn't see more than a door with tinted glass and security cameras above it swivelling in all directions, but she could imagine what it looked like inside. There was blood on the floor from the beatings.

Nicky sat in the front with Shamiela on the drive to the prison. Mrs Van Wyk was on the back seat with Shamiela's two daughters – Leila was eight and Nadia was six. They were chatterboxes dressed in identical pink dresses, white anoraks, white stockings and pink boots. All the way to Franschhoek they showed off the pile of drawings and cards they had made for their father, describing every picture and reading every card.

She had never been down the N1 before. She had never been to the Boland, although she had seen pictures in the newspaper and magazines. They turned off the highway before Paarl and headed south, towards Franschhoek. Rows of grapevines, slashed down to grey stick figures with arms outstretched, marched across fields and up the lower slopes of the mountain. Nicky hoped Kevin could see the mountains from behind the prison walls. It was probably beautiful in the summer if it looked so good under a cold August sky.

Shamiela braked sharply. Her rusted blue Mazda left the road and skidded onto the gravel verge. Nadia slid off the back seat onto the floor. Mrs Van Wyk clutched at her heart. "My goodness, are you okay?"

Nadia came up laughing, still holding onto the picture she had drawn for her daddy.

Shamiela took a deep breath. "Sorry everyone, I missed the turnoff." She reversed and turned into the prison. After a guard at the gate checked the permits and took down their details, they drove down a road lined with oak trees to the maximum security section where the detainees were being held.

Nicky was surprised how little she could see of the prison. She thought it would be one huge building with small windows surrounded by high walls and barbed wire. It was a collection of low buildings surrounded by fields of vegetables and wire fencing.

She thought she would wait in the car but Shamiela needed her inside. She alone had received permission for a visit, but she was planning to take her daughters in with her. She said it depended on the warder on duty. If he was a good guy in a good mood, there was a chance they could stay with her.

The cream-painted visitors centre didn't seem attached to the prison. Nicky didn't know whether she was glad or sad that they didn't have to walk through the jail. She imagined it to be a terrible place, full of dirty cells with small windows and air thick with the smell of unwashed men. If she didn't see the cells, she would keep dreaming about Kevin sleeping on a thin blanket on a cold cement floor. If she did see the cells and they looked like her dreams, all she would have was nightmares.

Mrs Van Wyk had a palpitation as they walked towards the waiting room. She waved her hand weakly across her face, which had gone pale and sweaty. Her knees buckled and she would have fallen to the ground if Nicky hadn't caught her around her waist. Shamiela saw what was happening and came to help lower Mrs Van Wyk onto the grass.

"I can't do this. I'm sorry, I just can't," the breathless woman choked the words out, waving her hand across her face. "I thought I was strong enough, but I'm not. It will be the death of me."

Nicky sank down to the ground next to Mrs Van Wyk. She reached into the sleeve of the old lady's cardigan and brought out a hankie to wipe the sweat off her face.

She looked up with a skrik when she heard Shamiela skelling. She looked just like a prison warder. Her jeans were tucked into black knee-high boots. Her legs were spread wide and her fists were in her waist. "This isn't the time for your hysterics. Stand up, Mrs Van Wyk. Stand up now!"

"I can't. I can't move. I think I'm dying," Mrs Van Wyk whispered.

"You not dying. Stand up."

Nicky couldn't believe the way Shamiela was talking. She had been admiring the woman, wishing she had her strength, but it seemed she got her all wrong. Shamiela was cruel. Mrs Van Wyk clutched her thigh, her fingers digging deep into her skin.

Nicky got cross. "Don't talk like that Shamiela. Can't you see …"

Shamiela interrupted before she could finish. "All I can see is a woman having the hysterics. Stand up Nicky, and help me get Mrs Van Wyk onto her feet."

"Shamiela, I think you being too hard. Mrs Van Wyk's heart isn't strong." Nicky was carrying all of Mrs Van Wyk's weight; she had collapsed against her like a corpse.

"There's nothing wrong with her heart," Shamiela said in a hard voice. "I saw Dr Finkelstein at last week's support committee meeting. He told me he examined her and her heart is as strong as a carthorse's. The only heart medication she's on is half a Disprin a day. Get up, Mrs Van Wyk. Visiting's in five minutes and we don't want to be late."

Nicky got to her feet, shocked by the news. Mrs Van Wyk's next best topic of conversation after Kevin was her dicky heart.

"You having a panic attack, Mrs Van Wyk," Shamiela said, crouching behind the old woman, circling her arms around her waist and pulling her onto her feet. "That's the only thing wrong with you. You have panic attacks and then you can't breathe. There's nothing wrong with your heart."

Mrs Van Wyk stared down at the ground. Nicky felt sorry for her. Even if she didn't have a heart ailment, she wasn't strong. She had been panicking about Kevin from the minute the security police arrived to take him away.

Shamiela's voice softened, but was still very firm. "We spoke about this, Mrs Van Wyk. Right now, Kevin needs you to be strong. He needs to hear from you that everything's fine. You gunna make it worse for him if you make him worry about you. If they interrogate him and all he wants to do is get home to you, then he won't be able to cope. He's going to piemp everyone just to get out. He's gunna make it harder for a lot of people."

Mrs Van Wyk shut her eyes tight. An eina moan started low in her throat and squeezed out of her mouth. She took a deep breath. Then another. She tried to talk but all that came out was another moan. Eventually she found her voice. "I'm so scared," she said softly. "You talk about interrogation like it's nothing. What if Kevin was assaulted? What if he's full of bruises? I couldn't bear it."

"He hasn't been assaulted. We would have heard if he was." Shamiela smiled and offered her arm. "C'mon Mrs Van Wyk. You got a letter from him telling you he's okay. There's nothing to worry about. The only thing you must worry about is being strong so you can give him the strength to get through this."

Nicky understood why Shamiela was so hard. It was important that Mrs Van Wyk's visit went well. Kevin was probably worried about her. "You can do this, Mrs Van Wyk," she said. "You can be strong for Kevin."

Mrs Van Wyk took another deep breath. "Okay," she said. She opened her handbag and took out a compact. She examined her face in the small mirror and patted down her steelwool hair with her free hand. Shamiela lifted her left arm and looked at her watch.

As Mrs Van Wyk started her careful steps towards the visitors centre,

Leila and Nadia ran towards her and each took a hand. Shamiela smiled at Nicky as they took up position behind them, "Kevin's going to be alright; you can stop worrying so much."

Nicky lowered her head, hiding her embarrassment. Could everybody see how her feelings had changed for Kevin? Would he see it in her face when he came out? How was he going to respond?

Nicky stationed herself and the two girls in the doorway between the waiting room and the visiting area when Shamiela and Mrs Van Wyk went in. The visiting area was divided into long rows of booths, the prisoners and their visitors separated by thick glass. Nicky couldn't see any telephones for the people to talk through, like they had in the films.

"There's my daddy, I can see him!" Leila shouted, jumping up and down. "Hello Daddy, here I am!"

"I can't see. Where's he?" Nadia sounded ready to cry. Nicky picked her up. She realised she couldn't help the child; she had never met Moegamat. Her eyes scanned the room until she spotted Shamiela in a booth on her left, about three booths down from where they were standing. "There's your mummy," she told Nadia. "Watch her, your daddy will come to her."

Nadia wriggled out of Nicky's arms. "I see him. Hello, Daddy!"

Nicky finally saw Moegamat. He was in the booth directly opposite the doorway, blowing kisses to his daughters above the heads of the young man seated on his side and the woman visiting him. He was dark and skinny, like Shamiela and the girls, tall enough to lean over his comrade's head to plant his palms on the glass. A warder in a khaki uniform came up behind him and pulled him away.

Before Nicky realised what they were doing, the girls rushed to their mother and climbed onto her lap. Shamiela lifted them up to kiss Moegamat through the glass. Nicky had heard a lot about him, from Shamiela and Dedda. Moegamat was a member of the neighbourhood watch and the Hanover Park Civic Association. Dedda said he had supported him when he spoke out about the students' attacks on women who broke the consumer boycott. Moegamat's detention made Dedda more determined to support Nicky against Mummy.

As she stepped out of the doorway, Nicky realised that Kevin was closer to her than he had been in five weeks, probably only metres away. She went back and looked up and down the visitors' room for Mrs Van Wyk. Maybe she could do what Leila and Nadia did – slip into the booth and visit without a permit. Nicky couldn't find her. She couldn't see into the booths at the far end of the room.

She hugged her arms around her waist. With all the drama of the palpitations outside she had forgotten to give Mrs Van Wyk a message to pass on to Kevin. As they drove to the prison she had worked out what she wanted to say. He shouldn't worry about anything at home; it was all under control. She wanted to say that she missed him, but she was too shy to tell his mother that. She had planned on telling him that she missed their arguments.

A warder with a boep spilling out of his khaki pants spotted Leila and Nadia in the booth with Shamiela. "Wat maak djy!" his voice was loud above the noise of conversations shouted through holes in the thick glass. "Only one visitor a prisoner."

Nicky took a step into the visiting area. She wasn't sure what to do, but Shamiela seemed to have the situation under control. She smiled at the warder. "I'm sorry, the girls ran in when they saw their daddy. I'm taking them out just now."

"Take them out right now or I'm cancelling your visit."

"Okay, they leaving. Say goodbye to your daddy."

The girls left the booth, blowing kisses to their daddy. Nicky couldn't believe how brave they were. She would have had the horries if it was her dedda behind the glass and she was told to leave him behind.

She took Leila and Nadia out of the visiting centre to sit on the grass outside. The clouds had opened up and the fields to their left were neon green in the sunshine. She gave the girls the chips and juice Shamiela had packed in for them and pretended they had come to the Boland for a picnic.

The visitors came out half an hour later. Mrs Van Wyk looked ten years younger. She danced on tippy toes towards Nicky and gave her a tight hug. "I told Kevin you were waiting outside and he said to give you his regards and this hug. He's fine; there isn't a mark on him. Isn't that marvellous? And he's in high spirits. He hasn't been interrogated at all and he doesn't know if he's going to be. Isn't that wonderful?"

Nicky relaxed in Mrs Van Wyk's arms, enjoying Kevin's hug. She hoped the woman would calm down now and give her a little bit of time off so that she could enjoy the last week of her holiday. She hadn't seen Shirley in three weeks.

Chapter Nineteen

The queues at the Strand Street taxi rank in front of Cape Town Station grew early on Fridays. From four o'clock there was guaranteed to be a wait, even with the rows of taxis lining up to cart passengers to the Cape Flats. People hung out of trains heading out of the station; the lines at the bus terminus were just as long as those at the taxi rank.

Neville walked as fast as he could across the Grand Parade, keeping his head down. The rain was coming at him. If there was a God, the angry voice in his head said, He had just washed His hands and was flicking His fingers directly into his eyeballs. His grey trousers and black windbreaker were soaking wet in the front and bone dry at the back.

He sighed when he reached the edge of the parade and saw the thick crowd at the corner waiting for the robots to change. There was going to be a moerse long queue at the rank. Friday night traffic flowed slowly down the four lanes of Strand Street towards the offramp onto the clogged Eastern Boulevard highway. Neville rushed across when the green man appeared. He hoped the Kentucky he bought on Darling Street would still be warm when he finally got a seat. He planned on keeping it on his lap.

His queue was always the longest. The Hanover Park taxi rank was a feeder for Mitchells Plain. Thousands of their people came through Hanover Park every morning and every night. Gaartjies hung out of the doors of the taxis lining the pavement, shouting out their drivers' destinations. "Wynberg! Step right up! Step right up for Claremont here! Quick Auntie, that's right, step up."

There was no shelter from the rain in the queue on the pavement.

Neville decided to keep facing it head on, holding the paper bag behind his back in the hopes of keeping the chicken warm. He didn't see who it was that grabbed his arm. He turned to find Herbert Ontong, the chairman of the neighbourhood watch. He smiled. "Herbert, nice to see you man."

Herbert looked very serious. "I was waiting for you, Neville. I got something I want to talk to you about."

Neville bent his head close to Herbert's lips so he could hear him through the wind and the gaartjies' shouting.

"The neighbourhood watch is branching out," Herbert announced. "We gunna be moving into prevention work. I plan to bring it up at the next executive committee meeting and I'm hoping to get your support. The plan is to work on reducing the number of young men who join the gangs. To cut them off from the head of the snake."

Neville nodded, it sounded like a plan. Get less people to join the gangs. It would make them easier to watch.

"People are approaching us all the time," Herbert explained. "They know we anti-gangsterism so they bringing all their gang-related troubles to us."

Neville nodded. "Ja, we get good intelligence most places we patrol. There's hardly a corner that's taken when someone comes to tell us about it."

"That's just one part of it. There's parents coming to us saying their children are associating with the wrong types but they don't know how to stop them. They complaining about the drugs. The boys are getting hooked on Mandrax. They causing problems for their families."

"Too true," Neville said. "There's a boy like that at Magnolia Court, Ricardo April. He got good parents; he's a clever boy. But he got addicted to Mandrax and he dropped out of school, now he just lies on the couch the whole day. Magda says his parents complain all the time about him. I been meaning to have a talk to the boy."

"Now's your chance. Ricardo's parents asked the watch for an intervention. It's happening tonight. I want you to come with me. Like you say, the boy lives on your block. You can keep an eye on him afterwards."

Neville reached the front of the queue, the conversation had to wait.

He shuffled to the back seat of the taxi and settled himself next to the window. Herbert and another man joined him on the bench seat covered in black vinyl. Just as they settled down, the gaartjie ushered a woman down the aisle towards them. When she finally squeezed her hol into a space half its size, Neville popped forward like a Toffolux from a tube. He nearly crushed the box of chicken on his lap.

He turned to Herbert, who was struggling to pull his right arm free from behind the woman's back. "What's a intervention?"

Herbert grunted as he got his arm out. "It's when you stop something from happening before it happens. It's a big thing in criminology right now. I been reading up on it. They call it diversion programmes."

Neville was still in the dark. "So what you gunna do to Ricardo?"

"Not just me, you also. We gunna talk to him; we must point out to him the error of his ways. But we must also listen to him. Might be something in his life is causing him to be this way. A lot of the time you find these youngsters got problems in the homes. You got to take away all his reasons to do drugs."

Neville nodded. The chicken was lekker warm on his lap. His brain was starting to defrost. He checked with Herbert to see if he got it right. "So we must make things right for the boy, is that it?"

Herbert shook his head. "No, that's only half of it. He must also listen to his parents. He must face what he is doing to them. He must decide if he wants to keep hurting them."

It sounded like a great manoeuvre. Neville liked the idea. There was all kinds of dangers on the street, and the young men ran towards it like fools. In Hanover Park you needed everybody to keep an eye on your children. Your eyes couldn't be everywhere at once. Sometimes your problems got so bad you needed the support of your community to get through it. Wasn't only the church that could offer help.

Neville checked his watch as the taxi drew to a stop at the Hanover Park rank and the gaartjie flung the door open. He had one hour with his family before he had to meet up with Herbert for the intervention. They would eat together at the kitchen table, away from the TV. He felt a strong need to check up on his children. Even with the best parents they could go wrong sometimes. Look at what happened to the Aprils.

The holidays were over; the children were back at school five days

166

already. He had to find out how it was going. Suzette had to get into a study routine now already. Matric exams started in four months. He let Nicky run all over the place during the holidays; it was enough now. Maybe she could keep checking up on Mrs Van Wyk. But this wasn't the time for meetings and protesting.

He hoped Anthony learned his lesson. The boy wasn't stupid. He just wanted everything to come easy. It was hard keeping him inside for the holidays, but the boy needed a skrik. He had given Anthony the hiding a month ago but he still felt kak about it. Every time the Catholic brothers at the orphanage where he grew up so much as looked at a boy they loosened their belts.

Neville reached Magnolia Court. He chased away the young men in damp denim leaning against the wall. He stared at the graffiti they had painted a week earlier. 'HOSH' filled the wall with thick white letters, above a hellavu kak painting of a fist holding a long, sharp knife. He thought of something else the neighbourhood watch could do to stop boys joining gangs. They could have a fundraiser to buy paint to cover up the slogans. He decided to suggest a fundraising dance at the next meeting. This time, he would take his girls.

It was lekker warm in the kitchen when the Fourie family gathered around the table for supper. Magda had reheated the Kentucky in the oven and left the door open when she took it out. There was one gas heater in the flat. It was only used in the lounge. The family squeezed themselves around it every night until Anthony went to sleep on the couch. They piled their blankets high when they went to bed.

Neville kept it casual over supper. His children were good; there was no need to come down heavy on them. He started his questioning with the child who gave him the least trouble. "So Nicky, is it good to be back at school?"

"Ja, it's good to see Shirley again. I hardly saw her in the holidays; I was so busy with Mrs Van Wyk. But it feels funny to be back at school. I keep expecting to see Kevin, 'cause school was the only place I ever saw him. I keep expecting him to be coming around the corner."

Neville wasn't expecting this. He didn't know Nicky had such strong feelings for the boy. He had to divert her from Kevin and talk about detainees; he wanted to find out if she was learning in class, doing well.

Madga came to his rescue while he worked out what to say. "I think your dedda was asking about your classes Nicky, not your friends."

Neville watched Nicky's face fall. Magda could be so abrupt. She didn't have to cut the girl off like that. Nicky was sharing her feelings. His children had to be able to talk to him at all times about anything. "Ja, it must feel strange," he calmed his daughter. "Any news about when Kevin is coming out?"

"No, there's nothing. They can hold him for three months without giving a reason. In the Transvaal, they had a emergency before us. Up country they releasing the detainees, then they rearresting them immediately, with new orders. It's cruel, what they doing; to the families also."

Neville kept his voice firm. "Now that you back at school you got to pay attention to your studies, Nicky. You of no use to anyone if you haven't got an education. Magda, I think we should let Nicky have Saturday afternoons for her meetings and her protests. But the rest of the time she has to help at home and do her schoolwork. You can still visit Mrs Van Wyk after school, Nicky, not every day and not for long."

Neville pretended to ignore Nicky until he got to the end of his speech. She kept trying to interrupt him while he spoke. When he stopped she jumped right in.

"But Dedda, that's exactly what I was gunna say. I think that's why I keep thinking I'm seeing Kevin wherever I turn. I'm feeling guilty 'cause I'm not doing so much for him anymore. I was getting very involved in his life."

Neville could see Suzette understood what Nicky hadn't realised she was saying. She was giggling behind her hand. Suzette was growing up; she was learning to read people. He wondered if Nicky was old enough to fall in love. He was nineteen when he fell in love for the first time, with Magda.

Magda didn't seem to get what was going on. "Concentrate on your studies, Nicky. You must put that first. You won't keep getting high marks if you don't work for them."

Neville thought of a way to divert Nicky from talking about detainees. He looked at Suzette. This time he was more direct. "How's your school work going, Suzette?"

Suzette shrugged. "Okay. The usual."

Neville spotted Nicky hissing. Was she trying to interrupt again? "What's it Nicky?"

"Nothing Dedda."

He turned back to Suzette. Her answer hadn't satisfied him. "Are you learning new work?"

"We started revision already Dedda, that's all we doing every day. Revision."

Suzette didn't look at all interested when she spoke about school. But she never did. Neville had to keep her motivated for just four more months. He planned on sitting her down soon and drawing up a study timetable.

He knew how to make one of his children excited. "Anthony, your house arrest is over. You can go out tomorrow. What you gunna do?"

Anthony shrugged. "Dunno."

Neville couldn't figure this one out. Before he brought the bad report, Anthony had to be fetched home almost every night. "What you mean you dunno? Don't you want to see your friends? What about Enver from next door?"

Anthony's lips moved but little came out.

Neville couldn't make out what he said. "What? I can't hear you."

Anthony's next words disappeared into a chunk of drumstick. Magda gave him a quick slap on the back of his hand. "Speak up!"

Anothony shouted when he lifted his head. "I said you must be glad I want to stay home!"

Neville didn't know what to say to that. The boy had a point.

As he headed down the stairs for his appointment with Herbert, Neville reckoned that his children were okay. Teenagers were difficult. It was hard to talk to them. They didn't know how to speak to adults. Nicky had given him something to think about. A boyfriend was sure to take her mind off her studies.

The clouds had dried up and the wind had gone to make another place miserable; patrol wouldn't be so hard tonight. Neville and Herbert were setting out later than usual; first they had to do their intervention. Neville shook his friend's hand when he found him waiting at the bottom of the stairs at seven o'clock.

Mr April opened the door wide when they knocked. He had taken his teeth out, half his face sunk into his skull with his wide smile. His grey hair stood out in all directions. Neville was shocked by how he looked; the man had aged overnight.

First thing Neville spotted when he stepped inside was a wall unit with an empty space in the middle. His eyes found Mrs April on a couch opposite the unit. He walked over and shook her hand.

After they were all seated and Herbert and Neville said no thank you to a cup of tea, Herbert explained how the intervention would work. "I came here tonight, with Neville also, to listen to the whole family. Sometimes people get so caught up in their problems they can't see a way out. It helps to have someone else to listen and to try to understand all the sides of the story."

Mr April rubbed his hands and his gums together. Neville couldn't look in his direction. This was no time to smile. He looked around while Herbert spoke. The Aprils were New Apostolics. There were three big photos of their saints on a wall. Coloured men, all in black suits and black ties with side paths combed into their kroes hair. New Apostolics paid their saints to pray for them, or the saints got a slice of the tithes, Neville wasn't sure how it worked. He had no truck with religion, not since the orphanage.

He tuned into the conversation again. Herbert was asking where Ricardo was.

"He's in the kitchen, I'll go get him," Mrs April lifted herself from the couch. She didn't dress like a New Apostolic. Her fleshy thighs rubbed together in her navy blue pants as she walked. Her shirt was tucked into the pants, showing off her broad hips and bum.

Neville stared at another picture on the lounge wall. Must be Mrs

April's grandparents; they were dark-skinned, like her. The photo was in a gold frame. The middle-aged couple was seated on a couch, both wearing cardigans. They looked like they just had a big fight with the photographer.

He turned his attention to Ricardo when Mrs April brought him into the lounge. The boy was tall and as thin as a pole. His torn, dirty jeans had a belt in the loops, but they hung low on his hips. His face was hidden under a peak cap pulled low on his forehead. The boy stared at the floor as he made his way to a chair in the corner of the lounge. He turned around and dropped down.

Mrs April took her seat on the couch again. The lounge was quiet as a coffin.

Herbert cleared his throat. "Folks, we here for a reason tonight. Can anyone tell me what that reason is?"

Everyone kept their mouths shut. Neville realised he didn't know enough about how interventions worked to know what to say. Herbert hadn't prepared him well enough.

Herbert leaned forward towards Ricardo, who slid down his chair. "Ricardo maybe you can tell us."

Ricardo balanced on his skinny shoulders, narrow hips and heels digging into the floor. "Dunno what's going on here."

Mrs April jumped in, her voice shrill. "You dunno what's going on here? It's all about you! That's all we talk about nowadays."

Herbert put up a hand. "Let's keep calm now. Give everyone a chance to talk. Mrs April, you sound like you got something to say. Why don't we start with you?"

Mrs April leaned back on the couch, making fists in her lap. Neville felt sorry for her as he watched her struggling to compose herself. It couldn't be easy raising a boy like this. He hadn't seen much of Ricardo's face, but his body showed he was bad news.

Mrs April took a deep breath. "I don't know when this business started. I noticed when my things went missing. First it was my small appliances. Then my video machine and my television."

Her voice grew more and more shrill as she listed Ricardo's crimes. Neville looked at Mr April. He was gumming furiously; his head bobbing up and down. He looked at the source of the problem. Ricardo was staring at his feet like it was a bioscope screen.

Mrs April was still going strong. "Ricardo denied it was him. He said people must of come into the house and taken the stuff when he wasn't looking. But I could see something was wrong. He stopped talking. He stopped eating. He stayed out all hours. We couldn't wake him in the morning to go to school. He didn't want to tell us what was wrong."

Mrs April had tears in her voice. Neville could appreciate that; she was right to be so upset.

Mr April piped up. "Then my wife's mother's ring went missing. It wasn't worth a lot, but it meant a lot to my wife. It was all she had left of her mother. Nothing else was missing in the drawer, just the ring she kept rolled up in her pantyhose."

Neville stared at Ricardo. The boy hadn't taken his eyes off his takkies while his parents spoke, their voices filled with pain. There was nothing special about them. The grey canvas probably once was white and the laces were missing.

Mrs April continued with the story. "The final straw was tonight. I'm glad you came here to help us sort this out. I can't take it anymore. I want him out of my house. Get out!"

Ricardo went from nought to a hundred in ten seconds. He was at the door.

Neville restrained him and brought him back to his chair. He didn't know what to do next; how to get the intervention moving. Maybe he should get Ricardo to talk. That was the point, wasn't it, to find out everybody's problems? "What happened tonight, Ricardo? Can you tell us? What is your mother talking about?"

Ricardo shrugged silently, his eyes glued to his shoes.

Mrs April couldn't hold it in any longer. "I'll tell you what happened, Neville. I found my lamb was missing from my freezer. I could take it when all my spare sheets and my towels were stolen by this … by this bastard. Even when the mattress disappeared from his bed one day, I could take that. Let him sleep on cold bedsprings. But I can't take this. Not my lamb. It's his sister's confirmation on Sunday and I invited all our family to lunch after church. Now what am I going to serve them? Rice and potatoes? Or will my rice be stolen by Sunday?"

Mrs April was tjanking by the time she finished. Neville was also upset. This was a vuilding. A confirmation lunch was a big thing in a young girl's life. Ricardo's Mandrax addiction was his whole family's problem. Neville stared hard at the boy. Ricardo showed no interest in anything that was being said.

Mrs April spoke through her tears. "I don't understand what kind of drug dealer will take meat from an addict. Or sheets, or towels. What they going to take next? I want Ricardo to go. He has taken enough. I want him out of my house."

This time Herbert jumped to stop Ricardo when he stood up and headed for the door. He pushed him back into his chair.

Neville could understand why Mrs April felt the way she did. But it wasn't helping Ricardo. He couldn't see what problem the boy had; all he could see was what a problem he was for his parents. It must be hard to live with him.

Mr April didn't think so. "You see, that's where you wrong, lovey. I think we must give the boy a chance …"

His wife interrupted. "Give the boy a chance, that's all you have to say! How many chances must we give him? 'Til there's nothing left to steal in this house?"

Mr April waited 'til his wife was finished. "I was going to say, give the boy a chance to say where the meat is. It's not too late; he can go fetch it. Tell us Ricardo, where's your sister's confirmation meat?"

Four heads turned to look at the teenager, who had slid his head sideways onto his shoulder. He grunted in the direction of his chest. "How must I know? I dunno nothing about confirmation meat."

Mrs April wailed. "I can't take it anymore! I want this boy out. He's gemors!"

Mr April coughed softly. "See my dear, that's where we differ. We can't throw the boy onto the streets. Where will he go? Probably to the people who got him into this state in the first place. They'll be only too happy to make him worse. We can't give up on him now that he's got a problem."

Neville didn't know what to think. He could see why Mrs April was so angry. But Mr April also had a point. Parents couldn't give up on their children; not even when they were rubbishes like Ricardo. The gangs were full of children whose parents had given up.

When Herbert adjourned the intervention, Neville was relieved, it didn't look like they were getting anywhere. Ricardo was up on his feet and out of the flat before they made a time for the next discussion.

While they patrolled through the bitter night Neville and Herbert struggled to come up with a way to help the April family. Neville wore his pyjama pants under his jeans, a long-sleeved vest, a T-shirt, a jersey, a jacket and a reflective vest but it wasn't enough to stop his bones from freezing. He hugged his arms around his chest.

There wasn't much activity on the streets. The young men on the corners stared at their sparking braziers like they were longing to climb inside. Only the most desperate alcoholics and addicts would go out on a night like this.

There was plenty of time to talk. Neville couldn't figure out what was the best way forward for the Aprils. He was leaning towards Mr April. The man was right. Parents couldn't walk away when their children were in trouble. He didn't think he ever would. "I had a talk with my children before we came out," he told Herbert. "Just checking on them, you know. No matter how vigilant you are the children can still go wrong."

Herbert nodded. "I'm with you on that. There's lots of people who complain about crime but they don't see what's under their own noses."

"I'm worried about my daughter Nicky. I let her run around the whole holiday supporting families of detainees. Now it sounds like she's fallen for a comrade. We been very lucky with Suzette. She's eighteen already and she never had a serious boyfriend."

"Your children are lucky to have you and Magda. You two got such dreams for them. There's too many parents who say nothing when their children drop out of school."

Neville had made himself a lot of promises in the orphanage. He had promised himself he would have children one day. He promised he would always be there for them. He promised he would never hit them. Half of the children at the orphanage had parents who were still alive. Neville had been left on the steps when he was a few days old.

This was something he never brought up, not with anyone besides Magda. "I was raised in an orphanage, you know," he told Herbert carefully. "I swore to myself that one day my children would have both parents and grow up in a loving home."

Herbert came to a standstill. A cloud of warm air escaped from his mouth. "I know you so long already and I never knew that! I never thought to ask you about your parents but I never realised you didn't know them."

"Ja, for all I know they could be the king and queen of England. But that wasn't my point. The priests at the orphanage gave us a hard time. Some of them were pure evil; I don't want to even tell you the things they did. I don't go to church because of them."

"Well, look at you today," Herbert said like a true friend. "Look how you turned out despite your hard beginnings. You could have easily become a Ricardo. You could have done anything and blamed your parents."

"Ja, that's why I'm with Mr April. It's a hard choice to make, to walk away from your children. I don't think I have it in me to do that."

"You, me and the Aprils – we the exception."

Neville patted his friend's shoulder. Herbert was still there for his son, months after his murder. The police hadn't arrested any suspects, and he wouldn't let it rest. He had written a letter to the Progressive Federal Party to ask them to ask Parliament about the status of the investigation. One of the lawyers at Neville's firm suggested that he try that to get answers from the minister of police.

At the end of their night's patrol, Neville promised Herbert he would keep a close watch on the April family and that he would support his motion to expand the work of the watch to include interventions. Herbert had heard of an organisation that was like Alcoholics Anonymous, but for drug addicts. He planned to track them down and ask them to help the April family and train the neighbourhood watch in diversion programmes.

Neville's children were all asleep in bed when he came in from patrol. He could spare some time to keep an eye on Ricardo. His children were doing fine, but that didn't mean that he could drop his vigilance.

Chapter Twenty

Suzette's life changed forever on the second week of August. Her school report, and Nicky's, came in the post. They were on the display cabinet, where she always dropped her keys when she came home from work. She would be in big kak if she looked at it before her parents. Besides, she already knew she failed, she hadn't written one exam.

She hadn't yet come up with a way to tell Mummy and Dedda that she had dropped out of school two months ago and found a job. But what was done was done, all they had to do was get used to it.

She knew she had it in her to be a fashion model. All her friends thought she could make it – her old friends from school and her new ones at work. Even Maureen, Neil's friend who worked at *Fairlady*, could see she had it. Mummy and Dedda didn't see because they didn't look at her properly. All they saw was someone in line with their plans, kak as they were.

Neil couldn't take his eyes off her a few hours ago when he came to the factory to see the new line. He winked when she came onto the ramp. She couldn't look in his direction while she strutted across the stage, her cheeks cooked when she remembered what he did to her. On her very last turn, before she came to a halt near the edge of the ramp, she looked at him and couldn't pull her eyes away. Melanie had to whistle to get her to move.

Neil's Golf was parked outside the factory when she came out of the gate. He jumped off the bonnet when he spotted her. His eyes crinkled. "Howzit?"

Suzette let him pull her into his hips when she reached him. His lips were just as soft as she remembered. Her eyes closed, the world disappeared. A shrill noise pulled her back. She turned to find Melanie among a group of women on the pavement. Her friend had two fingers between her lips; she was almost as loud as the factory siren.

Melanie pulled her fingers out and grinned. "Lekker show you putting on Suzette. It's like a Officer and a Gentleman. At Planet Fashions nogal."

Neil burst out laughing and pulled away from Suzette. "I should have carried you out. It's starting to rain. Let's go. Show's over, ladies." He opened the passenger door.

Neil leaned over the gearbox to give Suzette another kiss after he got into the car. This time, their tongues got involved in the action. He was as sexy as Richard Gere. It did feel like he came to carry her away.

She and Melanie loved *An Officer and a Gentleman*. They met at the Luxurama bioscope in Wynberg for the two o'clock show and stayed for the next one. Both times Melanie cried at the end. She really believed that if a factory worker in America could get a befokte guy in a film, it could happen to her also.

Suzette hadn't seen Neil for two weeks, not since the weekend that she first had sex with him. They had gone on a drive the next day. She had seen Cape Point for the first time, it was kwaai but she would have preferred it if he had taken her to his flat. She was jas for him.

She phoned him twice since, and he seemed all friendly, but he didn't ask her out again. In a way she was glad, she didn't know how she was going to get it right to see him. She had to wait a while before she asked Mummy and Dedda if she could sleep out again.

Neil looked at her meaningfully before he started the car. "I missed you girl. Thought about you a lot. Sorry I wasn't around. My sister got married; it was a week-long affair."

She wondered why he didn't invite her to the wedding. Maybe he wasn't ready to start going out with her yet. Maybe he didn't want his family to know he was seeing someone who wasn't white. She said it was okay.

He smiled at her. "We're not buying right now, but when I heard Planet Fashions had a new line to show today, I came to see you. How've you been?"

"I been good."

Suzette spoke easily to Neil as he headed down Prince George Drive. Christopher Cross's Sailing was playing on the car radio. At full speed, the windscreen wipers couldn't keep up with the rain beating down. It felt like she was with Neil on a yacht, like in the Peter Stuyvesant ad at the bioscope, the two of them drifting far away from the rest of the world.

Neil argued with her when they reached Lansdowne Road. He didn't want to leave her at the bus stop in the rain. He wanted to spend more time with her. His eyes ate her up like a puppy staring at a braai chop. "Why don't you come out with me tomorrow night? There's a great film on at the Labia."

"That would be kwaai ... very nice," Suzette sukkeled. When would the time come when she could talk to Neil without sounding stupid? Couldn't he hear in her voice where she was from, what kind of person she was? That was a problem. "Can we go to the bioscope together? I'm not white."

Neil stroked her cheek and laughed. "Don't worry about that. The Labia's different. Everybody goes there. It's kiff, you'll see."

Neil's car windows were misted up with kisses when he pulled away. Suzette had to find a way to get out of the house tomorrow night. She would tell Mummy and Dedda the church youth was having a meeting. She could always get away for that.

Neil's kisses sent her floating home on a soft, white cloud of smoke like the one that rose up the stage when the supermodels came together for a finale. There was no blerrie way Suzette was going to let her report spoil her mood. She went to lie on her bed with a magazine.

Her mind kept her too busy to read. She had a problem to solve before Mummy and Dedda got home. Neil said the bioscope was down the road from his flat. The film started at eight o'clock; they could go back to his place afterwards. She wouldn't take cocaine again. It made it hard for her to leave. Actually, she thought with a smile, it made Neil so hard she couldn't leave.

Nicky interrupted her jas thoughts as she rushed into the bedroom. The girl was in a state. The words came so fast out of her mouth that Suzette sukkeled to make out what she was saying.

"Our reports came! Did you see they came? Now what you gunna do? What you gunna say to Mummy and Dedda? You in big kak, you know that?"

Suzette leaned back on her pillow. "What you want me to do?"

"Dedda and Mummy gunna find out you been bunking. Don't say I didn't warn you. You didn't write exams. In minutes, they gunna find out."

"Ja, you already told me that. Go away. Can't you see I'm reading?" Suzette picked up the magazine and lifted it high to block out her sister's face. She listened while Nicky and Anthony spoke about her in the lounge. Anthony said he hoped she got a hiding. Nicky said she was in big kak. She kept repeating herself. Big kak.

Suzette heard the door opening a few minutes later. Dedda was home before Mummy; she must be working overtime again, the new season was coming. Anthony couldn't keep his big bek. "Hello Dedda. Suzette's and Nicky's reports came today. Must I fetch them for you?"

"Leave it, my boy. I will look at them when Mummy gets home."

Suzette tuned them out while she prepared what she was going to say later. She had plans. They weren't what Dedda and Mummy wanted for her, but they were good plans. Planet Fashions wasn't the dream job, like Maureen called it, but it was a start.

Mummy came to say hello after she came in, fastening the buttons of her pink-checked housecoat as she walked into the girls' bedroom. When she spotted the magazine in Suzette's hands she ordered her up to peel potatoes for the tinned pilchards smoortjie she was planning for supper.

Nicky and Anthony didn't get a chance to squeal about the reports at the supper table. Mummy got so worked up that no one got a word in edgeways. Sharnay – the oldest daughter of Mummy's only sister Violet – was pregnant. She was getting married next week. It was the worst skandaal that could have happened to the family.

Suzette knew what was coming next. Whenever Mummy heard something bad about other peoples' children she convinced herself hers were going to be next. She always thought the worst of her children, even when they did nothing.

"You children must make sure you say nothing to nobody at the wedding." Magda put down her fork to wave her finger at Suzette for a full minute like PW Botha, then she turned and waved it at Nicky and Anthony. "If people ask you why Sharnay got married so quickly, you say you don't know. You hear me?"

Then she asked the same thing she asked a million times before. What would people say? She knew all the answers. They would say that Violet was a bad mother. That Sharnay was a loose girl. They would say shame; she comes from such a good Christian family.

Mummy thought the worst of everyone, not just her children, Suzette realised. She tried hard to think about Neil, but she couldn't tune the lecture out. She looked across the table. Nicky had a finger twisting deep inside one ear, probably to block Mummy's voice.

"I expect to see a ring on all yours fingers when you bring grandchildren to my house, you hear me?"

Suzette nodded when she heard that for the two-hundred-and-fifty-nine-millionth time. Nodding like you agreed was the quickest way to get Mummy to shut up. This time it didn't work.

From the kitchen sink where she was washing up after supper Suzette heard big bek Anthony, in the lounge with Mummy and Dedda, reminding them about the reports. Nicky put the dishcloth down and went to join them. Suzette stared into the rice pot she was scrubbing without thinking, getting her story straight in her head.

She heard Dedda's voice. "Well done, bokkie. I'm proud of you." He must have read Nicky's report first.

There was silence again. Dedda must be reading her report while Mummy took a happy look at Nicky's. Wasn't long now. Was Dedda going to give her a hiding with his belt? She wasn't going to let him; she was a working woman, he couldn't treat her like a child.

Neville finally got the picture. "Suzette! Come here. Come here right now, girl!"

Suzette rinsed the pot under the tap and placed it on the draining rack. She shook her hands over the sink. She turned to pick up the dishcloth Nicky had draped over a kitchen chair and dried her hands. She took her time, making sure both were dry.

Neville was at the kitchen door. "Suzette! Didn't you hear me calling you?"

"Coming Dedda. Just drying my hands."

Neville waited 'til she got to the lounge before he waved the report in her face. "What is this? What is the meaning of this report?"

Suzette swallowed. Her mouth was full of spit. She didn't want to get it all over Dedda, he was already cross. She told her story carefully. "I dropped out of school, Dedda. I got a job. It's not the job of my dreams but it's a start."

Dedda was staring at her like she was mal. Suzette didn't want to look in Mummy's direction, she was too bang. She stared across the lounge floor. A carpet tile was coming loose near the front door.

Neville had more questions. "You got a job? Are you out of your mind? You got a job when you only got four months left in school?"

Magda reached out a hand. "Let me see that report. Neville, give it to me."

The lounge went quiet while she studied it. Suzette stared at Anthony and Nicky, sitting on the couch smiling like malletjies. What did they know about her life? Nothing. She turned to Mummy when she started shouting.

"You better tell me right now what's going on, Suzette. This report says you been absent from school for two months. For every exam, it says absent." Magda's finger poked into the paper with every sentence, breaking through at the end of the last one.

Suzette's explanation came out exactly as she had it planned. "I'm a model, Mummy. At a factory. It's not so bad, we got a dressing room and all. I'm saving up for a portfolio. I'm going to take it to agencies and then maybe I will even pose for magazines one day."

"You saving up!" Magda screamed, sukkeling to get out of her chair. She wouldn't let go of the report, waving it in the air as she made it to her feet. "When you start working you work for all of us. But you not working now. Do you know how much your dedda and I sacrificed to get you into matric? You could have been working for us almost two years already if we took you out in standard eight, like most parents. What you take me for? A fool? I'm not your fool."

Suzette had never in her life seen Mummy so bedonnered. She

looked like she was going to burst a vein in her forehead and drop down dead onto the floor. Anthony was laughing at her, the fokken bastard. What did he know about her life, her dreams? She was living with strangers. It was bad enough they knew nothing about her; but they also weren't interested.

Magda had a question. "What's this factory where you working?"

"Planet Fashions, Mummy. In Retreat."

Magda's face screwed up like she was chewing sour figs. "What they make there? What orders they got? How many lines?"

There was no use lying, not this time. Mummy could ask at work and someone would know something about Planet Fashions. The girls at Mummy's factory moved jobs all the time. They had relatives and friends in the clothing industry across the Cape Flats. It wouldn't take long for Mummy to find out. "Women's fashions, Mummy. Nightwear and lingerie."

Magda took a step back, her bottom lip curling. "You walking around in underwear in front of strange men! A daughter of mine! And I didn't even know it. Neville! Say something! Shut up!" She turned around to smack Anthony who was laughing like a baboon.

Hot tears burned Suzette's eyes. Her life wasn't a joke. She had it all planned out. She was finished with school. That she knew for a fact. Soon as she had the tears coming up under control she would show them how blind they were.

Magda wasn't finished, she had a line to lay down. "No daughter of mine is going to be an underwear model, finish and klaar. What will people say if they must find out my daughter is an underwear model? Who did you tell about this?"

Suzette got in the moer in. That was all Mummy ever worried about – what will people say? Maybe they would say what she was doing was kwaai. Mummy knew nothing. There was people in the world who didn't think the whole world started and ended in Hanover Park. People who thought it was normal to want to be a model.

Neville came out in full support of Magda. "Suzette, I think Mummy said all there is to say. Tomorrow you will go to school. And you will stay there for four months and you will leave with your matric. I don't want to hear anything more about modelling, you hear me?"

Magda brought the conversation to a close. "I will pray every night that God gives me the strength to forgive you for your lies Suzette, because I haven't got any. I'm sure He will, after a while. Say you sorry and go back to school tomorrow and that's the end of it."

Suzette faced her parents. And her tarty sister and brother. It was time they found out who she was and what she was made of. "I won't go back to school. I'm a model. I'm in a factory now but one day you will see me in the magazines. You will all see."

Suzette didn't see the klap coming before it shocked its way across her face. Mummy aimed for her head next, one klap after another. She headed away from the heavy hand, out of the lounge and into the passage. The klaps came chasing after her, pausing only for Mummy's ugly words.

"No child of mine is going to be a underwear model. *Klap.* You might as well stand on the corner in your underwear. *Klap.* It's the same thing. *Klap.* I didn't raise you to be a hoer. *Klap.* Say you will go back to school tomorrow. *Klap.*"

No mother should call her daughter a hoer. Suzette turned to face her. "Mummy I won't."

She grabbed Mummy's hand when it came up again to hit her. When Mummy raised her other hand she twisted her around and gripped both hands tight behind her back.

"Hoer!" Magda hissed. "Look what you doing! You lost all your respect for your parents. That's what happens when take your clothes off for strange men."

Suzette let go. She waited 'til Mummy faced her before she spoke, her voice strong. "I'm not a hoer. I'm just a stranger living in your house."

"You right. I don't know you anymore. Get out of my house."

Suzette stared at Mummy. They both realised the same thing tonight. She didn't belong. She turned to go to her bedroom.

Magda shouted at her back. "Where you going? I told you to get out!"

Suzette stopped but she refused to turn around. "I'm going to get clean panties and other stuff. Do you mind?"

"Get your things and get out."

183

From her bedroom she could hear everyone talking over each other when Mummy joined the rest of the strangers in the lounge. She emptied her school haversack and left her books on the bed. She packed the new jeans she had hidden in a packet at the back of the wardrobe. Some clean panties, bras, socks and her takkies. She needed jerseys; it was freezing outside. Her haversack was full; she couldn't fit them in. She took out her takkies and squeezed a jersey into the bag.

When she walked past the lounge to get a packet in the kitchen for her shoes, the room went quiet. They kept still while she fetched her toothbrush and facecloth in the bathroom. The voices started up again when she went back to her room. Nicky's room now.

She made plans as she packed her things. She could go to Neil, ask him if he would let her stay awhile 'til she found somewhere to live. Somewhere close to work. She couldn't stay in town, she would spend too much on train fare, money she could use for her portfolio. She was going to show the Fouries who they once had under their roof.

She lifted her heavy haversack onto her back and picked up two packets with handles tied tight, it was raining hard outside. She hoped Neil was home. Now she could sleep at his place anytime she wanted. She answered to no one. It was a lekker feeling.

Suzette heard Dedda drukking Nicky as she walked to the lounge. "You must of noticed she was bunking. You at the same school."

Neville stopped talking when he saw her come in. He wouldn't meet her eyes. Mummy was staring at her as if she had horns coming out of her head. Nicky was tjanking, as usual. Anthony's eyes were big in his head.

Suzette stared at Dedda. He hadn't said anything when Mummy attacked her and called her a hoer. He hadn't told her to leave. She didn't know what he thought. He wouldn't look at her. She walked to the front door. No one said a thing. She opened the door.

Magda spoke in the voice she used to chase dogs off pavements. "Leave your keys."

Suzette dropped her keys on the display cabinet, put her head down and walked out. The icy rain slapped her as she made her way down the concrete stairs of Magnolia Court. She was grateful she was out of the flat. She was leaving; she was free of them.

Chapter Twenty-One

Anthony didn't know how to get out of his appointment with Ougat. He didn't want to be a full-on Junky Funky, whatever that was. He thought about it as hard as he could and the answer he came up with was always the same. He was in enough kak already.

Ougat promised to fetch him if he didn't pitch up to join with the JFK. He didn't want the gangster to come to the flat. He didn't want Dedda and Mummy to find out he had been hanging out at the shebeen. Ougat might tell Dedda he was working for him. Dedda might find out he was smoking dagga and storing Mandrax.

Look what happened when they found out about Suzette's lies. Dedda sat like a statue and said nothing when Mummy threw her out. There was a good chance they would chuck him out if Ougat came. Where would he go? He couldn't look after himself; he was only thirteen.

There had to be a way. Anthony scratched through his brain until he came up with an answer. What if he threw himself down the stairs and broke his leg? If he landed in the hospital, Ougat might leave him alone. He went onto the landing to check out how to drop. The stairs looked hard. There was a good chance he would be brain damaged if he landed on his head, like Ishmael on the third floor across the way. He was twelve years old and he still wore nappies.

Nah, that was a kak idea but he didn't have a better one and time was up. He was supposed to meet Ougat at the shebeen in four hours. Anthony was so caught up in his search for an answer that he didn't hear the door open and skrikked when his sister's keys dropped onto the display cabinet. "Yoh, Nicky! Can't you say something when you come in?"

Nicky frowned. "Since when you so worried about greeting? Can you even hear anything with the TV so loud?"

Anthony dropped back on the couch as his sister tutted in his direction like an old woman and left the lounge. He was carrying a cement lorry load of worry. His next idea wasn't too bad, considering the concrete setting in his brain. Nicky could help. Since Kevin was detained she had been helping people in trouble with the law. She was so busy going to police stations and prisons she hardly had time for her family. It wasn't like he asked her for a lot.

He walked to the kitchen, dragging a body that felt as heavy as Hulk's. Nicky was doing her homework at the table. He kept his voice casual, he didn't want to show how desperate he was. "What you doing?"

Nicky scowled as she looked up. "You blind? I'm doing my homework."

Anthony shifted on his overworked feet. He had to get moving, get her on his side. "I'm making tea. You want some?"

"You are blind! Can't you see I already got tea?"

Anthony stared at Nicky's mug next to her textbook, steaming into the icy kitchen. "I didn't see, okay? No need to get so worked up."

He switched on the kettle and opened the cupboard for a mug. His plan wasn't working; Nicky was ignoring him, her head down in her book. When his tea was made, Anthony pulled out a chair across from his sister and sat down.

Nicky looked up after his second loud slurp. "What you want?"

Anthony didn't know where to start. This was hard to explain. "There's this big problem I got. I dunno what to do. When Dedda and Mummy find out they gunna be the hell in."

"What problem? What don't Dedda and Mummy know?"

Anthony could hear the suspicion in his sister's voice, and he hadn't told her anything yet. "There's this dingus I got involved in and I dunno how to get out of it."

Nicky's frown sunk deeper into her forehead. "Anthony, this isn't the time for your nonsense. We all got enough problems. It's not fair that you and me's under house arrest because of what Suzette did. Dedda's going on like it's my fault she failed. The way he talks you think I was supposed to look after her instead of him."

Anthony didn't mind that he had to come home straight from school and stay there. He didn't want to go anywhere. Ougat or his ouens might spot him. Nicky was right on one thing though; Mummy and Dedda didn't need more kak. The Suzette thing made them deurmekaar. Dedda wanted to go look for Suzette, to see if she was okay. Mummy wouldn't let him. She said Dedda was going to find Suzette 'lying under some man somewhere'. Yoh, Mummy was cross! If she found out he was involved with gangsters that would be the end of him also.

Nicky was tired of waiting. "What you want Anthony? What secret you keeping from Dedda and Mummy?" She put her hand up when he started speaking. "Stop. I don't want to be in trouble again because I knew something and I didn't squeal. Tell Dedda and Mummy yourself. Wait 'til I'm out of the room."

Anthony wasn't going to stand for any more of Nicky's attitude. Her comrade friends were all criminals in jail, and she wanted to be the judge of him. He gripped his mug tight to stop himself from chucking his tea into her face. Who in the hell did she think she was? He got up so fast his chair toppled onto the floor.

Nicky stood up. "What's wrong with you? Don't be so mal."

Anthony's words came out in a mixture of squeaks and grunts; he was so the moer in he couldn't control his voice. "What's wrong with me? Why don't you ask yourself that? I hardly ask you for anything and today when I wanna ask just one thing, you got no time for me. You got no time for anyone, just your fokken comrade criminals."

He wanted to klap Nicky but he was out of time and he didn't want to waste any on her. He ran out of the kitchen.

"Where you going? Anthony, where you going!" Nicky shouted at his back.

He tore open the front door and turned to shout. "None of your fokken business. You the one who don't wanna know what I'm doing. What you asking for?"

He banged the door behind him and rushed down the steps, almost tripping as he reached the second-floor landing. He held tight onto the rail as he found his feet. He didn't want to break a leg. He wanted to get the fok away from Magnolia Court.

In a crock parked in the courtyard of Klipspringer Court, Anthony slid down the front seat, clutching his arms across his chest. There was no glass in any of the car's windows. The wet wind swept down the torn vinyl, creeping along his spine and down to his freezing feet.

He had been sitting there for hours and he still hadn't figured out what to do. Dedda and Mummy were probably home already and in the moer in. He was sure Nicky squealed on him; they knew by now he was keeping a secret.

He didn't know any families in Klipspringer Court; he was safe for a while while he worked out what to do next. It got dark early in winter; maybe Mummy and Dedda just got home and Nicky hadn't piemped him yet. When a man walked past the car Anthony asked for the time. Half past seven. Dedda would have been home for more than an hour, Mummy for close on two hours. He was already in big kak.

Time was up. He hoped his new plan worked. All he had to do was convince Ougat that he wasn't ready to the join the gang. The metal skeleton of the car door creaked as he pushed it open. He headed for the shebeen, his feet dragging in the wet sand.

Anthony rushed to the blazing brazier soon as he got to the shebeen. He held his frozen hands as close to the flame as he could stand while he shook the cold off his back. Ougat came over with a big smile and slipped an arm around his shoulder.

"The main man has arrived. Tonight is the night, my man."

The ouens came over to join them, greeting Anthony with handshakes and backslaps like he was Jackie Lonte pulled up in a BMW. Anthony took the joint when Oegies passed it. Dagga made his words smooth; it would help him talk his way out of trouble.

Ougat was gaaning aan so much it was hard to get a word in. "You right on time, my man. I knew you wasn't gunna make me come get you. I know how to mos pick them. I can spot a Junky Funky Kid a mile away. Told you ouens, Anthony is a ware JFK."

As Ougat klapped him on his back, Anthony realised he had been promoted from a laaitie to a man. That was a worry, Ougat would expect more from a man.

He smiled. "Um Ougat, I was wondering … Can I have a word with you alone?"

Ougat checked a gold watch half the size of his fist. "No time, my man. We got places to go, people to see, things to do. I got something bemoer lined up for you tonight. Tonight's gunna be a night you will never forget, so waar."

He had no chance to halt Ougat as he got busy. Thursday nights were quiet at the shebeen, pockets and purses hardly ever made it until payday Friday. Riedewaan was put in charge while the rest of the ouens were rounded up.

Anthony let Ougat take him round the shoulder and lead him out of the shebeen. Oegies, Marewaan, Lippe and Skelm made a scrum behind them as they walked down Peach Street. He had no idea where they were taking him. He was scared but he couldn't explain it to the ouens in a way that they would accept.

They walked to a row of houses on the edge of Hanover Park, near the factories. Anthony could smell the fish smoking at Snoekies. When the wind blew hard they could smell it all the way to Magnolia Court. They went down the wet street to the last house on the row, right at the edge of Hanover Park. Ougat led the way through the front garden and down the side into the sandy back yard. A wood and iron shack took up most of the yard. He was still figuring out how to say that he wanted to go home when Ougat unlatched the door and led the way inside.

Anthony could hardly see where he was going. There was a light inside the shack but it gave up before it got to the door. He tripped over his feet as someone pushed him from behind. As he walked in he made out two men in the middle of the shack, seated on plastic crates. A lamp hissing on a crate topped with a board between them gave off a weak blue light and a strong paraffin smell.

One of the men had a tattoo on the base of his long skinny neck, a semicircle on a wavy line. It took a while to figure out what it was – a rising sun with four black rays. The big man seated to the right had left his teenage years far behind him, but acne had turned his face into the surface of the moon on the poster in Anthony's classroom. The light from the lamp was too weak to reach across his face – it had a dark side, like the moon.

Ougat introduced the men as Bra Mike and Boeta Toefie. Anthony shook their hands and stepped to the side to give the ouens a space to greet. They all sat down on crates arranged in a semicircle around the lamp. It was cold in the shack; his brain was too frozen to work out what was going on.

The men watched in silence while a pipe was lit. Bra Mike held two matches in the mouth of the bottle top while Boeta Toefie sucked at it, the tattoo on his neck rising and setting. When the inside glowed red, Boeta Toefie took a sharp pull. He made a small gap in his lips and blew out a steady stream of white smoke. He took another pull and passed the pipe to Anthony.

Anthony had never smoked a pipe. Only Mandrax rookers used them. They crushed the tablets and mixed it with dagga, stuffing the mixture into the narrow neck of a smashed glass bottle. Filters of rolled up silver paper, from the inside of cigarette boxes, were fitted into the mouth. The pipe Boeta Toefie passed on smelled like dagga. Anthony turned up the bottom to see what was inside.

"Hey laaitie! What the fok you doing?" Ougat asked.

Anthony looked up at the gangster seated across the way. "I never smoked a pipe before. I was looking to see what is in it."

Ougat lifted his fist to his mouth and sucked on it. "It was made special for you. Is your night man, trek 'n skyf."

The glass was hot. Anthony curled his thumb and forefinger around the top and lifted it to his lips. He sucked. He blew out. Nothing came out of his mouth.

"Trek reg. We came here to make you a man. Pull like a man." Ougat's eyes were bursting in his face.

Anthony lifted the pipe and pulled hard. He choked as bitter smoke scratched down his windpipe, but he kept it down. A respectable stream of white smoke came out when he exhaled.

Ougat leaned forward, his elbows digging into his knees. "One more. Wys wiesie man. Wiesie man? Anthony, the main man!"

The ouens leaned forward on their crates, stamping their feet into the ground. "Wiesie man? Anthony! Wiesie man? Anthony!"

He took another drag. He counted up to ten before he exhaled. The ouens chanted his name until the last whisper of smoke came out. Anthony passed the pipe to Oegies.

The shack went quiet while the pipe was passed around. Anthony could hear the wind pushing against the grey iron sheets nailed onto the structure's wooden frame. The sheets buckled as they blocked the wind whooing outside like an old-fashioned train.

He checked on the pipe's progress. Lippe had it, next and last in line was Bra Mike. The shack walls buckled but Anthony couldn't hear the noise it made. Something was pouring into his ears, filling the pipes. He put a hand up to find out what it was.

Sour vomit rose up his throat. He pressed his lips tight, swallowing deep as he could. He knew it was cold in the shack, but he was boiling under his skin. Flames of vomit licked up his throat.

Anthony got to his feet and stumbled to the door. His vomit sprayed into the doorway as he struggled with the latch. He stumbled outside and reached the vibracrete wall before he hurled again; his stomach hitting his spine. He held onto the swaying wall.

Ougat came out to join him, putting an arm around his shoulder. "You orrite laaitie?"

Anthony had to move away from the smell of his vomit; it was going to make him throw up again. Ougat followed him as he stepped away, holding onto the wall. He sucked the wet wind deep into his burning lungs. His hearing came back, he could hear himself panting like a dog. "What was in that pipe?"

Ougat smiled proudly. "It was a white pipe. Tonight we welcoming you into the kring. We making you a full-on Junky Funky. Is gunna be bemoer."

So far, joining the gang was a kak experience. He had gone deaf and vomited 'til his throat hurt. What was coming next? Anthony didn't think he had the krag for it. But he couldn't find the krag to leave.

Ougat took him back inside the shack. "Is orrite laaitie, we all hurl the first time we smoke a white pipe. Is gunna be befok now."

After he took his seat again, Bra Mike brought Anthony into the Junky Funky Kids. He learned what they expected from him. Rule number one was never betray a member. Rule number two: anyone who betrayed a member was vrek. He wasn't exactly sure what 'betray' meant. He had to find out and make sure he didn't do it.

The next rule was to protect the turf. Never let strays onto the territory; they made themselves a home quickly. Anthony told himself to remember to ask Ougat to remind him until where the Junky Funky Kids turf stretched. He was feeling better. He rolled his shoulders; they were lekker loose. He stretched his arms out behind his back and met Ougat's eyes; staring at him with looks that could kill.

Bra Mike stopped talking. "You with us laaitie? You got somewhere else to be?"

Anthony skrikked. "No Bra Mike. I'm with you. Protect the turf."

"I finished that a while back. You listening? This is serious business." Bra Mike stared hard before he continued. He recited a list of the enemies of the Junky Funky Kids. The Nice Time Kids, the Dixie Boys, the Naughty Boys. The list was long. Anthony worked out a way to remember it. Any gang member who wasn't a Junky Funky was an enemy.

After the lecture, Boeta Toefie brought out a bottle of ink and a long darning needle. He lifted the lamp's glass and held the tip of the needle to the flame.

"Take off your top," Bra Mikey instructed.

Anthony took off his tracksuit top, school shirt and his long-sleeved vest. The last of the Mandrax heat disappeared in the splinters of cold penetrating the zinc walls and cutting across his ribs.

Bra Mike pulled him across his lap, gripped his left arm and took the needle from Boeta Toefie. He dipped it into the ink and stabbed it into Anthony's upper arm.

"Eina!" Anthony wasn't expecting the pain. He tried to pull away.

Bra Mike's fat fist closed over his elbow. "Hou jou mond! Djy's a man."

Anthony wasn't gunna argue, Bra Mike was at least four times his size. He focused on the lamp. Purple flames jiggered in the glass hood and black smoke escaped from the top. His arm was fokken sore, not only where Bra Mike was working. The pain travelled at top speed down to his fingernails. He didn't think they would let him cry. Can't be more than five stabs before it was over. Was Bra Mike digging a hole into his arm? Five more. Now he was slicing into his skin. Eina!

He was about to start crying when Bra Mike pushed him off his lap. Anthony twisted his head over his shoulder to see how much of his arm had been cut away. The letters JFK were tattooed in black ink near his left shoulder. The skin around the tattoo was starting to swell.

Ougat jumped to his feet. "A vollende JFK! This tjap will show people who you belong to. Djy's nou myne!" He grabbed Anthony around his shoulders and gripped him hard.

Anthony winced as Ougat's shoulder dug into his sore arm. Oegies slapped him on his back, sending pain clawing into his new tattoo. The rest of the ouens walked over to admire the tattoo and shake his hand. He dressed carefully, shivering with cold and pain.

Boeta Toefie lit another pipe. "Now we anoint Anthony with a ceremonial pipe."

Anthony didn't know what a ceremonial pipe was but he took it from Boeta Toefie when it was passed. This time was different. There was no vomit, and he didn't go deaf. He sat loose and listened while Ougat told Bra Mike how the Nice Time Kids started a shebeen on Junky Funky Kid turf. Bra Mike asked what retribution he was looking for.

Ougat clicked his fingers. "I'm gunna fokken sort that Majiet out. I'm not his naai. Tonight already. I got it all planned."

Anthony tried to listen, but he couldn't concentrate. He was starting to boil again. He wanted to be outside in the wind. He should go home. He had forgotten to worry about Mummy and Dedda. He interrupted Ougat, took his hand and shook it. "Bye. I got to go home. I'm gunna be in big kak."

Ougat pulled his hand away. "Nooit, the night is young. You not yet a man. I told you we got something special lined up for you. Stay a while. Who got the pipe? Give it to Anthony, my main man."

The shack door burst open a few minutes later. Ougat's ouens Darryl and Malcolm came in, dragging someone between them. They walked to the middle of the shack and dropped the body onto the floor.

Anthony couldn't make out much in the light from the paraffin lamp. It looked like a young woman with Wella-straightened hair

193

hanging above her shoulders. He couldn't see her face. She tried to lift her head but gave up when Darryl pushed it down with his foot. Her crying disappeared into the sand floor.

Anthony moved closer to see what was going on. Ougat came to his side, rubbing his hands together. "Now we in business laaitie. A while back I promised to organise a kind for you. Tonight is the night, laaitie. Show my man what we got for him."

Darryl lifted his foot, bent down and grabbed the girl's hair, turning her face to the men crowded around her. Anthony knew her; she was Nicky's friend from school. What was her name again? She came to the flat a lot. Her name was Shirley; that was it.

Shirley's white jersey was smeared with the grey sand of the shack floor. Her eyes were flying saucers in her head as she stared at the men crowded around her. When her eyes lit on him Anthony could see how confused she was. First she looked like she was glad to see him, then she frowned. "Anthony! What's happening? Why'm I here? Help me."

Anthony swallowed. He shouldn't have smoked again. He couldn't think. What was Shirley doing here? "Ougat, what's going on? I know this girl. She's my sister's friend."

Ougat frowned. "You know her?"

"Ja, Shirley's my sister's friend. I known her for years. What you gunna do with her?"

Bra Mike cleared his throat. "Ougat?"

Ougat crouched down next to Shirley, grabbed her jersey and pulled her into a sitting position. He stuck his nose close to hers and growled. "Who you?"

Shirley tried to pull her wet face away. "Shirley. Shirley Martin. From Apple Street."

"Fok!" Ougat dropped Shirley, got to his feet and confronted Darryl and Malcolm. "This is the wrong fokken kind. You supposed to bring her sister!"

Anthony's blood ran through his veins like hot jelly. Shirley was still crying. Why were they so rough with her? What did she do to them?

"Ougat?" Bra Mike's voice boomed from a dark corner of the shack.

Ougat put up his hand. "Is okay. I can sort this out. Just give me a minute to think here." He kicked Shirley, who was kneeling on the ground, rocking backward and forward. "Hou jou bek, I can't think straight."

Shirley hukked silently while Ougat stared at her like a klipsalamander hungrily eyeing a fly. Anthony struggled to get his brain going. He was bang. He should leave now. But what about Shirley? "Ougat, what's going on? What you gunna do?"

Ougat smacked his lips. "Is not what I'm gunna do, you gunna do it. This kind is your ticket to the big time, laaitie. Her sister is involved with Majiet, that naai from the Nice Time Kids who thinks he can stroll onto my turf and take over. I wanna send him a message. This is it, my broer. This is where you haal uit en wys. You either with the Junky Funkies or you against them."

Ougat grabbed Anthony's arm and pulled him to the back of the shack, where Bra Mike leaned against the wall. Anthony made out the shine of a knife in his right hand. Ougat caught him in a vice grip while Bra Mike lifted the knife to his neck. Pain sprinted up and down his tattooed arm. He pressed his knees together. He felt a piss coming.

Bra Mike hissed: "Last thing. You must prove loyalty to the JFKs. Ougat here is asking for your help. You unnerstand?"

Anthony nodded his head carefully. He was scared to move, the knife looked sharp. Bra Mike grunted and dropped his hand.

Ougat spun him around and led him back to the centre of the shack where the ouens were crouched around Shirley. She stared at him with desperate eyes. He had to look away. There was nothing he could do. "Ougat, I got to piss. I'm gunna wet my pants if I don't go now."

Ougat gripped his arm hard. "Me too, let's go."

Anthony scratched through his brain while they watered the wall outside. Were they gunna hurt Shirley? Would they hurt him if he got in the way? If he ran home would they chase him down?

Ougat pulled him back into the shack. Shirley had been stripped while they were outside. She was naked from the hips down. Her white panties were stuffed into her mouth. Oegies and Marewaan had her arms pinned down.

Ougat pushed Anthony towards Shirley. "Let's go laaitie. You ready or you want me to warm her up for you?" His hands went to his fly.

Lippe and Skelm pulled Shirley's legs open. Anthony couldn't help it; his eyes went straight there. Her toet looked just like the pictures in the porno magazines. Bushy hair on the outside, hiding fat lips. There was one big difference from the pictures in the magazines. He could see some pink inside, but it was mostly brown and purple. He realised that all the porno magazines he had seen used white models. They looked different.

Shirley tried to kick free. Lippe and Skelm struggled to keep her still.

"Anthony, Anthony, Anthony," the ouens started up.

He couldn't look away from Shirley's toet. His piel was as hot as the penny polonies the halaal butcher kept in an urn and sold for ten cents each. Anthony pulled down his tracksuit pants.

"My main man!" Ougat slapped him on his back. "Naai her, Anthony. Show her what the Junky Funkies are made of."

Anthony's piel jumped out as he pulled down his underpants. He kept his eyes fixed on the toet. He couldn't think about who it belonged to, this one was available.

Oegies looked up with a wide smile. "You got the right weapon for a JFK, my broer."

Anthony took his piel in his sweating hand. It was difficult to keep it still; it was straining towards the hole. He lay on top of Shirley, closing his eyes after he made the mistake of looking at her wet face when he came down. He reached back to pull his pants down further. Lippe and Skelm helped. He held his piel in his hand while he tried to find out where to put it.

"Want a hand, laaitie?" Ougat asked. "Can't find the right hole?"

Anthony shoved his piel inside the toet. Shirley did nothing to help him; he had to do everything. He put his palms next to her head, pulled out and pushed in again. He couldn't get in deep enough. He tried again and made it all the way inside. What came next? He concentrated on pushing and pulling until he found a rhythm. He forgot it was Shirley under him; he was blind to the ouens surrounding him. He was doing it. Finally, he was doing it!

His face was wet. He opened his eyes. Oegies was leaning forward and spitting at him like a wild man. "Naai haar Anthony, naai haar!"

He closed his eyes and got going again. This was much better than his fist. The soft flesh inside the toet gripped his piel. Anthony went

196

deep, pulled out and went back halfway. He went in hard and soft to see which was better. Hard was much better. Hot pressure built up from the base of his piel. Not yet! He wasn't finished. He pushed in as deep as he could and boiled over.

"That's my main man!" Ougat shouted. He pushed Anthony off Shirley, threw his leg over her hips and started pumping. A scream came pushing through the panties in her mouth, but it wasn't strong enough to find help.

Anthony looked at Shirley's face as he got up from the floor next to her. Her eyes were tight shut but two rivers of tears leaked out and rolled down her cheeks. He took a few steps back until her face disappeared and all he saw was Ougat's skinny gat pumping up and down.

As he pulled up his underpants, Anthony felt sand on his gat from rolling onto the floor when Ougat pushed him off Shirley. His palms were also covered in sand. He cleaned his hands on his jacket and wiped off his bum. He checked his piel for sand. It was covered in dark brown blood. Vomit rose up again in his throat. He turned his back on the ouens chanting Ougat's name as he pulled up his pants.

He couldn't watch. He didn't want to see what he had done. He held his hand to his mouth and rushed out of the shack, letting go as he reached the wall. All he had left inside was a small stream of sour water.

He held his head in his hands and walked around the yard in a small circle. What had he done? How was he gunna look Shirley in the face again? Was she gunna tell Nicky? He lifted his face up to the rain to cool himself down and wash away some of his sin. The men's voices drifted from the shack. Must be Marewaan's turn, they were chanting his name.

Anthony's body pulled him in the direction of home. His mind pulled him towards the shack. He couldn't stop what was happening to Shirley but the least he could do was make sure she was okay when they were finished with her. He couldn't leave. He went to the outside tap to rinse his mouth.

He choked on his skrik when a light came on in the house. The back door opened and a pretty young woman came out. Her black hair fell down the back of her white gown. "You okay there?" she asked.

Anthony looked up. It hadn't occurred to him that someone was inside the house; a few steps away from where Shirley was being ...

197

He stopped himself, just in time, from asking her to call the police. He couldn't betray the Junky Funky Kids. He would be betraying himself also. "I'm orrite."

He stood outside the shack after the kitchen door closed and the light went off. The chanting had stopped, all he could hear was groaning and moaning. They were raping Shirley. He had started it. He couldn't watch, 'specially because he would have to look Shirley in the face again.

He thought he was in big kak when he tried to get Nicky to help earlier; now it was much worse. That fokken Nicky. She wouldn't help him find a way to escape Ougat, now look what was happening to her friend. This was also her fault, for only being interested in herself.

The shack door opened and Ougat came out. "Want another chance laaitie? The kind's lekker wet now."

Anthony dug his hands into his hair. "Ougat, what am I gunna do? Shirley knows me. She knows my sister and my parents. She's gunna squeal then I'm gunna be in big kak."

"That kind's not gunna squeal. Bra Mike is giving her a talk."

"Is he gunna kill her?"

"Nooit man, that kind is a message from the JFKs. Bra Mikey's tuning her that if she goes to the police, we gunna gryp her sister. If that vark Majiet don't fok off from our turf, her sister's next."

Shirley came stumbling out of the shack, a long moan coming up from deep inside her. "God help me. Oh God, help me."

Anthony moved towards her. He stopped. He couldn't think what to say. Something came into his head. "Don't tell anyone what happened here. Don't tell Nicky."

Shirley took two steps forward and spat in his face.

Ougat threw his weight into the klap that sent Shirley to the ground. Crying loudly, she struggled to her feet and ran out of the yard, her arms wrapped around her stomach.

Ougat turned to Anthony. "Why you let her do that? You a Junky Funky; people must respec' you."

Anthony sighed. He was tired. His arm was throbbing. This night had been the worst of his whole life, and it wasn't over yet. There was more kak waiting at home. He might get chucked into the street. "Ougat, I'm tired. I'm going now, okay?"

"Sure my man. It's not every day that a man has his first naai. Been a big night for you."

Mummy and Dedda were still awake when he got home after midnight. Dedda said he had been out on the streets, looking everywhere. Mummy said she was worried sick. She didn't look right; she was pale and sweating like a horse that won the J&B Met.

Anthony listened to their skelling, but he wouldn't give up anything. He couldn't tell them where he had been. He couldn't tell them what he had done. He couldn't explain it. He didn't fully understand why he was a JFK and a rapist.

Mummy begged him to tell her where he had been. Dedda screamed and shouted like a mal ding. Anthony hung his silent head.

Dedda finally gave up, took off his belt, pulled him into the kitchen and forced him to bend over a chair. It was worse than the hiding he got when he failed; more eina than anything Mr September the master caner gave at school. Anthony enjoyed it.

"Cry Goddammit! Why don't you cry?" Neville shouted, his arm getting lame.

"Because I deserve it, Dedda."

Chapter Twenty-Two

Nicky was the moer in. She had failed her geography test; she didn't know where to put her face when Mr Louw gave back her paper and she saw the mark. She had written it last week, the morning after Anthony disappeared for hours and came home silent. She had the test in first period, while she was still sukkeling to wake up.

Her classroom emptied fast when the bell announced the end of the school day. Mr Louw stopped in the middle of a sentence explaining the differences between sedimentary and igneous rock, picked up his bag and was first out the door. School finished early on Fridays; many of the male teachers rushed to get the weekend started on the benches of the tavern next to the taxi rank. Nicky stood up and slowly packed her geography textbook and classwork book into her haversack. She was in no hurry to go home to her problems.

She dropped back into her desk; too lam to face carrying her heavy bag downstairs and out the school gates. For the past seven days she had been climbing up a mountain of difficult questions and she could see no sign of the top. How did her life get so kak, so quickly?

She did nothing wrong but she was in trouble. It wasn't fair that she was under house arrest for what Suzette and Anthony did. She was trapped in the middle of Mummy's and Dedda's war; night after night their voices were brandy-bottle loud. What was wrong with Anthony? Why was he staring in silence at the walls like a zombie had taken hold of him?

Was she living in a broken home? She knew children from broken homes – where one or both of the parents were missing in action or were dronkies who never bought food. If it was really bad, the school got involved. Nicky worried she was next. There was a chance Mr Louw would say something in the staffroom about her geography test. He gave her a funny look when he handed back the marked papers; he was used to getting As.

Mummy would be the hell in if the teachers came to ask questions. She warned them to keep Suzette's skandaal a secret until she worked out what they must say when people asked after her. It was almost three weeks since Suzette left. Someone was sure to notice soon.

There was another problem sitting on Nicky's neck: Where was Shirley? At the time when she was the most desperate for someone to talk to, her best friend had stayed out of school all week. There must be something wrong. She pictured Shirley in a doek, trapped for eight hours a day on a long row of sewing machines in a factory.

She had to go to Shirley's house to find out what was up; they didn't have a phone. She would be in trouble with Mummy and Dedda for not going straight home after school but she didn't give a fok. Her friend would check on her if she went missing. She was expected to be Anthony's prison warder, but he wasn't going anywhere. He came straight home from school every day and planted himself on the couch to count the bricks in the wall. Nicky could spare some time to check up on Shirley, to talk to someone who might be interested in her kak life.

She had failed her geography test because of Anthony. There was no ways she could study last Thursday night when he hadn't come home. Mummy and Dedda went out of their minds with worry; so did she.

Dedda cross-questioned her again; the way he did the night Suzette disappeared, like everything was her fault. "Was Anthony here when you came home from school, Nicky?"

"Yes Dedda, he was here. I told you already."

"So tell me again. Did he say where he was going?"

"I asked him but he didn't want to say."

"Why didn't you go see where he went?"

"I dunno Dedda. He left so fast I didn't have a chance to think. I didn't think he was gunna stay out so long."

Neville went to all of Anthony's friends to check if he was there;

they said they hadn't seen him for weeks. Magda phoned the police but they said there was nothing they could do until the next day. They said it was only nine o'clock; teenagers stayed out late.

Nicky stood in the lounge doorway and watched Mummy and Dedda pacing up and down, passing each other in the centre of the room. Six steps, turn around, six steps back. They were both talking but they weren't listening. They hadn't been hearing each other since the night Suzette left home. Every once in a while one of them would stop to cross-question her again.

She said nothing while Mummy spread the blame on thick. "You older than your brother, Nicky. His whole life I been telling you to keep an eye on him. And what happened? You don't know where he is. You knew your sister wasn't going to school and you said nothing. What's wrong with you?"

Nicky couldn't see any space to set Mummy right; now wasn't the time for the fight that was sure to follow. Why was she alone expected to keep Suzette and Anthony in check? It was their job. She was burning to tell Mummy and Dedda how blind they were to their children's problems.

Maybe she was in the wrong when she didn't tell them weeks back that Anthony was up to kak, coming home late and refusing to say where he went after school. She knew he hadn't studied for the exams; his report came as no surprise. Why was she the only one to notice, to try to pull him straight? She couldn't exactly blame Mummy and Dedda for missing the signs that Suzette had a secret life. She knew her sister was bunking and she said nothing.

Neville stopped his pacing and turned to Nicky. "Bring my jacket and my torch. I'm gunna go look for Anthony again."

Magda flew into him again as Nicky left the lounge. "This is all your fault Neville. You spending so much time on the neighbourhood watch you don't have time for your own children. Your children disappearing on you one after the other. All of this happened since you joined that blerrie neighbourhood watch."

Nicky was shocked when she came back to the lounge with Dedda's things. Mummy never swore. Her face was made up with disgust as she pointed a finger at Dedda. "You up and down these streets night after night looking out for other people's children. You should have left hours ago to look for Anthony."

"I should have left hours ago to look for Anthony."

Nicky almost started a small celebration, until she realised that Dedda wasn't agreeing with Mummy. The same words just happened to come out of his mouth that came out of hers. Her parents missed the moment.

She tried to keep Mummy strong while they waited for Dedda to come back with Anthony. She made cup after cup of sweet tea and patted her back while she cried. She ran out of words to make it better. "Dedda will find him, don't worry so much."

Anthony came just home after midnight, a few minutes before Dedda returned, pale and silent like he had been gryped by a spook.

Nicky was sent to her room where she couldn't sleep. She was sure all the neighbours could hear every word Mummy and Dedda screamed over the howl of the wind and the rain outside. She didn't hear Anthony's voice, not once. There was only silence the few times he was given a chance to speak.

Then came the whistling of the belt. The phwaack as it landed. Nicky gripped her pillow over her ears. She felt sorry for Anthony, although he deserved a pak for making them worry so much. She also felt sorry for Dedda and Mummy, and for herself. Suzette's and Anthony's kak was making all their lives kak.

Mummy and Dedda skelled for a long while in their bedroom after Anthony was sent to bed. Nicky heard every word. When Dedda came to shake her awake the next morning her eyeballs felt like they had been dropped onto a beach and left there all night. When she reached her classroom she couldn't remember walking there. She was still half asleep when Mr Louw put the test paper on her desk.

Jirre! She really missed Shirley. Nicky lifted her haversack onto her back and forced her exhausted legs to take her out of the classroom. She hoped that whatever kept her friend from school was nothing big; if Shirley was up to it they were going to have a long talk. She had to tell someone about the guilt she carried, about her worry that she had robbed her brother and sister of protection. When she kept Suzette's and Anthony's secrets she stood in the way of Mummy and Dedda being the good parents she knew they were.

It was a lekker day for a walk. The sun had been bright for three days straight and was slowly drying up pools of winter rain littered with plastic. The warm rays evaporated some of the tension off Nicky's back.

She worked on her long list of questions as she walked to Shirley's house, blind to the people crowded onto the pavement to visit with each other and the sun. She came to a halt as a realisation hit her: she was desperate for someone to talk to about the kak in her life; Anthony was in the same situation. She wouldn't listen when he tried to tell her his problem the day he disappeared. Nicky decided to sit him down soon as she got home. There was something she could do to help make it right.

Nicky was so deep in her thoughts when she turned into Plum Street that she walked into a card game set up on the corner. Four men seated on milk crates slapped red Bicycle cards onto a piece of plywood perched on top of a paint tin. She bumped into the back of one of the players, knocking him into the rickety table and sending it sliding to the ground.

"Watch your step!" The man reached back and grabbed her wrist; pulling her around his body and onto his lap before she realised what he was doing. He tugged her wrist down when she struggled to get up. "Let's see, what do we have here? Who is this meid that come round the corner and drops onto Harvey's lap?"

Nicky checked out Harvey. She couldn't see much. Half of his skinny, dark face was covered with sunglasses that reflected back at her like a mirror. She could see her eyes in them, wide with skrik. She pulled away from his face. His smile showed off his missing four front teeth, flanked by brown stokkies. His breath smelled like a rat crawled inside his mouth and died.

She struggled to get off Harvey's lap. She didn't have time for his kak. She had enough kak in her life already. Nicky kicked her heels into his shin when he wouldn't let go.

"Eina!" Harvey's hand shot down to find his pain. Nicky jumped off his lap the second he loosened his grip.

The other players rose from picking up the scattered cards. They came to attention when Harvey shouted and waited to see what came next.

"Eina! I was just being friendly. Why you take it like that?" Harvey complained.

Nicky twisted her fists into her hips. She was so cross she didn't stop to think what kind of a man Harvey could be. "I haven't got time for your nonsense. I got a lot on my mind. My parents kicked my sister out of the house. My brother looks like his best friend was murdered but he won't say what's wrong. I'm going to see my friend who disappeared and I dunno why. Sorry I walked into you. Sorry I kicked you."

Nicky hoped Harvey took her apology the right way. Her worry floated in his sunglasses. She didn't know why she told him all her troubles like that. Maybe it showed how desperate she was for someone to talk to.

Harvey made her wait a while before he answered. "Is okay sister. Next time, be careful. Look where you walk."

"I will, I'm sorry." Nicky lifted up her hands and stepped back carefully.

There was something very wrong at Shirley's house. Her sister Karen had opened the door when Nicky knocked. The way Karen was performing made Nicky worry even more about Shirley. She was desperate to get inside.

Karen was planted in the doorway like Table Mountain. The frowns on her forehead were as deep and dark as its kloofs. Nicky had never seen her so ugly; she was one of the hottest girls in Hanover Park. Karen and Suzette were the reason why Nicky and Shirley became friends. They had the same problem – older sisters who thought they were beauty queens and much better than them.

Karen had a bemoerde body. Mummy said her hips were made for babies. When she swayed down the street men stopped in their tracks and hung their tongues out for some fresh air. Karen's boyfriend Majiet treated her like a queen. He bought her fancy clothes and jewellery.

Shirley said Majiet was the leader of the Nice Time Kids but her mummy said nothing because he bought food for the house.

Karen's made-for-babies weren't moving. Nicky was going to have to climb over her if she wanted to get into the house. She wouldn't explain why she couldn't come inside. Karen had only one line, and she said it over and over: "Shirley don't want to see you, don't come here again."

Nicky couldn't click what was going on. "Why not? We didn't have a fight or anything."

She had neglected Shirley when she looked after Mrs Van Wyk, but they were best friends again when school started after the holidays. She had been jealous of Shirley's friendship with Kevin, but recently she had been thinking the three of them could be best friends after he was released. When she fell asleep with her arms wrapped around her waist she woke up feeling his support.

This was no time for daydreams. Nicky lifted herself onto her toes to look over Karen's shoulder. Where was Shirley? Karen didn't say she wasn't home. The push caught her by surprise; her bum connected hard with the cement path when she fell. Shock stapled her to the ground.

Karen shouted before she slammed the door. "I told you Shirley don't wanna see you, now fok of! Voetsek! Don't come back here."

Nicky got to her feet and walked slowly down the path to the gate. After she closed it she stopped to stare at Shirley's house. It was smack in the middle of Apple Street, with neighbours' identical two windows and front doors joined like train carriages to the left and right. Nicky thought she saw the curtain move in Shirley's bedroom window. She stared at the window, hoping Shirley would see her waiting and still wanting to be friends.

There was no sign of her friend. She walked slowly down Apple Street, struggling to understand what just happened. Karen didn't say Shirley wasn't home. She said Shirley didn't want to see her. Something was very wrong. Nicky swung around, heading back to Shirley's house for the truth.

This time she pushed against Shirley's front door when it opened and got inside in two steps. It wasn't hard; her friend's eight-year-old brother Peter had opened the door. He had skinny shoulders like angels' wings. He said nothing when she asked where Shirley was.

Nicky walked through the lounge. "Shirley, are you here?"

As she entered the passage and turned towards the bedroom Shirley shared with her mother and sister, Karen again blocked the doorway. Her growl warned that her bite wasn't far away. "What you doing here Nicky? Didn't I tell you earlier to voetsek?"

Nicky stood her ground. "I'm here to see my friend and I'm not leaving 'til I set eyes on her. Shirley, are you here?"

She ducked to the right when Karen reached out to grab her and squeezed her way into the bedroom. Her haversack jammed her into the doorway with Karen. She almost fell onto the double bed after she jerked herself free. She would have landed on Shirley, who was curled up tight in the middle with her back to the door.

She fired out her questions while she had the chance. "Shirley! What's going on? What's wrong? Why did Karen say you don't want to see me anymore?"

Karen came up behind her and pulled her arm. Nicky wasn't ready to leave. She rukked herself free and knelt on the bed, shaking her friend's shoulder. "Shirley, look at me. What's wrong?"

Shirley wouldn't turn around. Nicky could hear her thick breath splashing through a snot-filled nose; she was crying.

"Time to leave, come!" Karen was pulling at her again.

Nicky held onto Shirley. If her best friend didn't want to see her again, she had to tell her to her face. This was rubbish. Shirley wouldn't even look at her. Again she was in trouble with someone and she did nothing wrong. She pulled hard on Shirley's shoulder and rolled her onto her back.

"Hooliha!" Nicky knew that was the wrong thing to say but she couldn't help it. The sun poured in through the bedroom window, lighting up Shirley's face like stained glass. Her skin was elephant grey. There was a bruise across her left cheek, starting above her swollen eyebrow and painted down to her chin. It was purple and black around her eye, green over her cheekbone and yellow near her chin. Nicky could make out some of Shirley's eye through the swelling. There were bruises on her throat, dark as a brinjal.

"Haai Jirre Shirley, sorry I pulled you like that. Did I hurt you?"

Nicky started to feel kak for bursting in. She changed her mind quickly. She wasn't sorry at all. Look at Shirley's face! What happened? She reached for Shirley's hand. It was pulled away violently.

Shirley sat up on the bed with a groan, wiped her tears and stared hard through one eye. "You seen me now. You satisfied? What you think of my new look?"

Nicky covered her mouth with her hand. Who moered Shirley? Why was she speaking in such a ugly voice?

Shirley turned her head from side to side. "Seen enough? I got more bruises in other places I can show you. You gunna go tell everyone how I look? Is that why you came?"

Nicky crept to the bottom of the bed. She looked nervously over her shoulder. Karen was in the doorway, arms folded like a nightclub bouncer. She was more worried about Shirley than her sister. "Shirley what happened? When did this happen? I'm sorry I didn't come earlier but I was under house arrest. I had to go behind Mummy's and Dedda's backs to come see you."

Shirley leaned forward and stared into her face like she was seeing it for the first time. Nicky held her in her sights and waited. She was going to stay as long as it took to find out what happened to her friend and to try to make it better.

Shirley spoke like a old man kept in solitary for a long time. "Can't you just leave me alone? Didn't you hear Karen say I don't wanna see you?"

Nicky knelt on the bed like a statue keeping guard at the top of a street. There was something in Shirley's eyes. She could almost believe she didn't want to see her again. If she left that was the end of it. Her friend would drop her and she would deserve it. "I'm not going anywhere. When you not feeling lekker, that's when you need friends the most. You don't have to tell me what happened Shirley. Just let me stay a while."

"Why you wanna stay? So you can study me and go to school and tell everybody what you saw?"

Nicky figured out what the problem was. Shirley was worried what people would say if they found out what happened. She would never squeal on a friend. "Shirley, I won't tell anybody. I promise I won't.

You don't have to tell me anything. I understand."

Shirley rose up on the bed like a cobra and hissed. "You don't understand nothing. I hope you never understand. No, I take it back. I hope the day will come when you feel the way I do. Ag, just get out. Voetsek! Fok of!"

Nicky got to her feet as Shirley started swearing. Karen pulled at her shoulder. She dropped to her knees and stared up at Shirley from the foot of the bed. "What's wrong? Why you going on like this?"

Shirley words came out like knives cutting her throat. "What's wrong? You never gunna know Nicky, why I don't wanna see you again. You dead to me Nicky, vrek. Take a good look at this face. You never gunna see it again."

Karen reached down and grabbed Nicky round the waist. She grunted as she lifted her to her feet and dragged her towards the door. Nicky let Karen pull her away. It was time to leave. Shirley was still hissing at her like a snake.

Shirley's words brought Karen to a halt in the doorway. "One more thing, Nicky. It's not only you I never wanna see again. I never wanna see anyone in your family again. Not one fokken Fourie. You fokken Fouries think you shit chocolate ice cream but you must see what your kak really looks like Nicky. You must smell your kak sometime. I never wanna see you again. You hear me? You hear me?"

Nicky could still hear Shirley's screams when Karen pushed her out of the house and slammed the front door. She must have been on her twelfth 'you hear me' and it didn't sound like she was gunna stop anytime soon. Nicky didn't linger at the gate. She ran down Apple Street, ignoring the stares of people sunning themselves on their front steps and howling like a baby hanging on a dry tet.

She forgot that she planned to talk to Anthony about his troubles. Her eyes burned too much to look at him when she got home and rushed into her bedroom. She lay facedown on her pillow and cried for Shirley. Who attacked her? Why didn't she want to talk about it? Shirley didn't have a boyfriend, except maybe Kevin and he was in prison; must have been a stranger who did that to her.

She cried for herself afterwards. She couldn't work out how she landed up in this situation. All the kak in her life was other people's kak. Suzette's kak and Anthony's kak made Mummy's and Dedda's lives kak. And her life also. Shirley's kak cut deep; it was the foulest of the lot. She had no one to talk to. Anthony was in the lounge, staring at the wall with blank eyes.

Nicky checked her eyes in the bathroom mirror when she went to wash her hands before supper. She looked like a vampire in the night. Mummy and Dedda would have paid her no mind if she had sharp fangs hanging down her lip. They were on Anthony's case for hours, trying to get answers out of him. He said nothing – not even when Mummy started crying.

Then Mummy attacked Dedda and he gave it back to her. It was the same story, night after night. Who was to blame for Suzette. Who hadn't kept an eye on Anthony. They were so involved with each other they didn't notice she had gone silent with pain. There was only one thing she wanted to talk about but Shirley made it clear she wanted nobody to find out what happened. Not that she knew what happened to her friend.

Nicky went to bed early and was about to fall asleep when she realised she hadn't told Dedda and Mummy about failing her geography test. She decided to spare them the news that another child was in trouble. She prayed that her teachers wouldn't come for a home visit to find out what was wrong. She prayed for Shirley; that she would get better and want to be friends again. She prayed that her home wasn't broken yet; she asked God to heal it. She wrapped her arms around her waist, closed her eyes and went in search of Kevin's dream hugs.

Chapter Twenty-Three

Neville placed his bike helmet on the shelf of his grey metal locker in the staff room at work. He took off his black leather jacket and hung it on a hook below the shelf. He checked his watch, knock-off time soon. He hoped he was done for the day. He was vrek moeg.

He sweetened a cup of tea with three heaped sugars and sank down onto a chair at the pine table in the staff room, cupping his chilled hands around the mug. He didn't want to get back onto his bike, 'specially now that peak hour had started.

The law firm was the busiest since he started working there seventeen years ago. It had developed a reputation for human rights work. Neville was sent to the Supreme Court several times a day to file urgent applications. One of the partners was representing twelve people charged with treason and terrorism. He drove the firm's motorbike up and down to Pollsmoor Prison to drop off files and collect signed affidavits for court applications, putting in the overtime required after the state of emergency was declared.

He scratched his itchy scalp as he thought of the struggle that was waiting for him at home. His conflict with Magda had to come to an end soon; it was doing Anthony no good. He had quit the neighbourhood watch; there wasn't enough hours in the day to fix his family. Herbert offered an intervention, but Neville declined. Magda would never forgive him if she found out he was talking about their problems outside the home.

Magda had her own idea of an intervention. She wanted to bring Pastor Williams from her church to pray over Anthony. Neville got the grille at the thought. There was no way he would let the pastor lay a hand on his boy.

He took a slurp of his sugary tea, soaking up the energy. He had a plan coming together; he needed a few minutes to get it straight. He reckoned he needed advice. The firm's lawyers helped hundreds of parents whose children were locked up, tracking down the detainees' whereabouts and harassing the government in the courts for their release. One of the partners, Andrew Silverstein, had children the same age as Anthony and Nicky.

Neville clocked out at five o'clock and knocked on Mr Silverstein's office door.

The voice on the other side sounded busy. "Come in."

He opened the door and took a squizz inside. Mr Silverstein's curly blonde hair stuck out behind stacks of files piled on his desk. "Uh, sorry to bother you, sir. If you have a few minutes to spare I would like to talk with you."

"Come in Neville, come in."

Neville held onto a chair in front of the desk and cleared his throat until he was told to sit down. He perched on the edge, getting his thoughts in order. "Uh, Mr Silverstein, I got this personal problem and I don't know what I must do."

He watched through the tunnel between the files on the desk as his boss put his fountain pen down, leaned back in his leather chair and folded his hands on his chubby stomach. Neville shifted his chair a bit to the left for a better view.

Mr Silverstein's blue eyes smiled from behind his gold-rimmed glasses. "Call me Andrew and tell me what I can do to help."

Neville looked at the photos of his boss's family lining the windowsill while he gathered his thoughts. His wife, son and daughter were also blonde and well fed. They had their arms around each other in most of the pictures.

"Mr Silverstein ... uh, Mr Andrew, I have this problem with my children. My daughter left home. I don't know how to bring her back. My son disappeared for a couple of hours recently and I think something bad happened to him. I can't work out what it is. We can't get a word out of him."

Neville swallowed hard before he said the thing that was driving him befok with worry. "I'm starting to think Anthony was molested."

212

Mr Silverstein frowned and leaned forward. "Have you had him examined?"

"No, sir, examined how?"

"By a doctor, or a district surgeon, to see whether he's been harmed in any way. When did this happen?"

"Over a week ago." Neville counted the days on his fingers. "Eleven days ago exactly."

"That's a while back. How old is he?"

"He's thirteen, sir, same as your child." Neville nodded towards a photo of Mr Silverstein and his son, their big smiles resting on arms draped on the rim of a sparkling-blue swimming pool.

"I don't think it will make much sense now, to have him examined. But you could take him to another kind of doctor, to a psychologist. They can find out what happened even after some time has elapsed."

Neville frowned. Wasn't a psychologist the same thing like a psychiatrist? A doctor for mal people? Did Mr Silverstein think Anthony was going mal? Maybe he was. Maybe losing his voice was the first sign, and he missed it. "I wouldn't know where to find a psychologist. I don't think I ever come across one. But I think you right; Anthony needs one. He hasn't spoken a word for eleven days."

"I know a fantastic psychologist. She works at the University of Cape Town, at the Child Development Centre. She's doing trauma work. There's lots of that going around right now; children who've been shot, detained, tortured. When children are exposed to trauma they often can't vocalise it. She can arrange for Anthony to have medical treatment, if he needs it."

Neville's shoulders drooped with relief. He knew Mr Silverstein would help. He admired the partners. His greatest dream was that Nicky would be like them one day. But how was he going to persuade Madga that Anthony had to see a psychologist? Could they afford it?

Mr Silverstein read his mind. "The centre is fully funded. There would be no cost to you. I'll call Anne in the morning and tell her to expect your call. That's the doctor's name, Anne Brixton."

"Thank you, sir, thank you." Neville watched as Mr Silverstein searched through his Rolodex. He reached through the tunnel of files and took the sheet of paper with the doctor's name and number. He cleared his throat again. "Sir, if I can just bother you with one more thing. There's my daughter ..."

"Ah yes, you said she had left home. Do you know where she is?"

"No, sir, she left without saying where she was going. She didn't exactly leave on good terms; my wife threw her out of the house."

Mr Silverstein frowned. "What happened?"

"You see, sir, we found out she dropped out of school and got a job behind our backs. She's a model, for underwear." Neville was embarrassed, but he had already told Mr Silverstein he thought Anthony was molested. What could be worse?

"How old is she?"

"Suzette is eighteen, sir."

"She's a major at eighteen; you won't be able to force her to come home. You can report her missing at the police station, but they're so busy doing apartheid's work I doubt they will do more than open a file. Where does she work?"

Neville slapped a hand against his forehead. How could he be so dof? He had been grappling with this problem for five weeks and Mr Silverstein solved it in two minutes. Magda got him so worked up that he couldn't think straight. "I know the name of the place where she's working. Planet Fashions."

Mr Silverstein paged through his telephone directory. "Ah yes, here it is, phone number and an address. I'm quite the detective, aren't I?"

"Yes, sir, you very good. Thank you. I did the right thing coming here."

Neville gave Mr Silverstein the piece of paper with the psychologist's name and took it back after Planet Fashions' phone number and address had been added. He rose from his chair. "Thank you, sir. I know you busy and I was asking a lot ..."

"Not at all. It was nothing. Let me know how it works out."

Mr Silverstein's head dropped back into the file on his desk. Neville left quietly. The partners worked long hours, some of them with families waiting at home.

Neville turned up the collar of his jacket as he made his way home from the taxi rank in the blustery wind. He kept his head down; he didn't want anyone to see what he was thinking.

Telling Mr Silverstein he thought Anthony was molested was the first time he had spoken his fear out loud. He had seen those dead eyes before, in the orphanage. Molested boys went quiet. Everyone else kept their tongues. He wasn't keeping silent any longer. He was there for his boy no matter what happened. If Anthony was molested, that was no reason to stop loving him.

He wanted to take his boy to the psychologist as soon as he could get an appointment. Magda had to see this was the right thing to do. She was as worried as he was; she was begging Anthony to tell her what was wrong.

Neville took Magda for a walk before supper. She didn't resist when he told her he needed to have a word away from the children's ears. She put on her jacket and tied a scarf around her head. Spring was weeks away but the wind hadn't let go of winter yet. The sun had taken the last of its weak shine behind Table Mountain; lights came on early as the day ended quickly.

The courtyard between Magnolia Court's two blocks was quiet. Washing lines flapped white sheets and shirts in the centre of the court, giving them cover from their neighbours' eyes. Neville steered Magda on a walk around the courtyard, hoping she wouldn't raise her voice when she heard what he had to say. He started carefully. "Magda, we can both see there's something very wrong with Anthony and it's getting worse by the day. We have to do something about it, more than we doing now."

Magda kept pace as they circled the washing lines. She nodded. "You so right Neville. I think something happened to him the night he disappeared. We didn't realise it at first 'cause we were so cross when he came home late. He looks to me like he's seen something."

Neville forgot to go slow. "His eyes belong on a corpse. I can see the signs, something terrible happened to Anthony."

Magda stopped in her tracks and turned to face him. "Neville, what do you know?"

"When people face trauma they can't find the words to explain what happened. Anthony's just like that."

"What trauma? What you talking about? What you know?"

Madga was getting loud. Neville tugged at her arm. Mr Van der Westhuizen from flat thirty-nine was walking towards them. Neville greeted him and Magda checked up on his sick wife before they continued on their circuit around the washing lines.

Neville tried to keep his voice light as he took up the conversation. "I don't know exactly what happened to Anthony. But I realised I seen boys like this before. I seen the dead eyes."

Madga kept silent. Neville had told her about his childhood, some of it. He didn't like to go back to that time. She knew he was mistreated in an institution with no help from outside but she didn't know too many details.

Neville was desperate to make her understand where he was coming from. "If the boy's arm was broken we would take him to a doctor. There's something wrong with his head. We must accept that he got a problem and look for help." He decided to come clean. "Mr Silverstein at the office gave me a name of a psychologist. I told him today how worried we are about Anthony."

Magda's eyes opened as wide as they could go. "You think Anthony is going out of his mind?"

"Looks like it. The boy can't talk; I don't think the problem is that he won't talk. We getting nowhere with him. I got the name of a doctor who specialises in children who got problems with trauma. I want to take Anthony to see her."

Magda nodded energetically. "You must phone the doctor first thing in the morning. I just hope we didn't leave it too late."

Neville came to a halt and pulled Magda into his arms. He buried his face in her shoulder, wiping his tears on her jacket. He rubbed his head against her palm when she stroked his curls. Their fighting had taken her away from him. He needed her, and he was going to need her more than ever when he found out who did this to Anthony. Magda would have to put the brakes on him; he could easily murder the bastard who hurt his boy.

He decided not to tell Magda about his fear that Anthony was molested. What if he was wrong? He hoped he was; he couldn't think of a worse thing that could happen to his boy.

A voice came out the darkness. "Hello, hello. What have we here? Look like a married couple vrying in the dark like teenagers."

Neville lifted one eye above Magda's shoulder. Their neighbour Moira had a wide smile on red lips and one eyebrow riding up her forehead.

"Evening, Moira." Magda's voice was flat. She never hid the fact that Moira wasn't one of her favourite people. She believed her neighbour was no example for her girls. Everyone knew she had five children from five different men.

Moira's smile stuck to her face. "You must tell me what your secret is, Magda. I could never get a man to hold tight onto me after so many years."

Neville wiped his eyes on Magda's shoulder and pulled away from her. He was scared to talk; Moira might hear the tears in his voice. And he was embarrassed to recall the feel of her soft breasts when he fell on her after he got drunk at the neighbourhood watch party.

Magda could handle Moira. "I don't think you need any lessons on men from me."

Moira folded her arms and stood her ground. "Is everything okay? Sounds to me like you two got troubles in your home. But now I see the two of you, vrying in public, and I wonder what's going on."

Magda pulled her lips tight. "There's nothing going on. As you can see, we just fine. Come Neville, it's long past suppertime, we got to get going. Good night, Moira."

Moira trapped them with her next question. "Is Suzette okay? I haven't seen her for a while."

Neville turned to face his neighbour. He could handle this. "Suzette? She's fine. She's studying hard. Matric exams start in three months. Good night Moira."

He admired Magda's generous bum as he climbed the stairs behind her. He was glad their talk went well. It was good to have her back again; he had been lonely since Suzette left. He planned on holding his wife through the night, her body might grant him the first peaceful sleep in weeks.

Dr Brixton could see Anthony on Friday. She needed two hours for her first session, one with Neville and one with Anthony. Mr Silverstein gave him the morning off and wished him the best of luck. Magda couldn't get away. Her factory had a big order and sixteen girls were down with the flu.

When Neville told Anthony that he had to miss school and go with him to see a doctor, it was like talking to a brick wall. But Anthony did everything he was told as long as he wasn't asked to speak.

They took a taxi to Claremont, a train to Rosebank and walked up the hill to the University of Cape Town. Neville had never been to UCT before but he had driven past it on the highway on his many trips to Pollsmoor Prison. Next time he went there he planned to make a stop in Retreat, at Planet Fashions. But first he had to sort Anthony out.

The Child Development Centre was on lower campus, behind the Baxter Theatre. Neville checked out all the buildings as he walked up the hill but he couldn't spot the law faculty where Nicky would study. It was probably on the campus above the highway, in one of the ivy-covered buildings he saw as he whizzed past on the firm's bike.

Dr Brixton's office was in a gabled and thatched building. It looked exactly the way Neville hoped it would. There was a child-sized table in a corner of the waiting room with four small chairs tucked neatly underneath. Crayons and paper waited on the table for small fingers. A toy box overflowed onto the floor.

The white-haired receptionist said Dr Brixton was running five minutes late, Neville and Anthony could take a seat. The boy slumped onto a chair and dropped his chin onto his chest, staring blankly at the carpeted floor.

Neville checked out the place. The wooden-framed windows across from the receptionist's desk had a bemoerde view of the back of Table Mountain. He counted three waterfalls rushing down the gorges; a week's rain had finally dried up this morning. He checked out a pinboard on a wall covered in children's drawings. Stick men pointed shotguns at stick children. A police helicopter hovered above a burning shack. A child had probably used up all of a red crayon on a picture of a man lying in the street, blood pouring from his stomach.

Dr Brixton was exactly five minutes late. She apologised as she came hurrying in. Neville stared, she was nothing like he expected; not that he had any idea how a psychologist looked. Put Bo Derek in the same room and Dr Brixton would score a twelve. Her curly hair had generous sprinkles of gold. Her skin wrinkled around her eyes, although she couldn't have been older than thirty. When she came to shake his hand, he saw why – she smiled with her eyes.

"Hello, Mr Fourie. It's good to meet you. And is this Anthony?"

Neville shook Dr Brixton's hand. He turned to his son. Anthony hadn't changed position since he sat down. "Anthony! Greet the doctor." The boy didn't move an eyelash.

"That's okay, leave Anthony for now. I need to speak with you first, Mr Fourie. Then I'll see Anthony, without you. Come into my office."

Neville followed Dr Brixton down a short corridor leading off the waiting room. He had no idea what was coming next. Between him and Magda they knew little about psychology. They hoped Anthony didn't need electric shock treatment; it looked eina.

Dr Brixton's office was similar to the reception area. There was another child-sized table in a corner, with two chairs, one child-sized and one for an adult. Two cloth dolls lay facedown in the middle of the table.

"Have a seat, Mr Fourie." Dr Brixton waved a hand to a chair in front of her desk. "I've opened a file for Anthony and I'm going to need your help."

Neville sat upright in his chair, taking confidence from Dr Brixton's respect. He was usually Neville, or my boy, to the whites. He was ready to start when she opened Anthony's file.

Dr Brixton's smile hit her eyes. "First, I'm going to take Anthony's history, then you and I will have a little chat about his problem, okay?" Her questions drew out the story of Anthony's life. When he was born and whether it was a normal birth. Was Magda depressed after the delivery? How long did she breastfeed Anthony? How many brothers and sisters? Any other relatives?

Neville leaned forward and described his family. Anthony was born at St Monica's Maternity Hospital, thirteen years and ten months ago. It was a normal delivery. Magda breastfed until he was nine months old. She had to go back to work after two months, but she fed him in the evenings. They didn't have many relatives. Neville was an orphan and Magda had one sister, Violet. She had a husband and two daughters.

It was easy to relate to Dr Brixton. She asked all the right questions and wrote the answers down on a sheet of paper in Anthony's file. They reached the bottom of the first page. For the first time since Suzette left home, Neville felt like he was doing right by one of his children.

"Very good," Dr Brixton said, turning over the page. "Let's start with Anthony's recent history. Tell me why you came here today."

Neville didn't know where to start. He pushed his sweating hands under his thighs. "Until recently Anthony didn't give us much problems. Ag, he's thirteen. You know what boys that age are like. You have to fetch them inside in the evenings, and they give you lip when they think they can get away with it. But he's not a bad boy. I seen boys in our neighbourhood that are bad."

Dr Brixton smiled. "That sounds good. Was he performing well at school?"

"He did well, although he can be lazy. You have to keep at him all the time. He didn't fail once until last term, and then he failed badly."

"Did you meet with his teachers to find out why he failed?"

Neville was embarrassed. Dr Brixton was spot on. "No, I didn't. I just thought he was lazy. I didn't think there could be another reason. You think there is one? Is that when his troubles started?"

Dr Brixton calmed him down. "I'm not suggesting that. But I think we should find out more. You should make an appointment with the school and speak to his teachers. Ask them about his attendance."

Neville was definitely going to the school as soon as possible. He and Magda should have thought of that themselves. He rocked back and forward on his hands. Far as he knew, the boy went to school five days a week and came straight home. He played with his friends at Magnolia Court or in the park nearby. Come to think of it, the night Anthony disappeared his friends all said they hadn't seen him for a while.

Dr Brixton was on the same track. Her next question was about Anthony's friends. Neville confessed that he wasn't sure if there were new friends, boys he hadn't met.

He told Dr Brixton about Suzette; how they found out that she had a secret life. He was beginning to realise he knew little about his son's life outside the flat. Anthony was also keeping secrets from them, *moerse* big ones.

Dr Brixton didn't seem interested in Suzette, except to find out how it affected Anthony. "Do you think her departure had an effect on his ability to communicate with you? Was there space for him to talk about his problems?"

Another bull's eye. He had been too distracted by his battles with Magda to pay Anthony much mind after Suzette left home. Dr Brixton's questions went straight to the heart of Anthony's problem, his problem, the whole family's mess. Neville had come to get help for Anthony, but she was also helping *him*.

Her questions took him back to when Anthony disappeared. Neville realised he should have spent the last two weeks asking around the neighbourhood. Someone somewhere must have spotted Anthony that night.

He told Dr Brixton the last words he heard from Anthony before he went dumb, that he deserved his hiding. Then, because she was so easy to talk to, he told her about his worry that Anthony had been molested.

Dr Brixton's face crinkled up, but there was no smile. "Why do you think that?"

Neville's Adam's apple worked overtime. This was gunna be hard. "I saw it, with my own eyes. In the orphanage in District Six when I was growing up. The fathers were hard drinkers and hard men. The things they did to the boys should never happen to children."

"Were you molested at the orphanage?"

Neville pulled his right hand out from under his thigh and blocked his mouth, trapping the words that came spilling out. It was hard to talk about his childhood. He hadn't told Magda the worst of it.

Dr Brixton asked if he wanted a glass of water. He said yes, his throat was dry. After he emptied the glass he wanted to tell Dr Brixton everything, for Anthony's sake and his also. "The fathers interfered with the boys. They were all into it, the lot of them. Then Brother Mike came, from Ireland. He was the worst of all of them. He was a vuil vark."

Neville took a deep breath. He smashed through the brick wall sealing away his most eina memories and carried them out into the open.

"Brother Mike targeted my best friend Kenny. He was twelve, but he had a small frame so he looked younger. Brother Mike was a big man. His nose was the first thing you noticed. It was red and smeared with broken veins. He took Kenny to his room a few nights after he arrived. We said nothing. The boys who went with the fathers didn't want anybody talking about them. The rest didn't want to know. Kenny cried when he came back. The next morning there was blood on his sheets. I saw it with my own eyes; I was in the bed next to him. Night after night that vuil vark came to fetch Kenny. Night after night Kenny cried. One night he didn't come to bed. I found him the next morning, in the bathroom. He cut his wrists with a kitchen knife."

Neville cradled his forehead in his hand as he shook with the pain he had locked away for years. Kenny's face came out of the dark cell he had built for him in his mind; the way he looked that morning. His lips were dark blue in his pale face. Ribbons of blood streamed down the floor into his brown hair; matting it like the coir in their mattresses.

Dr Brixton's voice brought him back into her office. "Mr Fourie, were you molested?"

"No. I wasn't. One of the varke, Brother Jude, used to get excited when he gave me hidings. But he never touched me with anything except his belt. The thing is, I know what a boy looks like when he's molested, like he's seen hell up close. I'm worried I'm seeing the same thing in Anthony's eyes."

Dr Brixton passed on a pile of tissues from a box on her desk. Neville was sure she ordered boxes in bulk; she was good at drawing out pain. He was convinced he had found the right person to help Anthony. He blew his nose and listened close to her next words.

"Mr Fourie, we have to wrap up. We only have five minutes 'til our hour is up."

There was a lot more Neville wanted to say. For every problem he had offered up, Dr Brixton had a solution. But he couldn't take up more of her time; Anthony was outside waiting for her help.

Her next sentence gave him some hope. "I think you could also benefit from counselling Mr Fourie."

222

He nodded. "Ja, I'm surprised at what happened here today. I never told anyone about Kenny before. Not even my wife."

Dr Brixton broke his aching heart. "I'm sorry, Mr Fourie, I'm not in a position to help you. I'm a child psychologist, I don't treat adults."

Neville's lip quivered. "So what must I do? There's no psychologists in Hanover Park."

"No, I don't think there are. But I know of an excellent support group for adults who were abused as children. It will be perfect for you. A colleague of mine, a trained psychologist, facilitates the group. They meet in Wynberg on Saturday afternoons; you won't have to miss work."

Neville settled for his hour with Dr Brixton. In that short time she had given him a lot to think about, a lot to do. He came here thinking he was doing a good job raising his children, he learned that he was a vrot father. What did he know about raising children? When Anthony got into trouble the first thing he did was pull out his belt like the varke at the orphanage.

He collected another phone number, for the facilitator of the support group. He promised he would attend their sessions, soon as he had Anthony and Suzette sorted out.

Dr Brixton had one last piece of advice. "Start your attendance this Saturday. Make yourself strong so you can be strong for your children. Believe me, Mr Fourie, attending that group will be the best thing you can do for your children."

Neville nodded. "I promise I will start this week."

Dr Brixton escorted him back to the waiting room. She squatted down in front of Anthony and peered into his face with her honey smile. "So who's next? Come Anthony, let's get to know each other."

Anthony got to his feet when Dr Brixton tugged at his arm. He didn't look once in his father's direction as he let the psychologist lead him into her office.

Neville couldn't stay in the waiting room. He needed fresh air to clear out the filth he had dredged up in the past hour. He paused at the receptionist's desk. "I'll be just outside the door if the doctor needs me."

The old woman shooed him out. She was probably Dr Brixton's mother; she had the same crinkly smile. "It's no problem at all, you won't be needed for at least an hour."

He walked outside and drew deep gulps of sweet air. A thick black headache filled the space between his brain and his skull, throbbing at his temples. His legs trembled as though he had run up the hill to Dr Brixton's office with Anthony on his back. It was worth the pain. Dr Brixton was going to fix his boy, of that he had no doubt.

Neville collapsed onto a bench in the garden outside the Child Development Unit. The smell of the lavender bushes under the window calmed his heart and the tumbling waterfalls on the mountain gave him something to focus on while his headache cleared away. When he walked back inside the waiting room an hour later, Dr Brixton's office door opened and Anthony came out, his chin digging into his chest.

Dr Brixton smiled when she saw him hovering at the end of the corridor. "Mr Fourie, if I can just see you again for a minute?"

Neville stepped forward as Anthony reached him. He put his hand on his boy's shoulder. "You okay?"

Anthony was as silent as before. Neville guided him to a chair in the reception area and headed into Dr Brixton's office. She was on the phone, waving him to a chair while she spoke. "Thank you. I'll send them right over. Goodbye."

Dr Brixton folded her fingers and leaned across her desk. "Mr Fourie, I think your diagnosis is spot on. Something has affected Anthony deeply. He's in shock. I'm not going to be able to work with him in this state, so I'm recommending you to a colleague. Dr Paul Martin is a psychiatrist; they have different skills and techniques from a psychologist."

Neville got a moerse skrik. Did Anthony need electric shock treatment? Was he so far gone already? "What's the psychiatrist going to do?"

"Dr Martin will examine Anthony and prescribe medication if it's required. I can't do that. We need to calm him down so that I can work with him. I'll need to see him twice a week initially. You will have to make sure he takes his medication. Dr Martin's rooms are in Claremont, it's on your way home. You have an appointment in half and hour."

Neville took the psychiatrist's address and established with Dr Brixton that it was okay if Nicky brought Anthony next Wednesday after school. He couldn't keep asking for time off, the state of emergency had everyone at the firm working their guts out. He would bring Anthony for his Saturday morning appointments and take him home before heading to his support group session in the afternoon.

Chapter Twenty-Four

Suzette knew how Cinderella felt on her wedding day. Polished like a princess. She looked at her face in the mirror framed by small white bulbs. Was that really her? She had never seen those cheekbones before, but there they were – on her face. Her eyes weren't usually such shining gongs.

It was amazing what a little makeup could do. Well, a lot of makeup. She had been sitting in front of the mirror for almost an hour. She was bursting to see how she would look when her hair was done.

Maureen wasn't satisfied. She leaned over the back of Suzette's chair, peering into the mirror with a frown. "Hmm. I think we need more around her chin, to define it a teensy bit, don't you think?"

Mymoena swung the chair to left and examined Suzette. "Let me see. Maybe you right. She can do with a bit more definition."

Maureen stared into Suzette's face in the mirror as Mymoena brushed dark powder under her jaw line. "A little more, just a touch more," she encouraged.

Suzette was amazed at the difference the powder made. Who would have thought that grey dust could do that? Her face looked five centimetres longer, and it suited her. She knew the fashion world had makeup artists, but until today she never realised that what they really did was make art.

Mymoena used mostly sponges and brushes that she dipped into trays of paint and powder. The only makeup she wore was thick black liner outlining the slant of her green eyes. No cosmetics could come close to matching the red and orange mane of curls that draped down her back.

Suzette stared at Mymoena's nose ring when she leaned forward to trace her lips with a dark pencil; she had never seen one before. Mymoena's spicy breath reminded her how lakker hungry she was. She hadn't had time for breakfast, and lunchtime had long come and gone.

Maureen was finally satisfied. "That's it. I think she looks amazing."

Suzette agreed, although she would have stayed put in the chair for another two hours if her new best friend wanted more work done. Maureen had planned the shoot. Suzette was getting her portfolio, for free.

From the first night they first met, when Suzette told her about her plans to become a model, Maureen had been busy. She said she believed Suzette could make it to the big time; Grace Kelly looks were timeless. Suzette had never heard of Grace Kelly. After Maureen brought pictures she stared in the mirror for hours, searching for the princess.

When *Fairlady* booked Marc Fontaine for a fashion shoot, Maureen went into action. Suzette had no idea who he was when her friend brought him to Neil's flat on a Saturday afternoon. She thought he had a nerve to stare at her like that.

Maureen babbled nonstop. "See, didn't I tell you? Wasn't I right? You can see it, can't you?"

Suzette didn't know where to look while Marc looked her over. The man was clearly a moffie, why else would he flap his wrist like that? His blonde hair was completely Andy Gibb. Still, he was looking at her like she was a sucker he wanted to lick.

"Hmm. Give me a minute, darling. I'm thinking." Marc took three mincing steps to the right, crossed his skinny legs and stared at Suzette's profile.

She had no idea what was going on. Maureen had asked her to stand in the middle of the lounge and the two of them had been staring at her ever since. Marc eyeballed her breasts and hips, then twirled around her one more time, pausing at the back. Suzette could feel his eyes on her bum. "What's going on? Why you looking at me like that?"

Marc was back in her face, wincing as she spoke. He lifted his finger to his lip like a librarian. "Shh. Don't say a word. Just stand there and be you."

Suzette kept her calm while Marc rubbed his finger between her eyebrows and stared into her eyes. He was tarty but harmless.

Marc spun on his heels and clicked his fingers. "Darling! Get me a drink won't you? I'm parched."

Suzette went to the kitchen to get Marc a glass of white wine and beers for herself and Maureen. What was going on? She had been expecting Maureen today; they had plans to see a film at the Labia. She didn't know what Marc was doing here. She tuned into their conversation after she placed the drinks on the coffee table and took a seat on the couch next to Maureen.

"I think La Mode would take her on, don't you?" Maureen asked and answered before Marc could reply. "They're based right here, on the foreshore. They represent all the top girls."

"Yes, but Nora and Partners are the best in the business," Marc replied. "There are such things as planes, darling. Joburg's not that far away. Besides, there are girls from Africa working in Milan and New York. Think Iman. Don't be so parochial."

Suzette took a sip of her beer. She had no idea what they were talking about. She was getting on fine with Maureen even though she was so clever; they were both mal about everything to do with fashion. She had taken up Maureen's way of speaking – everything was amazing and lakker. The girls at the factory laughed at her for talking white.

"I think we must get onto it right away," Maureen was talking like she was in a speed contest with Marc. "Before someone else discovers her. I told you, she's already working as a model. Neil discovered her on a ramp in a factory in Retreat. No wait, I should point out at this juncture that I discovered her when Neil introduced us."

Marc flapped his wrist. "I agree fully. I see exactly what you mean." He leaned across the coffee table towards Suzette. "Tell me darling, how serious are you about becoming a model?"

Suzette was amazed. She put her beer down carefully. "You talking about me?"

Marc frowned. "She has good teeth, but she will definitely need elocution. Can you arrange that, darling?"

Maureen nodded. "She's getting better already, she's quite the mimic." She turned to Suzette and took her hands. "Suzette, let me introduce you properly to my friend. This is Marc Fontaine."

Suzette pulled a hand free and lifted it to her wide-open mouth. Marc Fontaine! When Maureen introduced him she thought his name was Mark. She had no idea it was Marc staring at her! Look how she was dressed, a jeans and a jersey! If she had known he was coming, she would have put on lipstick. She slapped her friend's arm. "Haai Maureen! You should have told me you were bringing Marc Fontaine! Look how I look!"

Maureen laughed. "That's why I didn't tell you. I wanted Marc to see the real you. Don't worry, he's very impressed. He wants to shoot your portfolio."

Suzette lifted her hands to her burning cheeks. She couldn't look in Marc's direction. He worked with the top models in the business. She had seen what he had done with Anneline Kriel for *Cosmopolitan*. The woman was befok beautiful but he made her look spectacular. And he was staring at her!

The hairdresser, Cyril, was also a moffie. Suzette could see his leopard-skin underpants through his tight white pants. His white shirt was unbuttoned to his waist. Three gold chains hung in a dark chest sprinkled with peppercorn curls.

He pranced around her as he teased her hair into a bird's nest. She couldn't figure out what he was doing. Was he trying to give her an afro like his? Her hair didn't frizz, all he was doing was making it stand away from her head. After his comb had been through every hair on her head, he blowdried it with a fat brush, pulled it tight and went to work behind her. She couldn't see what he was doing. Mymoena helped, passing hairclips every time Cyril snapped his fingers in her direction.

Finally, Cyril swivelled Suzette's chair around to face the line he formed with Maureen and Mymoena. They all stared in silence.

"Perfect!" Maureen said, turning to Mymoena. "That's perfect, don't you think?"

Mymoena smiled. "You look poenangs, Suzette."

"*Princess Grace se ma se moer,*" Cyril piped in.

Maureen swivelled Suzette's chair again and held up a small mirror behind her head. Suzette saw the stylish bun on the back of her head, exactly like the one Princess Grace wore in her official engagement photo. She looked like a princess – a little bit darker, but she could pass for one.

Maureen shrieked. "Don't cry! I can see you want to. Don't, you'll ruin your makeup. C'mon guys, finish up, Marc's on his way."

Mymoena brought a soft white shower cap and held it over Suzette's face. Cyril sprayed what seemed like a whole can of hairspray on her hair. Mymoena touched up her makeup when Cyril was done. Maureen pulled her up from the chair. "Now for the best part – the clothes!"

As she was led across the studio, Suzette looked around. She hadn't seen much since she arrived with Maureen; she had been taken straight to the makeup mirror in the corner and trapped there for almost two hours.

Marc's studio was at the back of his house in Camps Bay, high on the mountain with a view of the half-moon white beach and the sea beyond. Suzette had never been to Camps Bay before; it was amazing. The studio on the top terrace at the back of the house looked like a shed from the outside. The walls were made of shining silver corrugated iron, like a very posh squatter shack. Inside, the sheets were lined halfway with dark wood and the back wall was draped in a black curtain. No sunlight found its way inside.

Maureen shuffled through clothing crammed onto four rails flanking a studio wall. "Let me see, what shall we try first?" She selected a dress and handed it to Suzette. "We'll do the classic black cocktail number, okay?"

Suzette would have done anything Maureen asked. She didn't know how she was going to thank her friend for this. She still couldn't believe Marc Fontaine was shooting her portfolio. It would probably take the rest of her life to return this befokte favour to both of them.

The dressing room was a shaky wooden frame curtained with black cloth. It had a bench and a full-length mirror on the wall. Suzette undressed to her bra and panties. The curtain swooshed open.

Maureen came in, offering a brown bag. "Good, you haven't put the dress on yet. Here, take this, put it on first. Be careful, don't smudge your makeup. Pull the dress up from the floor."

Suzette opened the bag and shook a pair of black stockings out onto the bench. Something fell onto the floor. She couldn't figure out what it was when she picked it up. She examined the lace frill, trying to work out what to do with it. What were those clips for, hanging at the bottom?

She opened the curtain. "Maureen, come here a minute!"

Maureen laughed when she realised Suzette didn't know what to do with a suspender belt. "Don't worry, I'll be your dresser."

For the first time in her life, Suzette rolled black stockings up her legs. Maureen knelt on the floor and showed her how to fasten the clips. She handed Suzette the black dress. Its shiny lining slid icily up her tummy. It stroked her thigh where there was a gap between her stocking and lace suspender.

Suzette stared into the full-length mirror. Mymoena and Cyril were magicians. They had found the princess inside her.

"Don't cry! Don't you dare cry!" Maureen laughed. "I told you, didn't I? You should have believed me when I first said you had it."

Suzette couldn't take her eyes off her reflection. The Hanover Park high school girl was gone; she looked years older and good enough to go anywhere. She came down hard on the happiness waltzing through her veins. Princess Grace didn't smile in any photos she had seen.

"You're beautiful," Maureen whispered in her ear. "Come, Marc has arrived."

Modelling was much harder work than Suzette expected. It was fokken difficult to keep her body in the same position for a long time. After twenty minutes her muscles hurt like a bricklayer's at the end of a working day.

Marc spoke nonstop while he shot her. "Hold that pose, hold it. That's it, that's it. That's exactly what I want. Hold it."

His camera clicked as fast as his mouth. He took several pictures of

Suzette in the black dress. He positioned her on a barstool on the low platform under the lights and asked her to stare over her left shoulder at the camera. He shot off a roll of film while she looked straight at the camera, her eyes opened wide enough to satisfy him and learning not to blink in the flashlights. Then he demanded that she part her lips in a faint smile, like she was keeping a secret. Suzette got that one right soon as he asked.

Marc changed cameras several times. His assistant, Lukey, removed and replaced film and passed on fresh cameras. Lukey was Mymoena's cousin, so his real name was probably Lukmaan. His tight black demin jeans hung low on his skinny hips and his short black T-shirt kept creeping up to expose his small naartjie navel.

Lukey was also in charge of the backdrops. He rolled down white sheets of paper when Suzette wore the black dress; black sheets when she changed into grey slacks and a white shirt.

Marc arranged her body and barked at Lukey to position the lights. Suzette had to hold her poses while he fiddled with white umbrellas and strobes. Mymoena came over several times to patch up her makeup. It was hot under the lights.

She changed into a sculpted trouser suit. It was the first outfit that fit her properly; Maureen had to adjust most of the clothes with dressmaker's pins. They pierced through her skin while Marc ordered her to hold her position.

Marc fired instructions. "That's right baby, that's the look I want. Hold that thought. Don't move! That's it, not too wide baby; I don't want to see teeth."

The grey suit jacket with padded shoulders rested on Suzette's waistband. Her hands spanned her hips, following Marc's instructions to push them forward.

"C'mon baby. You're standing at the top of the boardroom table. Tell those fuckers the bottom line is unacceptable. Tell them they should either shape up or ship out. Show those fuckers who's the boss. C'mon, show me who's the boss."

The only boss Suzette knew was the owner of Planet Fashions, Mr Strauss. The only look he had was staring like a hangdog at his models. She knew how to pull off a bossy look; she was a first-born child.

When Marc finally said he was done, Suzette was so lame with hunger her stomach growled in reply.

Maureen wasn't finshed yet. "The wedding gown, Marc. We should do it now. We can get ramp lessons after she's signed up. We might as well do the gown now."

Marc agreed. "We'll need to change her makeup and her hair. I'm taking a break. Lukey, a strong cup of tea please. I'll be in the house. Call me when you're ready."

Mymoena gave Suzette two bananas and a cup of sweet tea. She wiped away her hours of work with cotton wool dipped in Ponds cream. She gave Suzette a new look; dusting pale powder on her forehead, cheeks and neck. She laid down a base of brown on her eyelids and shaded it in with red eyeshadow.

Cyril took over when Mymoena was done. He brushed the hairspray out Suzette's hair before blowdrying it into fat curls. This time around she could see everything he was doing in the mirror. He piled her hair above her head and pinned the curls into place. He laboured more than an hour threading oyster-coloured strings of tiny beads into her hair.

Suzette had never pictured herself as a bride; tying herself to a man wasn't part of the plan. She stared in the mirror as Cyril crowned her with pearls. She could catch a prince looking like this – one a lot more handsome than Frog Prince Rainier, as Maureen called him – a prince who looked like Richard Gere.

The wedding dress was amazing. The bodice was beaded, matching the sparkles in her hair. The lined dress was off-white. Maureen couldn't get the zip to go all the way up, but it made no difference at the front. The tight bodice pushed her breasts into pole position and the wide skirt swirled from the waist down. The skirt's panels of fabric looked like they came from an upholstered palace couch. Suzette stared into the dressing-room mirror. A picture in a fairy tale stared back at her.

Marc circled her when he came back into the studio. "Wow," he said softly. "You were so right, Maureen. Wow. Remember, Suzette, who discovered you. Be sure you tell everybody I shot you first. What the heck, I'll tell everybody."

Suzette waited while Marc fussed. He made Lukey walk up and down to a cupboard in a corner. Lukey brought black velvety fabric.

Marc made him hang it before he changed his mind. He sent Lukey away with the blue cloth as he reached the platform. He chose the dark red velvet. He fussed while Lukey draped it, insisting that the folds weren't fat enough; then he flapped for half an hour because they weren't evenly spaced.

He flashed the strobes as he positioned them in a semicircle, bouncing some off umbrellas positioned above them. Suzette sat in the makeup chair while she waited for everything to be just so – just watching Marc was exhausting. Finally, after Mymoena fixed her lipstick again, he was ready.

Marc instructed her to walk towards him while he took her picture. "I want you to come down the aisle to the man you love. The man you're crazy about. I want you to think about your honeymoon. You're in a suite alongside a canal in Venice. The windows are open and the curtains are flapping in the hot breeze. He's waiting there for you."

Suzette knew nothing about Venice. She couldn't think where it was on the map. Who would want to have a honeymoon on a canal? The one in Hanover Park, behind the Snoekies factory, was slime-green and choking with rubbish, mostly empty plastic bottles. It was no problem, though; she could picture Richard Gere waiting to start his honeymoon with his princess bride.

The platform was small, it took only five steps to the edge, but she could strut them. She pushed her hips forward towards Richard on the four-poster bed 'til they ached.

Marc approved. "That's it, that's my girl. Again, do it again. Keep that pose. Hold it, don't move. That's it. That's just perfect darling. That's my darling, do it again."

Five rolls of film later the shoot was finally over. Suzette was desperate to lie down. Her shoulders hurt, her pelvis ached – even her mouth was sore. She wasn't surprised to find it was dark when they left the studio. It felt like midnight but it was only seven o'clock. She had arrived at the studio at eleven that morning.

Marc kissed her on both cheeks when she left. "Remember, Suzette, I had you first. But I think we will work together again. You're a stunner, darling."

Three weeks later, Maureen brought four copies of her portfolio to Neil's flat. It looked like a big photo album, but it was much classier. It had a soft black leather cover with Suzette's name in silver letters on the front.

Maureen, Neil and Suzette took one each and poured over the photos. Neil and Maureen argued about which agencies were best. Maureen wanted one that arranged ramp work as well as photoshoots. "The wedding photo is the clincher. Every designer I know will be after Suzette when they see that one."

It was late Sunday night; Suzette had to leave to catch the last train to Retreat. She spent weekends with Neil when he was available. Her friend Melanie at Planet Fashions arranged with her widowed neighbour, Mrs Van Niekerk, for Suzette to board with her. She could walk to work from her new home.

She sat on her bed with her portfolio on her raised knees. Her roommates had tucked their blankets over their heads. For once, they weren't complaining about keeping the light on. They couldn't believe the portfolio when they saw it.

Mrs Van Niekerk had two young daughters. Caroline and Marcia shared a bunk, Suzette had a single bed squeezed into the remaining space in the room. It suited her for now. Mrs Van Niekerk asked only eighty rand a month for her board, including meals.

She paged through her portfolio. The first photo was a portrait. The makeup and the lights lit up her cheekbones as they curved across her face, creating shadows in all the right places. Maureen said she looked chiseled. She explained it meant carved out of marble.

Suzette preferred herself in black and white; she looked dramatic and stylish. She was shocked at how much older she seemed, how much more sophisticated. She could recognise parts of herself – the ears and the nose were definitely hers.

She couldn't stop saving now that she had a portfolio. She had opened a bank account last Saturday. Maureen said she would find her a place to stay near town when she starting getting regular bookings. Woodstock and Observatory were mixed communities; the neighbours wouldn't complain when she moved in. She was saving for a deposit on her rent.

She lifted the tissue paper lining the last page in the portfolio. Marc had taken this shot as she reached the edge of the platform. The wedding dress swirled around her legs as she leaned forward with a promise in her eyes. She couldn't wait 'til the girls at the factory saw the portfolio tomorrow. They were going to be amazed.

Suzette wiped her wet cheeks. The one place she wanted to brag was a no-go zone. She couldn't take the portfolio to Mummy and them to show what a kwaai model she was.

Chapter Twenty-Five

Marewaan and Oegies were waiting at the gate after school. It was no use trying to duck, Ougat's ouens had spotted him. Anthony couldn't work out what to do. Since he started taking his tablets a screen went up between him and the world.

Mummy and Dedda came to his school to explain why he was silent. He didn't know what story they came up with and he didn't care. They got the teachers to ignore him; that was all he wanted. That, and a room where he could mix with other people for a few hours and take some time to think. When he was alone with his filthy body, all he could think about was how to hurt it. Throwing it down the stairs had been a good idea.

The ouens were waiting for him; he knew it. It was no use trying to run. His legs were so pap he was sure they couldn't make it anywhere. He couldn't see anybody when he looked around for help. A car started up in the teachers' parking area. It was Mr September, reversing out of his bay. The principal's car slowed when it reached the gate. Marewaan and Oegies were close enough to touch it.

Mr September would have to wait if there was cars coming down the street. Anthony prayed as he stumbled forward. He had never prayed so hard. "Please God, let there be a car coming. Please God, let him wait." His lips moved but he couldn't hear himself speak.

God wasn't listening. Mr September pulled away. Anthony was five steps away from the ouens. He froze. He looked over his shoulder. Nobody there.

Marewaan's biceps bulged as he gripped Anthony's arm and pulled him forward. "Kom. Ougat is waiting for you. He got no more patience with you, laaitie."

Anthony had to walk in step with the ouens. What else could he do?

The shebeen was a few blocks up from home; Anthony kept his eyes peeled for someone he knew all the way there. He couldn't pull himself free from the ouens' grip, the tablets made him lam. He could see himself and the things he did, but he couldn't feel anything. His life was happening in front of his eyes like a film.

He knew Ougat was gunna come for him. They were brothers in crime, like the Mafia. Ougat was probably worried that he would betray him. Anthony wouldn't; he knew that the day he talked about the rape was the day he signed his warrant. The JFKs would be on his gat.

They were on Peach Street. He could see the shebeen's black zinc walls. The woman walking towards them carrying two heavy shopping bags couldn't help him; she was crooked with arthritis. The two girls playing eight blocks on the pavement across from the shebeen couldn't help. Anyway, how was he supposed to let them know he was in trouble?

It was too late to try. They were inside the shebeen. The customers turned and stared in slow motion as Marewaan and Oegies pulled him through the shebeen and into the lounge. Ougat's mother was planted on the couch in front of the blaring TV. Her lips moved but they didn't keep up with her words, like a kung-fu film. Anthony heard what she said when he was already out of the lounge and in the kitchen. "Wat gaan aan?"

He didn't see much of the kitchen as they passed through but he smelled it. Someone was cooking liver; the onions soaking in the vinegar made his eyes water.

Oegies and Marewaan led him into the zinc-enclosed back yard and seated him on an upturned beer crate against the vibracrete wall. Oegies gripped his shoulder. "Wag hier. Ougat will come sort you out."

Marewaan left Oegies on guard and went back into the house. Anthony didn't need a guard. He was too lam to go anywhere. The tablet he took in the morning made the whole day disappear and the night one sent him to sleep right away. No more waking up alone in the cold lounge wet with sweat.

While he worked out what he would say if he started talking again, he couldn't do anything else. How was he going to explain why he raped Shirley? He was going to jail for sure after he talked. For weeks he had been sitting in silence, waiting for the police to knock on the door. He was going to lose his family. They were going to hate him forever, Nicky 'specially.

The smell of frying meat poured out of the kitchen in a greasy cloud. Ougat's sister Sylvia was the cook. Oegies leaned against the doorway, keeping her company while she stood over the spluttering pan. Anthony dropped his head when she came to stare at him through the kitchen window.

Oegies walked over and shook Anthony, thudding his shoulders into the wall. Another hard shake followed. "Hey laaitie, you orrite?"

Anthony closed his eyes as he recalled Oegies screaming into his face when he lay on top of Shirley. The ouens' chanting had made him think that he was doing something kwaai. Until he started taking the tablets Oegies had been in his dreams every night. He slid his bum up the crate, coming upright and lifting his eyelids carefully. He nodded.

Oegies seated himself on a crate and lit a fat joint. He took three pulls and passed it on.

Anthony lifted a hand and shook his head. Oegies shoved his elbow into his ribs, offering the joint again. "You look kak laaitie. Here, trek a skyf. Look like you can do with a skyf."

Oegies brought his face close for a good look, his eyes bouncing like the pinballs at the corner shop. "Dunno what's going on here. You don't look orrite laaitie, you got a shadow on your face. Ougat is gunna be here shortly. He will sort you out."

Ougat kept them waiting for hours. Oegies got the munchies after his joint and scored a plate from the kitchen. He offered to share, but Anthony was too naar to look at the food.

He wanted a tablet. The screen in front of his eyes was lifting. The noises Oegies made while he ate made him naar. Liver grease dripped down the gangster's chin and onto his chest. He left an oily smear on his jacket's sleeve when he wiped it away.

Was it suppertime? Were Dedda and Mummy home from work already? Anthony didn't want to think about it. It gave him a pain to think about how much they must be worrying. He couldn't work out a way to get home.

Oegies had just lit his after-supper joint when the boss arrived.

Anthony squeezed his eyes tight. Looking at Ougat would take him right back to that night in the shack. The screen was melting away, his hearing was clearer than it had been for a while. Oegies was talking about him.

"Ougat, there's something wrong with this laaitie. I can't figure out what it is; if he's contagious or something."

"What kak you talking?" Ougat's voice was calm.

"It's the laaitie. He's not talking. And there's something not right with his face. See for yourself if you don't believe me."

Anthony's body pulled tight into itself, hard as a rod of steel, as Ougat crossed the yard. He kept his head down and his eyes tight shut as Ougat came to a halt. He could feel muscles in his neck that he didn't know was there. They weren't strong enough to stop Ougat from gripping him under his chin and lifting up his head. His muscles couldn't stop Ougat's hand pinning his forehead to the wall.

"Ag, there's nothing wrong with the laaitie. All's wrong is that he don't wanna be here." Ougat slammed Anthony's head against the wall.

Anthony flared his nostrils. Evil smelled like offal coated in vinegar.

Ougat knocked his head against the wall one last time before he moved away, issuing instructions to Oegies. "Keep watch. I got to sort some things out. Got something bemoer lined up for this laaitie."

Anthony slumped down the crate. His head hurt. He could hear in Ougat's voice how much he wanted to hurt him. What could be more bemoer than a rape?

Could he make it past Oegies, through the crowded house and even more crowded shebeen? He doubted it. He knew only one thing for sure: Ougat couldn't make him do anything. He was finished with the JFKs. He would rather take punishment from them than do another crime.

He dropped his head onto his chin. What was gunna happen was gunna happen. He was back in the shebeen because he was stupid enough to come here in the first place. No one held a knife to his neck and forced him to do what he did to Shirley. He brought it on himself.

His life couldn't move forward until the truth that was choking him came borrelling out. It was going to come soon; Dr Brixton was digging hard to find out what happened and she almost got it when he last saw her. Anthony decided he was going to tell her everything; it would be orrite, she was on his side.

Dr Brixton had explained at his first session how shock worked; she said it was his brain's way of protecting him. She made him feel he made the right choice to say nothing. She had told him what his dedda thought, that he had seen something that traumatised him the night he disappeared. His brain didn't know how to process it, so it locked itself up.

She almost got him to talk when he saw her yesterday. She explained again how everything he told her stayed in her room. Psychologists had rules; they weren't allowed to tell anyone what their patients said, not their parents, not even a court of law. If he had done something bad, he could tell her.

Dr Brixton smiled at him like a yellow sun in a Sunday school book. "Is that what's wrong, Anthony? Did you do something bad?"

Anthony couldn't stop his head from nodding up and down, twice.

Dr Brixton kept going. "Can you talk about it?"

Anthony shook his head from side to side. Just once.

"Do you want to talk about it?"

Anthony nodded again. He dropped his head and examined his fingers, twisting like earthworms in his lap.

"Sometimes it's hard to know where to start. You should think about that. Find a place to start and then you'll find it will be easier to get it out."

Anthony stared at his fingers. The night he raped Shirley was like a poison inside him, paralysing his body as it spread. His throat wouldn't work, his tongue couldn't move.

Dr Brixton leaned across her desk. "Our hour is nearly up. You did well today, Anthony. You did really well."

Anthony stared at her. If his lips were working he would smile.

"I want you to do something for me. I want you to think about what you would like to say to me. Where you want to start. Can you do that?"

Anthony nodded and got to his feet when Dr Brixton stood up. She put her hand on his back as she walked him to the reception area. The pressure on his shoulder blade made him feel a lot stronger. As he travelled home with Nicky, he scratched through his brain for the best place to start when he saw Dr Brixton again.

The kitchen filled up with voices. Ougat was back. Anthony opened his eyes. It was okay; he could cope. He only had to make it through the night and tomorrow. He was seeing Dr Brixton again at ten o'clock on Saturday morning. She could help him find a way to break from Ougat and clean up his life.

Marewaan and Oegies lifted him up from the crate. Anthony let them drag him across the yard. His feet remembered how to walk as they reached the kitchen step.

Ougat was waiting in the lounge. He cocked his head. "Let's go."

Lippe and Skelm were waiting on the pavement with a boy Anthony hadn't seen before. He looked fifteen at most. Ougat grabbed Anthony's arm and marched him down the pavement, the ouens taking up position behind. It was dark, Mummy and Dedda were already home for sure. It was almost time for his next tablet.

Anthony had no idea where they were going until they got there. A grey mist, thick with the smell of fish and salt, smothered everything as Ougat pulled him down pavements and across streets. They were back at Bra Mike's house at the edge of Hanover Park. Anthony took a deep breath as Ougat pushed him into the shack.

The set up hadn't changed. In the blue paraffin light Anthony could see the crates were in the same position as the night he and Shirley were brought there. Boeta Toefie was seated to the left of the lamp, Bra Mike stood like a giant to the right.

Ougat dragged Anthony across the shack to stand in front of Bra Mike. "Brought the laaitie, as promised."

Anthony's legs just about held him up. He kept his head down. He was scared to look at Bra Mike. He heard a grunt.

"Why you let him take you so laag, Ougat? Laaitie, did you not

242

swear right here, to me, that you were a ware JFK? Did we not stand by you? Hey laaitie, look at me."

Anthony kept his head down. He stared at Bra Mike's black boots. The stitching was coming loose at the tips. His head shot up when a heavy klap landed on his right cheekbone.

Bra Mike stared into his eyes. "Don't you show me no disrespec' in my own place. You took Ougat's pille and you gave him no compensation. Why you didn't report for duty after we made you one of us? Who you talking to, what you vertelling?"

Anthony looked down again. Ougat's blow landed on his ear, sending shock and pain racing down his neck. He tried to move away but Ougat pulled him forward, into a punch in his gut. Tears rolled down his cheeks, past lips pressed tight together.

Bra Mike gripped his chin and lifted his face. "Did you say what happened here?"

Anthony couldn't nod or shake his head. Even if he had the strength, the palm cupping his neck didn't allow him to.

Bra Mike shoved him down onto the ground. "Sort out your kak, Ougat!"

Ougat kicked Anthony's ribs. "Moenie worry. This kak is gunna get sorted out one time."

Anthony's feet dragged on the sand floor as Marewaan and Skelm pulled him to the side of the shack. He gave no resistance when Marewaan tied his hands behind his back with rope and Skelm took care of his feet. His head hit the floor as Marewaan pushed him sideways. The pain in his head and his ribs kept him pinned to the ground.

His mind was focused on his pain but he forced it to get working on escape plans. There was a way to let Ougat and the ouens know that he couldn't betray them because he couldn't talk. He could ask for pen and paper and write it down. He would let them know that he didn't want to be a JFK anymore.

Anthony lifted his head and looked around. He had lost track of what was happening. The ouens were seated on the crates. The smell of dagga mixed in with the salty mist drifting in through cracks in the zinc walls. The ouens were silently passing a pipe, the same routine like when they first brought him here.

243

The new boy who had come with them from the shebeen was seated on the crate next to Boeta Toefie. The teenager looked like he lived in a house where the supplies ran out a long while ago. His skinny arms grew out of his neck; he had hardly any shoulders. Seated next to Marewaan who was as wide as a bus, he looked like a pigeon.

Anthony drifted out again as Bra Mike stood up to give the boy the same lecture about the JFKs as he gave Anthony. What was the time? Was Dedda out looking for him? What was the chances Dedda would find him in a backyard shack covered in thick mist? He tried to say Dedda. His lips moved but he couldn't get a whisper to crawl out.

What did Ougat have in mind when he said he was gunna sort him out? Did they plan for the new recruit to rape him? Anthony decided that was okay. He deserved to be punished for what he had done to Shirley; he had to feel what he put her through.

Mist curled through the gap between the shack walls and the floor, wetting the soil under Anthony. He wriggled forward carefully, sparing his tender ribs. He checked out how the initiation was going. The boy had taken off his sweater; his ribs made a narrow cage on his chest. He shouted when the needle pierced his arm. Bra Mike shook him as easily as a housewife smacking a mat against a fence.

Anthony remembered the pain. Could the skinny boy hold him down with his sore arm and rape him? The ouens would help, he was sure of that. The boy would take him in the gat. Would the ouens all join in? How eina would it be? His bum clenched in anticipation.

Dr Brixton could help after the rape. He decided that was where he would start with his story. He could tell her about the punishment before he told her about his crime.

Anthony looked up when the ouens crowded noisily around the boy, congratulating him on his tjap. Boeta Toefie spoke the same kak about the ceremonial pipe and they all took their seats again. The new recruit's pigeon chest puffed up to twice its size when he pulled hard enough to make the pipe glow red.

Ougat got to his feet and pulled the new man up to stand next to him. "One more thing, Alfredo. You got to prove your loyalty to the JFKs. One more thing before we make you a ware JFK." Ougat brought Alfredo across the shack to Anthony. "You got to sort out this laaitie for me."

Alfredo stared down at Anthony, his eyes as bloodshot as Ougat's. "Sure bra, anything you want. I'm with you guys."

Anthony tensed up as Skelm crouched down to untie his feet. He had to decide. Was he gunna make a run for it or would he let the ouens rape him? They didn't give him a chance to run. Skelm and Lippe grabbed his arms and led him out of the shack. Ougat and Alfredo followed. Where were they going? He had made himself ready for rape, not anything else.

He saw lights on in the house as they left the shack. He wondered if the woman who offered him a glass of water the night he raped Shirley was inside. Would she come out if he shouted? He was still struggling to get a shout past his lips when he reached the pavement.

The ouens took a left, leading him towards the factories at the border of Hanover Park. He didn't know how to ask where they were going. Dedda was out for sure, looking for him. Even with a torch, it would be hard. Waves of mist curled through the darkness. The smell of fish swirling in the grey soup grew stronger as they neared the Snoekies factory.

Anthony knew the canal was to his right but he couldn't make it out. He had raced sucker-stick boats there with his friends when he was younger, before it went green with slime and choked with rubbish. Mummy would have had the horries if she had known he was playing so far away from home. He tried to say Mummy's name but it wouldn't come.

His ribs screamed when Skelm and Lippe came to a halt and threw him facedown onto the sand. Anthony twisted onto his back. He made a sound as he spat sand out of his mouth, tried to do it again and couldn't.

There was a shine in the mist. Anthony looked up to find Ougat standing over him, stroking a gun before he handed it to Alfredo. The newly made JFK grabbed it, his index finger curling around the trigger.

Anthony pulled back as Ougat's face came down towards him. He saw his mouth tighten before the spit blasted into his face.

Ougat stood up and pulled Alfredo closer. "You see this gemors? I want you to clean it up for me. This laaitie swore he was a JFK but he dropped us like warm kak the very next day. He was warned, just like you was tonight. Maak skoon!"

245

Anthony pulled in his feet, trying to get them into a position for him to stand. It wasn't possible with his hands tied behind his back. He pushed his heels into the sand, digging for traction to slide his body away. The sand was too soft; he couldn't get a grip. He lifted his knees, dug his feet into the sand and slid away from Alfredo and the gun.

A sound came from deep in his gut and seeped out of his mouth. A puppy's whine, too weak to penetrate the mist. Anthony tried to force his lips around the word 'no'. It wouldn't come. He pushed his shoulders back a few centimetres.

Alfredo followed him, two fingers around the silver trigger. The gun shook in his hand.

Ougat's voice drifted out of the mist. "Pull the fokken trigger. Show your loyalty to the JFKs. Get rid of this gemors, one time."

Warm piss soaked into Anthony's tracksuit pants. He dug his heels deep and arched his spine like a caterpillar as he tried to get away. His whine grew louder. Alfredo was gunna shoot him. A new recruit would do anything for Ougat.

He could do nothing, he couldn't shout for help. The moans that seeped out of his mouth sounded like they came from behind Egyptian mummy bandages wrapped around his face.

Anthony felt the pain the same time he heard the shot. The fire in his side sent a message to his brain that half his hip had been blown away. He howled.

"Fok, I missed." Alfredo sounded surprised.

Ougat's shrill voice cut through the thick mist. "Aim for his head, dom fokker. Maak klaar before someone hears. Put the gun against his fokken head and pull the trigger. Do it now! You wasting bullets."

Anthony felt cold metal against his forehead. His howl set off the dogs across the street.

Chapter Twenty-Six

The call came at half past five, as the first cobwebs of misty morning light crept into the flat. The phone had been ringing all night. Magda jumped out of her skin at every first trill but she couldn't answer; Neville picked up every time. She searched his face while he listened, praying for the smile that would signal Anthony had been found. It never came.

Magda phoned the police soon as she found out that Anthony was missing. They told her to wait until morning; the new shift started at eight o'clock, they would open a file. Nothing she said got them off their lazy backsides.

Herbert mobilised the neighbourhood watch when he heard the news. Every member reported for duty, although Neville had quit the watch when Anthony's troubles got so bad. Close on eighty people went out in the dripping mist, their voices getting weary as they called in through the night with nothing to report. After midnight most of the calls came from people signing off, but a few hadn't given up yet.

Magda had no idea where Anthony could be. She hadn't reckoned on him disappearing again. The boy had hardly moved in four weeks. But every weekday morning he stood up like a robot, put on his uniform and ate breakfast in silence with his head down. Seemed like he needed routine, she never thought to keep him home. The only other place he went was Dr Brixton's office twice a week, where he never broke his silence.

She could get nothing out of Nicky. The girl had searched the neighbourhood for hours until it got dark. She went hysterical when Magda questioned her, and rightly so. Nicky threw her questions back into her face. Why don't *you* know where he is? Where do *you* think he went? Magda soothed her daughter against her chest, the only one of three children that she could account for.

Suzette was probably okay, wherever she was. The immoral path was paved with reward. Anthony was in danger, and it was getting worse by the hour. He wasn't strong enough to be out in the dark on his own. Why hadn't she kept him home, where he was safe, until he was better? Did the people who damaged her son four weeks back take him again? What was keeping Anthony away?

Magda lifted the curtain and stared out of the lounge window. Silver ropes of mist hung between Magnolia Court's two blocks. She could make out her neighbours' lights in the block across the way. People were up and getting ready for work.

She fetched Anthony's last school photo from the display cabinet. The police had told her to bring it along when she came to report him missing. Magda took a long, sad look at her boy. She should have taken him to the barber before the photo was taken; his brown hair curled over his ears. There was a smear of dirt on his shirt collar.

She joined Nicky on the couch and invited her husband to join them. "I want to pray for Anthony," she explained. "The sun will be up soon. I'm going to look for Anthony and I want to ask for the Lord's protection. Please Neville. Come join us."

Neville didn't argue, for once. He came to kneel in front of the couch and took her and Nicky's hands. Magda searched out Nicky's hand to close the circle. She bowed her head and closed her eyes. "Dear Lord, we ask that you watch over Anthony. Keep him safe in your loving care. We ask for your protection as we go out to look for him. Guide us to him, Lord. Give us the strength to rebuild our family."

Her nails sunk into Neville's flesh when the phone rang, interrupting her plea. Her heartbeat matched its screeching call – bring-bring, boom-boom, bring-bring, boom-boom. Neville got to his feet and reached for the receiver.

Magda studied Neville's face. Let it be good news. Dear Lord, let it be good news. She couldn't make out what it was. He wasn't saying much, just nodding from time to time and contributing a few ja's and one okay at the end. This call was longer than the others that had given her false hope through the night.

The dhoof-dhoofs of her heartbeat pounded loud in the silent lounge. Neville was mum after he put the receiver down. Couldn't he see she was worried? What was wrong with him? "Who was that, Neville? What do you know?"

Magda couldn't get a word out of him. She took his hands when he came to sit on the arm of the couch. She kept her eyes trained on his face. She couldn't read it. "Talk Neville, tell me what's going on."

"Herbert said they found a body."

Magda heard Nicky's scream but her eyes remained locked on her husband's face. She freed one hand and reached back to pat her daughter's lap. She couldn't turn around, she had to see every word that came out of Neville's mouth.

This was the thing that vererged her the most about Neville. The man didn't know how to get a story out. He took the long way round with everything he said. This was not the time to be langdraadig. "What else did Herbert say?"

Again Neville took the byway instead of the highway. "He doesn't know anything more than that. He's on his way to see for himself. He will phone to tell us what he finds out."

Magda had to druk Neville again to get the most important detail out. "Where is the body? Did Herbert say where it was?"

"A man tripped over it. He was on his way to work. He didn't see it in the mist. He alerted a member of the neighbourhood watch who was passing by. He contacted Herbert on his walkie-talkie. Herbert phoned the police, they said they coming shortly. He's on his way to the canal. He will let us know what he finds out."

Magda rose from the couch. "I'm going to the canal. I can prove that it isn't Anthony."

Neville grabbed her arm. "It's better to wait here, Magda. Herbert will call to let us know. What if we on the way there and he calls to say it's someone we don't know?"

Magda pulled free and turned to face him. "You stay here, Neville. You answer the phone. I'm going. You not going to stop me."

She could feel the beat of her heart in the soles of her feet, begging her to get moving. It was hurting to delay. The skrik and pain chasing each other across Neville's face and the tears racing down Nicky's cheeks stopped her in her tracks.

She had to make them understand, quickly before she got going. "It's getting light outside. We wasting time sitting here. I can prove it's not Anthony at the canal. It's on the way to the police station. I'm going to report him missing and then I'm going to look for him."

Neville pulled his face straight. "I'm coming with you. Nicky, you stay here to answer the phone. We will also keep in contact with you."

Magda's heart pumped like a brand new sewing machine motor, propelling her legs smoothly down the three flights of stairs and into the courtyard. She sprinted across it towards the street. A man stepped out of the mist, slamming into her. She knocked him to the pavement. She couldn't stay to find out if he was orrite or to apologise. She had to get to the canal.

Her arms clawed at her sides into the silver mist. The damp air tasted of the sour brown ice at the bottom of the fish shop's fridge. Magda's lungs roasted in her chest but her heart took no pity on them; it was pumping at full strength.

She came to a stop when she reached Downberg Road, parallel to the canal. In the distance a blue flashing light of a police van pierced the mist. A group of people gathered on the sandy field between the road and the canal. Magda couldn't make out how many shrouded shapes there were – four, maybe five.

She reached down and gripped her knees to stop her legs from sprinting forward. She almost crushed Anthony's school photo; she hadn't realised she was still holding it. She took another look at her boy. He wasn't smiling in the picture but she could see the mischief in his eyes. She put the photo carefully into her jacket pocket.

Her heart shrivelled into a small lump in her chest. Did it have nothing more to give after rushing her here? Not much further now. A quick look and she could be on her way.

Neville caught up, panting like a dog. He slung his arm around her shoulders and pushed his wet cheek into her neck. His weight was just what Magda needed; a brake to keep her steady. She waited while his breathing slowed.

Her eyes scoured the field. She couldn't see a body; but it had to be where the shadowy people stood. She slukked stale air into her lungs and pulled Neville forward. Her court shoes sunk into the sand as she made her way across the field. Every step was an effort. The brave energy that brought her to the canal was gone.

A breeze lifted the mist off the weed-choked water. The grey wall of the Snoekies factory appeared on the opposite bank. The footbridge that spanned the canal came into view as the sun arrived to beat off the mist.

Magda tripped over a brick and fell onto a heap of building rubble dumped on the field. She hadn't seen it coming; her eyes were fastened on the body. Finally, she could make it out, lying at the feet of the men staring down at it. Her eyes locked on the shape on the ground as Neville lifted her to her feet, wiped her grazed hands and pulled ripped pantyhose out of her bleeding knee.

Her fingers clawed into Neville's arm as they took the last few steps to the body. The legs were facing the street. The two men with their backs to them were policemen in blue uniforms. She couldn't make out who was on the other side of the body.

Magda opened her heart and begged like she never had before. "Don't let it be him Lord, don't let it be Anthony. Please don't take my baby from me."

Herbert was among the men gathered around the body. He rushed over when he heard Magda's voice. "Neville, Magda, you should wait there. Wait, I'm coming to you."

Magda froze and stared at the body. Anthony wore the same blue-and-grey tracksuit to school. Her heart shredded and tore out of her chest towards the boy lying on the ground. His lips were as red as the day he arrived on earth, his eyelashes just so long.

A thin, sour stream of meaningless words poured out of her mouth. She dropped to her knees. She couldn't take her eyes off her baby's face. She crawled forward on her hands and knees and rested her cheek on the grey sand next to his. "My baby, my beautiful boy. Mummy is here. It's okay, Mummy is here."

The sand was wet. Magda tucked a hand under Anthony's cheek to keep it safe and warm. A rough voice cut through her whimpers. "Lady, don't touch the body. We waiting for the photographer. You can't move the body 'til the pictures are taken."

Magda was confused. Anthony needed help, why wasn't anybody doing anything? Where was Neville? She looked up and found him kneeling across the way from her, a dead-eyed stare in his frozen face. He was good for nothing; it was all up to her. "Neville, pass me your jacket. We got to keep Anthony warm."

A hand gripped her shoulder. "Lady, I told you not to disturb the body."

Magda rose to her feet and turned like a whirlwind on the policeman behind her. "Don't you tell me what I can or can't do with my son. Leave me alone. You've done fokkol for him. Fokkol."

She whipped around and shouted at Neville. "Why's your jacket still on? Take it off right now and give it to me."

Neville came slowly to his feet. He kept his eyes peeled on his son's face as took his jacket off, struggling to free the left sleeve. He knelt down next to Anthony and draped the jacket over his face.

Magda dropped down onto her knees. She ripped the jacket off Anthony and flung it to the side. "Are you out of your mind, Neville! What you doing?"

She lifted Anthony's head onto her lap. It was as floppy as the day he was born. She cradled her hand behind his head, paying no mind to the hand shaking her shoulder.

"Lady, I told you not to move the body."

Magda glared at men gathered around her. "Where's the ambulance? Did you call for one? Is it on its way?"

No one answered. Madga reached for the jacket and covered Anthony's chest. She held his head carefully on her lap. "Herbert, help me. Use your walkie-talkie, call for the ambulance."

Herbert turned away. One of the policemen refused to catch her eye. The other one, who looked like he was sucking a lemon, leaned forward and placed a hand on her shoulder. "Lady, it's no use. The mortuary van is on its way. It's too late for the ambulance."

Magda covered Anthony's ear with her hand while she screamed. She didn't know where she found the foul language, but how else was she going to get these fokken bastards to do something?

Neville dropped down next to her and lifted her hand from Anthony's cheek. Madga wailed as he turned her palm up. It was red and sticky with blood and sand. She turned Anthony's face into her stomach and looked down at his ear. There was a hole behind it, leaking onto her powder-blue skirt. The bloodstain had something else mixed in. It looked like beef mince minutes after it was added to the pot. Her baby's brain was dripping onto her skirt.

"No! Oh my Lord, no! Anthony, no!" Magda cupped her hand over the hole to stop it leaking. There were flecks of matter on the sand where Anthony's head had lain earlier. She took the school photo out of her pocket and scooped up the pieces carefully.

Neville lifted Anthony's head off her lap and laid it gently back on the ground. Hands gripped both her arms and drew her to her feet. Magda struggled to free herself as she was pulled away. "Leave me alone you bastards! Fok julle almal! Let me be with my baby!"

"Mummy? Mummy, what's going on? What's happening?"

Nicky's voice silenced the foul words that poured out from the place she had never seen before. What was she doing here? The policemen kept a firm grip on Magda's arms as they turned her to face her daughter.

Nicky's eyes were wild in her face as she stared at the body. "Is it Anthony? Ooh jirre, it's Anthony!"

Madga rukked herself free and pulled Nicky into her arms, turning her away from Anthony. The girl shuddered in her breast as she cried, hoarse as a seagull.

She looked over Nicky's shoulder at her son. He was beautiful. He had been beautiful the day he was born. She searched out Neville. He was leaning against Herbert, crying into his shoulder. Madga took Nicky over to the men. She had a lot to do.

Neville complained bitterly when the mortuary van arrived three hours later. He tried to klap the driver for leaving Anthony lying like a dog in the sand, but he broke down as he lifted his hand.

Magda closed her ears to Neville's tjanking. He was talking kak; the van came too soon. She wasn't ready yet. She had cleaned up around Anthony. She collected three plastic bottles, five cans, a cardboard box, a worn-out shoe, three carrier bags, seven cigarette stubs and several shattered pieces of glass. She was stroking his hair into place when the van arrived.

She took one more look at her baby before she allowed the policeman to zip the body bag over his face. She kept her eyes away from the hole on his right temple and the thin line of dried blood disappearing into his hair. The policemen lifted the body bag onto the stretcher the mortuary van driver wheeled onto the field.

As they pushed the stretcher across the field Magda was surprised to find it crowded with people. There were mothers with babies on their hips; grannies in flannel gowns and slippers. A woman in a doek sat on a kitchen chair with a flask on her lap. Magda took the cup of tea she offered as the stretcher went past. She quickly forgot she had it. She couldn't take her eyes off her baby.

The crowd was silent as Anthony made his way off the field. Magda clung tight to the metal stretcher. A policeman prised her fingers off when they reached the mortuary van. The stretcher's legs folded as it was pushed into the back. She watched the driver climb inside to fasten the body bag with straps bolted onto the cold steel floor.

She didn't know where they were taking Anthony. She didn't have the strength to ask. She would find out later. She had to find out what time visiting hours were. As the doors closed she tried to become the silence at the back of the van, to keep him company. Anthony shouldn't be alone at a time like this.

People streaming off the field blocked her view as the van took Anthony away. The policemen offered them a lift home. Some of the spectators stayed to watch them climb into the back of the police van. A woman rushed up as Neville guided Madga inside. She was surprised to find she had an empty cup gripped in her hand and struggled to get her fingers free when the woman demanded it back.

How did she get to her bedroom? She remembered nothing of the ride home. She didn't recall climbing the stairs to the flat. How long had she been sitting on the bed? The last thing she saw before she got here was the body bag, strapped on the floor of the van.

Her hearing returned. Nicky's voice drifted in from the lounge, rough with pain. Neville was trying to calm her down. She could do nothing for the girl; she didn't have the energy to do anything.

She had to find out where they had taken Anthony, and what time was visiting hours. First, she had to ... She didn't know what she was supposed to do next. She stared at her reflection in the dressing table mirror. Her hair was deurmekaar, standing up in all directions on one side and plat on the other. She rubbed her dirty cheek and made a new smear. She looked at her hand. Anthony's blood had turned brown as it crusted into her palm.

She reached into her jacket pocket. The bottom edge of the school photo's yellow cardboard frame was also stained. Pieces of brown flesh speckled the photo. She reached for a tissue. She wiped the photo carefully and placed it and the soiled tissue in the drawer in her bedside table.

She looked down at her fingers threaded in her lap. Her skirt was filthy. There was a bloodstain on her right thigh and a lighter brown stain below. She lifted her skirt and sniffed. It was tea. How did it get there? Her pantyhose was ripped and her knees were grazed. When did that happen?

Magda stood up and took off her skirt and her pantyhose. Her shoes were finished; the patent leather had been scraped away in the front. She took off her skirt and lay herself on the bed, pulling her petticoat down to cover her knees. She zipped up her jacket to keep warm and folded her hands across her aching tummy. She had only been in surgery once in her life. The discomfort she felt after her hysterectomy was nothing compared to what she was feeling now – like her womb was being scraped out with a rusty blade.

Chapter Twenty-Seven

The state mortuary was off Main Road Salt River near Rex Trueform, the factory where Magda worked her first job. Neville used to meet her after work when they lived in District Six. When the weather was good they walked home to save their bus fare for the Saturday-night double feature at the Star bioscope.

Neville was grateful his brother-in-law Bernard had offered to drive him to the mortuary. He didn't want to go on his own. He stared out of the car window, taking nothing in, sukkeling to make sense of everything. It couldn't be true, what Sergeant Scheepers came to tell him about Anthony. This he had to see with his own eyes.

He hadn't told Magda about Sergeant Scheepers's visit. Even if he told her, there was no way he could be sure she heard. Magda was dead to the world – a zombie, just like Anthony had been. She went befok the day Anthony died.

At first, he couldn't make out what she was saying. She insisted there was visiting hours at the mortuary; that she was going to visit Anthony. Nicky had to help him hold her back – Magda was on her way out the door. When they finally got her into bed she stayed put and dead silent. Her sister Violet was at the flat keeping an eye on things while Bernard drove him to the mortuary.

Neville had found it hard to look at Anthony while they waited at the canal for the mortuary van. Twice he had tried to cover the boy's face, but Magda wouldn't allow it. He was grateful he was going to see him again, to prove the policeman wrong.

He had been glad to see Sergeant Scheepers when he opened the door this morning. He had expected to get an update on the investigation; to find out why Anthony had been murdered and who did it. What he found out was that it was Anthony the police were investigating.

Pastor Williams from Magda's church was planted on the couch. He had arrived on Friday, soon after the news got out. Mrs Williams was in the bedroom holding Magda's hand; Neville was stuck with the pastor. He had taken over the couch, his boep drooping down halfway to the floor. He constantly smoothed his comb-over plastered down with Brylcreem, wiping his hand on the couch when he thought no one was watching.

Neville didn't object when the pastor took on the job of telling the people who streamed nonstop into the flat how Anthony was murdered next to the canal. The way he told the story, it was like he had seen it happen with his own eyes. Neville hid away in the kitchen, making pots of tea for Violet and Nicky to serve to the visitors who hung onto every word from the pastor like thick snot on a lip.

He hadn't thought to take Sergeant Scheepers to the kitchen for privacy. He was expecting good news, not this strond. From the start, the policeman's tone was wrong. Neville was expecting sympathy as the father of a murdered boy. What he got was a blerrie interrogation.

Sergeant Scheepers didn't take up much space; he could squeeze onto the couch next to Pastor Williams. He leaned forward as he spoke, resting his elbows on his bony knees and turning his blue hat around in his hands. He stared hard at Neville. "Your son's shooting was execution-style, close range to the head. Looks to us like he got on the wrong side of a rival of the Junky Funky Kids."

Neville couldn't make out what Sergeant Scheepers was saying. He got the first part, how Anthony was shot, but he couldn't figure out what the rest was about. "The Junky Funky Kids? What's that got to do with Anthony?"

"Our information is that your son was a member of the JFK. What do you know about that?"

Neville's tongue hung thick on his bottom lip, he couldn't pull it back in. He stared at the policeman. There was something he had to say. "My son wasn't a gangster."

Sergeant Scheepers rested his hat on his knees and reached into the pocket of his blue jacket for a notebook. He licked his index finger before he ruffled through the pages. Finally, he found what he was looking for and lowered his ostrich-shaped head to read. Pastor Williams strained forward to make out the words.

The policeman looked up. "They found evidence that your son was a member of the Junky Funky Kids."

Neville knew what he wanted to say, he just couldn't find the words. While he sukkeled to get his tongue to work, Pastor Williams took it upon himself to speak. "What evidence?" he asked eagerly, pulling himself forward so he could see the answer for himself in the policeman's notebook.

"The boy had a tattoo. On his left arm. The letters JFK. The evidence is clear."

Neville was grateful for the interruption when Nicky came into the lounge to serve tea. While the policeman heaped spoons of sugar into his cup, he realised how stupid he was. He couldn't let Nicky hear what was going on. It wasn't true. He tried to picture Anthony leaning against the wall of a court, cigarette hanging from his lip, growling like a mongrel at everyone who walked past. He couldn't see it. He smiled at Nicky. "I changed my mind, bokkie, can you also make me a cup of tea?"

Nicky didn't move. She stared at Sergeant Scheepers. When he ignored her, she turned to Neville. "I also want to hear. Is he here because of Anthony? What happened?"

Neville put his arm around his daughter and steered her out of the lounge. "I will tell you afterwards, I promise. Just give us a few minutes. Forget about the tea. Go see how your mother is doing."

As he walked back into the lounge, Neville's head cleared. He had to get this straight, quickly. He planted himself in front of Sergeant Scheepers. "Can it be that they tattooed the letters on his arm after he died? Did they think about that?"

Sergeant Scheepers made him wait while he checked his notebook again. "The tattoo wasn't new. It was there for a while."

Neville thought it over. When last had he seen Anthony's arm? He couldn't remember. Winter was taking a long time to leave; it had been a while since the boy was in short sleeves.

Sergeant Scheepers seemed sure of his facts. "When did your son join the gang?"

"Never. I'm telling you there was no ways he was a gangster. Not Anthony. I don't believe you."

"That's the direction of our investigation. I'm coming here to ascertain the facts. I need to find out more about your son, what he was up to, who he was hanging out with."

Neville was desperate for the answer to that million fokken dollar question. For weeks, he had been asking himself and people in the neighbourhood the same thing. But there was no way the answer was that Anthony had joined a gang. He was so desperate to prove the policeman wrong he looked for help in the place he swore he would never go. "Tell him, Pastor Williams. Tell him what kind of boy Anthony was. He was in church every Sunday, isn't that right?"

Pastor Williams ran his oily palm across his scalp as he answered. "Oh yes, that he was. Anthony was a lamb of the Lord. A sweet lamb of the Lord."

Sergeant Scheepers hadn't come for a debate. "You can go see for yourself at the mortuary, Mr Fourie. They need you to identify the remains. They going to release it for burial as soon as they get your signature. You know where it is?"

Neville was still nodding when the policeman carried on to his next topic of business. "I need to search the premises. I can get a warrant, but you can also agree to a search. Where is your son's bedroom?"

"Here," Neville sukkeled to explain. "I mean, he slept there. On the couch. We been on the council's waiting list for a three-bedroomed place since he was born."

Sergeant Scheepers rose to his feet. "Where did he keep his things? Did you have a cupboard for him?"

Neville showed the policeman to his daughters' bedroom and pointed out the wardrobe where Anthony kept his clothes. He shooed Nicky and Mrs Williams away when they came to see what was going on.

Sergeant Scheepers piled Anthony's clothes onto the bottom bunk and squatted on the floor while he searched through pockets and shook out socks. Neville stood on his toes to watch over Pastor Williams's shoulder. He couldn't get the vetgat to move out of the doorway.

When the search was over, he followed the policeman to the lounge.

Sergeant Scheepers lifted the couch cushions and found a Chappies wrapper. He fired off questions while he looked around the lounge. "Was the boy at school? Where's his school bag?"

Neville fetched Anthony's haversack. He had no idea what the policeman was looking for. What did he think Anthony was hiding? Guns? If there was gang goetes in the flat he would have known. Magda would have found out, that was for sure.

Sergeant Scheepers emptied Anthony's haversack onto the couch and checked all the pockets. He searched the display cabinet next, but turned up nothing. He pushed the television stand away from the wall, looked behind it and pushed it out further. He bent down and pulled out a carrier bag, rolled into a tube and tied with its handles. He took a seat on the couch and emptied the bag onto his lap. There was a couple of five and ten rand notes and five plastic bank bags inside, filled with off-white tablets. Sergeant Scheepers opened the bag, took out one tablet and examined it. "Mandrax."

Neville's guts burned like he was being sliced with a panga. He signed the receipt for the tablets when Sergeant Scheepers pushed it under his nose, but he left the rest up to Pastor Williams. He couldn't function.

The morgue was filled with bodies. Anthony was right at the back, on a concrete shelf. After Neville spotted his son's face he kept his eyes fixed only on him. Bernard held onto his shoulders and steered him carefully past the bodies on the floor. Anthony's face was swollen, 'specially around the bullet hole on his forehead. His boy was naked; his shoulders stuck out from the plastic sheet covering his body. Bernard held onto him when he swayed.

Bernard's voice was calm. "Don't worry, I'll do it." He lifted the plastic sheet to show the tattoo, a black vloek on Anthony's pale skin.

"JFK," Neville whispered.

He was standing in a corridor, outside an office door. Bernard was with him. What were they doing there? He could hear shouting. A woman's voice; strong enough to carry through the louvred glass above the door into the corridor. Neville strained to make out what she was saying.

Bernard gripped his arm. "Just one last thing, you have to sign some papers then we can leave."

The office door opened. Neville saw a woman in Muslim dress, clutching onto a table while a policeman tried to pull her free. Her scarf was loose and her long hair swung over her face as she shook her head from side to side.

"No," she shook her head violently. "I'm not leaving. Not 'til I hear the truth. You all liars! I'm not leaving 'til I get the truth."

The policeman pulled her fingers free. The woman tried to kick his colleague as he pulled her to the door. "I'm not leaving without the truth! Mogamat was ghafees. He memorised the whole Qur'an. He was going to recite it in the mosque this Ramadaan. His Qur'an was on the ground next to him. I saw it with my own eyes, he was killed right outside our door. He wouldn't throw stones if he was carrying the holy book. How can you look me in the face and lie so?"

Neville and Bernard moved aside as the policemen dragged the screaming woman down the corridor. He let Bernard answer their questions when they returned. He asked nothing about the investigation. It had started and ended when they saw the tattoo. He signed the papers they put in front of him. They said he could fetch the body anytime. The sooner, the better – they had run out of space.

Bernard went into a café opposite the mortuary while Neville waited in the car, his mind working its way through the questions pouring into his head. Was it just a joke? Did Anthony get his friends to tattoo him? Why would he do that? A boy with a tattoo was a walking target in Hanover Park. Anthony must have known that. He didn't hear Bernard getting back into the car. He took the can of Coke that was pushed into his hand.

"You need the sugar, Neville. You in shock. That thing you just did was hard."

Neville opened the can and swallowed half of the drink. His hands were shaking, his whole body was a livewire. He rolled down the window. They carried the smell of the mortuary on their clothes; the car with thick with it.

His brother-in-law was a good man to have around in a kak situation like this. He called him Mr Brown behind his back. Bernard always wore brown suits and ties as dark as his skin. Neville hadn't seen him wearing black shoes once in the twenty years he had known him. Like Pastor Williams, Bernard was losing his hair, but he didn't try to hide it. There was nothing false about him.

Bernard sold insurance. He had everything Neville wanted. He had moved his family into Lansdowne a few years back. It was only two kilometres from Hanover Park, but it was another world. Bernard's neighbour had a swimming pool. He drove a Toyota Cressida and Violet had her own car.

Neville respected his judgement. "Where did I go wrong, Bernard? There was so much I wanted for my children. So much I wanted to do for them. I don't know what to think. Was the boy a liar? Suzette lied to my face and I didn't see."

Bernard was a man of few words, but he used them well. "All children are like that, Neville. They all hide things from their parents. My Sharnay was no different. We thought she was at evening classes 'til she came home pregnant."

Neville shook his head violently. "They don't all become gangsters and get murdered. Don't tell me all children are the same."

He cried for the first time since the morning Anthony died. He hadn't had a chance to cry in the past two days; he had to be strong for Magda and Nicky. His body jerked in the seat as he tried to hold it in. Bernard left him to it, handing over a handkerchief after he calmed down.

The questions in Neville's head poured out. "Was it me who went wrong? Maybe Magda was right; I should have been home keeping an eye on my children. Was there a gangster in my own house? In front of my eyes and I couldn't see? What kind of father am I?"

Bernard's voice was soft. "The best kind, Neville. Everybody thinks that of you. Anthony couldn't have asked for a better father. You did everything you could do."

Neville rocked backwards and forwards in his seat. "I didn't, don't fokken lie to me. My boy is lying on a slab with a tattoo on his arm, that's the kind of poes father that I am."

"C'mon Neville. Don't be so hard on yourself. I can't see what you could have done different to stop this from happening. You blame the neighbourhood watch but that was nothing. No. I'm wrong. That was the right thing. It showed just how good a father you were. I mean, you are."

"No, I scheme you were right the first time. I was a father. I thought I was a good father but I did a kak job."

"You talking pure nonsense and you know it, Neville. It's natural to blame yourself. I would do the same in your position. In time you will see for yourself that you talking nonsense."

Bernard's smooth insurance talk didn't wash with Neville. "You don't know what it's like, Bernard. When you lose a child, come talk to me."

"You so wrong, Neville. I'm Anthony's uncle. I also lost a child, one I love as much as my own children. You and Magda were in the wrong not to tell us about the problems you were having. You didn't give us a chance to help. How you think that makes me feel? "

Neville turned it down a notch. "Sorry. You right."

"You know I am. There's a killer out there we must blame."

Bernard was right. Neville had expected the police to find the killer but it was up to him. He knew where to start. The neighbourhood watch kept tabs on the gangs. He knew where to find the Junky Funky Kids. First, there was one more thing he had to do.

Neville cried all the way to Planet Fashions. He had planned on visiting Suzette, but not like this. He wanted to check up that she was orrite and tell her how much he missed her. Maybe see if he could get her to come back home.

The receptionist at the factory looked at him like he was dog shit under her shoe. She told him he had to wait until lunchtime to see Suzette. It took a lot out of Neville to persuade her it was a family emergency. She wanted all the details. Eventually, she reached over to the intercom to call out Suzette's name. Neville wasn't offered a seat but he dropped onto the couch. His legs couldn't hold him.

Suzette took one look at him and came running across the reception area. "Dedda? What's wrong? Why you here? What happened?"

Neville's legs gave out from under him as he tried to stand up. Suzette caught him and fell onto the couch with him.

"What's going on Dedda? Why you here?"

Neville bit his tongue as he realised he wanted to say sorry for the mortuary smell that clung to him like a cloak of manure. He was sure it rubbed onto her when he fell against her. He started carefully. "It's Anthony. Something happened to Anthony. Something really bad. He's dead, Suzette, he was murdered on Friday."

Neville pulled Suzette tight into his chest, forgetting about the smell. She was looking at him like he stabbed her through the heart.

Suzette pulled away violently. "Why you only telling me now? It happened on Friday already and you only telling me now!"

Neville leaned over and stroked her arm. "We didn't know where to find you. Nobody could tell us. I had to wait 'til the factory opened after the weekend. I'm sorry. I didn't know where you were."

Suzette rubbed her arm under her leaking nose. "I'm also sorry Dedda."

Neville answered all his daughter's questions. He told her about finding Anthony's body at the canal. He told her Magda and Nicky needed her badly. And he did. He didn't tell her what he found out at the mortuary; she was upset enough.

He stared at Suzette when she left to tell her boss she was leaving. She had changed a lot in the two months since she left home. She had done something with her hair, he couldn't figure out what. Her face was different; she looked older and much prettier.

Magda came back to life when Suzette walked in. She shot up on the bed like Frankenstein and burst into tears. She held onto her daughter like flesh clinging to spine as they cried together. Nicky climbed onto the bed, hugging them both and wailing just as loud.

The bedroom was crowded. Mrs Williams, Violet and their neighbour Moira gathered around the bed, stroking Magda and the girls as they cried. Pastor Williams was planted in the doorway. Bernard was on the phone in the lounge making arrangements with the funeral parlour. The only one missing was Anthony.

Neville wiped his cheek with the back of his hand. He wanted to join his family on the bed but didn't want to smear them with the stink of the morgue. Besides, he had to leave soon. The flat was filled with people who could look after Magda and the girls. He had to go find out about Anthony and the JFKs.

It wouldn't hurt to delay a while. It had been a helluva day. It was good to see Suzette back home, and Magda talking again. They were making each other strong. Magda must be starving; she hadn't eaten for three days. He went to the kitchen to make up a tray for his family; the fridge and the kitchen table were filled with food their visitors brought.

It was getting dark when Neville left home and walked to Herbert's flat. He wasn't stupid enough to go alone to the shebeen on Peach Street to confront Ougat about Anthony. He told Herbert the whole story; about Sergeant Scheepers's visit, the tablets and the tattoo – and the visit to the morgue.

Herbert responded immediately. "Of course I'm coming with you. We must find out what is going on. The police, they a fokken waste of good time. Ten months my son is dead and no one can tell me one thing about it. Let's go."

The shebeen was crowded. Neville went to order drinks. He looked around while he waited for the beers to arrive. What did Anthony see in this place? Most of the men on the wooden benches lining the walls were his age or older. Young men in their twenties circled the pool table.

He handed a Carling to Herbert and joined him on a bench. He turned to the man seated to his left and lifted his bottle. "Cheers!"

His neighbour lifted his long tom and smiled. "Cheers."

Neville got to work. "Lekker place this, hey? Lekker music." He pointed to the pool table with his bottle. "Suppose that brings the laaities in."

The man swayed, his boep spilling into Neville's lap. "Ja, the laaities take it serious. There's money on the table."

"You don't say?"

Neville took a long pull on his beer. His eyes scanned the shebeen. There was no sign of Ougat. He kept up with his questions. "Lot of laaities come here to play pool?"

"Nah. I wouldn't say so."

Neville lifted his bottle. He didn't know what to say next. He was getting nowhere. Where was Ougat? He wasn't leaving without questioning the gangster out about Anthony's tattoo. "So, whose place is this, then?"

"Ougat, is his place."

"Is he here?"

Fat boep looked around. It was a big effort. Instead of moving his head, he shuffled his body around on the bench as he checked out the shebeen.

Neville waited patiently. He heard a shout from the pool table. A player was taking high fives from the spectators. He had to be the winner, but Neville wondered how someone so skeel could focus on a shot.

His neighbour prodded him. "Nah, I don't scheme Ougat's here."

Neville nodded towards the pool table. "Who's the winner?"

Fat boep looked at the squint player lining up the balls for the next game. "I reckon that's Oegies. He's good."

Neville considered moving on. He should check out the pool table. The players were the youngest people in the shebeen. One of them might know Anthony.

There was another prod in his side, and a splash of spilled beer. "You know mos, I just thought of something. Oegies is good but there was this laaitie who could take him anytime. Haven't seen him for a while."

Neville bit his tongue to stop himself from putting Anthony's name into the man's mouth. He waited. Nothing. Fat boep had switched off again; he was staring blankly at the pool table, his eyeballs floating. He kept his voice casual. "So this laaitie, this one who could take Oegies, you know his name?"

Fat boep frowned as he lifted his bottle and drained it. He clicked his fingers. "Got it! The laaitie's name is Anthony. He's hot to trot on the table."

Neville interrupted Herbert, who was interrogating a customer to his left, and leaned in close to him, trying to keep his voice low. "This man says Anthony came here. He gave his name up, just like that. Why did Anthony come here? When did he come?"

Herbert lifted his fingers to his lips. "Shh. Keep it casual. What did he say? Did he see Anthony with Ougat?"

Neville was too agitated to listen. "I reckoned there was two nights Anthony could have been here. The night he disappeared and the night he died. But it sounds like he was here a lot."

Herbert rubbed Neville's arm. "Cool it. We gunna find out. Did he say anything about Ougat? You find out where he is?"

Neville shook his head. "Not yet. I was thinking of asking at the pool table. Anthony played here. Sounds like he was good. Another thing he kept from me."

"Wait a while. You too worked up. We said we gunna take this slow. Wait, Ougat could come any time."

Neville rubbed his beer bottle across his forehead. He took a slug and cooled down a little. "Don't worry. I can handle this."

The shebeen filled up with the weekend's customers returning to drink away their Monday hangovers. Smoke swirled around the naked light bulb above the pool table. Neville sauntered towards the table and leaned against a wooden pole holding up the roof. Herbert took up position at his side.

He squinted as a white cloud of dagga smoke passed across his face and seeped into his eyes. He pulled the sweet smoke deep into his nostrils to cover the smell of dead meat. He turned to his left and smiled at the rooker, a young man built like a brick house.

He watched the game. The squint player was lining up a shot. Neville couldn't see which hole he was aiming for; his eyes were all over the place. A ball slipped smoothly into the middle pocket. Squint eyes sunk another ball and then parked one of his balls near the bottom pocket.

Neville turned to the rooker. "Not bad. Not bad at all."

"Oegies is the koning of the table."

He put on a smile and reached out a hand. "Neville."

"Marewaan."

"That's not what I heard."

Marewaan stared at him blankly. "What you say?"

Neville went carefully. "I'm saying is that's not what I heard. There is somebody who can take on Oegies. A laaitie. His name's Anthony."

"What kak you talking?"

Herbert intervened, trying the keep the talk loose. "Cool it. No need to get uptight."

Marewaan pushed out his bull chest. "Who the fok are you?"

Neville was sure Marewaan knew something. Why else was he getting so upset? He kept at him. "You know Anthony? You seen him here?"

"Who the fok are you? Why you come here with such kak?"

Marewaan's braying voice brought the pool game to a halt. Neville watched nervously as the players put their cues down. The spectators watching the game also moved closer.

Oegies pushed his way to the front of the ouens. "Wat die fok gaan aan? Why you getting so worked up, Marewaan?"

Marewaan pointed a fat finger at Neville. "This naaier walks in here like he owns the place and asks stupid fokken questions. Who the fok is he? That's what I wanna know."

Oegies eyes looked fixed on Herbert, but Neville suspected he was looking at him. "What kinda questions? Who the fok are you?"

"Neville Fourie. Look, I don't want trouble. I just want to find out if my son came here. His name is … was Anthony. He was murdered last Friday. He's lying in the morgue, with a tattoo on his arm. JFK. I came to see Ougat."

Marewaan folded his arms across his chest. "There's no Ougat here. And no Anthony. Now fok off. Voetsek."

The crowd parted for Neville. He wasn't leaving. He held up his hands. "We don't want any trouble. We just looking for information about Anthony. To see if anyone knows what happened to him. We not saying anyone here had anything to do with Anthony's murder."

Marewaan's fist slammed into Neville's cheek. His head hit the edge of the pool table before he dropped onto the floor. He stayed down. He was sure his eyes were filled with blood – all he could see was red. He couldn't help Herbert when his friend tried to lift him. He raised his right hand to his head. He could feel a knop, already as big as a plum.

A foot connected with his thigh as he made it to his knees. "Fok off. Fok out of here."

Herbert's arms locked around Neville's waist. His legs trembled as he was lifted to his feet. He held onto the pool table while he sukkeled to find his balance. Drums were going doef-doef in his head.

A voice cut through banging in his brain. "What the fok is going on here?"

The shebeen went silent. Neville turned around, blinking to clear his sight. Ougat stood in the doorway of the house, staring into the shebeen.

"Is someone gunna tell me what the fok is going on or must I moer it out of you all?"

Oegies pointed at Neville. "This naai came here with a lot of questions. We telling him to fok off. He better not come here again or his gat is mine."

Neville swallowed hard as he watched Ougat walking towards him through a red haze with Satan's fire licking up his back.

Ougat planted his toes against Neville's. "Who the fok are you?"

"Neville Fourie. I came to ask about my boy, Anthony."

Ougat smiled. The light bulb above the pool table picked up a gold tooth in his mouth. "Anthony? Dunno Anthony. Who's he?"

The drummer in Neville's head pounded across his forehead. He stared Ougat down. "My son Anthony was killed on Friday. I'm looking for people who knew him. People who maybe saw him before he died."

Ougat's finger stroked his chin while he pretended to think. "Told you, I dunno Anthony. Now you can fok off."

Neville had no problem with begging. "If you can just give me a chance to ask around. Someone said he saw Anthony here. He came to play pool."

Neville shivered as Ougat draped an arm around his shoulder. He let the gangster show him to the door. He stood quietly when he was brought to a halt on the pavement.

Ougat's voice was low but clear. "A word of advice. Don't fokken come here again. You aggravate my ouens; they don't like your gevriet or something. You come here again I guarantee you there will be kak. You hear me? This is no place for a decent man like you."

Neville nodded. He watched in silence as Ougat went back into the shebeen and high-fived Marewaan and Oegies.

Herbert pulled on his arm. "Come, we must go."

Neville gripped the iron railing as he pulled himself up the concrete stairs of Magnolia Court. Herbert had walked him home and left him at the bottom. The dull ache in his head throbbed in time with the stabbing pain in his heart. There was nothing more that he could do tonight. His legs couldn't carry him any further.

Herbert said he would mobilise the neighbourhood watch; they would ask around and figure out what happened to Anthony. Neville had little hope. The watch could do nothing for Herbert, his son's killers were still out there.

He stopped to catch his breath on the first-floor landing. He could hear his flat was full of people. Sounded like Magda's prayer circle; her voice floated high above the others. He hoped there was a quiet seat in the kitchen.

Neville got a skrik as he stepped onto his landing and almost knocked Moira down. He hadn't seen her standing there.

"Shame Neville, look at you. Come here, let me see."

Like a child, he stepped forward.

Moira cupped his face in her hand. "Come inside for a while. I just left your place. There's no space to move."

Neville waved a hand weakly towards his door. "Magda and the girls need me, I got to go home."

Moira pulled his arm. "Come inside. You don't have to stay long. You can't go home like this, you look like hell. What happened?"

Neville let himself be pulled into his neighbour's flat. He stood like a statue while Moira stared at him. "What happened to you?"

"Nothing. I don't want to talk."

"Your face is all dirty and your eyes is wild. Is that blood on your cheek? You can't go home looking like this."

Neville shrugged. Anyone who had a day as kak as his would look like this. He stayed put when Moira pushed him onto her couch and left the room. The sad hymn floating across the landing from his flat matched the wailing in his heart.

Moira was back, handing him a glass with dark orange liquid. "Brandy. You look like you seen a spook. Drink it."

Neville lifted the glass obediently. His nostrils flared at the smell. He swallowed half the drink and tracked its hot path down to his gut. Moira's voice was bossy. It wasn't necessary. He had no krag to argue.

"I'm running you a bath Neville. You very dirty and you stink. You can go home when you done."

Neville finished his second brandy in the bath. He sank back in the steaming water and closed his eyes. He shouldn't fall asleep; he was needed at home. He still had to work out what to tell Magda and the girls about Anthony's tattoo, the Mandrax and his suspicions that the boy had been involved with Ougat. He wasn't sure that he should tell them. He didn't want Magda to lose her mind again.

The washing line strung above the bath carried mostly Moira's stuff; pantyhose, lacy bras and panties. It was strange, lying naked in his neighbour's bath, but he was grateful to finally wash the morgue off his skin.

Chapter Twenty-Eight

Nicky didn't want to go shopping. She didn't care what she wore to Anthony's funeral on Saturday; any one of her church dresses would be orrite. Nothing Mummy, Suzette and Aunty Violet said could get her to join them on their shopping trip to Claremont. She didn't want to help choose flowers for the service.

The flat was quiet, for once. Dedda was in the lounge with Pastor Williams and Uncle Bernard, finalising the funeral programme in low voices. Nicky stayed with them long enough to find out that she and Suzette would be two of the six pallbearers carrying the coffin out of the church. She left the meeting when Dedda asked Uncle Bernard to give the eulogy for the family because he didn't trust himself to speak without breaking down. Her heart couldn't take any more listening to their plans.

She closed her bedroom door, took Suzette's portfolio out of her bag and lay on her stomach on her bed, paging through it slowly. She was looking at the photos for the fourth time and she still couldn't believe what her eyes were seeing. Her sister looked like a white woman ten years older. If she had seen her in the street in that makeup with that hair wearing those outfits she would have walked right past her, no two ways about that. She would think as she went by that a woman so befok beautiful should be a model or a film star.

Dedda and Mummy hadn't seen the portfolio yet; there hadn't been a right time to show them. People had come to the flat day and night since Anthony died; most of them from Mummy's church. Nicky was tempted to show off the album when the next batch of visitors came. Mummy was wrong to worry about what people would say. They would say Suzette looked kwaai, like a model.

Nicky sighed when a knock came on the front door and slid the portfolio under her blanket. She hoped whoever it was didn't stay long enough to need a cup of tea. She didn't want to leave the bedroom. She was tired of hearing 'my deepest sympathy on your loss' from people who didn't drop a tear while they listened to Pastor Williams telling all the fine details of Anthony's murder. She was tired of Pastor Williams gaaning aan about taking a stand against gangsterism. Where was he when Dedda and the neighbourhood watch patrolled the streets at night? She wasn't coming out of her room; Dedda could make tea for the visitors.

Nicky heard a man's voice in the lounge but she couldn't make out who it was. Could be someone from Dedda's work. A few girls from Mummy's factory had come to sympathise. Dedda and the visitor were talking; they didn't need her. She turned onto her side and closed her eyes.

The bedroom door opened as she was about to fall asleep with her arms wrapped around her waist, sinking into Kevin's hug. She hadn't visited him once in her dreams since Anthony died and right now she was in need of his support. She rolled onto an elbow and saw Dedda's head peeping through the half-opened door. "Nicky, someone here to see you."

When Kevin walked into the room behind Dedda she got such a big skrik she burst into tears. Neville came to stand next to her bed and rubbed her back. "What kind of welcome is this? I thought you would be happy to see Kevin."

Nicky buried her face in Dedda's neck. She couldn't look at Kevin, he would see instantly what kind of thoughts she was having of him. Her feelings had changed so much since he was detained; he would see it on her face in a second if she looked at him.

She kept her face hidden when her tears stopped. Now she was skaam to look in Kevin's direction. She had let him down. She made a promise to look after his mother, but she hadn't kept it since Dedda and Mummy put her under house arrest. Then her problems got so bad that she didn't have a minute to spare for Mrs Van Wyk. Still, she felt kak guilty.

Neville pulled her arms from around his neck. "Jissus Nicky, don't be such a tjankgat. Say hello to Kevin, he came to greet us. He heard about Anthony, he wants to talk to you."

Nicky lifted her head and took a quick look at Kevin. He was taller since she last saw him. It was his hair; it had grown into a curly afro. His smile was the same, a crooked line across his dark face.

She pulled away from Dedda and faced him. "Hello."

Kevin's face lit up like a veldfire in the dark. "Hello, Nicky."

Her mouth was empty. She stared at Kevin's takkies. They were white out-of-the-box new. Who bought them? Mrs Van Wyk hadn't been to the shops for years.

Neville patted Kevin on his back and walked to the door. "I'll leave you two to catch up. Pastor Williams is waiting." He closed the door as he left.

Nicky had never been with a boy in her bedroom before. She and Suzette weren't allowed to bring boys to the flat, let alone into their bedroom. She climbed down the bunk and went to sit on Suzette's bed, taking cover from the feelings printed on her face.

Kevin bent his head under the top bunk and came to sit next to her. "I'm sorry about Anthony. Jirre, this is such a kak situation. I don't really know what to say."

She turned to face him. "It's okay. Sorry is the right thing to say." She ran out of words quickly.

"How you holding up?"

"I'm okay. Busy. There's people here all the time. They all drink tea." Nicky hoped Kevin didn't take that the wrong way. She didn't mean him to leave.

"My mother sends her sympathies. She's sorry she couldn't come. She didn't think she could make it up the stairs to your flat."

Nicky put brakes on her tongue. It wasn't her place to tell Kevin that there was nothing wrong with his mother's heart. Let him find out on his own. "How's your mother?"

"She's okay. Glad I'm home. It was hard for her. I want to thank you Nicky, for everything you did for her. Every time she came to visit she spoke more about you than anyone else."

Nicky appreciated his thanks but felt she didn't deserve it. "I tried to help, but Dedda stopped me. It was difficult, here at home. I couldn't get out, I couldn't ..." Her words dried up when Kevin put his hand over hers.

"Shh, it's okay. Your dedda explained. He's very proud of you. He said you worked hard with the Detainees Parents Support Committee. I dunno about the pastor though, he looked like he was chewing kak while your dedda was talking about your pickets and marches."

Nicky giggled. "Pastor Williams believes we must render unto Caesar what belongs to him. Romans is one of his favourite chapters in the Bible. PW Botha is his favourite president because he's kragdadig against the communists."

Kevin had a serious look in his face. "But you know different, right Nicky? You don't subscribe to that bullshit."

She nodded vigorously. "People can twist the words of the Bible to suit their ideology. I know that."

"It's not such a bad book. I read it inside; we had Bible study twice a week. There was this kwaai comrade at Victor Verster. Reverend Louw. Yoh, I didn't know Jesus was such a revolutionary! He stood for the poor and He believed in the redistribution of wealth."

Nicky's shyness was fading. "How was it? I forgot how long you were in, I lost track."

Kevin squeezed her hand again. "It's okay, I understand. You had a whole lot of kak in your life. I was in three months and five days. I came out yesterday."

Nicky couldn't believe it had only been three months. So much had happened since then. She wasn't the same girl he had last seen in June. Would Kevin still like her? A gavel came down in her head when he walked in, finding her guilty as charged for not keeping an eye on his mother. She stared at his warm hand, wrapped around hers in her lap.

"Hey, you okay?" Kevin shifted over and pressed his shoulder against hers.

She couldn't look up. "I'm sorry. I wanted to keep helping your mother, but Mummy and Dedda wouldn't let me. I was under house arrest. Suzette ran away and Anthony got very sick, I had to take him to the doctor and everything."

Kevin took his hand off her lap and brought his arm up around her shoulder. "It's okay. Your dedda explained. You will think this is strange, but it's easier for the people in detention than those we leave behind. We got the support of comrades, the same routine every day.

It's like a university of liberation inside. All we do is study and play and eat and sleep. We were insulated from the trauma of everyday life in apartheid South Africa."

Nicky hadn't thought of detention like that. Before her life turned to kak she had worried about Kevin every day, convinced that he was sleeping on a cold cement floor with blood dripping from his wounds. "But detention's still kak, isn't it? People get tortured. It's not like it's a picnic inside."

"Ja, but it's the security police who torture detainees, not the prison warders. Most of the warders aren't bad. Some of them are politicised, they even demanding rights for detainees."

Nicky turned to face Kevin. "Were you tortured?"

"Nah. They just wanted me out of the way for a while. They interrogated me, only once; they didn't moer me. Just one klap at the start. I gave them nothing, just a few details about my life they already knew."

Nicky looked at Kevin with respect. "So what you gunna do now?"

"Go back to school. Keep up the work. A luta continua."

She hadn't been to school for a week, not since last Thursday, the day before Anthony died. She didn't know when she was going back; no one was making plans for that. It was good that Kevin was out, school wasn't the same without him. She kept looking for him at every turn. And not only him; there was someone else she missed. "Have you been to school? Did you see Shirley?"

"Nah, I'm going back next week. I need to spend some time with my mother. And you. How's Shirley?"

Nicky shook her head slowly. "I haven't heard from her for a while, she isn't coming to school. Shirley isn't speaking to me. Something happened to her two months back. I saw her, Kevin, she was attacked and hurt bad. She doesn't want nothing to do with me, I dunno why."

Her tears ran so thick she was bang she was going to drown in her troubles. She cried snot into Kevin's chest when he hugged her.

His hands stroked her back like he was bringing up her wind. Nicky allowed herself to be soothed. He had a nice, clean soap smell. His hand drew circles in the place where she carried all her troubles – just above her hips.

She pulled away from Kevin and stared into his face. There were a couple of things she hadn't noticed before. His eyelashes were long fans on his cheek. He looked a lot like her; black eyes in a dark face with a helmet of curls on top.

She closed her eyes as his face came close. She opened her lips after he pressed his softly against hers. Just a little, she didn't want to rush her first kiss. She liked the way Kevin was taking it slow. She stared him in the eyes when he pulled away; saw the question he was asking. She answered by closing her eyes when he drew close again.

She didn't know where to turn when the second, longer, kiss ended. She was glad they were sitting in the shadow of the bunkbed; he couldn't see the stupid look she could feel on her face.

Kevin's voice came out like a lead singer in the Commodores. "I been wanting to do that for a long time. I been dreaming about it. That was much better than my dreams."

Nicky's cheeks burned. She had also dreamed of Kevin's kisses. The real thing was much, much better. She leaned over and kissed him again. This time, she put her arms around him. She was melted chocolate when he pulled away. She swayed towards him, eyes closed and lips half open, just like in the films.

Kevin put his hands on her shoulder and pushed her upright. "Hey, Nicky. Hold up. Your dedda and the tamaai pastor's in the lounge."

The gavel came down in Nicky's head. She was guilty on another count. "I can't do nothing right nowadays. My family's getting ready for a funeral and I'm vrying here in the bedroom. I can't do one thing right. It's my fault there's so much kak going on."

Kevin shot right back. "What you mean it's your fault? What you talking about, Nicky?"

She shook her head slowly. She wouldn't know where to start if she had to tell him everything that was wrong. She knew Suzette was bunking but she said nothing. She didn't keep an eye on Anthony. She didn't know how to fix things with Shirley, at a time when it looked like her friend needed her the most. It was better if she sent him away. She was good for nobody.

Kevin turned her to face him. "What you mean when you say it's your fault?"

Nicky still didn't understand why and how she had changed. How did it get so difficult to do the right thing? She never gave Dedda a thought while she was kissing Kevin. What was wrong with her?

"Nicky? Talk to me. What's going on?"

The best thing she could do for Kevin was send him away. Her whole life she had thought Suzette was selfish, but she was worse. Somehow, she had forgotten how to do things for other people. She never used to be like that.

She tried to explain. "I wasn't keeping an eye on Anthony. For weeks he disappeared after school and I did nothing. Then he came straight home from school every day and he didn't want to go out. Just sat on the couch and stared with dead eyes. When he disappeared I could do nothing to help. I knew nothing about his life, where he was going every day, who he was hanging with. He was my brother but he was a stranger to me!"

Nicky swallowed hard. Her throat and her eyes were dry. The way Dedda looked at her when he came home that night! He asked her over and over where Anthony was; all she could say was she didn't know.

"So why you think it's your fault?"

Nicky got irritated with Kevin, just like old times. Why was it so difficult to make him understand anything she said? Was he doing it on purpose? Kevin used to like getting her all worked up. That hadn't changed. "Don't start your blerrie nonsense, Kevin. I know what you doing. I haven't got time for this. I think you must go."

Kevin gryped her hands. "I'm just trying to understand. What you telling me is that you think Anthony is dead because you didn't know where to look for him. Am I right?"

Nicky nodded. Finally, he was getting it!

"Now listen to me, Nicky. I'm asking why you so sure you would have found him if you did go look. What if whoever got him had gryped him already? Did you consider that possibility?"

Nicky calmed down enough to listen. "I didn't think of that. But you didn't see him, Kevin. He was like a zombie. He was seeing a psychologist. He couldn't look after himself."

"And you couldn't look after him all the time, Nicky. I'm sure you tried. You only sixteen, there's only so much you can do."

Nicky nodded, although she didn't agree. Mummy and Dedda didn't say they blamed her for Anthony's death. They didn't have to. She blamed herself. When Mummy took to her bed in silence after Anthony died she was so bang. She was convinced Mummy would be the next one to go.

She shivered. Kevin's hand was on that spot on her lower back, kneading his fingers into her skin. She turned into him and rested her face on his chest.

"Just give me a minute," she mumbled. "One minute more, then we can go to the lounge. I can imagine what Pastor Williams is thinking."

Kevin's voice was smooth like Lionel Ritchie's. "I know what I want to do with that minute."

Chapter Twenty-Nine

Magda rolled her pantyhose up her thighs. She leaned forward as she pulled them over her panty and snapped them onto her waist. The petticoat came next. Her new dress was on a hanger hooked onto the wardrobe door. It was black, matching her pantyhose and the shoes she slid onto her feet.

She stared in the mirror. Her hair was a nest on her head. She had towel dried it after her bath but she forgot to comb it through. She dropped down onto the stool in front of the dressing table with a deep sigh.

Violet's face popped into the mirror next to hers. "Let me help."

Magda sat like a sack of potatoes while her sister pulled up her zip and reached for the comb. Violet had arrived early, just after the Fouries woke up. She made cups of strong tea for everyone, ran a bath for Magda and had another cup of tea waiting when she got out.

She stared in the mirror as her sister pulled a comb gently through her knots. This was a turn up for the books. Her whole life she had looked after Violet; for the past eight days she was the one in need of care.

Their mother, who had raised them alone, died when Magda was fifteen and Violet was twelve. After the funeral, Ma had taken them to her house in District Six. It wasn't long before she started complaining how much young girls ate. Ma took Magda out of school and found her a job at Rex Trueform, the clothing factory in Woodstock.

Magda stared at her reflection. She was fair, like Ma and her mother, with straight hair. Violet came out dark and kroes. From the things Ma said, the sisters worked out that they had different fathers. Ma hated Violet's father, but she never came out and said why. She just picked on everything Violet said or did.

Suzette came into the bedroom and took the comb from her aunt. "I want to do Mummy's hair. I chose the hat; I know what I want to do."

Magda examined her daughter's reflection in the mirror. Suzette favoured her in her looks but she had a streak in her that made her different and difficult to handle. The girl had strayed off the path but she found her way back home when her family needed her. Family stood together at times like this.

Her eyes found Violet, sitting on the bed watching the hairstyle emerge. For the sake of her sister, Magda became a fulltime mother at sixteen; on the day she came home from work and found Violet locked in the hoenerhok in the yard. While she was dusting the ornaments the child had broken Ma's mug commemorating Queen Elizabeth's visit to Cape Town in 1947. Magda plucked the feathers from her sister's hair, packed up and moved out.

She walked her sister through the dark streets to Milly Anthony, who worked the machine behind hers. Milly took them in, stood by them and cried at their weddings and the births of their children. Neville moved in after they married. Suzette and Nicky were born in District Six. Magda was pregnant with Anthony when the government's lorries carted them up and dumped them on the Cape Flats.

She had to pay attention. Suzette was saying something.

"So what you think, Mummy?"

Magda stared in the mirror. Her black hat's veil fell to the middle of her forehead. She turned her head to see what Suzette had done. A French plait was twisted into a bun at the back of her head. Magda lifted her chin and turned from side to side, admiring her neck for the first time in years. Violet and Suzette were reflected in the mirror, smiling like idiots. Neville came into view, his face as dark as his new black suit.

"The cars have arrived; it's time to go."

Magda stood in the doorway of the Church of Eternal Redemption, her hands folded across her stomach. The hearse was parked to her right, its open back door facing her. She could see the coffin. She wanted to climb inside and wait with Anthony until the funeral started. It didn't make sense that she wasn't allowed to visit him. This was her last chance. Neville pulled her back as she took the first steps towards her baby.

"Magda, Mr Paulse is talking to you."

She hadn't noticed the arrivals. Their neighbour, Mr Paulse, had his hand stretched out. His lips moved, but she couldn't make out a word he said. Mrs Paulse grabbed her hand next and shook it up and down. This time she heard. She was so tired of hearing it.

"My deepest sympathies on your loss."

Magda had nothing to say to the people who lined up to greet her, blocking her view of the coffin. Her arm was lame when Neville finally took her inside.

The church pews were packed with their neighbours and the congregation. Anthony's classmates were three rows of blue-and-grey school uniforms. Mr September and Anthony's teachers filled a pew behind the children.

Magda grabbed Milly Anthony's hand when it stretched out for a squeeze as she reached the front pew. Violet, Bernard and their daughters Sharnay and Bernalette were already seated with Nicky and Suzette. Kevin leaned forward in the pew behind Nicky, whispering into her ear. Magda gripped Neville's hand as she sat down.

The arthritis-hunched organist marched onto the stage, took her seat and drowned out the whispers. Magda stood up when everyone else did. She turned and watched the pallbearers, six pupils from Forest Glen Primary, carry Anthony slowly into the church. Two dark-suited attendants from Bournes Brothers funeral parlour helped them lift the varnished light brown coffin onto a trestle below the lectern. The attendants placed wreaths and flowers around the coffin before they tiptoed away.

As the congregation fidgeted back into their seats, Pastor Williams climbed the five steps to the stage and took up position behind the lectern. A purple robe covered his silver suit. He ran his hand across his comb-over before he spoke. "Let us pray."

Magda squeezed Neville's hand, dropped her head and closed her eyes.

The sound system, bought with proceeds of the church fete, sent Pastor Williams's voice booming across the church. "Lord, we ask for your strength today. We come here in the most difficult of times. A child has died. It is an abomination. Yes, an abomination."

Magda shuddered. Pastor Williams was spot on. He knew exactly how to describe what she was feeling. She hadn't been able to come to grips with her pain for days after Anthony died; she lay down in silence and mapped its path across her body and her mind as she tried to get the measure of it.

"An abomination like this leaves scars on a community. We need the strength of fellowship to heal. Yes, fellowship. We ask you Lord to help us search for peace, for truth. It is hard to understand the death of a child. It is difficult to suffer such a loss."

Magda rose to her feet with the congregation when the organist announced the first hymn. She didn't need the help of the programme; she knew all the words, this used to be Anthony's favourite. She raised her voice: "Jesus loves the little children/ all the children of the world. Red and yellow, black and white/ all are precious in His sight. Jesus loves the children of the world."

After they took their seats Pastor Williams introduced the first speaker – Anthony's principal and a deacon of the church, Mr September. Magda listened to his greeting before she tuned him out. The coffin was four, five steps away. This was the closest she had been to Anthony in nine days. She would have chosen a white coffin, if anybody asked her opinion. What did he look like, inside? Was he lying on something soft?

The rumble of the congregation getting to their feet broke into her visit with Anthony. Mr September was gone from the lectern and she hadn't seen him leave. She rose to her feet and moved her lips to the next hymn but didn't have the energy to get the words out. She stared at the coffin. She didn't want Anthony in a hole. She lifted her hand to her mouth to hold in her scream. Neville's arm came up and pulled her into his shoulder.

Magda forced herself to concentrate. Pastor Williams was introducing Rushdie, a school friend of Anthony. The boy stood next to the lectern, he was too short to see over the top. Half his face was hidden behind the microphone Pastor Williams held to his mouth.

Rushdie squeaked into the microphone. "Anthony Fourie was a good friend of mine. He was a good friend of many children. Some of them that I know and some that I didn't. When Anthony was your friend he was a friend for life. He would never cause trouble in the friendship or fall out with you for no reason."

Tears rolled down Magda's cheeks to her wide smile. She smiled at Rushdie and she smiled at the coffin. She was so proud of Anthony.

"Anthony Fourie was one of the kindest people I know. When he had money you counted yourself lucky to be his friend. He will spoil you like nobody's business. Everything's on him, anything you want, eksê. He was the best friend I ever had."

Magda frowned. What rubbish was this boy talking? Anthony got fifty cents on a Saturday afternoon for sweets. What money did he have? The boy was finishing up. Good thing, he might have more rubbish to say.

Pastor Williams ruffled Rushdie's hair. "From the mouths of babes and the truth shall set you free. Lord, we ask for your strength as we confront the truth today."

Bernard was called up next, dressed for the funeral in his usual brown suit. He cleared his throat. "On behalf of the Fourie family, I want to thank you all for coming here today. I 'specially want to recognise Milly Anthony, formerly of District Six. You are family to us, thank you for taking us into your lives."

Magda turned in her seat to smile at Milly, seated at the end of the row behind her. Anthony was named for her. If he had been a girl his name would have been Antoinette. She didn't know who decided Bernard must do the eulogy, but it was a good idea. Recognising Mrs Anthony was the exactly right place to start.

She leaned back in the pew as Bernard's gruff voice carried over her like a whooshing wind. The service had been good so far. She hoped the programme was long. She wasn't looking forward to what was coming next. Who decided the coffin must be closed? She had been to funerals where you were given a last chance to say goodbye. She would insist, after the service, that they let her kiss Anthony. Magda realised the church was silent and pulled her eyes away from the coffin. Was Bernard finished already? She forgot to listen.

Bernard was still behind the lectern, wiping his face with a white handkerchief. He blew his nose into the microphone before he started up again. "Sorry, sorry. As I was saying, I have no doubt, as someone who has known Anthony since the day he was born, that he would have been a credit to his family. Neville, Magda, you have every reason to be proud of the child you raised. It is a testimony to your strength, to the example you set, that you had such wonderful children. Three wonderful children."

Pastor Williams's loud snort brought the eulogy to a stop again. He walked to the lectern, put an arm around Bernard's shoulder and led him off the stage. "Thank you. That was very good, thank you."

Bernard tried to say something to Pastor Williams's back as he returned to the lectern but gave up quickly. He stomped back to the pew and whispered loud in Violet's ear.

Magda thought it was a wonderful eulogy. She must remember to thank Bernard. What was next? Everyone was getting up; another hymn. She sucked in her lips when she recognised what the organist was playing. She wasn't going to sing Abide With Me. It was for the funerals of people who lived past their time. Who chose this one? Her sulk hung heavy on her face when the hymn ended.

Pastor Williams opened his Bible and ran a hand over his comb-over. "Our scripture reading today is Mark's gospel, Chapter ten, verse thirteen. It will help us deal with the abomination we are facing. It is carefully chosen. Listen carefully." Pastor Williams fiddled with his thin strands before he started reading.

"And they brought young children to Him, that He should touch them: and His disciples rebuked those that brought them. But when Jesus saw it, He was much displeased, and said unto them, Suffer the little children to come unto me, and forbid them not: for such is the Kingdom of God. Verily I say unto you, whosoever shall not receive the Kingdom of God as a little child, he shall not enter therein. And He took them up in His arms, put His hands upon them, and blessed them."

Magda sat absorbed in the silence that followed the reading, digesting the words. The scripture was perfect for Anthony. Just perfect.

Pastor Williams continued. "Now what message are we to take from this scripture? People are often confused about the use of the word 'suffer'. They think this means that children have to realise that life is hard; that life can be cruel, even, at times. That is not what Jesus meant."

He paused and searched for the bookmark in his Bible. He found the page and stroked his head. "Matthew eighteen: But whosoever shall offend one of these little ones which believe in me, it were better for him that a millstone were hanged about his neck, and that he were drowned in the depth of the sea."

Pastor Williams paused again before he looked up. "The Lord says clearly who it is He would like to suffer. Those who offend children."

Magda pursed her lips and nodded knowingly. She was sure Jesus had welcomed Anthony with a big squeeze when he arrived in heaven. He was still a child; he had died without sin. Pastor Williams's words were a comfort wrapped around her hurts and pains.

"Now when we think of child abuse, what comes into our minds? Violence, yes; beatings. That is child abuse. Starvation, abandonment, even rape. Some of our children are unfortunately exposed to such abominations. Anthony Fourie, thirteen years old, was murdered. He was shot twice at close range. One of the bullets went through his brain. He died face down, on a field next to the canal."

Magda flinched as every last detail of Anthony's death roared through the speakers and rippled through the congregation. She pulled her chin into her neck to duck what was coming next. What Pastor Williams said was true, but did he have to say it so ugly?

Pastor Williams lowered his voice. "Anthony Fourie was only thirteen years old but he had already taken Jesus into his heart. He planned to be baptised this year. It would have meant he could bow his head before the Lord, confess his sins, and be allowed entry to the kingdom of heaven."

Magda lifted her chin and smiled at the coffin. Anthony wasn't lonely in there; he was seated with the Lord. So why was Pastor Williams talking about sin? A shiver with long nails scratched up her spine while she waited for what was coming next.

Pastor Williams took his time, he had more questions than answers. "We heard testimony today from a relative about the love Anthony's parents had for him. But what is a parent's love? Can depriving a child of Jesus's love be described as abuse?"

Magda was even more confused. Seemed like Neville had the same problem, he was leaning forward in the pew, his fists drilling into his lap.

Pastor Williams continued. "Every Sunday our church is filled mostly with women and children. Mothers know there is no greater gift they can bestow on their children than the love of the Lord. But we hear testimony from mothers about men who want to stop them from bringing their children to Jesus. Is that not a kind of child abuse?"

Magda put out a hand but she was too late to stop Neville as he got to his feet. What was going on? She pulled on Neville's arm. Why was he taking offence? He wasn't violent at home; Pastor Williams was talking about other people. Everyone knew Anthony came to church every week.

Pastor Williams's voice went tense. "Sit down, Mr Fourie. I'm not finished yet. Sit."

Magda pulled Neville's arm and patted his lap after he sank down again. His thigh clenched under her hand, rock hard and ready to pull him to his feet. She tsked him and turned to face the pastor.

"Now I said earlier that Anthony's death was an abomination. Tragically, he bore the mark of his sin. His young, child's body was marked ..."

Neville was up, his arms an elastic band stretching towards the lectern. Spit flew from his mouth as he screamed. "Hou jou bek! You hou your fokken bek! You a snake, that's what you are! You came sliding into my house, pretending to bring comfort, but you nothing but a spy! I should have never let you into my house, never!"

Magda jerked back in her seat. What was going on? Why was Neville performing like that? He turned to face her, his eyes searching for understanding. She didn't have any to give.

Neville gasped like a guppie drowning in tears. "Tell him to shut up. Magda. Tell him he must hou his fokken bek. I won't let him poison my family. Not my family."

Magda didn't know where to start. First thing, she had to get Neville to stop swearing in the church. Then she had to find out what set him off like that. But she couldn't do anything until she calmed him down.

Pastor Williams got in first, his voice like ice. "Brother, do my words offend you? I said at the start of the service that we were in search of the truth today. We offer you fellowship, sincerely, to help you get through this time of darkness."

Neville hissed up at the lectern. "The only darkness I see is you. You, who came sliding into my home with your vetsak filled with poison. Leave my son alone! You leave Anthony alone!"

Magda had to get Neville out of the church. He was tjanking, his whole body shaking against Nicky and Suzette while they held him up. She waved her hands at Pastor Williams when he started up again, but she couldn't get him to shut up.

"Anthony Fourie had a bright future ahead of him. But he was failed, in the place where he needed guidance most, in his own home. I'm sorry to say it, but it is true."

Neville wailed. "Djy praat kak! You got no idea what you talking about! Hou jou bek!"

Magda was grateful when Bernard took Neville's arm in a firm grip. She handed her girls into Violet's care and helped Bernard pull Neville out of the church. Milly was on her feet when they reached her; her plump face twisted with concern. She took up position behind them as they walked down the aisle.

A white woman waited at the church door. She came straight up to Neville when Magda and Bernard leaned him against the hearse. She rested a hand on his shoulder and brought her face in close. "Breathe Mr Fourie, that's all you need to do now. Breathe until you find a rhythm. That's right, that's the way. Breathe."

Madga wanted to help Neville, but the woman seemed to have the situation under control. That gave her some space to think. What was going on? What set Neville off like that, and in church nogal! Who was that woman with a hand on Neville's shoulder? She spoke like she knew him well but Magda didn't know her from a bar of soap.

After the woman sent Milly to find a glass of water, Magda stepped forward. "Sorry, but who are you?"

The woman smiled and stretched out her hand. "You must be Mrs Fourie. I'm Anne Brixton. Anthony's therapist."

Magda couldn't hold her smile, the doctor drew it from her like a magnet pulling on her fillings. "Nice to meet you. Is Neville going to be okay?"

Dr Brixton patted Neville's shoulder. His crying had stopped, he was staring at his foot kicking into the tar. "Your husband's fine. He's just angry."

Madga's confusion tumbled through her guts. There was something very wrong, and it started with the fact that she was alone in the dark. "What happened in there? What made him so angry?"

"He's being blamed for Anthony's death."

Magda tried to sort out what she had heard in the church. "Pastor Williams said Anthony died with the Lord in his heart, that was the truth he spoke. But I didn't get what he was saying about Anthony's sin. Why did that set you off Neville? What was he talking about?"

Neville turned to face his wife, his face screwed up like he had bitten into a cockroach in his samoosa. "Magda, there's something you don't know. I was planning on telling you, but later. Pastor Williams is skinnering about things he found out this past week."

Magda still didn't know what he was talking about. Seemed that was the whole point; he was keeping something from her. "So what is it Neville? What you got to tell me?"

Neville filled his lungs like a chainsmoker lighting his first for the day. "You never asked about the investigation Magda, not once. The police came to the flat, Monday already, when you were still comatose."

He stopped. Mrs Anthony had returned with a glass of water and the woman from the house across from the church who had provided it. The woman nodded greetings to everyone and leaned against the hearse with folded arms to watch the drama.

Magda could hardly believe that Neville took this as a good time to be langdraadig. "Talk," she said, grabbing the glass from his mouth while he was drinking. "Talk fast. I'm standing outside my son's funeral."

Neville wiped his chin. He spoke fast after Magda prodded him in his ribs. "The policeman said there was a tattoo on Anthony's arm. A gang tattoo. The JFKs."

"Nonsense," Magda snapped. "He lied to you."

Neville shook his head. "He didn't. I went to see for myself. Anthony had a tattoo."

Magda closed her eyes and stroked her forehead. Bad was getting worse by the second. "Where did you go, to see this tattoo?"

Neville looked down at his feet. Magda poked the words of out him, a hard finger in his ribs. "I went to the morgue. I saw the tattoo with my own eyes. On his arm."

Magda was ever sorry Neville wasn't drinking from the glass when she klapped him, she wanted to break his teeth. "You went to the morgue! After telling me I wasn't allowed to visit with Anthony!"

"I didn't go to visit, Magda! I went to identify the body. There was forms to fill in and things like that."

So that was what he was hiding. She would have to deal with that later. What else was Pastor Williams telling people about Anthony while his parents stood outside the church during his funeral? "How come Pastor Williams knew about the tattoo and I didn't know? That is if there is a tattoo. I don't know what to believe. I will look for myself and see what's going on."

Neville's eyes were goon marbles in his face. He turned to Dr Brixton. "Pastor Williams was in the lounge when Sergeant Scheepers came. And he was there when I phoned you and told you about the tattoo. He's been planted on our couch every day since Anthony died."

Magda wanted to scream but she was bang that if she started she wouldn't be able to stop. She turned to Dr Brixton. "So the police knew, Neville knew, Pastor Williams knew and you knew. Did you know, Bernard?" Her brother-in-law wouldn't look her in the face.

"Mrs Fourie …" Dr Brixton started.

Suzette and Nicky came borrelling out of the church, both wailing as they ran towards them.

Magda gripped Suzette's shoulders. "What's wrong?"

Suzette had to be shaken before she started speaking like a robot programmed to bring a message. "Pastor Williams says he's tired of people who say nothing about gangsterism. He says he's taking a stand, he's not going to keep silent any more. He says Anthony is a gangster. The last gangster he's burying in his church. He says Mummy and Dedda did nothing to stop Anthony being a gangster. He says parents like Mummy and Dedda are the reason people are scared to walk at night in Hanover Park."

Magda lifted a hand to her cheek, it was too late to say anything to comfort Suzette. She had left the girls alone with Pastor Williams. She hadn't been there to protect Anthony while strond was shovelled into his coffin for him to lie in for all of eternity. She had to stand by him, take her seat in the church he attended every Sunday, where he had been promised communion.

Dr Brixton took a step forward. "I think we should …"

Magda's stare stopped her in her tracks. "If you all don't mind, I came here today to bury my son. It's the hardest thing I ever done. None of you is making it easier for me. Now if you don't mind Dr Brixton, I'm asking you nicely to fok of. And you, Neville Fourie. You, most of all. Fok off. I don't want you here. As for the rest of you, get back inside the church. We must bury Anthony."

Chapter Thirty

Suzette didn't want to klap Nicky, but the girl was asking for it – she had chucked the portfolio across the bedroom floor. She picked it up and checked for damage, struggling to keep her cool. The clasp held, protecting the pages, and the thick leather cover wasn't scratched. Nicky was lucky.

She stared at her sister, curled up like a hundred-leg worm on the bed, crying snot en trane. It was hard for Nicky; she could understand that. It had been kak for her when she left. But still, why was she being so dof? Why couldn't she see it was in her best interests to leave now – while they had a chance?

Dedda hadn't shown his face since he disappeared halfway through the funeral yesterday. Aunty Violet had taken Mummy to her house for a break. Neighbours came to crowd the flat to pick up details of the skandaal as the news spread. Not one of them was offered tea.

Suzette packed up her things as soon as Mummy and Aunty Violet left. She hadn't brought much; she never planned on staying long. Tomorrow was Monday; she had to get back to work. Mr Strauss would replace her if she didn't turn up.

There was another reason she was in a hurry to leave: Maureen was waiting to tell her about her first assignment. She liked the sound of that word; she heard it for the first time in her life when she phoned Maureen earlier. Her friend wouldn't give off any more details – she said she wanted to see Suzette's face when she told her all about it.

She was bursting her broeks to find out what the assignment was. To hell with Nicky. She had tried to talk sense into the girl. She reached for her bag. "Goodbye. I'm going. Nicky? I'm giving you one last chance to change your mind."

She wasn't sure Nicky heard her; the girl was tjanking so loud. She put her bag down and waited on her sister. Nicky had to stop soon, there was no way she could have more tears inside her. All through the service and afterwards yesterday she tjanked when anyone so much as looked at her.

Suzette heard knocking at the door and ignored it. She wasn't opening up for more biss neighbours. Nicky's noise level had gone down; there was a good chance they would think no one was home and go away.

Nicky got to her feet with the second round of knocking.

Suzette pulled her arm. "Leave it, Aunty Violet said we mustn't open for anybody."

Nicky rukked herself free. "Let go, it could be Dedda."

"Dedda's got his keys, he can get in if he wants to."

"Leave me alone. I don't wanna listen to you any more."

Suzette followed when Nicky left the room. Her sister would be too polite to get rid of the visitors if it turned out they had come to krap in the family's files.

She recognised the boy Nicky let into the flat. He was her friend from school, Kevin, who got detained. She had seen him at the funeral yesterday. Hello, what we got here? Nicky was leaning into his chest, whimpering as his hands drew circles on her back.

Suzette checked them out. They looked cute together. The boy had grown up while he was inside, he had filled out a bit. Good for Nicky! It was about time, she was going on for seventeen. She smiled at Kevin. "When did you get out?"

Kevin replied over Nicky's head. "I was released on Wednesday, just in time to support Nicky. Hell, this is a really kak situation."

Nicky lifted her head from Kevin's chest and stared at her sister. "It's getting worse by the minute. Tell Kevin, Suzette. Tell him what you planning on doing."

Suzette showed her sister her teeth. Maybe the boyfriend could help her talk sense into Nicky. She turned to him to explain. "I'm leaving. I'm never coming back if I can help it. I want Nicky to come with me, but I can't talk to her without her getting the horries. You see what I mean?"

Like a cymbal clash in a marching brass band, Nicky started crying again. Suzette was losing patience. If Kevin couldn't help her get through to the girl in the next five minutes, she was gone.

Kevin seated Nicky and himself down on the couch and looked up at Suzette. "Where you going? Where you taking Nicky?"

"Right now, I'm going to Observatory to see a friend. But I'm living in Retreat, and I want Nicky to come stay with me."

Kevin frowned. "Why?"

Suzette sighed. Kevin was the perfect boyfriend for Nicky – he was just as dof as she was. "You still have to ask why, after what happened at the funeral? I want to get Nicky out of this house. I want her out of this kak environment. Dedda was right, Pastor Williams sprayed gif over the whole family."

Suzette tried to be patient while Kevin digested her words. She was in a hurry to leave. It had come as a surprise when she offered to take Nicky. She definitely didn't plan on doing that. Now that she had made up her mind, it was amazing how strong she felt. It would be hard to look after Nicky. Mummy complained all the time about giving up her childhood to take care of Aunty Violet. But she was no longer a child and she was sure she would start earning good money when her modelling assignments picked up.

Kevin put an arm around Nicky's shoulder. "I don't know. I don't think it's so bad here that she has to leave."

Nicky stopped crying and started arguing again. "I don't wanna go anywhere! And I don't want Suzette to leave. How can you leave Mummy and Dedda at a time like this?"

Waves of anger shot out of Suzette like hot flashes from a strobe light. She didn't trust Mummy and Dedda with Nicky; look what they did to Anthony. She was shocked by Pastor Williams's announcement that her brother was a gangster, but when she thought on it later it seemed totally possible. The boy was two-faced, a devil who smiled at Mummy with angel eyes. If he had JFK tattooed on his forehead Mummy and Dedda wouldn't have seen anything. They fucked up Anthony's life big time and they were so fucked, now that they realised what they did to their son, that they were going to crush Nicky.

Kevin intervened. "I think Nicky's right, Suzette. This is not a good time to leave your parents. They going through hell. All of you are. This is a time to stick together. Unity is strength."

Suzette's hand went onto her hip as she cocked her head at Kevin. "What kak you talking? Unity is strength. Huh! This is not a political dingus, this is my fucking life you talking about. And Nicky's. The only reason there's hell in this flat, and in this community, is because parents like mine make it like that."

Nicky lost it again, shouting through her tears. "That's not true, Suzette! You want to blame Mummy and Dedda for everything, but what about me? What about you? You also saw nothing wrong with Anthony. You only interested in yourself."

Suzette rubbed her temples and went to sit next to her sister. She put her arm around Nicky's shoulder and shook her gently. "Come with me Nicky. I know I wasn't always interested in you, but I am now. You not safe here. The whole neighbourhood is skinnering about you. It's mal, you know, when you think on it. Her whole life Mummy worried about what people would say, now look what happened. Turns out the people have a lot to say, and none of it nice. Fuck this place, Nicky; come with me."

Nicky twisted free. "There's good people here, it's not all bad. There's Kevin, and his mother. And the people from the neighbourhood watch."

Suzette finally understood what was holding Nicky back. She had a boyfriend, she didn't want to lose him to someone who was more available. "Kevin can visit you weekends, and you will see him at school every day."

"That's not why I'm staying. Kevin is right, unity is strength. It's gunna take me a long time to get over Anthony. I want to do it here, with my family. I want you to stay. You also family."

Suzette sucked her stomach into her spine. She hadn't thought about it that way. If she left without Nicky, she would have to digest Anthony's kak on her own. When she phoned Neil and Maureen she hadn't told them how her brother died. She lied when they asked, said he had meningitis, that was something that killed children. They thought she lived in Lansdowne; she would have a lot to explain. She had Melanie, at the factory, to cry with – she knew the whole story.

Her mind was made up, all her thoughts tucked neatly into place. She was leaving Hanover Park; she wasn't prepared to live like this one minute more. Maureen was waiting to tell her about the assignment. Nicky would be fine, she was a good girl. Her sister was staring at her with big hoping eyes. "Don't look at me like that, Nicky. I'm not changing my mind. I'm going. I think you will be alright. I can't see you getting up to nonsense, except this political involvement thing you got going."

She turned to Kevin. "You better keep an eye on my sister. I don't want to hear she's locked up."

Kevin nodded. "I will, I promise. If you will allow me, I want to correct something you said. I think you wrong about your parents. I think they did the best they could do, more than most, from what I can see. The problem isn't them, it's the system. The system created these ghettos, gave people kak housing and no hope. Then worst of all, they turned a blind eye to the crime that resulted. We working hard to change our communities, to get facilities and proper policing. That's why I admire your dedda. He wasn't turning a blind eye. He was out there, eyes peeled."

Suzette found herself agreeing, even though Kevin's preacherman voice scraped down her last nerve. "That's exactly the way I see it! This place is a breeding ground for gangsters. There was one hatching right here, in this flat – it crawled out and joined the ouens on the corner. Doesn't matter what the parents do, that's the way this place works. Now you see why I want to get Nicky the fuck out of here?"

"I hear you. But you not listening to Nicky. She got the best reason to stay. There's been a death in your family, Suzette, and her place is here. She can't leave now. Your parents need her. They need you also."

That was another thing Suzette was worried about. Mummy and Dedda were going to lean on Nicky, and she was going to let them. Mummy's colour hadn't been right after she had forced the funeral attendants to open the coffin after the service and stared at the tattoo on Anthony's arm. When she came out of her room this morning both her cheeks had bright yolks. She sat wrapped in a shroud of silence while people came to fling questions in her face. Suzette was ready to moer the next visitor when Aunty Violet said she was taking Mummy away.

She wasn't available for a rescue mission. She couldn't take her family's kak to her first assignment, unless it was a shoot for a funeral parlour. She wouldn't be allowed to go to any shoots if she came back home. Mummy and Dedda were guaranteed to fuck up her future, just like they destroyed Anthony's. Suzette stood up. "I got to go. I'm going to find out about my first modelling assignment. Don't think I'm not grieving. I am."

Nicky's scream halted her in her tracks. When Suzette had told her earlier about her assignment Nicky got just as worked up and chucked the portfolio across the bedroom. "I hate you! You false, Suzette, you make me naar! I heard you on the phone talking with your new friend. I heard your phoney voice; everything was so amazing and fantastic. You trying for white, I seen what you done to your hair. It's almost blonde."

"So what's wrong with that? Grow up Nicky, it's time you realise there's a whole world out there. There's places where people don't live like this. You believe you can be Hanover Park's first lawyer? Well, I believe I can be Hanover Park's first supermodel. You just watch me!" Suzette strutted out of the lounge to fetch her bags.

The night she first left Magnolia Court with her bags packed, Suzette had hurried through the rain to the taxi rank. This time round she was delayed time and time again. First off, Aunty Moira was waiting on the landing outside with big news.

Suzette hadn't been comfortable with her neighbour since she stopped seeing Mark. Aunty Moira took it so serious, even though she only went out with her son three or four times. For a long time after they broke up she had been bang Aunty Moira would say something to Mummy. She had lied every time she went out with Mark. She kept her eyes down as she walked across the landing. "Bye, see you."

A hand reached out to stop her. "Hold up, wait a minute. What must I do with your Daddy? Can you help me bring him home?"

"My dedda?"

"He's here, at my place. See."

Suzette saw straight away when Aunty Moira pushed her door open.

Dedda was on his back on the couch, wearing his black funeral suit – jacket, tie and all. His legs were draped over the arm, the couch was too short to fit them. His shoes were still on his feet. She could smell brandy fumes on the snore that blew out of his mouth.

"He knocked on my door after it got dark," Moira explained. "Said he had nowhere to go. He brought a bottle. He's in a bad way, Suzette. This week's been hell for him. Yesterday was the worst of it. When he passed out last night he was well on his way to finishing the bottle. I didn't want to be a bother to your mother, so I kept him here. When I came to your place this morning to say I had him with me she looked right through me like I was plate glass."

Suzette had been glad Dedda disappeared; she was the moer in with him. It was because of him the family was taken so laag in the church yesterday. All those eyes on her; all those 'ag shames' that came her way. She was sorry all those eyes couldn't see into Aunty Moira's flat. What would people say about this? She shrugged. "What you want me to do?"

Moira stared at her. "What's wrong with you, Suzette?"

"Nothing. I just want to know what you expect me to do with that." Suzette pointed at her dedda.

"Don't talk like that! He's your father!"

"I talk how I like. Sorry, I can't help you. I got somewhere to be. Try Nicky and her boyfriend, they inside. They can help you carry. Bye."

Suzette ignored Aunty Moira's cross face and set off down the concrete steps. The block across the way was grey against the blue sky. The winter rain had washed off the last of its yellow paint. The washing lines flapping between them were crowded to take advantage of the stiff wind. A woman soaking in the spring sunshine on the bottom step squeezed against the side rails to make way for her.

Magnolia Court's corner was crowded with young men. There was new graffiti on the wall, taller than Suzette's head. She couldn't make sense of the words. RAAK WYS. What did it mean? Wise up about what?

As she stepped into his line of sight a man squatting on the corner, his crack on full display, whistled between his teeth. "Hot to trot, sister! Hot to trot!"

Suzette stopped. Were these Anthony's ouens? Were they JFKs? She looked for tattoos; most were in short sleeves. One of them, an older man, had tattoos running like veins down both his arms, but she couldn't make out a JFK. The corner stank; it was a regular piss stop for the men in the neighbourhood. She wasn't going to ask the ouens about Anthony. Fuck them; they were too busy ragging her to listen.

The netball courts across the road were crowded with spectators. There were matches underway on all four courts. Referees' whistles blasted at the players. A girl was lining up a shot as Suzette reached the pavement. The shooter's straightened hair stood in all directions, waving in the wind like candyfloss. The yellow skirt of the defender blocking the shot blew up, exposing navy-blue panties.

Suzette stopped to watch. The girl with the ball mikked twice. When she sent the defender's arm in the wrong direction, she took her shot. Missed. The spectators moaned. The referee's whistle shrilled. The two teams took their positions on the court, hands on their knees, waiting for the whistle to send them on their way.

She turned towards the taxi rank. It was nearly two o'clock. After she saw Maureen, she had to make her way back to Retreat. She would only see Neil next weekend. He said he wasn't available to see her this evening; he was having supper with his parents. Again, he didn't invite her.

Someone shouting her name and cutting through the netball spectators delayed her again. It was Charlene, of all people. Suzette hadn't seen her friend since she left Hanover Park. She had meant to catch up with her at the Galaxy one weekend, but she hadn't been once now that she had money to pay at the door. She couldn't picture Neil at the nightclub in Rylands. She put her bags down and hugged her friend.

Charlene fired questions nonstop into her neck during the hug. "Are you back in Hanover Park? When did you come back? Why didn't you tell me? Where you been? I missed you, you know."

Suzette smiled. Charlene hadn't changed. "Sorry, I been meaning to call you. I just got so busy."

"So what you up to? You still got that job?"

On her last day at school, Suzette told Charlene she was dropping out to take up the job at Planet Fashions. Charlene used to be her best friend; she couldn't just disappear on her. "Ja, I still got the job. Even better, I got another one lined up. I'm on my way now to find out more about it."

She opened her bag and brought out her portfolio to bring a halt to Charlene's long list of questions about her work. It was easier to show her than explain everything.

Charlene's loud response to the photos attracted a crowd that leaned over her arms and her shoulders while she paged through the portfolio. "Yoh Suzette, I can't believe it. This is bemoer! Yoh, look at that outfit! Is this really you?"

Suzette smiled. "Ja, I also couldn't believe my eyes when I first saw it."

Charlene turned the page. "It's befok. It's bemoer. It's so kwaai I'm running out of words to say. Yoh, look at this wedding photo. I sommer want to marry you myself."

The crowd aahed.

Suzette's cheeks were close to exploding in her face, her smile was so wide. She took the portfolio from Charlene and put it back in her bag. The tissue paper between the pages wasn't strong enough for the wind.

Charlene was as excited as Suzette when she heard about her first assignment. "If I wasn't looking after my sister I would come with you, I swear. She's playing here, for the Royal Rovers. My granny's in hospital and my parents went to visit. I can't leave Berlina alone."

Suzette promised to phone Charlene later to tell her about the assignment. It was an easy promise to make, something in Maureen's voice told her she would have something to brag about later.

She made her way down Apricot Street. The two-storeyed maisonettes on both sides of the street were protected by zinc fencing, the grey sheets striped with brown rust. The warm sun drew people out of their homes onto the pavement. Suzette dodged the dominoes game that took up a corner. The men stopped playing to shout what they wanted to do to her as she hurried past. She twisted around children playing on the pavement, their legs coated in the grey dust of the sand.

She heard her name being called. Not again! Why was everybody trying to delay her?

"Suzette? Are you Suzette Fourie? I know you mos. We go to the same church." A short, dik woman got to her feet. She had been sitting on an upturned bucket on the pavement. The two women visiting with her had car tyres for seats.

The fat goffel took up the whole pavement, blocking her way. A blue smock covered her Sunday church dress and a pink doek kept her Saturday morning hairdo in place. Suzette knew her face, she had seen those small eyes staring at her at the Maitland Cemetry when they buried Anthony, but she couldn't remember the name.

The woman grabbed her wrist. "You know me mos, Mrs Carelse. We go to the same church. Shame, how you keeping up?"

Suzette didn't know what to say. Charlene hadn't asked about Anthony, it was clear she hadn't heard yet. She hadn't told her friend why she had come back to Hanover Park; that would have delayed her even more. Now what was she going to tell this fucking bitch? "I'm okay. Bye."

She rukked her hand free, pushed past the woman and went on her way. She could hear Mrs Carelse telling her pavement companions about Anthony. She knew exactly what would happen; the women would sit for hours and enjoy the drama of Anthony's murder and Pastor Williams's condemnation. Then they would rush away to pass the skandaal on to everybody they knew. Suzette picked up her pace, desperate to outrace the dark cloud of skandaal that followed her. Fuck, she hated this place!

As she neared the rank, Suzette could see there was no chance of getting out of Hanover Park any time soon. The queues were peak-hour long, fewer taxis operated on Sundays. A brown Casspir parked alongside the rank, its back door open. Two soldiers sat on the floor with their legs hanging out, their fingers on the triggers of the rifles between their legs.

One of the uniformed men, his face messed up with a bad attack of bright red acne bommels, jumped out of the armoured vehicle and blocked her way. "Hello, beautiful. Going anywhere special? Can I escort you?"

Suzette stopped in her tracks. It was bad enough that the local men whistled at her like she was a dog. What the fuck did this idiot think he was doing? Trying to fit in? He had a face that could make a mother cry and hide him away. The head of the bommel above his right eye hung loose, capping a thin stream of blood and yellow pus running into his eyebrow. She lowered her eyes from the naarheid and took a step to the left.

The soldier followed her lead and pushed his rifle into her chest. Suzette looked up but she kept tjoepstil. He sounded asthmatic, his nostrils flared with every breath. She wasn't looking for trouble; all she wanted was to get on a taxi out of Hanover Park and never come back. The queue for the Claremont taxi was a few steps away. Some people in the line had spotted what was happening and were checking to see what she would do next. From the corner of her eye she saw soldiers pouring out of the Casspir to join the show.

The soldier lowered his rifle and stretched his lips wide. "Ag c'mon, don't be like that. We're here to protect you. The least you can do is be friendly. What do you say? You want to be friends?"

Suzette tried to keep her cool. The only words jumping around in her head sounded like they were put there by Kevin. She wanted to shout: Oppressors! Think I'm inferior to you? Think I'm just going to get into your Casspir and lie down and open my legs for you? And nogal in front of the whole taxi rank?

The soldier was getting desperate. His mates gathered behind his back shouted out advice to chaff her. He stepped forward and pulled on her arm. "C'mon! I'm just trying to be friendly. What's your name? I'm Daniel."

Suzette rukked her arm free and stepped back. Who the fok did Daniel think he was? What protection did he bring? Where the fok was he when Anthony was murdered, huh? Chasing down non-violent people like Kevin while armed killers went free to roam. She crooked her hand on her waist in preparation to give this ugly vark a piece of her mind.

A voice behind her got in first. "Suzette, is that you? I thought it was you!"

She looked up at the tall man who had come to stand next to her. The dark face under the red fez was familiar; she had seen him at the flat a few times in the past week. He was a friend of Dedda's from the neighbourhood watch. He had been detained with Kevin. She couldn't remember his name.

He smiled and spoke nonstop. "How you doing? Shame, I was at your brother's funeral yesterday. Your mother is a brave woman, I tell you. One of the bravest that I know."

Suzette nodded. She couldn't speak. If she opened her mouth now she would tjank forever.

The man put his arm around her and pulled her into his chest. She turned her face into his ribs and took a deep sniff of his Old Spice. When he pulled her forward she followed him. Daniel stepped aside. The soldiers at his back were silent. Suzette lifted her head. All the eyes in the Claremont queue were fixed on her.

The man hissed through the side of his mouth. "Keep walking. Don't look back."

Suzette insisted that Moegamat leave her in the queue. Her mind was made up. She was getting the hell out of Hanover Park. One day, soon, she was going to give them a reason to skinner and stare, give them something bemoer to talk about when the Fourie name came up.

She hoped a taxi came soon. She hated spring in Hanover Park, when the wind brought the pig manure stench from Phillipi's fields. She held her bag tight to her chest. She didn't want the smell on her portfolio.

Chapter Thirty-One

Nicky stood outside the Cosy Corner restaurant in Wynberg. The spicy smells drifting out of the door made her mouth water. Cars pulled up and left in a steady stream as people came to buy salomies, curries and vienna sausage-and-chip parcels from the takeaway section. The pavement was a safe place to wait. Ottery Road, lined with shops and houses with gardens, was busy as people made their way home from work.

She was waiting for Kevin. The new year had started badly for him. The security police came at four o'clock one January morning with an order to detain him in terms of Section 29 of the Internal Security Act. It allowed for indefinite detention in solitary confinement. He received a phone call minutes before they arrived, warning him that the boere were on the way. He slipped out the back door and over his neighbour's wall.

Nicky looked up and down the street for Kevin, she was haas to see him; it had been two months. A note came last night. Mummy said she found the envelope on the lounge floor; someone must have slipped it under the door. Kevin wrote to tell her to meet him outside Cosy Corner at six o'clock. She had to be on time and tell nobody she was meeting him.

She didn't notice the young man until he tapped on her shoulder and spoke fast in her ear. "Walk to the Luxurama and wait there for further instructions." He ran down the street before she could see his face.

Nicky made her way up Park Avenue and sat on the bioscope steps for almost half an hour. She had memorised every word on the current and forthcoming attractions posters by the time a nervous girl in a doek came to tell her to go to an address in Innes Road. She was to walk round the side and knock on the back door.

Kevin opened the door and pulled her inside on her first knock. While she had waited at the two checkpoints, Nicky organised in her head the news she had tell him – who was also detained, who was on the run, how successful the consumer boycott was and the plans for the rent boycott. Kevin wasn't interested in anything she had to say, he pushed her against the kitchen wall and locked his lips on hers. It was a good while before they stopped vrying and started talking.

Kevin pulled his hand out from under her T-shirt and stepped back. "Happy birthday. I forgot to tell you not to wear your UDF T-shirt, you more conspicuous like that."

Nicky reached behind her back to fasten her bra. "Sorry, I didn't think. You think we safe here?"

Kevin smiled. "I think so. The front door is still on the hinges."

Nicky looked around the kitchen for the first time since she came in. The fridge was plastered with photos of Indian-looking children and their messy works of art. "Whose house is this? Are you staying here?"

"They comrades. You don't need to know their names. They gone to Durban for the weekend, to a wedding. Now tell me about my mother, how's she holding up? When last did you see her?"

Kevin seated Nicky at the kitchen table for the birthday feast he had prepared. He had made all her favourites – roast chicken, sweet potatoes, carrots and yellow rice with raisins and almonds. She had never been spoiled like this before; this was the first time she ate roast on a weekday. How lucky was she to have Kevin for a boyfriend?

Nicky took a fat forkful from the plate Kevin put in front of her. She chewed thoroughly and swallowed before she answered. "Your mother's keeping strong. I was there this afternoon. You should see her giving the boere hell. They still parked outside your house; that fat vark of a boer and the skinny coloured sellout. She went up to them and asked if they haven't got better things to do. She told them to go track down real criminals."

Kevin laughed. "Ja, nuh? All those years she had me running backwards and forwards for her thinking she was sick."

Nicky put down the chicken wing she had chewed down to its bones and shined with her teeth. "She was scared. She didn't want to lose you also after your dedda died, so she made a plan to keep you close."

Kevin's mouth drooped like a banana. "That didn't work, did it?"

Nicky reached across the kitchen table and took his hand. She had no idea where he had been for the past two months. Comrades never spoke about those who disappeared. They knew not to show their connections to people in hiding; the boere would set their sights on them next. "How you doing, Kevin? You staying here?"

Kevin shook his head. "I move from time to time. It's hard, I'm cut off from everybody, but I can't take any risks. Those people caught up in the sweep the night they came for me, I'm linked to all of them. If the boere catch me I'll go away for a long time."

"What you up to Kevin? What you involved in?"

He tried to distract her. "Eat your food, Nicky, it's getting cold."

In the seven months since Anthony died, Kevin had drawn Nicky deeper into the struggle. He showed up at the flat every night after the funeral, but he could never stay long. She went with him to his meetings because she was lonely. Mummy and Dedda were so caught up in their war they said nothing when she went out, night after night.

Kevin was a member of the executive committee of the Hanover Park Youth and the Western Cape Youth Congress. Nicky kept silent at the first few meetings she attended, her head swivelling from speaker to speaker in the Catholic Church hall as she tried to keep up with debates that went on for hours. Before she got her head around them, she was being counted for the quorum. Kevin often disappeared on other mysterious appointments after the meetings. She learned to stop asking where he went; he gave her nothing.

As they finished their supper, Kevin caught up on her life. "How's your parents? Getting better?"

Nicky shook her head. "They getting worse. Not one of them remembered my birthday today. I never saw Dedda take a drink before Anthony died; now he's gesuip most weekends. Mummy told me to tell him that she won't allow liquor in the flat so he takes his bottles to Aunty Moira and passes out on her couch."

"Sorry, Nicky. I really like your dedda. He will recover, just you see. Anthony's murder hit him hard. Give him time."

"It's been seven months already. How much time do he need?"

"How you been coping? Is it getting better for you?"

Nicky shrugged. "I'm okay. I got the youth and the advice office work to keep me busy."

Kevin had introduced Nicky to his friend Abigail at the Hanover Park Advice Office. She was the very one who tracked down Shirley's father's pension so she didn't have to leave school to work.

The advice office provided the people of Hanover Park with free services, sorting out their problems with the rent office and the council and offering legal advice for their other troubles. Abigail took Nicky in like a mother and sent her on a training course, where lawyers shared their education with twenty volunteers from advice offices across the Cape Flats. At the end of the weekend Nicky had taken the first steps to becoming a paralegal.

Kevin kept up with his questions. "How's the advice office doing?"

"Yoh Kevin! We had a couple of bad cases recently. I can't believe how much kak women take before they complain. There was this one woman who was beaten on her wedding night and she stayed married to the vark for fifteen years. When she came in she could hardly speak. I sukkeled to find a place at a shelter for her, but she went back to the vark three days after we placed her. I don't think I can take another case like that."

Kevin reached across the table and took her hand. "People got a democratic right to fuck up their lives, Nicky. They get used to their oppression, they don't know any other way. Your job is to show them a better life, but you can't force them to accept it. You got to keep conscientising them, eventually they will get the message, like we did."

Nicky nodded. "Ja, it's not all bad. We organised a protest outside the council offices last week. They want to put up the rent by fifteen per cent; people can't afford it. We hired two buses to take protesters to town and we filled them both. It was bemoer. The mayor wouldn't come out, the coward, he sent a junior official to collect the petition. The women were so in the moer in they took off their shoes and threw them at the poor man!"

Kevin laughed. "With our shoes, we will free our land!"

Nicky's birthday supper ended with a chocolate cake that Kevin had baked with his own hands. As she blew the candles out she closed her eyes and wished that her life, and Kevin's, would be normal again, soon.

Kevin moved them to a couch in the lounge where they cuddled and caught up on all the news from Hanover Park. It wasn't long before they were vrying again. The separation made Nicky desperate to take as much of Kevin as she could. Her body pushed up against his as he came to lie on her. She hadn't noticed him loosening the button of her jeans and pulling her zip down until his hand slipped into her damp broeks. She had been too focused on his mouth on her nipples; they were growing as tall as skyscrapers under his lips. She lifted her bum off the couch to help him pull down her jeans.

After Kevin removed all their clothes, he made her wait. He had a condom and a speech at the ready. "This is not the time to be making babies, Nicky. We don't know what challenges tomorrow is going to bring."

Nicky pulled him back down onto her. The couch was deep enough to accommodate him between her wide-open legs. The first time was okay; the second sent her falling backwards with arms outstretched into sparkling space. They hardly rested in between. Nicky went from melted chocolate to electrocuted as Kevin's hands and lips kept up their travels across her body.

She was shocked at how much noise she made; they stopped and burst out laughing when they realised the neighbour's dog was barking in time to her moans. Nicky tried to keep it down but she couldn't, her feelings poured out of her mouth and every other part of her body. Kevin solved the problem by turning on the radio. Lionel Ritchie's Three Times a Lady was playing when he came back to the couch. They tried to keep pace with tempo but soon gave up; it was too slow for their need.

Nicky finally realised what Suzette had been so worked up about. Now that she had done it for the first time, all she could think about was when she would do it again. She pulled her nose away from Kevin's and frowned at him. "How long you gunna be in hiding?"

Kevin sat up. He started speaking; then he stopped. He excused himself and left the room. He came back with a soft blanket and covered Nicky. He sat across from her on the couch, his bare feet stroking up and down her calves under the blanket as he spoke.

"I can't do this anymore, Nicky. It's driving me mal. There's work to be done, and I'm stuck inside day in and day out. The time has come for the final push against apartheid and I can do nothing while I'm in hiding. That's why I wanted to see you tonight. Other than the fact that it's your birthday. I got something I need to tell you."

Nicky pulled herself upright and clamped Kevin's roaming toes. They were distracting her at a time when she needed to concentrate. "You can't come home! The police is still parked outside your house."

"I know I can't. That's not what I'm talking about. I'm leaving."

"Leaving for what? For where, I mean? Where you going?"

Kevin swallowed hard before he spoke. "I'm leaving the country, Nicky. It's all arranged. I'm leaving tomorrow. First to Swaziland, then Mozambique and then, hopefully, Lusaka."

There was a silence while Nicky digested his travel plans. She gave up for something more urgent. "You leaving tomorrow and you did this to me tonight! You know what you are? You a typical naai-her-and-leave-her naaier. I can't say it was nice knowing you."

Nicky rukked off the blanket and bent down to sort out her pile of clothes on the floor. It took a while to find her broeks; they had dropped down the leg of her jeans. Kevin pulled her back onto the couch as she stood up.

She twisted in his grip. "Let me go, you bastard! Let me go! I wanna go home! You can't keep me here! Let go! "

Kevin held fast, pinning her arms to her side. When she tried to twist and knee him in the balls he pinned her down with his body.

"Get off me! Let go! Leave me alone, you bastard!" Nicky's shouting was driving the dog next door befok; its nails were scraping frantically on the wooden fence.

Kevin gripped her hands above her head and covered her mouth with his free hand. His voice was serious. "Nicky, listen to me. I'm going to take my hand away, but first you must promise you won't shout. Listen to me, what if someone calls the police? Right now, you probably think good riddance to bad rubbish. But I'm asking you please, just calm down. I'm sorry; I planned to break the news in a better way. It's just, I was so nervous. We not supposed to tell anybody. We supposed to leave without saying goodbye. Now you promise you won't shout? Nod your head if you promise."

Nicky stared daggers at Kevin while she shook her head up and down. She was too in the moer in to say anything when he removed his hand. To think that a few minutes ago she had been dof enough to think this was the best night of her life. He had planned it all; he had gone out of his way to make sure she would remember her kak seventeenth birthday forever.

She managed to get a few words out. "So talk, I'm waiting."

Kevin climbed off her and sorted out their clothes. He handed hers over piece by piece before he got dressed. He switched off the radio and came to sit on the couch with his fingers locked tight in his lap. "How can I explain? The way I'm living now, the boere have defeated me. I've locked myself up. But if the boere get me they will put me away for a long time, you understand?"

Nicky realised after a while that Kevin was waiting for an answer. He still hadn't explained why he had got together with her tonight if he was leaving tomorrow. She nodded, more because of what she was learning about him than to show that she understood.

When he realised she wasn't going to speak, Kevin took the gap. "Nicky, I'm of no use if I stay in hiding. If I leave the country I can get involved again. It won't be long, I reckon a year or two. Three years at the most. Then I will come home and raise the ANC flag on the Union Buildings. It's better than going away from you to sit in a prison cell."

Nicky heard him fully. Everything he said so far had to do with him. He hadn't even realised how kak he made her feel. She was surprised she wasn't crying; she who tjanked at the drop of a hat. Must be that Kevin wasn't worth it. She had to tell him that before she left; let him listen to her for a change. She got to her feet and turned to face him.

She took it slow and cold. "You a naaier. All you can think about is yourself and the fokken struggle. How could you do this to me? How could you naai me and the next minute talk about going away for years? Fok off to Lusaka, I don't want to see you again long as you live."

She held her head high as she walked to the door. It was locked and there wasn't a key in the hole. She turned around and headed for the back door. Kevin blocked the kitchen doorway, arms and legs stretched out like he was preparing for a star jump. She slammed her palm into his chest. "Get out of my way, Kevin. I told you, I never want to see you again."

"Nicky, please listen to me," Kevin pleaded through fat tears in his voice. "I can see why you feel like that. I'm sorry. I'm begging you, give me one last chance to explain. I love you Nicky. Don't you know how much I love you?"

She didn't want to hear another word from his mouth. He was a liar on top of being a naaier. If he loved her he wouldn't leave. "Get out of my way, Kevin. I wanna go home."

"One last thing, Nicky. Just let me say one last thing then you can leave. Please?"

She crossed her arms over her heavy heart and nodded. Her legs gave way; she was vrek moeg. She held onto the table as she lowered herself onto a chair.

Kevin came to sit across from her and went on pleading his case. "Nicky, you got to understand. All I want is a normal life with you. I want to come to your house and take you out, to bioscope or something, not meetings. The main reason I'm doing this is for us. What kind of a life have we got now? We haven't seen each other for two months. I worry about you all the time and I can't check if you okay, your phone might be tapped. I'm going to miss you like hell. I'm already missing you. I wanted to show you how much I love you before I leave. I will have the memory of tonight to motivate me to come back quick as I can."

Nicky ploughed her hair with her fingers. She was starting to understand why Kevin wanted to leave the country. Why hadn't he realised how much his news would hurt her? What did he expect her to say? Hamba kahle comrade?

When the fist in her throat disappeared she interrogated him. Was there no other way out? How much trouble was he in? Was he sure they would lock him away if they got him? Was he sure he would come home in two to three years? How was she gunna cope without him?

Her voice broke. "You my family, Kevin. Since Anthony died I got no one but you. How am I gunna get by without you? You made me love you now you leaving; just like everyone else I love left me."

Kevin reached for her hands. "You got me, Nicky, no matter where

I am. I promise I will keep loving you and I will come home to you. You got to believe that."

Nicky had lots more questions, but Kevin was short on answers. He couldn't tell her more about his involvement with the African National Congress. He didn't know how he was getting out of the country. He was leaving for Johannesburg tomorrow to meet a contact who would smuggle him across the border. He didn't know how long it would take to reach Lusaka. He wasn't sure if he could send word that he had arrived safely but he promised he would do his best.

The sunrise was a milky blue when Nicky left. She held onto Kevin in the kitchen, kissing goodbye. After a while they made it into the lounge, where they ended up back on the couch, grinding desperately into each other. At the front door her lips wouldn't stop kissing. At the gate her arms refused to let go.

She cried all the way home for the loss of another person she loved, ignoring the stares of the early-morning commuters at the Wynberg taxi rank and the people crammed with her into the Hiace to Hanover Park.

Friday afternoons were usually quiet at the advice office. Nicky was on her own for the first time; Abigail had gone to coloured affairs to sort out a problem for a client. She checked her watch again, it was almost five o'clock; she had to find a way to get rid of the woman who had arrived more than an hour ago. There was nothing more she could do to help; the woman wasn't getting the message.

Mrs Julies came with a long complicated story, but Nicky quickly worked out she was looking for a handout. She wasn't interested in any of the solutions she was being offered.

The woman brought a sour smell into the office; soap hadn't touched her body for days. Her floral dress was stained like a tablecloth, with smears of beetroot, yolk and tea. She walked with difficulty; her ankles were fat tree trunks growing out of her tight shoes. Mrs Julies reached the end of her speech and went straight back to the start.

Her watermelon breasts lifted as she sighed deeply. "You see, if my boy hadn't been murdered, I wouldn't be here today. It's because he was stabbed, by that fokker Majiet from the Nice Time Kids. Everyone know who murdered my Tyrone. Majiet did it in the middle of Peach Street on a Saturday afternoon. But can I get the police to do anything?"

Nicky jumped in. She had to get home before it got dark. The war between the Nice Time Kids and the Junky Funky Kids had been waging for three weeks. After sunset anyone on the streets was a target for the wild shooters on both sides. "Mrs Julies, I already told you that you must follow up with the police to check if there's any progress on the investigation. It is your right to know what they doing; tax money pays their salaries."

There was another reason she wanted the woman to leave; she was staying close to home in case a message came from Kevin. It had been three weeks since he left and she was out of her mind with worry. She watched the news every night, expecting to hear about a shootout on the border and the death of a terrorist. She played Gloria Gaynor's I Will Survive over and over on the tape deck Kevin had given her as a birthday present and slept with her arms wrapped around her waist.

Mrs Julies sighed and continued as if there had been no interruption. "My Tyrone was the breadwinner of the home. He was a good boy, a hard worker. I can't work because of my arthritis, you see. And my daughters, they can't go out to work 'cause they all got small babies, and more on the way."

Nicky couldn't listen to this again. She looked around the advice office. The walls were covered in posters; they were running out of space. Many contained information, like the Declaration on Human Rights and the rights of workers to join trade unions. There were invitations to meetings and rallies, splashed in the bright red, yellow and black of the United Democratic Front. Her favourite poster celebrated the thirtieth anniversary of the Freedom Charter. The artwork showed the clauses of the charter: a mother cradling a child, mielies growing on a farm and workers marching into factories and mines.

Mrs Julies cleared her throat. She waited until Nicky looked her in the face before she started up again. "It's victimisation, you see. My daughters and me, we victims of a victimisation. That's why we entitled to compensation, the way I see it. Our Moslem neighbours next door, the Slamdiens, had problems with the shebeen from the day Tyrone opened for business. When Tyrone died, me and my daughters tried to keep the business going, but the police was working with the Moslems next door and chased away our customers."

Nicky rolled her eyes. What would Abigail do to get rid of the woman? Despite long lists of troubles Abigail heard day in and day out she kept a smile on her face; 'specially when she was laying down the line for people who stepped over it. Nicky couldn't figure out where the line was, but she was sure Mrs Julies was on the wrong side of it.

"Tyrone must of bribed the police to keep the shebeen going, but me and my daughters couldn't figure out who to bribe or how much to pay. We gave every policeman who came with the Slamdien's complaints twenty rands. That's a lot of money. But still, the police came with the rent office people and pulled down the structure in front of our house. It's those fokken Nice Time Kids. They must be paying the police more. They on a mission to take out the JFKs and they started with Tyrone."

Nicky lost the little patience she had left. "You say your son was an innocent victim, so why is a gang coming to destroy his illegal business?" She lifted her hand when Mrs Julies tried to talk. "Let me finish. I listened to you. I gave you a lot of advice already. I just thought of another thing you can do. You can look after your grandchildren while your daughters go to work."

Mrs Julies looked at Nicky like she was out of her head. "Isn't there someone else I can talk to? Someone older? I already told you I can do nothing because of my arthritis now you saying I must look after five children?"

Nicky kept her voice strong. It was time to show Mrs Julies the line. "I already told you. You can come in next week and see Abigail if you want to. But I don't think she can give you any more help than I did. This is an advice office. We not a welfare organisation. Abigail will tell you the same thing."

Mrs Julies tried one more time. "Can't you organise food parcels for my family? We don't need cash, even though we haven't got a cent between us. The funeral took a lot. Tyrone left strict instructions. He wanted a see-through glass cart pulled by white horses and a coffin that cost almost three thousand rands. I won't even tell you how much we spent on the clothes he was wearing when we buried him."

Nicky's mouth opened wider with every sentence Mrs Julies spoke. Maybe she hadn't been paying attention earlier, she only realised now that the woman was Ougat's mother. No one knew him as Tyrone. People were still talking about his funeral. Hanover Park had never seen anything like that before. Jackie Lonte had pulled up behind the horse-drawn cart in a white stretch limousine, followed by a convoy of BMWs and a Porsche.

Nicky sukkeled to hide her satisfied smile. Ougat's murder two months ago got her parents talking again, if only for a while. Dedda was convinced Ougat knew something about Anthony's murder; he remembered the gangster's threat to get him a year back when he confronted him at the park. Mummy said she didn't think that quarrel was cause to murder a child, but if Ougat knew something about Anthony's death they were never going to find out now.

Anthony's murder was still unsolved. Sergeant Scheepers hadn't been seen again after he brought the news of the tattoo and took the Mandrax. He was never at the police station to take phone calls and he didn't return messages. The neighbourhood watch stayed on the case for months but they got nothing from the community.

Nicky had watched, impressed, as Mummy and Dedda tried to work out together what Ougat's death meant for Anthony's murder. It was the first time in months that they spoke without spitting at each other. Until Dedda left the flat and came back with Aunty Moira and a bottle of Klipdrift to celebrate Ougat's death. Mummy chased them out with a rolled up magazine. She said Ougat was also some mother's child. His death took away none of her pain; Dedda had no right to laugh lekker over a dop.

The advice office door opened as she got to her feet to march Mrs Julies out. Nicky got such a skrik she dropped back onto her chair. Shirley was the last person she expected. She carried a baby, tightly wrapped in a receiver blanket. Shirley closed the door carefully and walked slowly to the desk.

Nicky got up and found her voice. "Shirley! Long time no see! Did you hear I came looking for you again? No one wanted to tell me where you were."

Shirley walked in, holding the baby in an arm held stiff away from her body. She didn't seem to notice Mrs Julies, who was spilling out of her chair, she headed straight for Nicky and stared with blank eyes when she came to a halt.

Nicky stared back at her friend. Shirley's skin was grey and her forehead was wet with sweat. She reached for the baby. "Are you orrite? You don't look so lekker. Come, sit down. Give the baby to me. Whose baby is it?"

Nicky took the small bundle from Shirley. She pulled the blanket aside and peeped inside. The baby was sleeping peacefully; long eyelashes curling softly onto its cheeks. It was dark, like Shirley, but its mouth was a light pink rose. "Ag moeder, how pretty! What is it, a boy or a girl?"

"It's a boy," Shirley's voice was flat.

"How old is he? He's so small. What's his name?"

"His name is Anthony. He was born this morning."

Nicky looked at her friend, skrikked. Shirley hadn't taken the seat she was offered. She was staring at the baby like it was gemors.

Shirley held onto the desk for support as she forced out through tight lips what she had come to say. "You so desperate to find out what happened to me? I'm gunna tell you Nicky. Your brother raped me. Him and his friend Ougat and other members of the JFK. They couldn't get to Majiet so they planned on raping my sister Karen 'cause she was involved with him. But they got me instead. You said you wanna help me? Here's your chance. I don't want that thing. He's yours. For all you know, he might be a fokken Fourie."

Nicky had forgotten Mrs Julies was in the office. She was surprised how fast the woman rushed out the door; she had complained nonstop about her kwale. Should she stop her? Shirley had just named Ougat as her rapist, explained how his war with the Nice Time Kids started. But she also named Anthony. Nicky stared down at the baby. She couldn't tell if he looked like her brother. He had peppercorn hair, but then so did Shirley, when she didn't slather on straightener and comb it through until her scalp burned.

When Nicky looked up from the baby's face Shirley was gone. She rushed out of the office and down the first-floor corridor, trying not to wake the baby as she speedwalked past the hair salon and the loan shop with the security gate. She went carefully down the town centre's stairs. Shirley was nowhere to be seen when she reached the pavement. She wasn't in any of the queues at the bus stop or the taxi rank.

Nicky checked on the baby. He was still asleep. She covered his face with the blanket and cradled him against her chest. Shirley's house wasn't far; she hoped he didn't wake up before they got there.

Shirley's mother was home but she wouldn't let Nicky past the front door. Mrs Martin's shouting woke the baby up. It was hard for Nicky to argue with the woman while she struggled to soothe him.

Mrs Martin's voice was thick with disgust as she closed the door in Nicky's face. "Voetsek. Take that thing with you. No product of rape is gunna be my grandchild. Give him to your mother."

Nicky managed to get one sentence in. "Please Mrs Martin, this is Shirley's baby."

The wailing baby started screaming when Mrs Martin slammed the door. Nicky lifted him to her shoulder and patted his back. His cries cut through her heartstrings. Nicky felt like crying herself. What was she supposed to do?

She knocked on Mrs Martin's door. No answer. She pulled down the handle and pushed. The door was locked. She knocked again. "Mrs Martin?" she called above the baby's howls. "Open the door. Please help me; I dunno what to do. Is Shirley there? Shirley! Mrs Martin!"

The baby's head wobbled as she banged her fist against the door. Nicky stopped knocking and tried to soothe him. She didn't know it was possible for a baby to be so loud, although she often heard her neighbour's babies through the walls at home.

She sat on the doorstep and placed him on her lap, opening the blanket to check if anything was wrong. His white babygro was too big for him, the sleeves covered his hands, and his feet didn't make it all the way down to the bottom. She could see all of his pink gums as he screamed. She ran her hands over his body. How would she know if there was something wrong? She knew nothing about babies.

Nicky swaddled the baby again and held him against her shoulder, rocking from side to side. She tried one more time to get Mrs Martin's attention. "Mrs Martin, please. Help me. I dunno what to do. Please help me."

The volume of the crying dropped a bit, but holding a pathetic baby was worse than holding an angry one. His wah-has hurt her as much as he was hurting. She had to do something.

She knew what to do. Natalie in flat thirty-nine below them had a small baby. She would have supplies. She would wait there until Mummy came home from work. Nicky gave up on Mrs Martin and headed to Magnolia Court for help.

Chapter Thirty-Two

Magda's corns were hot coals in her shoes. She always arrived early for the Woolworths sale; she had joined the queue outside the Claremont shop an hour before it opened. It was worth the pain, she pulled a nice frock for church off a rail as another woman reached for it. She chose underwear for herself and Nicky and draped the dress over it as she made her way to the other side of the shop to look for more bargains.

She headed for boys' wear. She couldn't resist the blue pyjamas with the yellow stars; she took two sets. She chose two T-shirts and a pair of takkies; they never lasted long. What did the boy do? Kick everything he passed on the street?

Her corns complained as she joined the long queue for the tills. There was a nice restaurant nearby where she would go for a cup of tea to rest her swollen feet before she headed for the taxi rank. She shuffled forward as the queue inched towards the tills. Flames of pain raced up her legs as something crashed into the back of her shins. She turned around to face the woman clutching a pram, apologising nonstop. She was about to start skelling when she realised who it was that lit her pain. "Suzette! Is it you?"

"Yes Mummy."

Magda hadn't seen Suzette since the day after Anthony's funeral, ten years back. She had set eyes on her, but not in the flesh. Magazines featuring her daughter piled so high on her coffee table that it couldn't be used for anything else. Her eyes shot down into the pram. She had read about Justin's birth in *Cosmopolitan* two years ago. The framed cover with mother and baby hung on her bedroom wall.

She crouched next to the pram and examined Justin's curly blonde hair and fair skin. The toddler's blue eyes crinkled as he smiled and offered her a bite of his soggy rice cake. She looked up at her daughter. "He's poenangs, you must be very proud of him."

Suzette smiled down at her son. "You should see him when he's throwing a tantrum, which he does a few times a day."

"He will grow out of that. They all do."

Magda's corns cried from the weight they carried as she crouched next to her grandson. She smiled at Justin and stroked his soft cheek. Her feet wouldn't allow her to stay down much longer. She gripped the pram as she sighed and stood.

She stared at Suzette. Her daughter was beautiful and normal at the same time. She had no makeup on her face, not even lipstick. She was two years away from thirty but she didn't look a day older than twenty-one. Her hair was as light as Justin's. The ponytail down her back had a natural shine; you would never say it came out of a bottle. Magda couldn't make out what Suzette was thinking; her eyes were hidden behind big, dark sunglasses.

Why would her daughter come hunting for bargains at Woolworths? She always looked so posh in the pictures in the magazines; she was always in the company of the big names. "Why you come to the sale? Surely you don't need to …" Magda stopped herself. She was speaking such nonsense; she got like that when she was nervous.

Suzette bent down and tickled Justin's cheeks. "This wretch grows so fast. I thought I could make a quick dash in and out. I didn't know there was a sale, I hadn't reckoned on this queue. Still, the clothes I found are so fantastic it's worth the wait."

Magda examined Suzette's finds. She had a pile on the hood of the pram, all of it for Justin. She lifted her arm to show off her choices. "These pyjamas are lovely; I see you also took them."

Suzette stared in silence at the two pairs of pyjamas.

Magda had been planning on a conversation with Suzette since the day she found out about Justin. She had worked out every word she wanted to say. It wasn't right that the child had a family he knew nothing about. It wasn't right that she had a grandson she didn't know.

She was at the front of the queue. The next available till was hers.

She gripped her daughter's arm. "Have you got time for a cup of tea? I want to speak to you, if you can spare the time."

Suzette looked at her watch. "Okay, a quick cup. But I have to get home soon. I've got people coming for lunch."

"I won't keep you long, promise."

A few minutes later they settled at a table at a restaurant facing the Woolworths parking lot. Magda looked around at the crowded tables after the waiter took their order. "I like this place. It's owned by coloured people, did you know that?"

"No I didn't. I seldom come this side of town. Justin had an appointment with his paediatrician this morning; her rooms are in Claremont."

Magda looked into the pram parked next to the table. Her grandson had fallen asleep with the rice cake crushed in his chubby hand. "Is he orrite?"

"He's fine, it was just a checkup. He's perfect, actually."

Magda swallowed hard. For Justin's sake, she had to tell Suzette what was on her mind; she had to make sure she got it right. "Listen Suzette, I got to tell you something very important. I been meaning to get hold of you for a while, since Justin was born. I didn't know how to approach you, or if you wanted to hear from me."

She couldn't see any expression on Suzette's face; she was still hidden behind her sunglasses. Magda shrugged. "Ag, I don't know why I'm taking so long to say it. I'm sorry for the way I treated you. I didn't believe in you when you were starting out. I want to tell you that I'm very proud of you. I understand that you don't want contact with us. But since I saw the write up about Justin in the *Cosmopolitan* I been meaning to call you. I wanted to congratulate you on your beautiful baby. I wanted to make sure you were doing okay. I want to say sorry that you had a baby on your own, without your mother to help you."

That was all she wanted to say. She hoped it came out properly.

Suzette said nothing. Magda watched nervously as she reached under Justin's pram, pulled out her handbag and scratched inside. She brought out a pack of tissues, took off her sunglasses and wiped tears from her eyes.

Magda bit her lip. This wasn't going well. Less than five minutes gone and Suzette was already crying. She wasn't one to cry. "Sorry, I didn't mean to upset you."

She waited quietly while her daughter composed herself. There was nothing more to say. She couldn't force Suzette to make contact or allow her to have a relationship with her grandchild.

Suzette blew her nose, smiled and reached across the table to grip Magda's hand. "Thank you, Mummy. That was the most perfect apology I have ever heard."

Magda was lost for words. Thankfully, the waiter arrived with their tea and her scone. She made herself busy, moving Suzette's sunglasses and the ashtray to the side to make space for their order.

Suzette started first after the waiter left. "I also have an apology for you, Mummy. I'm sorry that I wasn't there for you after Anthony died. I've been thinking a lot about him since Justin was born. I think I'd die if I lost my baby. I don't know how you coped."

Magda patted Suzette's hand. "It is the worst thing that can happen to a woman, believe you me. I knew you would think that after you had your baby. It was like that for me after all three of you were born. The worry never leaves you."

Suzette nodded. "That's why I stopped working. I need to be with Justin. My job involved far too much travelling. I used to wake up in hotel rooms not knowing what city I was in. I can't live like that anymore, especially with another one on the way."

Magda smiled. "You pregnant again? Congratulations! When you due? You hardly showing yet."

Suzette's hand went to her stomach. "We only found out two weeks ago. You're the first person I've told, after Cameron."

"Cameron's your husband, right? What does he do?"

"He's a software developer."

Magda had no idea what that was, but it sounded very bigshot.

Suzette spotted her confusion. "He makes programmes for computers, you know?"

Magda had seen computers but she had never used one. Nicky knew how to operate them; they had them at her work. She frowned as she tried to think of something to say about computers.

Suzette laughed. "You don't need to know any more than that. I don't understand a word Cameron's saying when he talks about his work. I just fake it. He's a fantastic father. He works from home, which is good for Justin."

Magda had a son-in-law she had never met, knew nothing about. She had seen only one photo of him, in the *Cosmo* story about Justin's birth. "How did you two meet?"

Suzette took a sip of tea before she started. "It's a complicated story. I had a friend who overdosed on drugs, and I was the one who found him. Cameron came to help me; they were friends. He got Neil to hospital in time, took him to rehab after he was discharged. It wasn't long before he relapsed, and it wasn't the last time. Years later I met Cameron again, bumped into him at a bookshop. We went for coffee and connected immediately. It was quite intense, what we had been through together."

Magda sighed. "He sounds like a good man."

Suzette's ponytailed flicked up and down the back of her chair as she nodded. "Yes, he is. I regret that my job kept me away from him also. I took three months off after I quit. We went to Greece for a month and I stayed home and cooked supper for my family every night for the next two months."

"Sounds wonderful." Magda wondered if she would ever be invited to one of those family suppers. She would very much like to come, to spend time with her grandson. And her daughter. Suzette had changed so much, 'specially the way she spoke. You would never say she was from Hanover Park when she opened her mouth. Still, so much of her was familiar, was the child she made.

"I'm setting up a business," Suzette announced. "A modelling agency. I've found offices in Athlone. It was a bit run down and it's been hard finding contractors who can do the job properly the first time."

Magda was confused. It was the new South Africa; Suzette could trade anywhere she liked. "Why Athlone?"

"It's the perfect location. It's a huge intersection for the Cape Flats. Advertising agencies are desperate for black talent nowadays, and the talent agencies haven't yet tapped into that market. I'm going to offer training, and I may branch out into an agency for musicians and actors. I've earned a fortune and I want to give back to my community.

Magda struggled to work out why Suzette was claiming the Cape
Flats for her community. She never lied in the interviews she had given
over the years; but she was always vague when she asked where she was
from. She never once mentioned her family. Why did she want to come
back now? She could live like a white person if she wanted to; Nelson
Mandela made it possible when he became president two years ago.

Suzette broke the silence. "How's Nicky?"

Magda shook her head. "She thinks she's okay, but I worry about
her. She's old long before her time. She never goes anywhere, never
does things with people her own age. Just lies in her room and reads
thick books."

Nicky would have the horries if she knew she was talking about
her to Suzette. But the truth had to be told, and it was easy to connect
with her oldest daughter. If only she could find a way to hold onto the
thin thread that held them together over a cup of tea. She wanted time
to mend the break between the sisters. Nicky swore she would never
speak to Suzette again after she called her for advice and was told to
dump the baby and walk away.

Suzette seemed interested in her sister. "Did Nicky become a
lawyer?"

"No, she never studied law. She's a social worker at the welfare. It
doesn't pay much, but she got good government benefits. She bought
a house last year, in Ottery. I'm staying there with her."

"A social worker? That's terrible! She wanted to be a lawyer her
entire life."

"Ja, but it was difficult. She dropped out of school in standard nine
when she got Anthony. Just for a year, then she went to night school
while I cared for him. She got two As in her matric. She got a job at
the advice office and studied part-time through Unisa. It would have
taken six years to get a law degree, so she did social work. She can get
a bursary from the government now she works for them, but she says
she's happy where she is. Maybe you can talk to her about taking up her
studies again. Anthony will be fine; I will help with the boy."

Magda worried she was drukking too hard when Suzette went quiet
again. She could have kicked herself, but her corns were burning. She
slipped off her shoes carefully and wriggled her toes, watching her

daughter. It was hard to work out if Suzette was interested in keeping contact. Just because she asked after Nicky didn't mean she wanted to see her again.

Suzette got to her feet. When she gripped the pram handle Magda expected her to say goodbye and walk out of the restaurant. Instead, she lowered the back of the pram, removed the rice cake from Justin's hand and settled him. Magda sighed with relief when she took her seat again.

Suzette learned across the table and spoke quietly. "So whose child is Anthony? Yours or Nicky's?"

Magda smiled. "Oh, Nicky's his mummy. It's all legal. When she went to register him for his birth certificate they just accepted what she told them."

Suzette frowned. "What name did she give as the father? She didn't tell them it was her brother, did she?"

"She said the father was unknown. It doesn't matter, Suzette. Anthony is a Fourie, that's all that matters."

"And his real mother? What happened to her?"

"We went to the Martins' house the night we got Anthony. They had packed up and left. No one knew where they went and we never seen them again. Anthony knows nothing about them. Nicky is his mother, that's all he has to know."

Magda knew where Suzette stood on the boy. She had given Nicky hell when she heard they had taken him in. She hadn't spoken to any of them again. She lived in the same city but she hadn't once set eyes on Anthony.

The boy was as much her grandson as Justin was, she had to make that clear. "Anthony is a wonderful boy Suzette, you should meet him sometime. He's so clever! Like his mummy, he's always first in class. And he's good at sports, the top goalscorer in his soccer team."

"Why did Nicky name him Anthony?"

"She didn't. Before she disappeared, Shirley told Nicky his name was Anthony. We decided to keep it."

Magda held back while Suzette poured herself a cup of tea from the pot. She kept her voice soft when she started up again. "At first, we didn't know what to do when Nicky brought the baby home. Shirley and her family were nowhere to be found. We couldn't go to the police. They just good for nothing, they did nothing to find Anthony's murderer. Besides, we couldn't tell them we suspected that Anthony raped Shirley."

She stopped talking when Suzette winced. She waited while her daughter added a splash of milk to her tea and took her first sip. She had never heard of Earl Grey before Suzette ordered it. It was funny-smelling stuff, with hardly any colour, not like the golden rooibos in her cup. When she realised Suzette wasn't going to say anything she continued with her explanation.

"While we tried to figure out a solution, the baby found a place in our hearts. You must see his mouth Suzette; it's exactly the same as Anthony's. He's much darker than Anthony but the shape of his face is the same. I took out Anthony's baby photos to check. Even if there was only a chance he was Anthony's baby, I wanted him. Nicky felt the same way."

Suzette put her cup carefully back in its saucer and looked up. "What did people say, when they found out about the baby? Surely people asked questions? You can't turn up with a baby and not say anything."

Magda smiled. "The neighbours solved our problem. They had it all worked out and their skinner quickly became the facts. Everybody believed Nicky was pregnant and she hid it 'til she gave birth. We couldn't come up with a better explanation than that, so we sent Nicky to register the birth of her son."

Suzette frowned. "You can find out for sure if you want to. There's tests that can be done nowadays to establish paternity. DNA tests, have you heard of them?"

"It doesn't matter, Suzette. I already told you, as far as we concerned Anthony is a Fourie."

"And what if he asks about his father?"

"He already asked. Nicky told him his father died before he was born. She told him he was a freedom fighter and the boere killed him."

Suzette tapped her forehead and frowned. "What happened to that boy Nicky was seeing? What was his name again? The one who disappeared, did she ever see him again?"

"Ja, Kevin pitched up in Hanover Park in 1990, already a grootkop in the ANC. He moved to Johannesburg a few months later, to work at

326

the ANC head office. He wanted Nicky to go with him, but she refused flat out. She didn't want to take Anthony away from me. She didn't want to go away. Our family is too small now to be broken again." Magda leaned over the pram and ate up Justin's sweet rosy cheeks with her eyes.

A woman and a teenaged girl came to a stop at their table, slicing through the thick silence that caked it. Both were tall, with green eyes in sharp-featured faces. The red streaks in the mother's hair came out of a bottle but her daughter had natural sunset in her long curls.

The woman's hands fluttered in the air. "I'm sorry to interrupt, so sorry. I can see you're deep in conversation. But I have to ask, are you Suzette Fourie?"

Suzette smiled. "Yes, I am."

The woman turned to her daughter. "See? Didn't I tell you it was her?"

The girl hid behind her mother's shoulder. "Yes, Mummy."

The woman stretched her long, red fingernails across the table and shook Suzette's hand. "I'm Avril Coetsee, and this is my daughter Miranda."

Avril stepped to the side and pushed her daughter forward. "Miranda wants to be a model. She's won a few pageants and talent shows. Her greatest wish is to follow in your footsteps, Suzette. Her bedroom wall is covered in your photos."

Magda knew Suzette was famous; her face was in almost every magazine she opened. But she hadn't realised what it meant; people were going to recognise her wherever she went. Avril was smiling at Suzette like she was a film star.

The woman's red nails swung around to point at her. "And you must be Mrs Fourie. I can see where Suzette got her looks."

Magda was struck dumb. This was the first time she was acknowledged by a stranger as the mother of a supermodel. Everyone who knew her knew that, of course, Suzette was always a major topic of conversation. Did she really look like her? She wanted to ask Avril where she saw the resemblance but she worried that would be like bragging. She looked at her daughter. Suzette was talking to Miranda like she knew the girl for years.

"It's hard work. You know that?"

The girl nodded.

"You have to get up for shoots before sunrise. You have to wear summer clothes in winter and learn not to sweat when you're all dressed up for winter and its boiling hot outside. You have to keep in shape, say no to ice cream."

Miranda nodded at the end of each sentence.

"But if you're serious, I can help you."

Avril jumped up and down, waving her hands in the air and squealing with excitement. "Do you mean that? Oh my God, I can't believe it! Did you hear, Miranda? Suzette says she's going to help you."

Suzette smiled at Avril. "As it happens, I'm opening an agency soon. Miranda's just the kind of girl I'm looking for, someone who's serious about modelling as a profession and who isn't scared of hard work."

Magda didn't know how Suzette could tell, the girl hadn't said a word. But she knew nothing about the modelling business. Maybe there was something in Miranda that Suzette saw. Her eyes were unusual; the green was flecked with fynbos. She got those eyes from her mother. Magda wondered what Suzette got from her. What did Avril see?

Suzette favoured her more than Neville, but she was much, much more beautiful. There was nothing out of place on her head, her face or her body. Her trouser suit emphasised her slim waist and her long legs. What was that word for her skin? Flawless, the name of the cosmetics range her daughter launched last year.

Avril grabbed Suzette's business card with two hands when it was offered. "Thank you. Thank you so much. We'll be calling you. You can be sure of that. Say bye-bye Miranda, we've taken up enough of Suzette's time. Nice to meet you, Mrs Fourie."

Avril wobbled off in her stillettos, her arm crooked into her daughter's.

Magda smiled at her daughter. "You were very kind to them."

Suzette put her sunglasses back on. "That girl is stunning. Did you see her eyes?"

"Yes, I did. Do you think she can be a model?"

"Oh yes I do. I would never have given them my number if I didn't. Girls like her are the reason I'm setting up my business in Athlone.

Cape Flats girls are an outrageous mixture of beauty from around the world. That one has Indonesian blood, you can see it."

Magda liked Suzette, for the first time in years. She had been a big admirer, but she hadn't liked her for a long time. It took years to forgive her for walking out after Anthony's funeral. The only way she coped was to set aside what her daughter had done while she mourned for her son. When Anthony's death stopped lashing her heart she brought out her anger against Suzette and let it settle for a while.

Suzette was so normal it was easy to forget she was famous. "Does that happen a lot, people stopping and talking to you?"

"Yes, it does. It will stop soon. I haven't taken on any work for six months. It's the L'Oréal campaign; it still has three months to run. When I disappear off people's television screens I'll disappear out of their lives."

Magda only realised now what it meant when Suzette said she had stopped working. Since she left them she hadn't disappeared; it was easy to keep track of her in the magazines. No more work for Suzette meant no more photospreads in magazines to show off at work. No more pictures taken at celebrity parties and weddings around the world. She had framed the photo of Suzette with Naomi Campbell and Nelson Mandela and put it on the lounge wall. She had to find a way to keep in touch. But how?

Suzette looked at her watch. "I have to go soon, I'm sorry, Mummy. I really do have people coming for lunch and I can't leave it all up to Cameron, it's not fair."

"Of course, yes. You did say. I didn't mean to take up so much of your time. Can you see our waiter? We need to ask for the bill."

Suzette waved her fingers in the air like she was signing her name. She turned to face Magda. "One more thing before I go, Mummy. How's Dedda? You haven't said a word about him."

Magda covered her mouth with her hands. How could Suzette know? She had been away from them for ten years.

"Mummy? Is Dedda okay? Did something happen to him?"

Magda shook her head slowly. "How would you know? We had no way of contacting you. Your dedda and I are no longer together. We divorced, eight years already. He took up with Moira; remember her?

He's still in Hanover Park, staying in the flat. Soon as I heard he made Moira pregnant I asked for a divorce. People chewed on that skandaal a long time. I was glad to get out of Hanover Park, I tell you."

Magda's divorce had driven her out of the Church of Eternal Redemption. Her new community, the Anglicans, didn't crane their necks in her direction when she walked into church. They didn't pull their children out of her way if she so much as looked in their direction. She was sure they would accept Anthony but Nicky wouldn't hear of it.

Suzette's mouth hung open. Was it incest if the daughter slept with the son and the father slept with the mother? "Dedda made Aunty Moira pregnant? From next door? Mark's mother?"

"Yes. Their son Michael is seven, he lives with your dedda. He goes to the same school as Anthony, York Road Primary in Lansdowne. They play for the same soccer club. Michael sometimes spends weekends with us. We visit with your dedda occasionally, birthdays and Christmas and such."

Magda pointed down to her Woolworths bag on the floor. "That's why I got two pairs of that pyjamas you also chose at the sale – one for Anthony and one for Michael."

"So Anthony is Michael's ..."

"I suppose Anthony is Michael's nephew, although he's older than him. Michael is yours and Nicky's brother, so that would make him Anthony's uncle. But they more like brothers, they so close."

The waiter came to interrupt and bring the bill. Suzette insisted on paying for their tea. She brought out a gold credit card from her purse. It was the first time Magda had seen one being used. It was so much better than carrying cash everywhere.

She got to her feet reluctantly. She was enjoying the time with Suzette and had been hoping to spend more time with Justin. The child should know his grandmother.

Suzette slung her large handbag over her shoulder and carefully manoeuvred the pram out of the restuarant.

Magda followed her out into the parking lot. Justin didn't wake up when he was lifted out of the pram and carefully strapped into the car seat in Suzette's silver BMW. Magda leaned in and gave him a soft kiss on his warm cheek while Suzette packed the pram into her boot. She sniffed his sweet neck. Her daughter came to stand at the car door, keys in her hand.

Magda pulled her head out of the car. "He's beautiful."

Suzette smiled. "Yes, he is."

There was nothing more to say. She was out of time. She didn't know if her apology was enough to bring Suzette back into their lives. She didn't know if Suzette thought she was too famous to associate with them. She had seen her face when she told her about Anthony and Michael; she looked like she had stepped on something. Would she bring Justin to their birthday parties?

Magda watched as her daughter got into the car. She stared at her flat tummy while she fastened her seat belt. She had another grandchild on the way, and she had no idea if she would meet this one. The car window rolled down smoothly. She leaned forward. "It was good to see you, Suzette. We must have tea again sometime."

Suzette nodded. "Yes we must, Mummy."

Magda watched and waved as her daughter reversed out of the parking bay and drove away.

Acknowledgements

I give thanks to the Cape Flats that birthed me and my huge, fascinating family who shaped me. I'm thankful for my comrades in the struggle against apartheid – they taught me to care, think and speak my mind.

It was a very good fortunate fate that found me a space in the University of the Witwatersrand's creative writing masters' class of 2011/2012. The group intimidated the mediocre out of me, lifted me up and kept me afloat 'til the last word was set down.

I recommend heartily that you seek out all the other writers in my masters' group; their work shines with heart and craft: Ingrid Hurwitz, Jeanette Malherbe, Lauren Royston, Dominique Botha, Sue Warring, Veruska de Vita, David Gordon, Arja Salafranca, Rohan Dickson, Kevin Bloom, Leon de Kock, Michael Titlestad, Christopher Thurman, Craig Higginson, Elsie Cloete, Gerrit Olivier, Michelle Adler and Veronique Tadjo.

My spice, Julia Grey, has the best set of eyes. For two long years she moulded, kneaded and shaped my clumsy manuscript with infinite patience and dedication.

If any lessons are imparted here, they are drawn from my family. My mother Fareda and my son Jihaad teach me daily how to love unconditionally. My father Eric and I are both storytellers and we love family stories best. My life is entangled with my siblings' lives. My children are tied firmly to me for the rest of my life. And Julia draws a protective circle around us all.